John Williston Cook, James V McHugh

A History of the Illinois State Normal University

ISBN/EAN: 9783337326845

Printed in Europe, USA, Canada, Australia, Japan

Cover: Foto ©Andreas Hilbeck / pixelio.de

More available books at **www.hansebooks.com**

OF THE

ILLINOIS

STATE NORMAL UNIVERSITY

NORMAL, ILLINOIS.

———

BY

JOHN W. COOK AND JAMES V. McHUGH.

———

Normal, Illinois.
· 1882.

PREFACE.

The close of the first quarter century of the history of the Normal School, and the celebration of that event, suggested the idea of the following volume. The work was begun by Messrs. James V. McHugh and George Howell. When about four-fifths of the work had been printed, Mr. Howell disposed of his interest to John W. Cook.

The thanks of the publishers are especially due to those who have contributed articles and have assisted in the collection of information.

The types are not quite intelligible in a few instances. On page sixty-three, Grennell should have appeared instead of "Gunnell;" on page sixty-four, read Stanard instead of "Standard;" on page seventy-one, change "Harwood" to Hurwood; on page ninety-five, change "Levett" to Swett, and on page ninety-six, change "Benton" to Wilder. The above are the only errors of especial note.

It is hoped that the "History" will be of interest to the friends of the school, and that it will contribute to a correct appreciation of an institution that has done its share in promoting the general welfare.

The Publishers.

Table of Contents.

EARLY HISTORY.

Previous to the adoption of the constitution of 1848, Illinois was peopled with emigrants who had generally come from the States of Indiana, Ohio, or Pennsylvania, where, at that time, there existed no system of common schools worthy of the name. These settlers brought with them the ideas and usages prevalent in their old homes. They were favorable to schools, but these schools were either academies, seminaries, or subscription primary, or district schools, supplemented generally by a little aid from the limited public funds. Our school laws were, however, an improvement upon those of many of our sister States, and our school funds were being provided for on a liberal scale by the donation of the sixteenth section of government land, which donation dates back to the admission of our State into the Union, in 1818, when the foundation was laid for the magnificent school system which we see to-day. This fund, however, though very well in theory, proved, in too many instances, a delusion and a snare in practice. Its management, in a great many instances in the older counties, fell into the hands of men who had no conception of the free school system, and even if they had foreseen the present value of the rich lands, they lacked the financial capacity to manage properly the great trust confided to their care. The settlers, in many instances, banded themselves together to purchase these lands at a mere nominal figure, thereby defrauding their posterity of the full benefit of this magnificent provision. Even where honestly and carefully managed, this fund often fell short of its capabilities, owing to the quality of the soil, the low value of all real estate, or to the inevitable losses resulting from panics, paper money, and incompetent supervision.

It therefore happened that from a variety of causes the college and seminary funds, and the general common school funds of this State, previous to 1848, were far below what the great men intended who provided for the original grant. Slowly and surely, however, our common schools were progressing. The cultured emigrants from southern States, liberally educated entirely with their parents' or guardians' money, and the descendents of our first settlers here, who were fortunate enough to enjoy the advantages of an education derived, in part, from public aid, were largely reinforced by emigrants from New York and New England. The latter were fresh

1

from States where common schools were free, and where the great principle of the Republic—free education of the masses—had been long enough in force to bring forth ripe fruit for western exportation.

These liberally-educated elements existed throughout the length and breadth of our State. Northern Illinois and the region west of the Illinois river, with scattering settlements in central and southern Illinois, were peopled largely with these New York and New England emigrants. Educated southerners were found all over the State, but more especially in southern Illinois.

The best educated native Illinoisans were most numerous in St. Clair, Madison, Monroe, Randolph, Gallatin, and the Ohio river counties. These elements did not, perhaps, strive with a common plan, but they were animated with a common purpose. They were widely scattered, and enjoyed few means of public discussion, either in convention or newspapers. But when their representatives met at our Legislature, and the school laws were being amended or re   it was found that there was a pressing demand for the passage of laws as should favor the free education of all the childre   the State. The efforts of these pioneers were finally rewarded when the new constitution of 1848 was framed. This provided a State tax of two mills on the dollar, which should be annually levied by the State Auditor, without the intervention of the Legislature, and a great step was at once taken in the cause of education.

This tax, though not large in itself, when added to the revenue of the school funds, in counties where these funds had been successfully managed, was at least a nucleus. Legislation provided for the raising of money to erect school houses, and, eventually, by further amendments, our most advanced communities were enabled to present successful instances of well-managed public schools. The great impetus given to the cause of public instruction in New York, New England, Indiana, and Michigan, exerted a powerful effect upon the public mind of this State, and the act of 1854 placed our system far in advance of its previous condition.

The friends of education were scattered all over the State and counted our most energetic and most influential citizens among their number and were fast advancing to the supreme control of our State school legislation. They could now begin to point to hundreds of most admirable free schools, in various parts of the State, taught by the best teachers in the Union. These schools were very numerous in the extreme northern counties, where the settlers had brought with them, almost perfect and entire, their eastern schools and eastern ideas. These had become naturalized and matured under the liberal laws of Illinois. Scattered through the State were a few bright examples in other counties. LaSalle, Peoria, Knox, Morgan, St. Clair, Madison, and other counties, had brilliant illustrations to add to the general stock, and free schools had not only become popular, but the demand of the hour. This was the period, embracing the year 1854, when our leading educators began to realize that, in order to make our schools all the public were now demanding, they must furnish some system, or source, through which more and better teachers could be provided.

There were teachers then in this State whose superiors have, perhaps, never been found. But it was undeniably true, and is, perhaps, true to-day, that many, many thousands were upon the teachers' platform, whose qualifications were far below the proper standard. Our best teachers were then mostly from the older States, and were those who had been educated at colleges or academies of a high grade, though there were not wanting numerous examples of home growth fully equaling the foreign article.

New England enjoyed almost a monopoly of supplying the best teachers, and had already commenced their regular production, Normal Schools having been in operation there for several years. Ohio was not far behind, while the best colleges of Virginia and Kentucky forward ed a goodly proportion.

The idea of obtaining a State Normal School began to take root and grow about 1856, especially among the teachers of the State who had by this time commenced holding annual conventions. The formation of the Illinois State Teachers' Association marks an era in our educational affairs. Previous to that time the schools of the State were almost entirely without organization. The general management was in the hands of the Secretary of State, and the schools formed simply a department in his office. Of course they could receive but little intelligent attention from that officer. The free school law itself met with bitter opposition in many parts of the State. Its principles were either misunderstood or misrepresented. County commissioners were elected in the several counties, but their salary was extremely low in nearly every instance. Free high schools were unknown. Under these circumstances, three men, H. H. Lee, of Chicago, J. A. Hawley, of Dixon, and Daniel Wilkins, met at the home of the latter, in Bloomington, for the purpose of trying to devise some plan by which the condition of popular education might be improved throughout the State. As a result of this conference, a call was issued for a general meeting of the friends of free schools to meet in Bloomington, December 26-9, 1853. The convention assembled pursuant to this call, and D. Brewster, of Kane County, was chosen president, and Wm. H. Powell, of LaSalle County, secretary. It was reported at our late meeting in Springfield that the president is still living. The secretary has not been heard from for several years.

Three topics were thoroughly discussed at this meeting: It was resolved to ask the Legislature to establish, as a separate office, the State Superintendency; to establish and maintain a Normal School;

and it also determined to organize a State Teachers' Association, and secure, if possible, the publication of a journal devoted to the cause of free schools in the State. The Normal School question seems to have provoked a long and spirited debate. It is a curious fact that the same objections were then urged that are biennially reproduced in our Legislature against these schools. Can it be that we are never to reach a period in the discussion when these questions will be settled by the logic of events? It does seem as though the actual workings of these schools, in the past twenty-five years, has abundantly demonstrated the weakness of the arguments put forth against them in 1853.

After the adjournment of the convention, the Illinois State Teachers' Institute was organized. The name was changed to Illinois State Teachers' Association, two years afterward, at the second annual meeting, held in Springfield.

Rev. W. Goodfellow, of the Illinois Wesleyan University, was the first president, and Rev. Daniel Wilkins, the first secretary. A constitution was adopted, which contained nothing remarkable, except that it made provision for the appointment of a committee on almost every conceivable department of school work. After providing that the first annual meeting should be held in the city of Peoria, in December, 1854, the meeting adjourned.

The most prominent topic in all the early meetings of the Illinois State Teachers' Association, was the organization of a Normal School. At the Peoria meeting, in 1854, and again at Springfield, in 1855, the discussion was continued with much warmth. There seem to have been really three parties to the contest: The Normal School men, who contended that the great want of the State was trained teachers, and that these could be secured in no other way than by establishing a separate institution for that purpose; on the other hand, a large and influential class of educational workers, headed by Prof. J. B. Turner, of Jacksonville, who maintained that either an Industrial University, with a Normal Department, should be established, or else that an Agricultural Department should be attached to the Normal School; lastly, those who thought it would be disastrous to the best interests of all parties if education and religion were divorced, and who favored the founding of Normal Departments, by the State, in connection with all the sectarian colleges already established. The discussion of these various views was so long and bitter at the Springfield meeting that the following resolution was adopted:

Resolved, That the Association does not wish to discuss any university question, but occupy themselves (*sic*) with the interests of common schools and Normal Schools.

When the Association met in Chicago, in 1856, Prof. Turner sent a letter, gracefully withdrawing from the contest. The following extract will contribute to a clearer understanding of the whole controversy:

"It has ever been my opinion, and the general opinion of the friends of the Industrial League, that a Normal School, with an Agricultural Department connected with it, would be more strongly bound to the interests and feelings of the masses of our people, and therefore more popular and prosperous than if it stood entirely alone, for precisely the same reason that such institutions do not so well prosper when standing beneath the shadow of a college or university, or higher order of school; for it is a law of nature that the stronger and higher should draw from the weaker and the lower. Still, if this is not agreeable to the teachers of the State, or the friends of the Normal School, I wish them to organize it in such manner as they think best; and in any plan the Teachers' Association may devise, the friends of the League will most heartily coöperate, provided it is effectually separated from such partisan political control as would render it a curse instead of a blessing to the State.

It is high time, my friends, that you had your Normal School, whether we ever get an Agricultural Department to it or not. Let us all take hold together and try to obtain it in such form as you may, on the whole, think best.

Respectfully submitted, by yours most truly,

J. B. TURNER."

After a long and animated discussion, the Association passed the following:

"*Resolved*, That the educational interests of Illinois demand the immediate establishment of a State Normal School for the education of teachers: and, in the language of the Board of Education, 'We therefore recommend an appropriation, by the next Legislature, of a sufficient sum annually to support such a seminary of learning.' In the following February, the Legislature passed, and the Governor approved, 'An act for the establishment and maintenance of a Normal University.'"

Before giving a history of the University, its organization, etc., allow us to introduce a letter received by C. E. Mann at the quarter-centennial of the State Teachers' Association, held at Springfield, December 26, 1881. It contains many interesting facts respecting the

ILLINOIS PIONEERS OF EDUCATION.

CENSUS OFFICE,
WASHINGTON, D. C., December 26, 1881. }

C. E. MANN, *Chairman Executive Committee, S. T. A.:*

DEAR SIR: C. E. Hovey insists that I shall explain his failure to write and myself respond for him. He is in a great pressure of work just now, and regrets he did not begin when your note first came, when he might have written something. We have recalled many things in view of the anniversary at hand. I knew most of the men prominent in the first meeting, and I had an early part in the Association's work.   Joliet, Jacksonville, Quincy, Dixon, Rock Island, and Rockford have each been the place of meeting at least once.   Decatur, Ottawa, Galesburg, and Peoria, each at least twice. Bloomington and Springfield at least three times each.   I cannot locate all the war-time meetings.   Mr. Hovey's reminiscences freshen up my knowledge of matters mostly known to me as they occurred, and so little wholly new to me that this may pass for our joint production, without separate credit for each item possibly due to him. Some of the men prominent in those early meetings are yet prominent. The first meeting was at Peoria, the year Hovey came west, and while he was yet a teacher of a stock school, the germ of the present school system of Peoria.   There was W. H. Powell presiding as first vice-president, in absence of O. Springstead, president.   Although afterward State Superintendent, his record can only be followed as a warning to teachers not to be too fond of money.   Then there were men with the teachers in interest, but not in school-room work at the time.   A strong force of such men was represented at that Peoria meeting by one of eccentric enthusiasm, who attracted attention by the balancing of his short name with the initials before and after it: W. F. M. Arny, D. V. M., the latter part not interpreted to this day so far as heard from.   He was afterward active in "Bleeding Kansas;" yet later, acting governor of New Mexico; went to England to look after one of those great estates so often left to unknown Americans, and is reported to have died after his return.   Bronson Murray, active in agricultural ideas as applied to education, was there. He left the State for an eastern residence after spurring others to the work.   Representing these agricultural men on the one hand, and the school-room teachers on the other, the champion of agricultural education, with broad culture, a sympathizing perception of the needs of the actual teacher, serving to check impracticable notions, with a bull-dog pertinacity, and a pride of independence in his ideas, was J. B. Turner, of Jacksonville, of whom an opponent in debate, in his vexation, said "he wanted to go in a gang all by himself."   However, he was not always found alone in his many undertakings.   Hovey insists that from a speech in Putnam County, delivered by J. Turner, whose ideas had gathered force meantime, came a rally and a petition from the Illinois Legislature, which inaugurated the national grants for the Industrial Colleges.   It was the momentum of the movement of J. B. Turner and Bronson Murray, and their associates, that made the Normal School an early possibility, supported with the university fund, granted to the State by the general government forty years before.

The State Superintendent of that day was at Peoria—Ninian W. Edwards, first Superintendent of Illinois Public Schools, yet living to link the great State of to-day with the infant Territory, of which his father was the only Governor.   At other early meetings, John F.

Brooks, yet of Springfield, and Horace Spalding, of Jacksonville, helped give form and force to the new order of things.

Uncle Sim Wright was at that Peoria opening. A wonderful man for hard work, he had made a little village school, that even yet is not reached by railroad, the nucleus for the young people forty miles around. The sense of his power was even then upon the book agents, who there showed the mighty zeal that has characterized them in greater or less degree ever since. The prospects of the new era in Illinois made them almost as zealous as in a recent year when they gathered in Missouri to aid in determining, for the good of the people, what books would be used for the next five years. Uncle Sim had good qualities for us to copy, and he would sacrifice himself to his work. He had his faults too, and died too soon, himself his own worst enemy. The school attendance of Illinois was not before, nor since, so high in proportion to population as when Simeon Wright, as agent of the State Association in 1857-8, preached an educational revival in the free school-room day and night.

Newton Bateman was at that formation meeting, and his formative influence was already shaping the first graded school of the State, and to the younger teachers the name has become so much a matter of course that they hardly know, even as a matter of history, that the system and Newton Bateman have not always been synonymous terms.

Not to dwell especially farther on the individuality of that Peoria meeting, except to notice that Charles Davis, the mathematical professor at West Point, was one of the speakers, and that Lucy Stone and Henry B. Blackwell were there, the meeting must be characterized as giving form and vitality to at least three movements of great importance. 1. A Teachers' Journal. 2. The Normal University. 3. The character of the State Superintendency. Mr. Edwards had been appointed to the office by the governor.

In the early years of the Association, questions that have passed so long that some teachers of many years experience think they were always settled, stirred up the very depths of zealous excitement. The men who met at Peoria did not represent the free schools. It was only exceptionally rich districts that had free schools, through lucky sales of their township land or accumulation of their funds. Nor were the graded schools represented, for there were hardly enough in the State to make a plural number. Many Illinois public schools were under the plan of signing a certain number of scholars to be paid for whether they came or not, and the patron received some credit for any allowance there might be on the schedule. The early public schools of the graded form even were not free. Tuition was paid in Jacksonville, in Peoria, and in Springfield for some time after the graded methods were introduced. The one idea, educate the people, drew those pioneers together, and all the questions of *how* were yet fresh for discussion and possessed an intense vitality that those who come to reap the fruits of others' planting cannot realize.

Insurance and law, as well as death, have taken off some who did zealous pioneer work. There were Tabor, of Aurora, and Heywood, of the same place, and now I find my memories flashing all about till I will drive a peg at the war and dismiss most this side of it as modern history. C. H. Dupee, then at the head of the Chicago High School, has not been known by this generation of teachers, but he can help them out of legal difficulties. D. S. Wentworth still wears the armor of an old warrior. W. H. Wells yearns for schools enough even now and then to take official relation to them, as also does J. F. Eberhart. The great apostle of Egypt is known, in the benignant name of Father Roots, to the present teachers who do not know his fighting capacity of the formative days. There is N. C. Nason, long a power, not known by his face to half so many as read his name as publisher, for many years, of the *Illinois Teacher*,—a man of sound education, and rare taste as a printer. There is Willard, the painstaking professor of history in the Chicago High School, who helped more than most men know in shaping the system of Illinois. There was, J. D. Low, first principal of the St. Louis High School, superintendent briefly in Springfield, of larger influence in Illinois than to be measured by the years of his teaching in the State. There was the sturdy A. M. Brooks, whose ratio of boys among graduates, in Springfield, has been rarely excelled in any similar school. A. M. Gow is now editing a paper at Washington, Pennsylvania. James Gow edits a paper and raises corn in Iowa. S. H. White, a hard-working, devoted man, finds his long form valuable in overlooking sheep on an Iowa prairie.* President Edwards was known to us as of St. Louis, when war came. He and President Hewett are a part of present, as well as of former history. Matthew Andrew and J. B. Roberts are names that come easily together as of Galesburg, where one still does good service, while the other teaches yet in Indianapolis. Trade, especially in books, has taken some strong men, as Woodard and Cook, who both sat in the Legislature, and Herrick, who did not sit in the Legislature.

Every State Superintendent of the State was identified with the record before the war. J. V. N. Standish was a faithful pioneer, of whom the present Association sees little. There were B. M. Reynolds, of Rock Island, now of Wisconsin, the earnest Kelly, of Whiteside, Wescott, most wonderful in power of minute investigation, now at the head of the Racine schools, Dr. Sewall, now in Colorado, and Ira Moore, now of Minnesota.

The Normal School was just beginning to show its results. Your

---

*Mr. White died March 15, 1882.

presiding officer (Gastman) and P. R. Walker, who went to war in the Ninety-Second Illinois Mounted Infantry, and Gove, of Denver, who was in the Thirty-Third Illinois Volunteers, and Norton, of the California Normal School, were of the men just putting their hands to the work. There were M. L. Seymour, true to his friends, and W. B. Powell, who has won distinction at home and abroad, and almost obliterated the memory of a Powell of a very different stock.

And there were many more doing valiant service in those days, to some of whom apparent injustice may, I fear, be done. In a record of the schools many names will have high position which were not so closely identified with the history of the Association.

Chicago has done herself honor in putting the grandest old bachelor of the profession, of fine scholarship, and very long, faithful service, in charge of her schools. It needs to be chronicled as an instance of public recognition of such service. He plead the sorrows of woman to some of us before the war, and the women in the Chicago schools never had a more appreciative friend.

The story since the war is better known, but those who know only the modern history know very little of the days when personal pledges of work and of money were the means to secure general success. This Association, one year, paid $1,500, and traveling expenses, to an agent. Pledges to *The Teacher* meant something, and among all the demands many a one put $25 and $50 at a time into the funds. Discussions and resolutions only pointed the way. The great school opportunities of to-day rest upon the foundations thus laid. Will the teachers and the people of to-day work with so much zeal and so much self-denial, upon the superstructure? Are the teachers, and the preachers, and the people, ready for the labor, and the sacrifices, and the self-denial, that shall make the moral and the intellectual growth of the country equal the marvelous physical development recorded in these census reports under my hand? Labor, and sacrifice, and self-denial, laid the foundation, and they are needed for solidity in the progress of to-day.

Yours, very heartily,
JAS. H. BLODGETT.

NORMAL UNIVERSITY.

ITS LOCATION AND CONSTRUCTION.

The location of the State Normal University at North Bloomington, May 7, 1857, marks a period of history that is not only important to Normal Township, but also in an equal degree to the city of
Bloomington and McLean County. At the time indicated, Normal
was North Bloomington, or "The Junction," the six miles square
now called Normal, not having been named until after the location of
the University, its first existence as a town dating from April 6, 1858.
The early history of the Normal Institution, its location, its first
years of struggling effort, its vigorous childhood, belong to Bloomington, and this sketch is as well calculated to honor that city as it is
fitted to reflect credit upon Normal. As we proceed with our account, we shall reach a period when the newly-built village became
in reality Normal, with a definite future and prospects of its own,
after which time, its acts and doings shall be credited to the proper
source as zealously as its most earnest friends can desire.

We might state, that in 1857, the township was generally occupied by farmers, the village of North Bloomington having been
platted and a few houses built, but to all practical intents, the entire
township was simply an agricultural district.

The Illinois Central and Chicago & Alton Railroads were finished and in running order several years before the location of the
University, an excursion train having been run on the 4th day of
July, 1854, from Bloomington to Lexington. The cars of the Illinois
Central passed this point without stopping, from May 23, 1853, to
the time of the completion of the other line. It was thought, in
1852, that there would be a railroad crossing near this place, and after
the definite location of the Chicago & Alton line through the western
part of Bloomington, in 1853, the point of the junction was fixed.
North Bloomington was projected and platted in the early part of
1854. There was a sale of lots on the 15th of June, 1854, at which
about thirty lots sold at prices ranging between $30 and $50, and
public attention was thus attracted to the new town of North Bloomington. The sale took place under the auspices of W. F. M. Arny

& Co., but it was understood that Mr. Jesse W. Fell was the moving spirit in the enterprise.

In 1855, a large addition was made to North Bloomington by a company composed of Jesse W. Fell, R. R. Landon, L. R. Case, C. W. Holder, and L. C. Blakesly. The place had all the prospects common to a railroad "crossing," or "junction," which were never very brilliant, when it is considered that the important town of Bloomington, with two depots, was only two miles away. Here, at the point of greatest natural beauty, Mr. Jesse W. Fell commenced, in 1855, his family residence, and finished it the next year, when he made it his permanent home.

In the enterprise of building a new town at the "Junction," he had taken into partnership, about this time, the several gentlemen whose names we have given; and in the course of a few years thereafter, acquired from them nearly the whole of their interests in the town site.

Mr. Fell, from the first, had plans for bringing to North Bloomington something more than the ordinary business of a common railroad crossing. He intended to spare no effort to build here a town that should have for its characteristics, sobriety, morality, good society, and all the elements for an educational center. Previous to the passage of the act to establish a Normal University, which dates from February 18, 1857, Mr. Fell was laboring, with some prospects of success, to establish at North Bloomington a college or seminary of learning, and was in correspondence with Hon. Horace Mann, and others, in regard to the matter. Had he succeeded, the institution was to have been located upon Seminary Block, shown on the plat of North Bloomington, as the block next east of Mr. Fell's residence. This particular piece of ground, at that time, before the trees and shrubbery had made their appearance, commanded a fine view of all the land in the neighborhood, being a part of that beautifully-rounded, elevated prairie upon which Mr. Fell built his family residence. In fact, the whole tract was one of striking beauty, long before North Bloomington was projected, in the days when, for more than a mile in either direction, not a house or improvement of any kind was visible. As long ago as in 1833, when on his way to what is now the township of Money Creek, in company with Mr. Kimler, one of the early settlers of Blooming Grove, Mr. Fell rode over the beautiful elevation which his residence now occupies. The public highway then passed in that vicinity. It was early in the morning, and as they surveyed the beautiful prairie landscape, Mr. Fell remarked, what a fine location this would be, at some day, for a residence. His companion replied that it was not probable any one would ever be fool enough to build at such a great distance from the timber, echoing thereby the common sentiment of the early settlers. Over twenty years after, Mr. Fell built his family residence at that point, and commenced to plant trees, which, in a little more than another twenty years, have made at that location the most beautiful grove, or park, that can be found in Central Illinois, and he has lived to see the prairie landscape converted into a beautiful village, shaded by many thousand trees tastefully adorning the whole. We question if the history of our rapidly growing State can furnish a parallel, a town built entirely on the prairie, and, in so short a space of time, to be covered with more large trees than can be shown in most cities of older growth, though they were built on land originally occupied by those grand monarchs of the forest, which the early settlers delighted in destroying as fast as possible.

Mr. Fell took a remarkable step toward bringing to the new town a desirable class of residents, by providing in all deeds to purchasers of lots in North Bloomington, that intoxicating liquors should never be sold on the premises; and this stringent prohibition was afterward re-enforced by a town charter, which was intended to be entirely prohibitory. This charter needed amendments, however, in 1867, to make it as fully operative as the inhabitants desired, and a petition was circulated, asking the Legislature to make such changes as should perpetually restrain the town or city authorities from ever licensing the sale of intoxicating liquors. It is remarkable that this petition was signed by every man and woman, and every child over seven years old, in a town which then contained 1,800 inhabitants. This incident, though rather out of the proper historical order, is valuable, as we thus discover that the foundations for the gathering-together of a very superior class of citizens, were laid broad and deep, and the subsequent character of Normal can be traced quite plainly to those early efforts. North Bloomington, in 1857, was barely started—scarcely known—called indiscriminately by its proper name, or the "Junction;" a town site without a town, and no special reason for its existence. There was one inhabitant previous to 1855; this was Mr. McCambridge, whose residence was at the crossing of the railroads, where, as agent, he attended to all the interests of the railroad lines crossing at that point. Mr. Fell moved into his residence in 1856, and, during the year, the new town was augmented by the arrival of L. R. Case and family, and a few others, but no great growth took place till after the events of the year 1857.

Normal Schools were new in the West at that time, Illinois being the pioneer in this grand enterprise. Massachusetts, New York, and New Jersey, and a few other States, had inaugurated Normal Schools. None of them were equal to the demands of the times. Still, their success had been such as to warrant the public in expecting that institutions for the education and training of teachers of our common schools would aid the cause of education to a desirable degree. Some of the ablest friends of this new project for the proper education of the teachers of the public schools, lived·in McLean County, among whom we might mention W. F. M. Arny, Jesse W. Fell, Prof. D. Wilkins, and J. H. Wickizer, the latter being member of the Legislature from this district.

The public mind was ripe for the proper appreciation of the needs, designs, and scope of such a school, although even its own advocates differed somewhat as to the course of study and plans for its development.

The act of the Legislature provided for a university, although what was established is, in fact, a Normal School. The intention was to gather around the new institution the different colleges,—classical, agricultural, industrial, law, medical, and the other departments of a university,—until, in the end, the State should have here a grand university, equal to any in the land. The full design has not been carried out, but there are many who still have hopes that the future may yet see its realization.

The law provided a Board of Education of the State of Illinois, with power to carry into effect its purposes. This Board consisted of N. W. Edwards, of Springfield; W. H. Wells, of Chicago; John R. Eden, Moultrie County; A. R. Shannon, White County; Simeon Wright, Lee County; W. Sloan, Pope County; George Bunsen, St. Clair County; George P. Rex, Pike County; Charles E. Hovey, Peoria; Daniel Wilkins, Bloomington; C. B. Denio, Galena; F. Mosely, Chicago; S. W. Moulton, Shelby County; and J. Gillespie, Jasper County. This Board had full power, and it was made their duty, "to fix the permanent location of said Normal University at the place where the most favorable inducements are offered for that purpose, provided that such location shall not be difficult of access, or detrimental to the welfare and prosperity of said Normal University."

This body of gentlemen soon organized, and it appointed a committee to receive proposals for the location of the Normal University, which committee published notices in several newspapers, stating that the Board would, on a certain specified day, open, at Peoria, all bids that might be made.

Several cities and towns entered into competition for what was understood to be a valuable prize. That the value of the new institution was thoroughly appreciated by the inhabitants of Bloomington is shown by the following extract from the Bloomington *Pantagraph* of April 8, 1857, then edited by E. J. Lewis:

The advantages to be conferred by such an institution upon the place of its location are too obvious to need enlarging upon. Richly endowed from a government fund, collecting within its walls every year the flower of the youth of every part of the State, and organized with a full corps of the ablest instructors, the Normal University will doubtless take rank among the noblest institutions of learning in the country, and give to the town which contains it a degree of prominence at home and abroad scarcely second to that enjoyed by the State capital itself.

In the light of subsequent events, how prophetic this statement!

Mr. Fell and his co-workers did not rely on appeals made through the public press. On the contrary, they were willing that the competing points should labor under the impression that Bloomington was not thoroughly aroused. These gentlemen labored incessantly with individuals; argued, pictured, pleaded, taught, both by precept and example. They set the fashion by giving liberal subscriptions, and so far succeeded that they brought the amount of donations, in land and money, up to $50,000, from private individuals. They had previously obtained a pledge from the members of the County Commissioners' Court, A. J. Merriman, of Bloomington, Milton Smith, of Pleasant Hill, and H. Buck, of LeRoy, who formed the County Court at that time, that they would appropriate from the proceeds of the swamp-lands funds an amount equal to that subscribed by individuals. This made the total offer $100,000, and it was thought amply sufficient to secure the location.

In order to be fully aware of what Peoria—the principal competitor—was doing, one of the most active of our party went to that city, quietly, and rather in disguise, dropped into a back seat of a meeting of the County Board, held in aid of the project, mixed with the crowd in the streets, and, in various ways, learned almost exactly what Peoria was preparing to offer. Its liberality alarmed him; he returned to Bloomington, and aroused his friends to still further efforts. Mr. Fell and other gentlemen increased their subscriptions until they reached $20,000, or $70,000 in all. The County Court was speedily called together again, the county's part increased by $20,000, and when the final effort was completed, at about the last day, in the afternoon, the total offer amounted to $141,000, made up of $70,000 from the first proceeds of the sales of McLean County's swamp-land, and $71,000 in money, lands, and town lots from individuals.

But the gross amount was kept a profound secret. Mr. Fell, and a very few others, were aware of the total, as it was highly important that competing points should remain in ignorance until too late for them to make additional subscriptions.

On the 7th of May, 1857, the State Board of Education met at Peoria to open the bids and decide upon the location. The first offer was that of Batavia. This bid embraced $15,000 in money, and the land and buildings of the Batavia Institute. There were between twenty and twenty-two acres of the land, and a building seventy by fifty feet, three stories high, the whole estimated at $30,000, making Batavia's bid, in effect, $45,000. The citizens pledged themselves to raise $25,000, in order to pay a debt of $10,000 now resting on the buildings, and to give the sum of $15,000 for the Normal University direct. There were several propositions from Bloomington, six sites being offered. The tract of 160 acres at the junction was the favorite, and the particulars of that proposition were as follows:

General subscription, ... $ 7,875
Local cash subscription for Junction site, ... 25,850
Real estate: 160 acres land—60 acres at $300 per acre, $18,000;
   100 acres at $200 per acre, $20,000, ... 38,000
McLean County subscription, ... 70,000

     Total, ... $141,725

There were offered also, by K. H. Fell, thirty acres west of Sugar Creek; by Judge Davis, ten acres, near his residence; by William Flagg, ten acres, on the north hill above the city; by Thomas, Young & Sears, forty acres northeast of town; by K. H. Fell and John Nicolls, eighty acres, two and a half miles east of the city, each of these on condition the University be located upon them. By the citizens of Washington, Tazewell County, and the Trustees of Washington Academy were offered $12,000 in cash, and the lot 430 by 120 feet, with brick building 47 by 62 feet, and three stories high, of said Academy, in said town; real estate at $20,000, making the bid $21,000. Peoria offered in money:

Individual subscription, ... $25,032
City Corporation, ... 10,000
County Board of Supervisors, ... 15,000

     Total, ... $50,032

There were several offers of land for sites. Phelps, Conklin & Brady offered 15 acres, of which appraisements were unsettled, the first rating it at $18,000, the second at $30,000; the twenty-acre site was valued at $20,000; 120 acres two miles from the Court House, at $18,000; 200 acres three and a half miles from the Court House, at $20,000, and there were two minor offers. Taking the highest valuation of the principal site, the total bid of Peoria was $80,032.

The bid of McLean County was so far ahead of Peoria, the next competitor, that the Board of Education located the Normal University in accordance with the conditions of the subscription, on the 160 acres of fine rolling land within three-quarters of a mile from the junction of the Illinois Central and Chicago & Alton Railroads.

Great must have been the rejoicing at Bloomington on receipt of the glad news of success, after a contest of such intensity; but we, who look back over twenty years, can scarcely imagine the interest of the occasion.

The Board of Education made the location upon the condition that the full amount of the McLean County subscription of $70,000 should be legally guaranteed within sixty days, in default of which, the location was to be made at Peoria. They employed Abraham Lincoln to draw up a form of bond or guaranty to be signed by responsible citizens of Bloomington. This guaranty is a matter of such historical interest that we produce it entire, with the list of guarantors, prefacing this with the remark that this bond was thought to be necessary on account of the danger that a future County Court might reconsider the appropriation, and the further doubt whether the swamp-lands would be sold for cash soon enough to meet contracts for the building about to be erected.

GUARANTY.

WHEREAS, On the 15th day of May, 1857, the Executive Committee of the Board of Education of the State of Illinois passed a resolution in the words and figures following, to-wit:

"*Resolved*, That we require of the citizens of Bloomington a guaranty that the sum of $14,000 be paid on the 1st day of August next, and the further sum of $14,000 on the 1st day of November next, and the further sum of $14,000 on the 1st day of February next, and the further sum of $14,000 on the 1st day of May next, and the remaining sum of $14,000 on the 1st day of August, 1858, if called for by the Board, to enable them to erect the building of the Normal University, on the McLean County subscription."

Now, therefore, we, the undersigned, in consideration that the said McLean County subscription be accepted by said Board of Education, and the said Normal University be located at the place and in accordance with the conditions indicated in and by said McLean County subscription, do hereby guarantee, each, to the extent of the sum set opposite his name, and no further, the payment to said Board of Education the several sums specified in said resolution, and to be made at the times therein required. And in case of any actual default, we are to share with each other, *pro rata*, according to the several sums set opposite our names.

May 15, 1857.

K. H. Fell,	$5,000	James Bronson,	$ 500
Jesse W. Fell,	5,000	Edward D. Benjamin,	1,000
J. E. McClun,	5,000	F. W. Bakewell,	5,000
A. B. Shaffer,	5,000	Dr. H. Schrœder,	1,000
A. Gridley,	5,000	H. H. Painter,	3,000
George Bruener,	1,000	H. J. Eager,	5,000
R. R. Landon,	5,000	Z. Lawrence,	2,000
R. Leach,	500	John Magoun,	5,000
W. McCullough,	3,000	Leonard Swett,	3,000
H. Rounds,	5,000	James Grover,	3,000
George Park,	5,000	A. W. Moore,	3,000
J. H. Moore,	3,000	O. Ellsworth,	1,000
A. J. Merriman,	1,000	L. Bunn,	1,000
John Dawson.	1,000	Z. S. Hoover,	3,000
William R. Chew,	500	S. E. Kenyon & Son,	1,000
A. W. Rogers,	2,000	David Brier,	5,000
E. R. Roe,	500	A. Johnstone,	500
R. T. Stockton,	500	R. Thompson & Co.,	1,000
J. C. Walker,	2,000	S. G. Fleming,	1,000
J. H. Robinson,	1,000	C. W. Lander,	500
William F. Flagg,	5,000	John Rouse,	2,000
Overman & Mann,	1,000	S. S. Adolph,	1,000
William E. Foote,	1,000	J. C. Slening,	1,000
D. D. Haggard,	500	E. H. Rood.	1,000
Denton Young,	3,000	John J. Price,	5,000
W. W. Lusk,	3,000	Joseph Ludington,	1,000
C. Baker,	3,000	O. Rugg,	1,000
Joseph Payne,	5,000	N. B. Heafer,	2,000
M. Pike,	1,000	Keays & Brother,	500
S. B. Hance,	5,000	S. Galagher,	1,000
C. W. Holder,	2,000	Birch & Brothers,	1,000
S. P. Morehouse,	1,000	Elihu Rogers,	2,000
N. Dixon,	1,000	E. M. Philips,	1,000
Charles Roadnight,	5,000	J. F. Humphreys,	1,000
Franklin Price,	3,000	C. Wakefield,	1,000

William W. Orme,	5,000	W. Wyatt,	5,000
W. W. Lusk & Company,	5,000	A. J. Warner,	5,000
William T. Major,	5,000	J. N. Ward,	5,000
D. L. Crist,	2,000	E. Hartry,	5,000
Theron Pardee,	5,000	James L. Rice,	1,000
George W. Stipp,	5,000	W. P. Withers,	1,000
W. H. Temple,	3,000	Jesse Adams,	1,000
James Niccolls,	3,000		

Their guaranty was never enforced, as it was found that some of the lands were sold for cash, others on credit, and the proceeds used in the building, and it also happened there was no trouble about the county appropriation, as it was confirmed by the new court in the spring of 1858. This new court consisted of a Board of Supervisors, the county having adopted township organization at the fall election in 1857. This guaranty, however, was made in good faith, was of great value at the time, and is one of the important steps taken to secure the Normal University.

It will also be interesting to read the list of subscribers, which we give. The following is a list of subscriptions that were nearly all given with the single condition that the institution should be located at some point within one mile of the corporate limits of Bloomington:

Jesse W. Fell, $500, payable in six and twelve months after location is made; also, ten acres for site, to be selected anywhere, valued at $2,000.
C. W. Holder, $200, payable in six and twelve months.
S. D. Rounds, $300, payable in six and twelve months.
William W. Orme, $100, payable in six and twelve months.
R. O. Warriner, $100, payable in six and twelve months after the building commences.
A. B. Shaffer, $600, payable in six and twelve months.
Park & Brother, $100, payable in six and twelve months.
Robert Leach, $100, payable in six and twelve months.
R. R. Landon, $100, payable in six and twelve months.
George Dietrich, $50, payable in six and twelve months.
Leonard Swett, $100, payable in six and twelve months.
W. Thomas, $100, payable in six and twelve months.
A. and O. Barnard, $100, payable in six and twelve months.
J. E. McClun, $500, in real estate at cash prices.
Isaac Mitchell, $50, payable in six and twelve months.
William E. Foote, $100, payable in six and twelve months.
James P. Keen, $100, payable in six and twelve months.
S. B. Hance, $100, payable in six and twelve months.
Hance & Taylor, $100, payable in six and twelve months.
Corydon Weed, $100, payable in six and twelve months.
John R. Smith, $50, payable in six and twelve months.
R. Y. Stockton, $50, payable in six and twelve months.
O. Ellsworth, $100, payable in six and twelve months.
Lewis Bunn, $100, payable in eight and twelve months.
E. Thorp, Smith & Co., $100, payable in six and twelve months.
John Magoun, $100, payable in six and twelve months.
C. P. Merriman, $50, payable in six and twelve months.
F. K. Phœnix, $100, payable in one and two years.
F. Price, $100, payable in one and two years.
E. Thomas, $200, payable in one and two years.
Denton Young, $100, payable in one and two years.
W. W. Taylor, $200, payable in one and two years.

K. P. Taylor, $150, payable in one and two years.

K. H. Fell, $100, payable in good notes, to be made payable in one and two years from the 1st of June next, provided the said institution is located within two miles of the corporate limits of the city of Bloomington.

Jesse W. Fell, $500, payable by the conveyance of 100 acres of land, of average value, in Range 4 west, of Jackson County, Ill., on completion of building.

The list which follows is made up principally of those who limited their subscription to a location within three-fourths of a mile of the junction of the Illinois Central and Chicago & Alton Railroads. These individuals owned land in North Bloomington, or adjoining, or near by, and hence had, most of them, a direct interest in the location. Several of these made smaller unconditional subscriptions. C. W. Holder, for instance, would give $200, wherever the institution might be located, and $800 more provided North Bloomington were the fortunate point. The most of this, with that in the preceding list, was limited, practically, to the site which was chosen, it being within one mile of the corporate limits of Bloomington, and also within three-fourths of a mile of the crossing of the two railroads:

Jesse W. Fell, $2,000 (including a subscription of $500 already made), payable in one, two, three, four, and five years: *Provided*, not less than $10,000 more can be added to this subscription, and not less than eighty acres of land; the first $500 to be expended in making a good side or foot walk to the Junction from University.

Swett & Orme, $1,500 (including a subscription of $200 already made), payable in one and two years: *Provided*, not less than $10,000 more can be had to this subscription, and not less than eighty acres of land.

C. W. Holder, $1,000 (including a subscription of $200 already made), payable in one and two years: *Provided*, not less than $10,000 more can be had to this subscription, and not less than eighty acres of land.

F. K. Phœnix, $1,500 (including a subscription of $100 already made), payable one-half in nursery stock or ornamental planting on said site, and the balance in one and two years.

R. R. Landon, $1,000 (including a subscription of $100 already made), payable in one and two years.

F. Price, $300 (including a subscription of $100 already made), payable in one and two years.

Robert Ulrich, $300, payable in one and two years.

William Dooley, $500, payable in one and two years.

A. Gridley & Co., $1,150, dischargeable by a conveyance of eleven and one-half acres of land situated in North Bloomington, and in tracts adjoining on the north.

John Magoun, $700 (including a subscription of $100 already made), payable in one and two years.

William Hill, $400, payable in one and two years.

O. M. Colman, $1,000, payable in one or two years, or dischargeable by the conveyance, within one year, of ten acres of land in North Bloomington.

Joshua R. Fell, $500, payable in one or two years, or dischargeable by the conveyance, within one year, of five acres of land off the south end of my home farm, east of the railroad, at my option.

O. T. Reeves, Jr., $500, payable in one and two years.

Elihu Rogers, $500, payable in one and two years.

William E. Foote, $200 (including $100 already subscribed), payable in one and two years.

Robert A. Dalzell, $250, payable in one and two years.

Thomas Junk, $500, payable in one and two years, or dischargeable by the conveyance, within one year, of five acres of land in the northwest corner of my farm, at my option.

Norvel Dixon, $200, payable in one and two years: *Provided*, I succeed in getting a good title to the northeast quarter of Section 22, Township 24 north, Range 2 east.

W. W. Taylor, $600, payable in one and two years, including a subscription already made of $200.

K. P. Taylor, $500, payable in one and two years, including a subscription already made of $150.

J. S. Walker, $200, payable in one and two years, if located on the Arny property.

Overman & Mann, $1,200, payable in one, two, and three years, one-half in nursery stock, hedging and ornamental planting, first and second years; and balance cash, second and third years.

L. R. Case, $200, payable in one and two years in cash, or dischargeable within one year by the conveyance of two acres of ground in North Bloomington, and adjoining on the north, at my option.

K. H. Fell, $500, payable in notes to be due in three years from the 1st of June next.

John Rouse, $200, payable in one and two years from the 1st of June next.

W. H. Allin, $1,100, payable on the completion of the building, by the conveyance of the following lots: Lot 7, Block 1; Lot 5, Block 2; Lot 13, Block 13; Lots 14 and 15, Block 23; and Lot 9, Block 24—all of Western Addition to Bloomington.

William T. Major, $600, payable on the completion of the building, by a conveyance of Lot No. One (1), Section 16, Township 25, R. 2 east, containing 40 acres.

George P. Howell, $150, payable in one, two, and three years, equal installments.

Jesse W. Fell, $7,000, payable, on the completion of the University Building, by the conveyance of 1,450 acres of my Jackson County lands, situated in Towns 8 and 9 south, Ranges 4 and 5 west of the Third Principal Meridian, and to be of average value with my other lands in said townships, to be selected by disinterested persons.

The next list is mostly made of those who subscribed on condition that the institution should be located at some point within three miles of the corporate limits of Bloomington.

Dietrich & Bradner, $200, one-half payable in nine months and balance in eighteen.

Poston & Didlake, $100, one-half payable in nine months and balance in eighteen.

S. P. Morehouse, $100, one-half payable in six months and balance in twelve.

D. L. Crist, $100, within one mile of Bloomington, one-half in six months, balance in twelve months, and $100 more if located within one mile of Junction.

A. C. Washburn, $50.

Harwood & Rugg, $200, one-half payable in nine months and balance in fifteen, if located one-half mile from Junction.

John Denman, $100, on condition that said school is located within one and one-half miles of Bloomington.

E. K. Crothers, $50, one-half in nine months and balance in one year.

R. E. Woodson, $50, one-half in six months and balance in one year.

Thomas Carlile, $200, one-half in six months and balance in twelve months, if located within one mile of the corporate limits.

C. Weed, $500.

Samuel Watson, $200, in one and two years.

O'Donald & Warner, $300, in one and two years.

C. W. Lander, $50.

E. Barber & Co., $50.

R. B. Harris, $25.

A. Steel, $25.

E. Martin, $100, in one and two years.

T. J. Karr, $25.

C. Wakefield, $50, in one and two years.

Giles A. Smith & Graham, $50, in one and two years.

Samuel Colvin, $25.

John McMillan, $25, in one and two years.

A. J. Nason, $25, in one and two years.
J. Bronson, $25, in one and two years.
A. Sutton, $25, in one and two years.
J. W. Lichenthaler, $25, in one and two years.
J. B. Crouch, $25, in one and two years.
K. Thompson, $25, in one and two years.
J. W. Moore, $50, in one and two years.
Orin Small, $100, in one and two years.
James Grover, $100, in four yearly payments.
E. M. Philips, $100, in four yearly payments.

The subscriptions in this last list, as well as those in the first and second classes, were, by the terms of their subscription, included among the donations to the Normal University.

In addition to the above, we find that Joseph Payne and Meshack Pike donated the site where the institution was located, consisting of about sixty acres, with enough more on the west to make their gift about eighty acres, the whole valued at about $22,000. Mr. E. W. Bakewell and Judge David Davis, each gave forty acres, valued, together, at $16,000. The whole of the last-mentioned eighty acres, and some of the other, is west of Main street, and is the land designed to be used by the agricultural department of the institution.

The list we have given speaks for itself. It is a record of liberalty, which, at the time it was made, was unparalled, and caused great comment all over the country. We should not forget that the most valuable part of the subscription—that which really was of the most solid importance—was the county subscription. This was voted by the County Commissioners—Judge A. J. Merriman, of Bloomington, and his Associates, Hon. Milton Smith, of Pleasant Hill, and Hon. H. Buck, of LeRoy, in a quiet, almost private session, with no opportunity to consult their constituents.

In the fall of 1857, these gentlemen were all re-elected to the same positions; and when the Board of Supervisors, in the following year, ratified their proceedings, appointing A. J. Merriman Swamp-Land Commissioner, it was seen that McLean County fully sustained the County Court in its disposition of so large a portion of the swamp-land funds.

The Board of Education appointed an architect—George P. Randall, of Chicago—who prepared plans and specifications, upon which bids were called for in the papers of Alton, Galena, Springfield, Peoria, Chicago, and Bloomington. Fifteen bids were made, ranging in price from $80,000 to $115,000. The contract was awarded to Mortimer & Loburg, and T. H. Soper, of Chicago, for the sum of $83,000, the work to be completed September 1, 1858. The corner-stone was laid September 29, 1857. On this occasion there was quite an impressive ceremony. Rev. H. J. Eddy, of the Baptist Church, of Bloomington, offered a prayer. Prof. D. Wilkins read a letter from Gov. Matteson, appropriate to the occasion. W. H. Powell, State School Superintendent, deposited in the corner-stone a copy of the school laws and of the different educational journals of the day.

Mr. Jesse W. Fell deposited a list of all the contributors to the location of the Normal, and hoped to see the institution develop into a complete' State University, with a model farm and Agricultural College.

Dr. E. R. Roe, the editor of the *Illinois Baptist*, deposited all the Bloomington papers of the time, and made a very appropriate speech. Judge A. J. Merriman, of the County Court, placed the upper stone in position when the ceremony was completed.

Before winter, quite a large amount of work had been done upon the stone foundation of the lower story, and about $30,000 was expended before the work was suspended for the winter season.

The financial crisis of 1857, which commenced in the month of September, was the means of causing a discontinuance of the work on the building. The county lands could not be sold for cash; many of the subscribers were crippled, and it was thought best by the State Board to wait a few years, till money matters might become easier, and hence the buildings were not fully completed until the early part of 1861. During 1859 and 1860, the work was pushed with sufficient vigor to see the building inclosed in the winter of 1859, and far enough advanced so that the graduating exercises of the first class were held at the new building in June, 1860.

Temporary rooms had been secured by the State Board at Major's Hall, in Bloomington, where, on the 5th day of October, 1857, Charles E. Hovey, Principal, and Ira Moore, Assistant, opened the Normal School with 29 pupils, whose numbers increased during the academic year to a total of 127. Major's Hall continued to be used until the fall term of 1860, when the Normal building was far enough finished to be occupied by the entire institution. Several of the rooms were not completed till late in the winter, at which time the State made an appropriation of $65,000 to pay debts which had accumulated against the Board of Education. The building cost more than the sum first agreed upon, owing, in part, to advanced cost of materials. Included in the appropriation is a large sum for heating and furnishing the building, and for miscellaneous matters. A portion of this money was lost by the failure of so many banks in 1861, and for other reasons it was found necessary for the next Legislature to appropriate $35,000 more before the debts were fully paid. The total cost of the building, with all the incidental expenses, and the amount asked for books and furniture up to 1863, was about $200,000; but had the building been completed near the time it was started, the total cost would probably not have exceeded $100,000, reckoning simply the cost of the building. It should be stated that McLean County honorably met its subscription according to its terms, and that nearly all the private individuals paid, though, as before stated, the State Board of Education did not enforce the subscriptions at the time most of them were payable.

The Normal building is located about two miles north of the McLean County Court House, on an elevated plateau, commanding a splendid view of Bloomington and the surrounding country.   At the time of its erection, the adjacent lands were principally utilized for agricultural purposes; but since that time, the beautiful suburban village of Normal, with its elegant villas, lovely parks, classic church spires, and wealth of flowers and shade trees, has clustered around it, making as fine a combination of natural and artificial landscapes as can be found in the entire West.

The building is admirably arranged for collegiate use.   Its dimensions are 160 feet in length; the end wings are 100 feet in width, and the central portions, 80 feet.   The distance from the basement to the extreme height of the tower is 140 feet.   The basement is divided into apartments, used, respectively, as a chemical and zoological laboratory, scientific lecture room, and dissecting rooms. These are furnished with the necessaries for thorough, practical tests and demonstrations in the various branches.   The remainder of the basement is occupied by the janitor's rooms and the heating apparatus, hot air and steam being both utilized.   Here, also, may be found reels of hose, connected with the reservoir, located near the roof, which furnishes sufficient water-pressure to extinguish any ordinary outbreak of fire.

The first floor is exactly symmetrical in its divisions, the adjacent sides and opposite ends corresponding precisely with each other in the size of the apartments. The north side is divided into four recitation rooms, occupied by the grammar and high schools. The corner rooms on the south side are large, convenient dressing rooms. The primary department serves as a training-school for teachers. Here, the pupils of the Normal Department witness the theoretical, practical, and diciplinary work of teaching, demonstrated by Prof. Metcalf and his assistants. Pupils are required to take charge of primary classes, affording them an excellent opportunity to put into practice the theories imbibed by observation. The reception room, in the central front, is a neat apartment, carpeted with Brussels and furnished with upholstered chairs and sofas, the walls hung with portraits, and, on one side, adorned with an elegant gilt-framed mirror.

Ascending to the second floor, we find the assembly-rooms occupying the entire width of the building, with seats and desks for 270 pupils. The remainder of this floor is divided into eight recitation rooms, the library and reading rooms. The library contains about one thousand four hundred volumes of choice, standard reference-books. The reading room contains files of prominent literary and news journals.

The third floor contains five departments—the museum, Normal Hall, and the two society rooms, the latter occupying the west end; they are 30 by 50 feet each, and seat 250 persons. They are similarly furnished, each with a well-selected library, a piano, and other appropriate articles, all of which are the property of the societies. The Philadelphian and Wrightonians hold their regular literary exercises once a week. The Normal Hall is 80 feet square and 20 feet in width, with a seating capacity of about 800 persons. The museum occupies the east end, and contains a very valuable collection, of great interest to the student as well as interesting to visitors.

When the Normal building was ready for occupancy, in the fall of 1860, the village of Normal comprised only about thirty houses, and a large number of the students resided in Bloomington during the first two years; but by the fall of 1862, there were enough tenements to accommodate all who desired board at Normal. From this time forward, the number of permanent residents in Normal rapidly increased, and probably the year 1863 may be taken as the time when the village had become in reality, distinct and separate from Bloomington, with definite aims of its own. Houses went up on every side, retail stores began to be started, and Normal was a town of 1,000 inhabitants as early as 1865.

AUTOBIOGRAPHY OF GEN. C. E. HOVEY.

(From the SCHOOLMASTER, 1869.)

DEAR WENTWORTH:

You say "your (my) history may be autobiographical or otherwise (let it be otherwise), for I know lots of your old friends who would be glad to do you the honor, if you would furnish the facts concerning your early life, with dates, etc." Said history to occupy "about two pages or eleven hundred words."

Don't you think that limit will squeeze the story dry?

You remember the cider-press in use when we were boys. The pomace, made into cheese, and bound together by wisps of straw, occupied a liberal space, and held the juice; but when compressed to a pancake, by huge wooden screws, the cider oozed out.

However, these are the facts and dates, or some of them.

I was born in the town of Thetford, in the State of Vermont, sometime during the twenty-sixth day of April, eighteen hundred and twenty-seven. My mother was a Howard. I had four sisters and six brothers. My parents called me Charles, but, after a while, observing other boys had two Christian names, I appropriated Edward, which, having got into print, has adhered since.

At or about the age of seven, I was sent to the public school, distant some two miles. The "fragrant birch" grew hard by the school house, and was held in high esteem by the "master," nor did the gentle "mistress" confine her admiration wholly to the beauty of its slender twigs. One custom, however, operated in mitigation. The victim of the birch was usually selected to fetch the stick, and if he fetched *too tough* an one, he alone had to answer for it. So there were not many mistakes made.

In that old school house, ornamented with curious jackknife carvings, I met my ideal teacher. She died long ago. But her memory lives, and lingers bright as ever; and her image comes unbidden to "my mind's eye," whenever I think of my a b c's.

My father was a farmer, and did not neglect to instruct me in the the principles and practice of his art—especially in the practice. So it came to pass that, up to the age of fifteen, the farm and the school house bore about equal sway. I preferred work to study, but do not now recollect to have had any great liking for either.

At fifteen, I began "to keep" school. It was in a country district, high up among the green hills. The neighborhood was small, requiring but a single teacher, and it happened that some of the young folks who attended the school were seniors to me in age. On this account the committee raised an objection; but, as I had solved their arithmetical puzzles, spelled their hard words, and read with some fluency, it was agreed to waive the objection and give me a trial. The fear was that I could not govern the big boys; nor is it probable I could, had not the big girls come to the rescue; and the "boarding round" may have had something to do with that matter.

I had stipulated to teach the school for nine and one-half dollars a month, and board; but, was to board around with each family in turn.

I cannot tell whether this custom still exists, or how it affected others; but it subjected me to many and funny adventures, exposing all sorts of secrets, and uncovering hidden views of such social institutions as apple parings, sewing circles, and match-making.

The thing, however, which affected me most, outside the daily duties of the school room, was the evening spelling school. Nearly everybody became interested and attended. There was contest and victory in it. The boy or girl who "spelled down" all others, triumphed as really as the conqueror at the Olympic games; and when the rival school, a little way up the valley, sent down a challenge, and one of our girls out-spelled them all, there was glory enough. Even the "master" came in for a share. This may have been wrong; it certainly was delightful. I noticed that girl secured her choice of young beaux from and after that event.

I was next employed in a village school, on a salary of twenty dollars a month, and board. This was in 1843, and when the Millerite, or Second Advent mania had driven whole settlements crazy. From Friday night to Monday morning, Mr. Miller's disciples were allowed, the use of the school house for meeting, and they used it uninter-mittingly, day and night. These saints insisted that I should join and *go up* with them; but were quite indifferent about the progress of their children in knowledge; nor am I aware that they made any great progress. Nevertheless, their teacher was popular; and promoted to a more important school for a third trial.

> "The third day comes a frost, a killing frost;
> And—when he thinks, good easy man, full surely
> His greatness is a ripening—nips his root,
> And then he falls as I do " (did).

I had ventured too far, got stranded, and was taught a lesson in adversity. It was dictated roughly, with the moral of the Scotchman's poem about a louse, in a church, on a lady's bonnet, for a text:

> "O wad some power the giftie gie us
> To see ourselves as ithers see us
> It wad frae mony a blunder free us
>   An foolish notion."

It was thought I lacked the "giftie," whereupon the parson pro-ceeded to inquire privately; the critic printed his notes or notions in the paper, and the young people waxed perverse in the school room. There were gusts all around; and the gossips ran wild, and lost their breath in the hurry to spread the news. It began with ominous looks and whisperings, social ostracism followed, then confidence fled, and both sides prepared for war.

3

I kept that school through to the last hour of the last day of my engagement, but it was a failure, and a load rolled off my spirit, when it ended, bigger than fell from the back of Bunyan's pilgrim.

Sore over this result, and suspecting some mistake in selecting a calling, I escaped to the woods and went to work in a saw mill; and being rather tall, but not rather stout, my comrades seemed disposed to disparage my ability as a lumberman almost as much as others had as a pedagogue. It cost a great effort *to work* that conceit out of them; but I did it, taking my turn at felling trees, playing John, tending mill and rafting lumber. I had to learn something of the mill-right's trade and of navigation. It was an absorbing business for a green hand, but it could not exclude the "bitter memory." Again and again would the thought of *failure* obtrude, obstructing all consciousness of the great, blind, live force at work in the mill. Again and again did some board or scantling come to grief in the same way as bruin did, when he undertook to dine, sitting on a log which was moving under the saw.

Such a state of things could not last long, and did not. The lumberman resumed the ferule, and rarely afterwards had cause of complaint against pupil, parent or people.

In 1848, at the age of one and twenty, I was admitted to Dartmouth College, and, four years later, graduated; having paid expenses by teaching three or four months each year.

Now came the election of a profession. I preferred the law, but was tempted away to another calling. Resolving to be a lawyer, I became a teacher. Looking southward, towards the Old Bay State, that "paradise of pedagogues," I "brought up" in Framingham, the most charming town in the State. The people were highly cultivated, the students of the Academy and High school, over which I presided, were wonderfully intelligent, and the preceptress was a paragon of all the graces. You may have seen her. She sits by the other lamp, just over the table, quite unconscious of what I am saying. Late in the autumn of 1854, I emigrated to Peoria. *The preceptress went with me.*

When I reached Peoria she must have numbered twelve or fifteen thousand inhabitants. Such schools as she had were "kept" in deserted breweries, shanties, cabins, anything which furnished an excuse for shelter or mimicked a house, with three exceptions; two of which were private, and one public.

The private school buildings were constructed by an association of the more intelligent citizens, mostly of northern origin—one for males, and one for females. The school for females had been in operation several years under the care of Miss Sarah Mathews, a most excellent lady and teacher; and the school for males was about to begin in charge of "your humble servant" and the "preceptress."

The public school building referred to was a long, narrow, one story brick, whose walls were fast crumbling, under the influence of moisture from the swampy mud hole beside which it stood.

Here Mr. ——— was monarch of all he surveyed, the great man, "Sir Oracle," head and embodiment of the current ideas, and county superintendent of common schools.

To his mind, things educational were as near right as they well could be; even to the squalid barrack, where he held his court, didn't seem to disturb his sense of æsthetics, or the pool to offend any sense nature had given him. He exemplified ideas indigenous to southern and servile latitudes, and championed the chivalry. He was a Methodist, and had the backing of that compact and powerful organization.

I found in Peoria, also, Dr. J. A. Sewall, sick in body and at heart, and Doty, and other "lesser lights."

In the contest about school matters, which soon opened, Mr. ——— stood firmly by the chivalry; I fell into line with the Yankees.

Serving in a private school, my suggestions in regard to public schools were looked upon as meddling, and were sturdily resented by the aforesaid chivalry. But what was to be done? Here was a city already rich and populous, and needing no prophet to tell of great expansion in the near future, whose school buildings were execrable, whose ideas of common public school education were "villainous low," and whose teachers were contemned as pedagogues "with none so poor as to do him (them) reverence."

What was to be done? Personally, there seemed little to gain, and much to lose. I had a comfortable school room, a very good class of students, and a liberal salary; but I could not escape the public schools, if I would. My school was envied, epitheted, and compared. It was the rich man's school, the aristocrat's school; relied upon show and clothes. Mr. ———'s, per contra, was the people's school, eschewed all show, and relied upon solid merit. ——— was a great man; Hovey, "nix." All this was human and very natural. Æsop explained it centuries ago, in his fable about the fox and the grapes.

But what was to be done? The great, serious facts kept rising up, and would not down, at anybody's bidding, that a wrong was being perpetrated upon the school children of Peoria for a want of proper school facilities; that there was no proper appreciation of public duty in regard to public education; that there was no suitable public spirit, or buildings, or teachers; that there was needed some sensible system for the organization, conduct, and support of the schools for the city.

I resolved to make a suggestion. I began with Mr. A. P. Bartlett, president of the association of citizens who employed me. He talked with his associates; we all talked together; Judge Peters drafted a bill, in the nature of an amendment to the city charter. It was quietly put through the Legislature, though our member trembled for his head for doing it. But these citizens agreed to back him in case any troubles came of it—such men as Hon. A. P. Bartlett, Judge Onslow Peters, Judge Jacob Gale, Hon. Jonathan Cooper, and J. W. Hansel, Esq. So the deed was done, and the chivalry woke up to find themselves superseded. A new charter was in force, and the chivalry were not. But they didn't see it,—didn't get the hang of the thing,—didn't scent where the power had gone. Meanwhile those who did put forward a ticket of good and true men for the School Board, elected them. Pickett edited the Republican paper, and Raney the Democratic paper, and both opened their columns to the friends of free schools. It is but fair to say, however, that Pickett had by far the best appreciation of the system, and did it the greater service. Largely through his judicious management,—through what he kept out quite as much as what he put in his paper,—our ticket was elected practically without opposition.

The chivalry didn't understand it even then, but if they had it would have been too late. The law was passed and gave nearly all power to the School Board. The Board was elected, and an excellent one it was, too, with Bartlett at the head.

The private school buildings, the only buildings suitable for school purposes in the city, were at once purchased, and in one of these was organized a high school, in the other a grammar school. I naturally enough fell in charge of the former, and was also appointed superintendent of all the schools. There was work enough to be done—school houses to be built, temporary accommodations to be provided meanwhile, schools to be organized, courses of study to be mapped out, text-books to be selected, teachers to be found, tested, aided, and started on the road to glory. Lively times were these. Night and day, week-days and Sunday, I worked on. The Board backed me, and worked and planned with me, and without me.

New school houses went up, teachers' reputations went up, scholarship went up, morals went up, and so the present school system of Peoria was begotten, born, and christened. How well the bantling has thrived since I am not able to say, but I have heard, "as well as could be expected."

Even the chivalry have got the hang of the thing at last.

I have stated how I was involved in the public schools at Peoria, and what came of it. I may here explain some matters which led to other changes.

On the last days of the year 1854, the State Teachers' Association held, in Peoria, its second meeting. It was by no manner of means wholly composed of or controlled by teachers, although sailing under their colors. It was a wild, western gathering, full of vim and schemes—a huge grindstone, on which each man who had an axe to grind, ground away, or tried to. (Bear in mind that these are recollections of fifteen years ago.) Among actual teachers were Wright, Bateman, Wentworth, Brooks, and Wilkins. Among others, many of whom had been teachers, were Turner, Powell, Eberhart, Murray,

Arny, and, among distinguished scholars from abroad, Prof. Charles Davies.

Turner, Murray & Co. wanted some action which would aid them, at Springfield, to gobble up the College and Seminary funds of the State for an Industrial University. The old college men desired action looking to the distribution of these funds among existing colleges. Both parties suggested Normal *Departments* as a lure to the friends of Normal Schools.

Arny & Co. urged a manual labor scheme, as near as I could understand them, volunteering to superintend the experiment, if somebody would furnish the money. The member from Springfield insisted that phonetic spelling was the great reform, the coming event. The member at large waxed eloquent about his "chain of commercial colleges," and challenged debate—a Stratton strategy. He got, what he wanted, advertised. Several gentlemen intimated a willingness to endure an endorsement of eminent fitness for the office of State Superintendent of Public Instruction.

Several publishers of text-books hinted, warily, that now was the time, and this the body, to render a signal service to the people of Illinois, by recommending *their* wares for exclusive use, thereby securing the blessings of uniformity. The agents of said publishers exhibited surprising tact and ability, rising even to the plane of "grand strategy" in some of their movements to capture the convention. They were clever, obliging, companionable, and had there been but one, he would certainly have got my vote; but as there were a score or more, a vote for one became a vote against nineteen, and could not be indulged. As well might a man be expected to choose between equally bewitching women.

I was a new comer, and, for the most part, a looker-on; and, in truth, vastly taken by the free and easy way these people had of pushing their hobbies, both at the court house and the hotel; and no man could properly appreciate the former who had not the *entree* at the caucus rooms, in the latter. I was a stranger, but they took me in; and once in, uncovered the situation.

On the one side were all these "reformers," not peaceful, but resolute to rule the Association, and seize upon its power, whatever it might be, to mould public opinion. and legislation. On the other, were the great body of teachers not quite prepared to ignore the ways of the fathers, or the gathered wisdom of years, but eager to adopt any measure which promised to better their calling or themselves. They didn't appreciate, or if they did, they didn't take kindly, the joke of playing second fiddle to Bronson Murray, W. F. N. Arny, *et id omne genus.* True, there was the great-brained Turner, apparently leagued with these men, whom all delighted to honor. This man we could follow. He was of us—had been a life-long teacher. He was the orator whose tongue uttered, at Granville, in Putnam

County, the outline of an Industrial University, which was the origin of the magnificent institutions now springing up in every State by the munificence of Congress. Had he stood alone, his scheme might have prevailed; but he did not. At his heels howled a pack of self-seeking zealots, lacking culture and modesty, and casting a shadow of doubt over even the orator himself. So it happened that the hobbyists were not pleased, and shaking the dust from their feet, departed. Nor am I aware that they ever again returned,—certainly not in such force.

One project, however, did prevail at Peoria. It was agreed *nem. con.*, to publish a monthly journal, to be called the *Illinois Teacher*, as the "organ" of the Association. Wilkins and Arny were chosen local and managing editors, with a corps of monthly editors, and the editor of the Bloomington *Pantagraph* as publisher. A thousand copies were subscribed for on the spot, and the "organ" started off with great expectations. A year later, at Springfield, this same "organ" gave its friends no little trouble. It had not proved a financial success; was not elegant as a work of the printer's art; had not been issued very punctually, nor on very fine paper; the monthly editor was not regarded with favor, and no one was satisfied. I may as well say it was a failure. Those who had been more directly responsible felt compromised. It was clear the Association did not care to have *such* an organ, and would not assume financial or other responsibility under such auspices. But some there were who liked not the word failure, and resolved not to have it thrust upon them. Besides, they believed an exclusively professional journal was needed. They held a caucus and decided that the *Teacher* should go on, and that I should be editor, with control over manner and matter, and should be privileged to pay all the bills, and might pocket all the proceeds, which, when the former publisher learned, waked the spirit of prophecy within him, and he prophesied, saying, "If Hovey has got fifteen hundred dollars to throw away, he has now an excellent opportunity to do so."

A year before I had desired this office, had time to devote to it, and fancied the business would suit me, and I it. But now I had not the time to spare, and was not a little fearful lest my friends should be disappointed. But I "waded in"—and swam as well as I could. Luckily, the printer was a man of rare taste, scholarship and business habits, from whose eye a typographical blunder had but a slender chance of escape, who used new type, and clean white paper, and issued "on time." Of course this man must have been Nason—and Nason it was. My caucus friends "kept the faith," and subscriptions came tumbling in by every mail, until at the end of the year there was money enough to pay all the bills, and I think a trifle more. The next year showed a balance on the credit side also. This "*Teacher*" business forced attention to matters outside of Peoria, and threw upon me the responsibility of advising what should be done. In procuring instructors for the schools in Peoria I had found difficulty, and had been compelled to go abroad for them. The same difficulty existed elsewhere. There were not enough well qualified teachers in the State.

The discussions at Peoria in regard to the College and Seminary funds were fresh in memory. Why could not these funds be used to endow a Normal School? I could find no valid objection, nor did any one else suggest a good reason why they could not be so used. On the other hand, those teachers with whom I had opportunity to confer, favored the idea, and it is likely some of them may have suggested it to me originally. Be that as it may, I approved the scheme and fought steadily for it, with the quill, on the stump, and in the lobby. At Chicago, the Association moved in the matter, and appointed a committee to visit the Legislature and urge this disposition of these funds. Simeon Wright was the leading man of this committee, and is entitled to the highest credit. I should weary you to tell how the Normal University bill was finally enacted into a law; how one objection after another was removed or quieted, and how the great stumbling block—the location—was at last got over, by leaving it to competition and the Board. But the fact has passed into history, and I—pass on.

Peoria and Bloomington were the leading competitors for the location. Peoria made the best cash bid, but was overborne by a swamp land grant by McLean county.

I was chosen principal, Mr. Phelps, then of the New Jersey Normal School, receiving the minority vote.

It was summer in 1857. I accepted the office, resigned all others, except that of editor of the *Teacher*, and gave notice that I should resign that as soon as a successor could be chosen.

[This event took place in Decatur the following Christmas, after an exciting contest. Bateman and Eberheart, then, as now, acknowledged leaders, were the candidates.]

Having shaken off other occupations, I began to concentrate all thoughts upon the Normal. Much had been already accomplished; the live teachers were its friends; the Legislature had endowed it; McLean County and people had subscribed a site and fund for building purposes; it was nearly half founded.

But that man was ignorant of interests at work in the State, who supposed the College and Seminary funds could be diverted to this purpose, unchallenged. These interests warred against the passage of the Normal University act, and failing, belittled whatever was done under it. The end aimed at was repeal.

Large numbers of men opposed educating teachers at public expense;—let them pay for their education like other people, or like men preparing for other callings. McLean County was overrun with thinkers of this sort. Citizens, respectable in numbers and intelligence, regarded the enterprise as an experiment; were willing to be convinced, but would take nothing on trust. Among these were eminent lawyers.

Enthusiastic friends looked for *immediate* results. In vain did we plead inability to beat nature, which grows not men from babies in a day. Something telegraphic had been promised, and must be performed. Some, misled by the name, were disappointed not to find included in the curriculum all branches of knowledge. A few expected grand discoveries in science, such as would add to the sum of human knowledge; and savans offered their services, and felt aggrieved that they were declined. Inventors and manufacturers paid their *devoirs* and deposited their wares. There are now, or lately were, a highly-finished plow, and harrow, and roller, and horse-rake, and I recall not what other implements—gifts to the University. Many suggestions came with them, and proffers of service to explain their peculiarities, and *were for sale*.

No one will know how I was besieged with advice and intimations. It may be true enough, that in a multitude of counsel there is safety; but it does not follow that a multitude of counselors are safe, even if Solomon did say so.

On the question of aims and ends, of what should be done or attempted, there was a difference of opinion in the Board itself.

One party proposed to borrow a curriculum from existing institutions—to imitate the wise men of the east. It was in part the party which proposed to borrow a man of that longitude for principal.

Another party, unwilling to snuff out "the lamp of experience," did, nevertheless doubt whether all possibility of progress died with "Father Pierce," or existed only at Trenton. Something more generous and broader than had yet been achieved was deemed possible, and should be attempted. These ideas and expectations were by no means calculated to put the principal at ease, for upon him would fall the task of realizing them. He must found an institution for, and entitled to, leadership. Beside these parties, individual members held individual views.

Good old Father Bunsen, learned in all the methods and courses of study and of training in Germany, made primary education his hobby; and I will do him the justice to say, was master of it. He was an enthusiastic and learned Dutchman, and rode his hobby eternally. It was the beginning and ending of any proper system of Normal training (a proposition half true, certainly). But he took mortal offense because I could not, or would not, read through his spectacles, and once even introduced to the Board a resolution of inquiry, looking to my removal from office. What came of it I never know.

Ninian Edwards was rather ambitious in his notions. His father had been Governor of the State. He himself had heard somewhere of Oxford, or Cambridge, and was chagrined that our chief officer should be styled principal instead of chancellor. To me he appeared to be a little "at sea." His ideas and words were as two kernels of wheat to two bushels of chaff. I think that is the scriptural way of putting it. But great lawyers are not required to be great in everything.

Father Mosely didn't trouble his head about courses of study, but was nervous to learn whether my salary, which he had fixed at $2,500 per annum in specie, was satisfactory; *id est*, he wanted, through the Board to be himself complimented for liberality. I am afraid I was never forgiven the stupidity of not catching his drift. But let that pass.

The general scope of the institution and a course of study having been considered informally, and a committee of supervision appointed, the whole matter was handed over to the principal to be put in form and "put through."

Embarrassed by conflicting counsels and extravagant expectations, there seemed to be a "right smart chance" of a first-class muddle. However, as the smoke blew away, I was able to map the work to be done with tolerable accuracy, and, having rented a hall to do it in, and given notice of the day for beginning, and secured Ira Moore and Charlton T. Lewis as associate instructors, began to feel that I was getting my appropriate work well in hand, nor intended to be drawn outside of it. Almost from my advent in the State I had lived in a hurry, doing double, triple, often quadruple duties. Now I determined to do but one. 'Twas useless.

> "There's a divinity that shapes our ends,
> Rough-hew them how we will."

Scarcely had said determination been recorded when I was startled by the presentation of a plan or sketch for a university, by a member of the Board, so singularly inappropriate that I presume its adoption was not seriously expected, even though backed by a strong local influence. But the bare presentation of such a plan exposed the importance of the subject, A mistake here would be a calamity.

For the purpose, therefore, of defeating any hasty action, quite as much as of killing off this plan, I joined Dr. Rex in urging the propriety of sending a committee to inspect the more notable school edifices of our and other States. Dr. Rex, as chairman, made a careful examination of the school architecture in Philadelphia, Trenton, New York City, Albany, and in many towns of Connecticut and Massachusetts; and on his return submitted a written report in which I concurred, and also recommended for adoption the plans of the New Jersey Normal School Buildings, in which I did not concur. I was the other member of the committee, and, although I had seen nearly all the prominent edifices in the country for educational purposes, or plans of them, yet I made the tour and studied them over again. It was not enough to select the best existing edifice, and model after that; and if it had been I should still have non-concurred in the Trenton plans; but it was required to discover the best plan, existing or not,—in matter or only in mind,—for an institution such as we were founding.

Given, five hundred adult students: required to find how to construct an edifice wherein they could be comfortably accommodated and *assembled* in one room and *separated* therefrom into several rooms, or *vice versa*, in the least possible time and confusion, and with the greatest possible ease. That was the problem. It was not proposed to organize or conduct the institution on the college system, in which students occupied—*studied in*—their private rooms exclusively, and could as conveniently go from these to one place, or to different places, for recitation and for "prayers." A chapel and class rooms, whether *adjacent* or not, satisfied this system. The class rooms might as well be, and often were, in different buildings from each other, and from the chapel. Had it been proposed to conduct the University on such a system, it would have varied the problem.

But as it was, whoever will take the trouble to examine the *second* story of the Normal University building, at Normal, will find my solution. The plan of that story was the seed from which the building grew—the nucleus around which the architect grouped the balance of the edifice. The building, as it now stands, is not my ideal, nor that of Mr. Randall's, the architect, in two particulars. Something had to be yielded to secure the adoption of our plan over that of Dr. Rex, and something also to local prejudice. The local influence will be better understood by recalling the fact that the money for erecting the building had been subscribed by, and was expected to be realized from, McLean County and her people. Hence, the very natural desire on the part of the Board to conform to local humor, prejudice, or taste. The two departures from the original ideas of Mr. Randall and myself —two blunders I have always thought—were these:

1. Placing "Normal Hall," the *third* story hall, over the main school room. This change, or *addition*, compelled *the lowering* of the ceiling of the main working room of the building, which should have been spacious, airy, and proportioned, ten or twelve feet, and the putting into it of columns to support the floor above. The *upper* hall hardly compensates for these blemishes.

2. Changing the belfry tower from an *angle* to the *center* of the building. This change was made in deference to local feeling, but in defiance of taste and architectural effect. Whoever has seen the Smithsonian building, in this city, will understand what I mean.

It is not unlikely that the varied relief at first contemplated would have added to the expense; but that had nothing to do with the change, which was made purely in deference to local feeling, but in deference to local ideas of taste, and possibly of grandeur.

Further, the *center* tower has nothing to roost on but a bridge; the angle tower could have rested upon solid ground. There might have been several towers, varied in form and size. But even one would have suited me better than the present *baseless* belfry.

Saving these variations, the building, as it now stands, fairly represents my ideas, and the views of the architect. Such is the way the plans were made, modified, and finally adopted.

A contract was at once entered into for the construction of the building, and work vigorously begun in the fall of 1857.

I went back to the school, but did not expect to have much to do with the University building until it should be ready for occupation. The sequel will show how I was disappointed.

I need not tell how Ira Moore and I began to instruct a score or less of students in a tumble-down hall, tumbled-up on the top of a grocery house, at an out of the way corner, in the city of Bloomington; how the students increased in numbers; how other teachers were added; how Mary Brooks "run" the experimental school (primary), and made it a model; how said hall was fitted and furnished and grew to be comfortable, bating the surroundings; how here we pursued the even tenor of our way, biding our time; for these things are well enough known.

But there came a time when we were not permitted to go on in peace. Questionings, which would not be quieted by plain answerings, came again and again. I tried hard to bar them from the school room, but could not. The great fact that not a blow had been struck on the University building for eighteen months, was known to everybody. It acted and reacted on us depressingly. Were we to remain cooped up in Major's Hall forever? Must we, after flattering the public and ourselves with the grand idea of a model school in a model edifice, confess failure? The thought was wormwood, and the fact, if fact it should prove to be, was full of peril. We had carried the Normal School bill "by the skin of our teeth," and who knew but that the opposition might rally and repeal the law, armed with such a failure, to carp at.

But what could be done? We had neither money nor credit. What we did have, applicable to building purposes, was a subscription which could not then be collected, and perhaps never. The suspension of work on the building, in December, 1857, was brought about by our inability to collect, from this subscription, six or seven thousand dollars to pay the contractors the first installment due them on their contract, for work done. They reasoned, and sensibly, that if the subscribers to the building fund, in the first flush of victory, while yet the ink was hardly dry with which they had recorded their "promise to pay," would not or could not pay seven or eight thousand, out of one hundred and fifty thousand dollars (I use round numbers,) it would not do to rely upon them, or their subsciptions;

and the sooner they (the contractors) stopped work the better it would be for them. So they stopped, and the suspension continued until the summer of 1859—more than a year and a half. Meanwhile matters grew worse. A great financial revulsion had swept over the country, carrying ruin to some subscribers, and greatly crippling others. Moreover, from this cause, or the lapse of time, or some other reason, the great body of donors seemed to carry their obligation more loosely, if possible, than at first. Some who had subscribed lands refused to deed them until the building should be fully completed, which was a repudiation of their subscription so far as any aid in erecting the building was concerned. The most prominent of these was David Davis, then Judge of the Circuit Court, and now one of the Justices of the Supreme Court of the United States. His example was disastrous. After the building should have been built, it was quite immaterial whether he deeded his land or not. Everybody knew, the State, in the end, would pay all necessary bills. The need was present aid, the immediate and honest payment of the subscription, on the faith of which the Board had located the institution in McLean County. When a ship is once launched, it will float itself, but it takes *power* to launch it. Davis, in bad faith I have always thought, refused to furnish the *power* he had promised, until such time as it should not be needed. And yet this same Judge Davis is reputed to be worth four millions of dollars, and his subscription was only forty acres of land. Adjoining it, a comparatively poor man, Mr. Bakewell, gave twice as much, and didn't higgle about deeding it, either.

That part of the subscription made by the county of McLean was undoubtedly good, but remote. It was payable out of the *proceeds* of the sales of her swamp lands. These lands could not, by law, be sold for less than their appraised value, and would not then sell for that. Of course there were no proceeds, and nothing due on her subscription. This subscription was seventy thousand dollars,—nearly one-half the entire amount.

What, then, was the situation at the close of the school year, in June, 1859? We had got a charter, a fund to pay teachers, a plan for a building, and a subscription, but no money for building purposes.

Mr. Moore might have stated the case, so far as relates to the building, as follows:

Given, a sixty-acre site, a plan on a scale of two hundred thousand dollars, and and an unavailable subscription of one hundred and fifty thousand dollars.

Required, to construct an edifice, in pursuance of said plan out of said subscription.

Could it be done? Of course nobody but a Yankee school-master would be fool enough to undertake it; but could it be done, if undertaken?

You ask, Why not go to the Legislature for funds to build with?
For two reasons:

1. We had promised not to do so; and that was one of the considerations which secured the passage of the Normal University act. We could not "eat our own words" and go back to the very next Legislature and ask for more money. We were too modest for that.

2. We had not grown strong enough to risk the institution in the Legislature at that time. It might take the idea into its head to modify, or even repeal the charter itself. We needed a little more time for development and results before going again to Springfield for money.

If the people of Bloomington and McLean county could not or would not comply with their obligations and pay up, why not change the location to some town or city that would?

I was of the opinion that this might be done. But there were objections. The site had been given and accepted in good faith. Some donors had complied or stood ready to comply with the terms of their subscriptions; others had failed only because of financial reverses beyond their control. McLean County did not agree to pay her subscription until she should obtain the money therefor by the sale of her swamp lands; and this subscription alone was nearly equal to the greatest bonus offered elsewhere, for the location—*and was sure to be paid some time.* Under these circumstances, the suggestion to change the location to some other county could not be maintained.

When the Board met, therefore, in mid-summer of 1859, on occasion of the annual examination and commencement, and reviewed the situation of affairs, the following facts were found:

1. The "Normal University" bill became a law on the 18th day, of February, 1857.

2. The interest on the College and Seminary funds was, by said act, set apart for the maintenance of said University.

3. The location of said University was to be made by "the Board of Education of the State of Illinois," where, other things being equal, the largest bonus should be offered therefor; and *was* made at Normal, in McLean County—said county, and the people of said county, having offered the biggest bonus.

4. The bonus, or subscription, for the location was the only fund given to the Board for the erection of a permanent house, or home, for the institution.

5. A plan for a building had early been considered and agreed upon, a contract for construction entered into, work begun, and foundations laid, in 1857.

6. Work was suspended in December of said year, because of the inability of the Board to pay the contractors the first payment on their contract, as it fell due.

7. Said suspension continued during all of 1858, and half of 1859.

8. During this interval the availability of the subscriptions had considerably deteriorated.

9. A distinguished judge, and a few others moved by his example, refused to pay his subscription until after the completion of the building; that is, until it was not needed.

10. McLean County's subscription was, at present, unavailable, unless, indeed, it could be used as collateral on which to borrow money.

11. Nobody had yet been found willing to lend money to the Board on that or any other collateral, or on any terms which the Board could offer.

12. In January, 1859, two years after the passage of the University act, and during the suspension of work on the building, the Legislature met, but it had not been deemed advisable, by the Board, to ask of it further aid at that time.

13. The proposition to change the location to some other place, in the hope of getting money to build with, was decided to be unwise.

14. The Legislature would not meet again until January, 1861.

15. We could not afford to wait, in temporary quarters, until that time, nor to risk the effect of failure to provide a suitable edifice, for four years after the inauguration of the institution.

16. We were, therefore, remitted to the subscription, and it alone, for means to build a permanent and creditable house; and we believed a failure to erect speedily such a house would peril the whole enterprise.

With such a retrospect and prospect, with growing doubt in the public mind, and restlessness in the school, the Board might certainly be pardoned for an occasional out-look for breakers ahead.

But what did they do?

You remember what the Roman Senators did when the Republic was seriously menaced. They chose a dictator and ordered him to see that the Republic received no harm. [*Ne quid detrimenti respublica capiat.*]

So comparing small things with great, our Board made its Building Committee dictator, and decreed that it should take care that the University received no detriment; in other words, that the building should be constructed anyhow and now—and said committee should do it.

I was the local member of the committee, and for about twenty-nine days in each month, the only member 'comeatable,' and of necessity was compelled to act for the committee.

Never did man have worse means, or better backing. I remember especially Messrs. Moulton, Powell, Wright, Denio, and Rex, as taking a decided interest, and a full share of responsibility. They would leave their own business at any time, on call, and repair to Normal. Powell spent months there. Moulton joined me on notes to borrow money for the work, on our individual responsibility. Rex came to the rescue in 1861, when our treasurer got timid and refused to handle the money, just appropriated by the Legislature, for fear bills of broken banks might get into his custody. But I must not delay upon others. It is a long story, and would weary us both.

The first step was to get clear of existing contracts, based upon cash payments, because we had no cash.

The second, to substitute other contracts, based upon barter—so much subscription for so much work or material.

The third, to accept labor or material of subscribers who could not pay money, but could pay these.

The fourth, to compromise with those not able to pay all, for a part.

It was purely a matter of barter. We traded, "made turns," compromised and got all out of the subscription there was in it, then laid it aside.

Such is a general statement of the case. But, perhaps, it does not satisfy a reasonable curiosity to know some of the particulars. How was all this done, and who did it?

To the last half of the question, I answer, the Building Committee; but "how" will take more than three words to tell.

1. How we got our first start:

The Board authorized the sending of an agent east to effect, if possible, a sale of the county lands, and thereby hasten the payment of the county subscription. It was intended and expected, by the Board, that the State Treasurer, Mr. Miller, a resident of Bloomington, and well acquainted with the lands and their value, would be the agent. It was believed his knowledge, wealth, and office would give him influence enough to find a purchaser. But he would not go, or have anything whatever to do in the matter. Other "solid" men were applied to, but would not go. They seemed quite unaccountably tender of touching these lands or our subscription. I had faith that somebody could be found to buy these lands; and, inasmuch as the "Honorable" men and the "rich" men would not undertake to find said somebody, I concluded to try "Young America."

At that time, C. M. Cady, Esq., was instructor in vocal culture in the University, a man of tact and pluck, and not afflicted with any serious tenderness about investing his skill in an attempt to negotiate the sale of the county lands. So to Gotham he went, with a list and description of the lands in his pocket. He made something of a stir there, I judge, from the letters of inquiry which, soon after his arrival, began to come by every mail. But he needed something more than a list of the lands. He could do nothing without the bonds for deeds which could be passed by simple endorsement. With these he could effect a sale, in fact, had virtually done so already.

I tried to get the bonds from the county authorities, but could not. They would enter into no transaction, save only to sell the lands. There was one way in which I could comply with Cady's suggestion. I could *buy* the lands myself, paying for them by a small cash advance, and the balance by time notes, and could take the bonds and do what I pleased with them. As this was the only path, I walked into it, and bought seven or eight thousand acres of the land, at a cost of twenty-five or thirty thousand dollars. The purchase was made in the interest of, and intended for, the Board, but without any authority, and it was never recognized. I had to shoulder the whole transaction. My notes, to the amount of twenty-five thousand dollars, or thereabout, were turned over to the treasurer of the Board by the county, in part payment of her subscription; and the Building Committee paid them to A, B, and C, for labor or material. So they became widely scattered and gave me a "heap" of trouble to take them up as they fell due.

But I got the bonds, and notified Cady. Meanwhile, the parties with whom he had been negotiating failed, and the bargain fell through; nor did he succeed in finding another purchaser. I was now in a fix. As Deacon Homespun, or some other wise man, said, or might have said, "I had brought my pigs to a fine market." I could boast of numerous broad acres of swamp land, which nobody would buy, and for which I was in debt, and had nothing to pay. Besides, the transaction, in the turn it had taken, pretty clearly impeached my discretion, and might involve my honor. At any rate, it was a delicate matter, for my notes were held by the Board, and should they fail to be paid promptly, or not to be paid at all, the Board would have cause to complain of my unauthorized and rash purchase.

But, however it may have affected and embarrassed me, it proved a Godsend to the University. The sale got noised about as a big speculation. Over twenty-five thousand dollars worth of the county lands had been bought up by one party. (*Mum* about the party.) The transaction grew on every tongue, and soon reached colossal proportions. There must be something in these lands, after all. (*And they will soon be gone*, I took care to have suggested.) The wave was rising. Through Powell, we got the State officers at Springfield to invest (Hatch, Dubois, and Miller), and took good care to have this fact related to Madam Rumor, who forthwith spread it through all the country round. Others took heart and bought lands; nor was it long before the funds in the treasury enabled us to begin operations.

2. How we proceeded:

We paid off Mortimer & Loberg, the contractors for the mason work, and they surrendered their contract. Mr. Soper, the contractor for the carpenter work, elected to retain his contract, go on with the job, and take his chances about getting his pay.

It was now necessary to find some mason who would undertake the construction of the walls of the building, and take his pay in the subscription. . A man who could and would do this was hard to find. But by dint of much talk, of appeals to local pride and interest, and aided by the eclat of the recent sales of the county lands, we found him in the person of S. D. Rounds, Esq. He exacted the "pick" of our assets, and took the *cream* of the subscription, leaving the *skim-milk*, and not much of it, to pay the carpenter, painter, plumber, and plasterer. But it was the best we could do, and we did it. Even with this choice, the mason found great difficulty in completing his job; and, although he succeeded, the walls crept up at a snail's pace, sometimes forgetting to creep at all for many weeks together, so that the heart grew sick at hope deferred.

It was absolutely necessary to provide some money. Work could not go on without it. It could not be obtained on the credit of the Board. That matter was fully tested. Nor could it be obtained on private notes, based for security on the assets of the Board. There was but one way. The friends of the institution must loan it money or credit. At first Moulton and I borrowed a few thousand dollars, which was soon gone. Then Messrs. Fell and Holder came forward and put their names to paper on which we got more money, and in this way, from time to time, when hard pushed, money was raised. I remember especially in this connection, Jesse and Kersey Fell, and Charles and Richard Holder. Without them I see not how we could have succeeded.

I next went among the merchants of Bloomington, and told them I would be personally responsible that they should be paid out of the first money the Board should receive for building purposes, if they would supply our carpenter, Mr. Soper, with what he needed, on a credit. The Legislature was to meet the ensuing January, and I told them it would appropriate for any deficiency there might be in the means to build the University building, and that they should have their pay out of said appropriation. So much I pledged. They consented, and by this arrangement Mr. Soper was enabled to supply himself with hardware, paints, oils, glass, some lumber, groceries, and all kinds of provisions and clothing for his family and his workmen; and when the appropriation was made, as I said it would be, I redeemed my promise, and caused them all to be paid. I considered this a lucky piece of financiering, and it was lucky for the institution; but it bequeathed to me one first-class lawsuit, and sundry smaller ones, and has cost me a good deal of money and trouble.

Perhaps it is not necessary for me to relate more particulars. I have stated enough to show you how the deed was done. In January, 1861, the edifice was still incomplete, and I estimated the debt then due at sixty-five thousand dollars, which was granted by the Legislature. During the spring and summer of 1861, the edifice was

4

fully completed, and an additional debt of some thirty odd thousand dollars, as near as I can now remember, incurred, which has since been paid. We realized some hundred and ten thousand dollars out of the subscription, so the edifice cost a little over two hundred thousand dollars. The time occupied in building the edifice, after the resumption of work in 1859, was two years, although the bulk of the work was done in 1860.   Chas. E. Hovey.

Washington, D. C., May, 1869.

BIOGRAPHICAL SKETCHES OF THE FACULTY.

Richard Edwards, LL. D., president of the State Normal School from 1862 to 1876, was born at Aberystwitch, Cardiganshire, Wales, December 23, 1822. His parents were classed among the common people. His father was a stone and brick-mason, and his mother, *nee* Jones, was the daughter of a thrifty farmer in moderate circumstances. Owing to the limited means of his parents, his early education was sadly neglected. At the age of ten, his father became interested in the New World, and moved westward. Pleased with Ohio, he located in the northern part, on a tract of land known in history as the Western Reserve. Richard, until he was twenty-two, worked on a farm, sometimes turning the soil and sometimes plying the trade of a carpenter. These industries, however, were not suited to his taste and character. He desired something more elevating. At this time it was his good fortune to meet two scholarly gentlemen who had completed the classical course at Harvard. They gave him some wholesome advice respecting the advantages of an education, and after carefully considering their counsel he determined to go to college. After much hard work he succeeded in gaining admission to the Freshman class at Harvard. He remained at Harvard only a short time. Afterward, he completed the Normal course at Bridgewater, Massachusetts, and in 1847 became a student in Rensellaer Polytechnic Institute, at Troy, New York. He has taught at Hingham, Waltham, Bridgewater, and Salem, Massachusetts. After leaving Bridgewater he became the agent of the State Board of Education in visiting schools. For three years he was principal of the State Normal School, at Salem, Massachusetts. In 1857 he was appointed principal of the city Normal School of St. Louis, Missouri. In January, 1862, he became president of the Illinois State Normal University. In 1876 he resigned this position and accepted a call to the Congregational church at Princeton, Ill., where he is engaged at present.

Edwin C. Hewett, LL. D., president of the Illinois State Normal University, was born in Worcester County, Massachusetts, November 1, 1828. His childhood was spent on a farm with his parents, who are still living. At the age of thirteen he learned the shoemaker's trade, and began to do for himself. The day he was twenty-one he engaged his first school, and received as a recompense, $13 per month. He has had wonderful success as a teacher. His services have ever been in demand. Be it said to his credit that he never engaged but one school, and that was his first. In 1852 he graduated at the State Normal School in Bridgewater, Massachusetts; in 1853 he became an assistant teacher in this school, and remained four years. In the fall of 1858 he came to Illinois and entered upon his duties as Professor of History and Geography, in the Normal University; in January, 1876, he was appointed president; in 1863 he received the degree of A. M. from the University of Chicago; in 1877 he received the title of LL. D. from Shurtleff College. As an instructor, Dr. Hewett has few equals in the Union. His practical experience, keen perception, and laconic forms of expression, have gained for him an enviable reputation among the educators of this nation.

Thomas Metcalf was born in Norfolk County, Massachusetts, in 1826. His father was a farmer in poor circumstances, but was able to give his children the advantages of attendance, for one or two years, at an academy, in addition to the meager opportunity afforded by the district school. The latter was seldom kept for more than five months each year, and this in the warm season, in order to save the expense of fuel. During the long winter, in common with nearly all the children of that vicinity in those days, the Metcalf children braided straw for bonnets, having their daily stint from eight to twelve yards. The subject of this sketch must have been so employed for not less than seven winters. The morning of his sixteenth birthday, when, with hoe in hand, he was cutting weeds amongst the corn, he was called to take charge, "just for to-day," of the school in his own district. Homesickness kept the teacher away, and gave the young farmer-boy eleven weeks practice in school-keeping, at her wages—$3 per week. For five years teaching district school, alternated with attendance at an academy, not without occasional experiences at home with scythe, rake, and plow. At the age of twenty-one came the year's course at the Bridgewater Normal school, followed by an immediate engagement as sub-master in a grammar school on Bunker Hill. Two hard, but helpful years, here were followed by seven years as principal of a grammar school in West Roxbury. He came west in 1857, leaving the last named school for the assistant's position in the St. Louis high school, where, as professor of mathematics, and afterward as principal of the combined high and Normal School, he taught five years. From that city he was called, by President Edwards, in June, 1862, to this University as professor of mathematics; then, in 1873, the Board established the training department on a new footing, and he was appointed to the new chair. Prof. Metcalf has taught nearly forty years. In the spring of 1871, he visited England, Scotland, and Continental Europe, returning in August with health much improved.

Albert Stetson, professor of language and literature, was born in Kingston, Mass., in 1834. One year of his boyhood was spent in pegging shoes, and during the summers of his fourteenth and fifteenth years he was employed in a tack factory. In 1852-3 he took the Bridgewater Normal course. The next year he had charge of a grammar school, situated at the extreme end of Cape Cod. The following year Mr. Stetson went to Yellow Springs, Ohio, where he entered the preparatory department of Antioch College. Here circumstances afforded him an excellent opportunity of becoming acquainted with the distinguished president of the college, Horace Mann. In July, 1858, he was admitted to the Freshman class of Harvard College. The college vacation of six weeks was spent in hard study, and at the beginning of the school year he entered the Sophomore class. His expenses at Harvard were paid with his own earnings, save a little assistance received from the college. While at college, he was one of the editors of the *Harvard Magazine*. He graduated in 1861, and in 1862 was suddenly transplanted from the shores of the Atlantic to this University in the midst of the prairies. The *Illinois Schoolmaster* was founded and edited by Mr. Stetson. In 1878 he visited Europe.

In the order of entering the Bridgewater school, the names of our presidents and professors stand thus: Edwards, Metcalf, Moore, Hewett, Stetson, spanning the period from 1845 to 1853. All these men were assistants in the school for at least one term,—Edwards and Hewett for several years; and all ascribe a large share of whatever success has attended their labors to the influence of that quiet, thorough, honest graduate of West Point, Nicholas Tillinghast.

Joseph Addison Sewall was born in 1830, in Scarborough, Me. He graduated from Harvard in 1852, and received the degree of M. D. In 1860 he completed the scientific course, in the same college. Between the years 1852 and 1856, he practiced medicine in Bureau and LaSalle Counties. In the fall of 1860 he was appointed professor of natural science in the Normal University. He went to Colorado in 1878. He is now president of the Colorado State University.

W. L. Pillsbury was born in Derry, N. H., November 4, 1838. He was brought up on a farm. He went to Pinkerton Academy, in Derry, for about a year, and when nearly eighteen, went to Phillips Academy, at Andover, where he prepared for college. Entered Harvard in 1859, and graduated in 1863. He came to Normal as principal of the model school, in 1863, and remained until 1870. His teaching was all done in the high school, and he seldom had anything to do with the other departments. From 1870 to 1879 he was engaged in the insurance and real estate business. In 1879 he received the appointment of chief clerk in the office of Mr. Slade, State Superintendent. He was married December 26, 1866, to Miss Marion Hammond, of St. Louis, who had charge of the primary department in the Normal University.

John W. Cook was born in New York, April 20, 1844, and is the son of Col. H. D. Cook. In 1851 Mr. Cook came west with his parents, and settled in McLean County, Illinois. He entered the State Normal University in 1862, and graduated in 1865. He then began teaching school at Brimfield, Peoria County, Illinois. Here he remained but one year, and returned to Normal, and became principal in the model school department. In 1867 he was married to Lydia Spafford, sister of Mrs. Gen. Hovey. In 1868 he became a member of the Normal Faculty, and taught history and geography. In 1869 he changed to reading and elocution. In 1876 he was appointed professor of mathematics.

Stephen A. Forbes was born in Stephenson County, Illinois, in 1844. He worked on a farm until the age of fourteen, when he entered the preparatory department of Beloit College. In 1861 he enlisted as a private in Company B, Seventh I. V. C. He was honorably discharged at the close of the war, bearing the title of captain. Immediately after the war closed, he entered Rush Medical College, of Chicago.. In 1867 he taught school in southern Illinois. Before receiving the appointment of curator of the museum of the Illinois Normal School, which he did in 1872, he was superintendent of the public schools of Mt. Vernon. He is now State Entomologist, having been recently appointed by Gov. Cullom.

Lester L. Burrington was born in Burke, Caledonia County, Vermont, March 24, 1838. He attended the district school of his native State, and graduated at Tufts' College, near Boston, in 1866. For a short time he was professor of ancient languages in Dean Academy, at Franklin, Massachusetts. He held the same position in Goddard Seminary, Vermont, for four years. From here he came west. In January, 1874, he accepted a position in the State Normal University as principal of the high school. He resigned in 1879. He is at present president of the Dean Academy, at Franklin, Massachusetts.

Edmund J. James was born May 21, 1855, at Jacksonville, Morgan County, Illinois. His parents settled on a farm near Normal, in 1863. He entered the lowest class of the grammar school in the model department of State Normal in the spring of 1866. He remained in the model department six years and one term, graduating from the high school in 1873. He then spent two terms in the classical department of the Northwestern University, at Evanston.

After holding a position for one season (six months) in one of the field parties of the U. S. Lake survey, he went to Harvard College in October, 1874, and remained one year, making a specialty of the classics. He went to Germany in August, 1875, attended the universities of Berlin and Halle, studying history, political science, and philosophy. He graduated at Halle in August, 1877, with the degrees of A. M. and Ph. D. He then took charge of the Evanston high school, January 1, 1878, and entered on his present work in September, 1879. He is turning his attention to political economy, and is one of the contributors to the Encyclopedia of Political Science, now being published.

Minor L. Seymour was born in Genoa, New York, in 1835. He attended a district school till the age of nineteen, afterward Owego Academy, Ithaca Academy, and the Illinois Normal University, each one term. At present he is our professor of natural science.

Henry McCormick was born in 1837, in Mayo County, Ireland. In 1853 he came to America, spent two years in Ohio, one in West Virginia, and then went to Wisconsin, working on a farm in summer and going to school in winter, until the winter of 1859-60, when he taught his first school in a log school house for $16 a month, "boarding around." The school house being on the line between Illinois and Wisconsin, he had to undergo examination in both States. The next year he was promoted to a stone school house and $23 a month. This school he had four months of every year until the spring of 1865, when he came here as a student. In 1869, one year after graduation, he was appointed professor of geography. In the intervening year he was principal of the Normal public school. Now he is professor of history and geography at the University. Last year, 1882, he received the degree of Ph. D. from the Wesleyan University.

B. W. Baker, a farmer's boy, was born in Coles County, Illinois, November 25, 1841. He entered the army at the age of twenty, and served from 1861 to 1864 in the Illinois Volunteers. He entered the Normal University in 1867, and graduated in 1870. Since graduating he has taught in the grammar school of the University, and is now preaching in Colorado.

Charles DeGarmo was born in the State of Wisconsin in 1849. At the age of two his parents moved to Sterling, Ill., where he lived ten years. Afterward he lived at Lebanon, St. Clair County, Illinois. He enlisted in the army at the age of sixteen, and served one year. He saw all the great battle fields of Georgia, *one year after the battles*. He entered the Normal University in the fall of 1870, and graduated in the spring of 1873. He was married in 1875 to Miss Ida Witbeck, of Belvidere, Ill., who was for two years a student in the University. He has worked in institutes for eight years. At various times he has done institute work in Shelby, Jo Daviess, Lee, Fayette, and McLean Counties; also, in the State of Iowa.

Mrs. M. D. L. Haynie was born in Danville, Kentucky, in 1826, the daughter of Dr. Duff Green. At the age of five she entered the primary department of an Episcopal Seminary, and remained there seven years, having completed a year of high-school work. She was then placed in a Presbyterian Ladies' Seminary, where she completed the course, after which she spent several years in southern Tennessee. When she was twenty years of age her father moved to Mt. Vernon, Illinois, and soon after she, in connection with her sister, now Mrs. Gray, opened a school. The experiment succeeded. She taught in Mt. Vernon about one year, and a year and a half in Salem, Illinois. In October 1849, she was married to Dr. A. F. Haynie, of Salem, who died in 1851. In 1855 she accepted a position in an academy in Mt. Vernon, and soon after was given the entire control of the young ladies' department. She resigned in 1866, and became teacher of language in the model department at Normal. Since 1876 she has held the position of professor of modern languages in Normal University.

Flora Pennell was born in Putnam, the smallest county in Illinois, in the town of Granville, which, in the early history of the State, was one of the centers of education. She began attending school at the age of four, and has not been out of school (either as a pupil or a teacher) any whole year since. At the age of twelve she moved to Normal, and entered the grammar school of the University. She entered the Normal in the fall of 1869, and graduated in 1872. The next year she taught a country school, one mile west of Bloomington. In the fall of 1873 she went to Vassar College, and in the year 1874 she became an assistant in the high school at Elgin, Illinois, where she remained for three years. From Elgin she came to teach in the Normal Department in the fall of 1877.

Julia E. Kennedy was born in southern Illinois. She attended the district school and the spelling school, where she often "spelled down" all competitors, until the age of fifteen. At this time her father died, and she taught her first school in a log school house. She entered the Normal at seventeen, and graduated in 1871, valedictorian of her class. Since then she has taught in Missouri, as principal of a school in St. Louis, and as professor of rhetoric in Cape Girardeau. In 1879 she came here and took charge of the primary department.

Rosalie Miller was born at New Haven, Connecticut. She graduated at the Westfield, Massachusetts, Normal School. Entered upon the profession of teaching in Massachusetts, and in 1874 came to Normal. At that time there was in the Normal Department only one lady teacher, Miss Case. Before this time there had been no regular teacher of drawing, and there were no casts, or any of the apparatus used in that department now. Since she came here, Miss Miller has been constantly studying and perfecting herself in the different branches of her art.

M. Emma Skinner, the most youthful member of the faculty, was born on a farm, one mile from Princeton, Illinois. She attended the district school, later the Princeton high school, from which she graduated at the age of sixteen, valedictorian of her class. Still later, after a two years' course of study, she graduated from the School of Oratory, of Boston University, under the late Lewis B. Monroe, being one of twelve to represent the class of forty. The two years following she taught reading, in the high school at Princeton; thence to Normal, in the fall of 1881.

CHANGES IN THE FACULTY.

At the breaking-out of the rebellion, Gen. Hovey, then president of the University, entered the army as colonel of the Normal regiment, which he had organized. Ten of those who had been instructors took up arms on the right side. Leander H. Potter was made a colonel in the army, and afterward president of the Soldiers' College, at Fulton. Ira Moore was a captain, and at the close of the war he became principal of the Normal School at St. Cloud, Minnesota. J. H. Burnham was a captain, and Aaron Gove an adjutant. Julian E. Bryant and Joseph G. Howell were made lieutenants. Bryant was drowned on the Texan coast, and Howell was shot at Fort Donelson. Edwin Philbrook was made a sergeant, Dr. Samuel Willard a surgeon, and Dr. E. R. Roe a colonel. When President Hovey entered the army, Perkins Bass, of Chicago, consented to act as principal until a permanent appointment could be made. In 1862 Richard Edwards, formerly principal of a Normal School in St. Louis, became president. During Gen. Hovey's last year there were ten members of the Normal Faculty. In President Edward's first, there were five, Mr. Hewett and Mr. Sewall being the only members who served in both administrations. Mr. Hewett was instructor in geography and history, Mr. Sewall in natural science, Leander H. Potter in language, Thomas Metcalf in mathematics, and Margaret F. Osband in grammar and drawing. During the next year, Mr. Potter was succeeded by Prof. Stetson, so that twenty years ago the faculty contained three of its present members.

Of the preceptress, Miss Osband, now Mrs. Stetson, Dr. Edwards says: "She was a faithful and capable teacher, and her discontinuance was altogether owing to her unaccountable preference for another position." She was followed by Miss Emaline Dryer, who resigned in 1870, Miss Myra A. Osband taking her place. In 1874, Miss Case (now Mrs. Morrow) became preceptress.

At the head of the model school, in which the high-school grade had just been established, was Charles F. Childs, who is described as a man of rare power. Miss Levonia E. Ketcham was teacher in the primary department, but shortly after she "went the common way," and married. Her example was followed by her successor, Miss Marion Hammond, who took for "better or worse," William L. Pillsbury, who had succeeded Mr. Childs in the high school. After Mr. Pillsbury, Miss Mary E. Horton occupied the position for one year, followed by Prof. Coy, who, in turn, gave place to Mr. Burrington. Prof. James has been principal of the high school for the last three years.

The grammar school was organized as a separate department in 1866, with E. P. Burlingham, as principal. Previous to this time the model school was entirely under the supervision of the principal of the high school, and included all children of school age in district No. 2, of the town of Normal. But the rooms of the University became too small for their accommodation. Accordingly, a school house was built by the district, and the grammar and intermediate grades of the model school were removed to the new building in 1867, with John W. Cook as principal. Two years later, Joseph E. Carter became principal, and by a vote of the State Board of Education, the University ceased to exercise control over the new building. In 1870, Mr. Baker, familiarly known as "Big Baker," took charge of the grammar school. Mr. DeGarmo came next. Miss Edith F. Johnson had, in 1865, succeeded Miss Hammond in the primary. In 1868, Miss Lucia Kingsley took the position, but she "preferred Indiana with a husband to Illinois with single blessedness," and passed her work into the hands of Miss Martha E. Hughes. Miss Gertrude Case, Mrs. Joseph Carter (sister of Miss Flora Pennell), and Miss Paddock, successively occupied this position until Miss Kennedy came in 1879.

Miss Baudusia Wakefield, of the Normal Department, was appointed in 1875. She resigned in 1881, and her place was filled by James V. McHugh, who also resigned in December, 1881, to accept the principalship of the Normal public school.

PRESENT FACULTY.

Edwin C. Hewett, LL. D., President, Professor of Mental Science and Didactics. Succeeded Dr. Edwards in 1876.

Thomas Metcalf, A. M., Principal of Training Department. Appointed in 1862.

Albert Stetson, A. M., Professor of Language and Literature. Appointed in 1862.

John W. Cook, Professor of Mathematics. Appointed in 1868.

Henry McCormick, Professor of History and Geography. Appointed in 1869.

Stephen A. Forbes, Director of Scientific Laboratory. Appointed in 1872.

Minor L. Seymour, Professor of Natural Science. Succeeded Dr. Sewall in 1878.

Edmund J. James, Ph. D., Professor of Latin and Greek, and Principal of the High School. Succeeded Prof. Burrington in 1879.

Mrs. Martha D. L. Haynie, Professor of Modern Languages. Appointed in 1865.

Miss Julia E. Kennedy, First Assistant, Training Department. Appointed in 1879.

Charles DeGarmo, Second Assistant, Training Department. Appointed in 1870.

Miss Rosalie Miller, Teacher of Drawing. Appointed in 1874.

Miss Flora Pennell, First Assistant, Normal School. Appointed in 1877.

Miss Julia Scott, Second Assistant, Normal School. Appointed in 1881. Resigned in 1882.

Miss M. Emma Skinner, Teacher of Reading. Appointed in 1881. Resigned in 1882.

The museum of natural history, formerly belonging to the Natural History Society, was, in 1871, transferred to the State, and is now under the control of the Board of Education. In 1872 the collection was estimated as being worth, in money, nearly $100,000. The first collections were made by Prof. C. D. Wilber, who had charge for several years. He was followed by Maj. John W. Powell, whose explorations in Colorado have since become so famous. In 1873 Stephen A. Forbes took his present position, and has added much to the value of the museum, both by arranging the mass of material already collected, and by adding greatly to the variety of specimens.

The changes in customs, methods of instruction, etc., have been few and gradual. The institution has never been

> "The first by whom the new is tried,
> Nor yet the last to lay the old aside."

Reappointment has been the rule, both in the Faculty and Board of Education. Spelling has *never* assumed a very mild form. In Dr. Edwards' time, he occupied one platform in the assembly room and Mr. Hewett the other, alternately hurling verbal missiles at the first and second classes in spelling.

In those halcyon days, there was no "observation work," but in its place, every Friday afternoon, one of the classes taught by a pupil-teacher was, without warning, whisked up to the assembly room, and after the exercise was performed as well as the fright of the teacher and children permitted, every pupil was expected to criticise if called upon. The small drop of self-confidence, possessed by the poor teacher, entirely evaporated when the concentrated wisdom of all the faculty was brought to bear on the work. There was no training teacher, as now, but each member of the faculty gave what time he could to visiting the pupil teachers. Occasionally one would teach a term without receiving a visit.

ALUMNI ASSOCIATION.

In June, 1863, I sat an intensely interested spectator at the Normal commencement. I had been a student in the institution for one year, and had regarded Section A as a superior sort of people. My interest in them was in no sense diminished by the conspicuous part they played on that occasion..

At the close of the exercises, Dr. Edwards announced that the Alumni would meet in the Wrightonian Hall, and the happy seven, who had been in the focus of the public gaze for three or four hours, filed into the society room, and the closing door shut out the inquisitive gaze of at least one "yearling." That was the first time I heard of the Normal Alumni Association.

The succeeding year the scene was reënacted, and a year later, in 1865, I, in common with my classmates, accepted the president's invitation. We found a dozen or fifteen of our forty-one predecessors. They received us with great cordiality and with many congratulations, and, after a social meeting of an hour, we adjourned to receive the compliments of our admiring friends.

It will be seen that the Alumni Association had not, as yet, a very thorough organization nor a very definite purpose. A few years later,—two or three perhaps,—the plan of a private business meeting and banquet in the afternoon, and public exercises in the evening, on the day preceding commencement, became the settled policy of the Association. Before that time, it had been customary for the literary societies to employ some lecturer of national reputation, to deliver a public address upon that evening. The new arrangement dropped into place very naturally. This plan was followed, more or less faithfully, until 1880, when the change in the school calendar, by which the annual commencement occurs in May, made it impossible to secure a full attendance. About 1870 an attempt was made to raise a permanent Alumni fund, but only two or three classes took any interest in the matter, and the scheme was abandoned.

. At each session of the Legislature the institution was obliged to encounter more or less hostility to its appropriation bills. A stock argument, employed by our enemies, was the charge that the graduates did not teach. The Association determined to settle the question. To this end the constitution was so amended as to provide for an additional officer,—a sorresponding secretary,—whose duty it should be to communicate annually with the Alumni, and to keep a record of their work. I undertook the task in 1876, and the result appears in the following pages. It is needless to say that the charge that the graduates do not teach has been abandoned.

JOHN W. COOK.

THE NORMAL ALUMNI REGISTER.

Those marked "H. S." have paid their tuition in full, and are under no obligation to teach.

CLASS OF 1860.

1. Sarah M. (Dunn) Strickler taught in the Peoria high school one year, in the Bloomington high school one year, and in a private school in Peoria two years. She married Mr. Strickler in August, 1862. They have two children. Their present residence is Philadelphia. Mrs. Strickler can always be reached by addressing her in care of Miss Hattie Dunn, Bloomington, Illinois.

2. Elizabeth J. (Mitchell) Christian taught in the Bloomington schools two years, and in the Decatur schools two years. She was married in 1865 to M. L. Christian. They have two children, a son and a daughter. Address is Bloomington, Illinois.

3. Frances A. (Peterson) Gastman was born in Sublette, Illinois, in 1839. She entered the Normal School on the 5th day of October, 1857—the first day of the first term. She continued her studies until June, 1860, and graduated with the first class. Evincing unusual power as a teacher, she was retained as preceptress of the Institution, and remained in that position until June, 1862. On the 24th of July succeeding, she was married to E. A. Gastman, who was teaching in Decatur, and removed to that city. With the beginning of the school year of 1862-3, she took a position in the high school which had just been organized. About the twenty-second of February following, she was taken sick in the school room, and after an illness of a little less than a week, she died.

4. Mary F. (Washburn) Hull was principal of the primary department of the model school in 1860-1. Her health, always delicate, became so poor that in 1862 she was obliged to resign. In April of the same year she was married to John Hull. They have two children. Her present address is Carbondale, Illinois.

5. Enoch A. Gastman, immediately after graduation, went to Decatur and commenced teaching in a primary school at forty-five dollars a month, six months in a year. In May, 1862, he was elected superintendent of city schools, and has held the position continuously since, nearly twenty years. He has been twice married—in 1862 to Miss Peterson, mentioned above, and in 1864 to Miss Caroline Sargent. They have four children. He is a member of the State Board of Education, treasurer of the State Teachers' Association,—a position which he has held for several years,—president of the Normal Alumni Association, is especially interested in bee culture, and manages a farm near Hudson. He has been tendered positions in both of the State Normal Schools, but prefers to remain in Decatur. He was president of State Teachers' Association in 1880.

6. Peter Harper taught a district school in Peoria County until the war. He then entered the army, and remained until the close of the war, finding himself much broken in health. He remained in Louisiana, was elected a member of the State Legislature, and in 1876 was elected Parish Judge. He was a candidate for the same position in 1878, but was defeated on the "Louisiana plan." His health is not good. He is living on a farm purchased ten years ago. His address is St. Charles, Louisiana.

7. Silas Hays, Jr., after graduation, taught in the Wenona schools four months, in Elm Grove two years, and in El Paso one year. He traveled for Harper Brothers one year, and spent two years selling goods. He was principal of the Fairview schools one year, after which he bought a farm near Odell. Since 1869 he has taught seven winters, five of them in the same school, and two of them in "breaking-in" mutinous schools. His address is Odell, Illinois. He has taught seventy-four months since graduation. He is now farming at Rugby, Illinois.

8. Joseph Gideon Howell was born in Bethel, Bond County, Illinois, September 4, 1838, and died from the effects of a rifle ball through the head, on the bloody field of Donelson, February 15, 1862. He entered the Illinois Normal University, October 5, 1857, and graduated with his class, June 29, 1860, receiving the first diploma ever issued. During the fall and winter of 1860-1, he taught in the model school, but resigned his position to enlist as a private in the first company that left Bloomington, under the command of Captain Harvey. After the expiration of the ninety-days service, he was elected first lieutenant of Company K., Eighth Illinois Infantry. At the time of his death, he was serving as aid to Gen. R. J. Oglesby. He was a noble, Christian man in every sense of the word. He despised a mean, low act in anyone. His mind was singularly clear and decided. He reached a conclusion in a moment, and never hesitated to carry it out with his whole soul. Probably no one ever left the University with brighter prospects of usefulness than Joseph G.

Howell. Had he lived, there can be no doubt that he would have stood in the front rank of teachers. He was a warm and devoted friend. Always happy and joyous, his very presence was an inspiration. The girls said that "he always laughed with his eyes." He was brought to Bloomington and buried in the cemetery, although he had often expressed the wish that he might rest where he fell.

9. John Hull taught, 1860-1, at Salem, Illinois; 1861-2, in the model department of the State Normal School, and 1862-4 in Bloomington. During 1864-5 he was agent for Brewer & Tileston. The next four years he was in business in Bloomington. In 1869 he was elected superintendent of McLean County, and was re-elected in 1873. He resigned this position in 1875 to accept the chair of mathmatics in the Southern Normal, which he still occupies. He was married in 1862 to Mary F. Washburne, mentioned above. Mr. Hull edited the *Illinois Schoolmaster* in 1868, was chairman of the executive committee of the State Teachers' Association in 1873, president of the Association in 1874, chairman of the executive committee again in 1879, and is now the secretary of the Association. His address is Carbondale, Illinois.

10. Edwin Philbrook taught one year in Pana, was four years in the army, spent four years in various kinds of business at different points, teaching, meanwhile, one year at Heyworth. He was principal of the Maroa schools three years, of the Sabetha, Kansas, schools three years, of the Blue Rapids, Kansas, schools four years, and is at present principal of the third ward school in Decatur Mr. P. was married in 1871.

CLASS OF 1861.

11. Sophie J. (Crist) Gill was born in Perry County, Ohio, in 1840. She entered the Normal School in February, 1858, and graduated with the second class, in June, 1861. After graduation, she taught a year and a half in a female seminary in Greenfield, Illinois. In November, 1862, she was married to Cary Judson Gill. She accompanied her husband south, he being at that time in the army, and remained eight or nine months. She returned to Bloomington in July, 1863, suffering from disease contracted in the south. She died in November, 1863.

12. Amanda O. Noyes was born in Landhoff, New Hampshire, in 1830, and entered the Normal School in September, 1858, and graduated in 1861. Immediately after graduation she took a position in the schools of Jacksonville, and remained there for two years; but her health failed, and she was obliged to resign. She went to La Porte, Indiana, and resided with a brother there. After a painful illness of several months, she died on February 7, 1864.

13. J. H. Burnham, immediately after graduation, entered the army as lieutenant of the Normal company of the Thirty-Third Regiment. He subsequently became captain of the same company. In April, 1863, he resigned on account of ill-health, and returned to Bloomington. He was superintendent of the Bloomington schools one year, was editor of the *Pantagraph* two years, and since 1867 has been agent of the King Iron Bridge Company. In 1866 he was married to Almira S. Ives. His address is Bloomington.

14. Aaron Gove entered the Thirty-Third Regiment immediately after graduation, and soon became adjutant of the regiment. He remained in the army two years, was in business two years, was principal of the Rutland schools two years, and principal of the Normal public schools for five years. In August, 1874, he was elected city superintendent of the Denver, Colorado, schools, which position he still occupies. He purchased the *Schoolmaster* of Mr. Hull, and the *Illinois Teacher* of Mr. Nason, and consolidated the two journals. Mr. Gove was married to Cora Spafford, of Massachusetts, in 1865. They have four children—two boys and two girls.

15. Moses Morgan, immediately after the battle of Bull Run, entered the army and remained a year and a half, when he resigned with prostrated health. In 1863–4 he was principal of the third ward school in Peoria. In 1864 he again entered the army, in a civil capacity, and served until June, 1866. He removed to Brecksville, Ohio, and commenced farming, and in two years recovered his health. In 1865 he was married to Miss Laura Green. They have buried one child, and have two living. His address is Brecksville, Ohio.

16. Henry B. Norton taught one term in the model school, in 1861. In 1862–3 he taught at Warsaw. The year 1864 he was editor of the Bloomington *Pantagraph*. In 1864–5 he was county superintendent of Ogle County. In 1865 he resigned, and accepted a position in the Kansas State Normal School, at Emporia. He remained there five years. The years 1870–73 were spent in newspaper work and traveling. In 1873 he returned to the Emporia Normal School, where he remained two years, resigning to accept a position in the San Jose, California, Normal School, where he has since remained. He was married in 1864. They have three children. Address is San Jose, California.

17. Peleg R. Walker taught in Dement, 1861–2. He enlisted as private in Company K, Ninety-Second Illinois, in 1862, and was made lieutenant in April, 1863. He commanded the company in nearly every battle in which they were engaged, "Marched from Atlanta to the Sea," and thence by way of Carolina to Virginia, and was on an advanced post when Johnston surrendered. On his return, he was elected principal of the Creston schools, where he remained for seven years. In 1872 he resigned, to accept the principalship of

the Rochelle schools, which he has held continuously since. He was married in August, 1865. They have one girl, born in 1871.

18. Harvey J. Dutton entered the Thirty-Third Regiment immediately after graduation, and remained four years, becoming captain before the close of the war. On his return to Illinois he commenced farming, and removed to Missouri in 1860, where he had purchased a farm. He has taught from four to six months each winter for nine successive winters. In August, 1866, he was married to Louise V. Brinsden. They have four children—three girls and one boy. His address is Virgil City, Missouri.

CLASS OF 1862.

19. Sarah E. Beers taught four years at Normal Center, and part of 1866 in the Canton high school. In 1868, she opened a private school in Canton, and has conducted it continuously since, excepting the year 1878-9. She owns a neat little school house of her own. She is librarian of a circulating library and teaches some. She writes, February, 1882, "I do not propose to teach at all, on the account of deafness, but the people insist upon keeping me in the harness. I love the work, and would gladly spend the remainder of my life in it."

20. Elizabeth Carleton for four years following her graduation, was first assistant in the Griggsville high school. During the next four years she was principal of the grammar school in the same town. For ten years she was employed in the Hannibal, Missouri, schools. From September, 1881, to April, 1882, she was traveling. She then resumed work in Hannibal.

21. Helen (Grennell) Guild, immediately after graduation accepted the position of first assistant in the Peoria high school, where she remained for the succeeding ten years. In 1872 she resigned to take a similar position in the St. Louis high school. In 1874 she was married to Albert D. Guild, Chicago. Her present address is Lakeside, Michigan.

22. Esther M. Sprague, for four years after graduation, was principal of the intermediate department of the fourth ward school in Peoria. During the year 1866-7 she was principal of the model school in Platteville, Wisconsin, Normal School. The six years succeeding she was head assistant in the Kinzie school, Chicago. She was for seven years principal of Lincoln street school. From September, 1880, to March 1881, she did not teach. Since then she has been in the Foster school.

23. Emma (Trimble) Bangs in 1862-3 taught in York, Kendall County; in 1863-4 in Washington, Illinois; in 1864-5 in Lacon; in 1865-6 in Sparland; in 1866-7 in Lacon. She then learned the printer's trade from the "devil" to the editor's chair. She was postmistress

of Hillsboro for eight years. She is now local editress of *Montgomery County News*.

24. Lorenzo D. Bovee entered the army in 1862, and served one year in the One Hundredth Illinois Volunteers. In 1863 he was discharged on account of ill health. He taught only one year, his health having been impaired by service in the army. He is now engaged in farming near Chelopa, Kansas.

25. James F. Ridlon taught at Abingdon in 1862–3 and at Henderson during the winter of 1863–4. He entered the army in 1864, and at the close of the war taught in Monmouth during the winter of 1865–6. In 1866 he went to Kansas, and taught in Lawrence the winter term of 1866–7, and at Lanesville during the winter of 1868–9. In 1869–70 he was a member of the Kansas Legislature, and took an active part in all legislation affecting educational matters. He was married in 1870, and had charge of the DeSoto schools during the succeeding year. He then went on his farm, surveyed one year, and taught every winter until June, 1878. He is now farming during the summer, and acting as Grange lecturer in winter.

26. Logan Holt Roots was principal of DuQuoin schools before receiving a diploma. In the summer of 1862 he entered the army and served till the close of the war; "Marched to the Sea;" was in "grand reunion" at Washington; went south with Sherman, and remained in the army a while after the close of the war. He resigned, bought a plantation, raised cotton, and was successful. He was a member of the Fortieth and Forty-first Congress, and was afterward U. S. marshal in Arkansas. Since 1872 he has been president of the Merchant's National Bank at Little Rock.

CLASS OF 1863.

27. Mary A. Fuller was born in Tazewell County, Illinois, in 1841. She entered the Normal School, April 13, 1860, before the occupancy of the new building. She remained until her graduation, in 1863. Immediately after graduation, she commenced work in Decatur, as assistant in one of the grammar schools, and remained there for seven years. Resigning, she accepted the principalship of the Magnolia schools, which she retained three years. This proved to be the last of her work as a teacher. Her family had moved to Normal, and there Miss Fuller joined them to enjoy the quiet of her pleasant home and to devote herself to the further development of her cultured mind. After a visit to England and the Continent, and a rest of three or four years, she spent a year in the Boston School of Oratory, and was seriously thinking of resuming her teaching work, of which she was ardently fond, when she was suddenly attacked with a fatal illness, and in a few hours she had entered into a new life.

5

She was a woman of rare poise of character. Her habits were those of the scholar. She loved the seclusion of home and the companionship of books; but she was no recluse. She felt the currents of our busy modern life, and shrank from no duty that came to her door. The thoughtful, earnest, sincere, clear-faced little woman, impressed herself with singular force upon her associates, for she always brought with her suggestions of higher living and purer atmospheres ·of thought. To scores of young lives she gave such trend and inspiration that she still lives in many a home to enrich and bless it by the potency of her character. She was buried at her old home in Tazewell County.

28. Sarah F. (Gove) Baldwin taught one year in Granville, and two years in Peoria. In April, 1866, she was married to Eugene F. Baldwin. They have three children. Her address is Peoria, care of *Journal*.

29. Abbie R. (Reynolds) Wilcox taught one term in Bloomington. In June, 1864, she was married to Mr. Wilcox. They have three children living, and have lost two. She has since studied Kindergarten work, and is now a Kindergarten teacher in St. Louis.

30. Sarah Hackett Stevenson taught in Bloomington, Mt. Morris, and Sterling, aggregating four years in these places. She studied medicine in Chicago, and subsequently went to England, where she continued her studies with Prof. Huxley. In 1875 she was elected to the chair of Physiology in the Woman's College, in Chicago, which position she still retains. She is quite widely known as a lecturer and writer, and also as the author of a charming book, "Boys and Girls in Biology," published by D. Appleton & Co. Her address is Woman's College, Chicago.

31. W. Dennis Hall began teaching at Granville, Illinois, in September, 1863. He remained there during the year 1863-4, excepting the last two months, spent in the army. He left the army about the first of November, 1864, and began teaching in Brimfield, Illinois. He remained there three months. During the spring term of 1864-5 he had charge of the second ward school, in Peoria. During the year 1865-6 he had charge of the Elmwood schools. In September, 1866, he took charge of the Clinton schools, and remained there nearly five years. From 1869 to 1872 he was superintendent of LaSalle schools. During the years 1872-3, and 1873-4, he held a similar position in Centralia. In 1874, and a part of 1875, he did not teach. The last five months of 1875-6 he had charge of the Farmer City schools. Since June, 1876, he has been in the employ of D. Appleton & Co. He was married about 1868, and has one daughter. His address is 340 State Street, Chicago.

32. Ebenezer D. Harris, the three years succeeding his graduation, had charge of one of the ward schools of Peoria. He then engaged in market-gardening on a somewhat large scale, near Lincoln,

Nebraska. Since February, 1880, he has taught two terms in Lancaster County, Nebraska. He is now teaching.

33. John B. Thompson was born in McLean County, Illinois, in 1842, and entered school in 1860. He graduated with the fourth class, in 1863. Desiring to fit himself more fully for teaching, he remained the succeeding year, continuing his studies in the high school, and acting also as assistant in the same department. In 1864-5 he taught in El Paso, and in 1865-6 in Charleston. In the fall of 1866 he went to Kansas and taught there in 1866-7, returning to Illinois in the summer of 1867, with his health much impaired. He gradually declined, and in January, 1869, died at his home near Bloomington. He was an intense worker, and carried into his chosen profession a high degree of enthusiasm and earnestness.

CLASS OF 1864.

34. Hattie E. Dunn has taught constantly since graduation, as follows: 1864-5 in Springfield; 1865-71 in Bloomington ward schools; 1871-2 in Carbondale; 1872-3 in Carrollton; 1873-5 in Bloomington high school, as assistant, and since November, 1875, she has been principal of the same school. Her address is Bloomington.

35. Anna (Gunnell) Hatfield taught one year in Bloomington, and two in Peoria. Her address is Mrs. William Hatfield, care of Merchants' National Bank, Chicago.

36. Edith (Johnson) Morley taught one year in Aurora, three years in the model school, Normal, and two years in Bonham's Female Seminary, St. Louis. In 1871 she was married to Rev. John H. Morley. She writes in January, 1882, "Taking care of a good husband, two sons and a daughter." Her address is Winona, Minn.

37. Isabella More taught four years in Conover's Seminary, Bloomington; one year in Cairo, one year in Perry, and about three years in ungraded schools. On account of ill health, she did not teach for a few years. She resumed work in June, 1876. In 1877 was a candidate for county superintendent of Pike County; opposite party had a majority of 1,000; she was defeated by a little over 100. Since June, 1879, she has taught as follows: Six months in Perry, and four months in Independence, Perry township, where she is now teaching.

38. Harriet E. Stewart. No report has been received from this lady.

39. George Colvin was principal of Atlanta, Illinois, schools two years, of the Pontiac schools two years, and has had charge of the Pekin schools since September, 1871. In May, 1865, he was married to Miss Sallie Bergen. They have two children. His address is Pekin.

40. Lyman B. Kellogg continued his studies at Normal for a time after graduation, teaching meanwhile. In 1865 he was elected principal

of the Kansas State Normal School in Emporia. He organized the school and remained at its head for seven years. Since 1872 he has been engaged in business, and the practice of law. He was married in 1866. His wife died in 1873, leaving two boys. His address is Emporia.

41. Philo A. Marsh has taught but one year since graduation, and that was at Magnolia in 1864–5. Since then he has been engaged in railroading and milling. He was for a time passenger conductor on the P., D. & E. R. R. He is now agent for the I., B. & W. R. R. at Urbana, and is interested in a flouring mill near Atlanta. His address is Urbana.

· CLASS OF 1865.

42. Olinda (Johnson) Nichols taught nearly all the time until her marriage in 1869. Her address is Mrs. N. F. Nichols, Aurora, Illinois.

43. Almenia C. Jones has taught every school month since graduation. She taught two years in Pekin, two in Lewistown, and the remaining time in Canton, where she resides.

44. Lucinda (Standard) Johnson taught in 1865–6 in Centralia; the succeeding three years she taught in Charleston; in 1869–70 she taught in St. Cloud, Minnesota, Normal School. After this she taught one year in Ft. Smith, Arkansas, six months in Little Rock, and two and a half years in the Arkansas State University, at Fayetteville. The summer of 1874 she spent in Europe. On her return she was married to A. O. Johnson, Esq., a lawyer of Drake's Creek, Arkansas.

45. Bandusia Wakefield has taught as follows: Four terms in the model school; one term in Farmer City, Illinois; one term in Atlanta, Illinois; two years in Winterset, Iowa; one year in Emporia, Kansas; one term in Farmington, Illinois; two terms in Bloomington, Illinois; six and a half years in the Illinois Normal University. She resigned at the close of winter term, 1880–1, to take charge of her brother's children. Her address is Sioux City, Iowa.

46. Thomas J. Burrill had charge of the Varna schools three years. Since September, 1868, he has occupied a chair in the Industrial University at Champaign. For the last few years he has been professor of Botany and Horticulture. He is widely known among the leading agriculturists and horticulturists of the State, as he spends considerable time in lecturing upon topics of great economic interest to that part of our population. He was married in 1868.

47. John W. Cook. See page 49.

48. William Florin, 1865–6, was principal of the grammar department of the Lebanon schools; 1866–7 he was principal of the Highland schools; 1867–70 was principal of Lebanon, and 1870–2 of the Highland schools; 1872–3 he had charge of a grammar school in Belleville;

1875-6 he was assistant in the high school at the same place; 1876-7 he had charge of the Edwardsville schools, and in 1877-9 he held a similar position in St. Jacob. In the summer of 1879, after teaching steadily for fourteen years, he concluded to go into business. He is now selling drugs at Altamont.

49. David M. Fulwiler, 1865-6 was principal of the Lexington schools; 1866-9 he held the same position in Hillsboro. In 1869 he left teaching and went into business. In 1876 he became a short-hand reporter. He has taught one year since. His address is Lexington.

50. Oscar F. McKim taught one year in the model school, and for three years was principal of the second ward school in Decatur. He served four years as county superintendent of Macon county, and was associate principal of Decatur high school one year. In 1874 he commenced practicing law. He removed to Kansas in 1875, and taught in Oxford in 1875-6. He was principal of the Wichita schools 1876-8, and of the Wellington schools 1878-9. The next year he was an attorney-at-law agent. He is now teaching at Dallas City. Mr. McKim was married in 1866.

51. Adolph A. Suppiger, in 1865-7, was principal of the Maine schools, and 1867-73 of the Highland schools. He served four years as county superintendent of Madison County. After his term expired he taught six months in Venice, and one year in North Alton. He is now in business in Pierson. He was married in 1870, and has three children.

52. Melancthon Wakefield taught two terms in the model school after graduation. In 1866-7 he had charge of the Buda schools; 1867-8 of the Carrollton schools, and 1868-9 of the Cherokee, Iowa, schools. He has not taught since June, 1869, but has been practicing law in Cherokee. He has served three terms as mayor.

53. William McCambridge (H. S.) was station agent at Normal until 1871. He has been engaged in newspaper work since, and is now editor of the *Pantagraph*, Bloomington, Illinois.

54. Gertrude K. Case (H. S.) taught six years in Bloomington, and was three years principal of the primary department of the model school. She was married in 1875. Her address is Mrs. Wesley Young, Dayton, Ohio.

55. Howard C. Crist (H. S.) studied medicine, and, with the exception of one year spent in Arizona as United States Mission Surgeon, has been practicing in Bloomington.

56. Charles L. Capen (H. S.) entered Harvard University in 1865, and graduated in 1869. He then studied law in Bloomington, and is now a member of the law firm of Williams, Burr & Capen. He married Miss Nellie Briggs, in October, 1875.

57. Robert McCart (H. S.) graduated at the Ann Arbor law school, in 1867. He practiced in Bloomington until 1877, and then settled in Fort Worth, Texas.

58. Clara V. (Fell) Fyffe (II. S.) married James Fyffe, now deceased. Her address is Normal.

59. Hosea Howard (H. S.) is in the office of the Wabash, St. Louis and Pacific Railroad, St. Louis.

CLASS OF 1866.

60. Harriet (Case) Morrow was principal of the high school department of Hadley's Normal Academy, in Richmond, Indiana, in 1866-7. For four years, 1867 to 1871, she was principal of a grammar school in Ottawa, Illinois, except part of one year when she was assistant in the high school. For two years, 1871-3, she was teacher of mathematics in the Leavenworth, Kansas, high school. From September, 1873, to January 1878, she was preceptress in the Illinois State Normal School. In January, 1878, she was married to Mr. Morrow, of the lake survey. They have one son. Their home is Tonganoxie, Kansas.

61. Martha Foster taught two years in the intermediate department of the Yates City schools, one year in the intermediate department of the model school at Normal, two terms in country schools near Yates City, one year in Boone, Iowa, one year in Lindsay, Kansas, five years in Dexter, Iowa, and one year in Ottawa, Kansas. She also taught in six Normal Institutes, one month each, and three months in Junction City, Kansas. Her health having been somewhat impaired, she was obliged to give up teaching for a time. Since June, 1880, she taught seven months at her home in Maquon, Illinois.

62. Harriet A. Fyffe taught two years in Menard County, two years in the public schools of Normal, and for three years was principal of the Magnolia schools. She is now engaged in the drug business in Magnolia, Illinois.

63. Margaret (McCambridge) Hurd taught in the Cairo schools in 1866-7. In 1867 she was married to Charles R. Hurd. They have three daughters. Their residence is in Denver, Colorado.

64. Mary E. Pearce taught one year in Carrollton, one in Shelby County, one in Farmington, six in Lexington, and two in the public schools of Normal. The year 1877-8 was spent in California, and in 1878-9 she did not teach. In 1879-80 she was principal of the West Side school in El Paso. In 1880-1 she taught six months near Hudson. Since September she has been teaching in Lexington. Her address is Normal, Illinois.

65. Alice (Piper) Blackburn taught six years in the public schools of Macomb—two years in the grammar school and four in the high school. In 1872 she was married, and removed to California. They have one daughter, six years old. Her home is in San Buena Ventura, California.

66. Helen (Plato) Wilbur, from October, 1866, to March, 1867, taught in Kaneville; from September, 1867, to February, 1868, in Elgin; from February, 1868, to March, 1871, in Chicago. In 1871, she was married. Mr. Wilbur died a few months after their marriage. In December, 1874, she resumed teaching in Chicago, and has been so employed constantly since. Her address is 256 Ontario Street.

67. Sarah E. Raymond, in 1866–8, taught in Fowler Institute, Newark, Illinois, as assistant in the English department. 1868–9, she was assistant in a ward school in Bloomington. From September, 1869, to March, 1873, she was principal of the same school. The spring term of 1873, she was assistant in the high school. 1873–4, she was principal of the high school, and since September, 1874, she has been city superintendent of the Bloomington schools.

68. Olive (Rider) Cotton, 1866–7, was principal of the intermediate department of the model school at Normal. The six years succeeding, she taught in the schools of Griggsville. In 1873, on account of poor health, she gave up teaching. The succeeding three years were spent in California, New York, and Massachusetts. In January, 1878, she took a position in the Normal public schools, and remained there until June. In 1879, she was married to Alfred C. Cotton, of the class of 1869. Since then, she has spent two years in California, and one year in New York. They reside in Turner Junction, Illinois.

69. Julia (Stanard) Frost taught one year in Charleston, Illinois, one in Whitehall, one in Jersey County, one in Ottawa, two in Atlanta, and five months in Bureau County. After resting three years, she began teaching in Atlantic, Iowa. She taught one year in the primary department, two in the grammar, and since 1879 has been assistant in the high school. She was married in 1867 to R. H. Frost. They have one child.

70. Nelson Case was principal of the Tolono schools in 1866–7. He has not taught since. He studied law at Ann Arbor, and since his admission has been practicing in Oswego, Kansas. He was married in 1872. He is now judge of the probate court.

71. Philo A. Clark was principal of the Chillicothe schools one year, of the Neponset schools one year, one year near Davenport, and one year in county schools in Kendall County. For two years he was agent for school apparatus and furniture. He was a wholesale merchant and resided in Peoria; was then in the school furniture business. He left Peoria in October, 1878, to travel for a spice and tea house of Omaha. In 1879 he removed to Madison, where he has inherited considerable property.

72. John Ellis, jr., for three years, 1866–9, was principal of the Naples schools. The next three years, 1869–72, he was principal of the West Side schools in El Paso. In 1872 he went to Beatrice, Neb., and engaged in real estate and loan business. In 1878 he was elected

county treasurer. He was married in 1872, and has two children.

73. Joseph Hunter was born in New York in 1843. He entered the Normal School in September, 1863. In 1866-7 he was principal of the Pontiac schools. The next year he took a position in Washington University, St. Louis. Here he commenced the study of law. In 1869 he was admitted, and located at Rockford, but soon changed his residence to Mendota, where he remained until 1875, gaining, meanwhile, a lucrative practice. In 1873 he was married to the only child of J. C. Crocker, Esq., of Mendota. Thinking that a change of climate would improve his enfeebled health, in 1875 he removed to Lincoln, Nebraska, and formed a partnership with a leading attorney of that place. In the year 1880 his old friends at Normal were shocked to learn of his sudden death, which occurred on the 17th of April. He leaves a wife and four children. Mr. Hunter was an unusually modest, quiet man, gentle and tender as a woman, and generous to a fault. The rich treasures of his deep, true nature were hidden from the many to be revealed to the few. During his school days he was often called "Lincoln," from his resemblance to the martyred president in personal appearance, and in the general cast of his intellectual and social nature. Once known he could not be forgotten. His individuality was strongly marked. He was universally esteemed, and his untimely death brings the keenest sorrow to hundreds of his early mates, as well as to the friends of his maturer years.

74. Richard Porter taught one year in Perry, one in Rantoul, one in Monticello, and three years in country schools. In 1877 he removed to Kansas, and is now farming near Bavaria. He is married and has two children.

CLASS OF 1867.

75. Emily (Chandler) Hodgin, immediately after graduation, was married to her classmate, Cyrus W. Hodgin. She has taught only one term. They reside in Terre Haute, Indiana.

76. Emily (Cotton) Collins taught in Griggsville, Collinsville, Cairo, and Decater—nine years in all. In September, 1876, she was married to Wm. H. Collins, of Quincy. They have one daughter.

77. Nellie Forman, immediately after graduation, began teaching in West Bridgewater, Massachusetts. She remained there a year and a half, when her health became so poor that she was obliged to resign. She spent two years in the study of music, and three years as a teacher in Lynn, Massachusetts. For seven years she held a position in the Mercantile Savings Bank, Boston. Since October, 1881, she has been teaching at Hampton Institute, Virginia.

78. Mary W. French, in 1867-9, taught in the Cairo schools. Since 1869, she has been an assistant in the Decatur high school.

79. Eurania (Gorton) Hanna, from September, 1867, to June, 1869, taught in the Rock Island high school; from 1869 to June, 1871, in the Peru high school; from 1871 to June, 1872, she was principal of the Aurora preparatory, and from September, 1872, to May, 1874, was assistant in the Aurora high school. In May, 1874, she was married to John R. Hanna, of Aurora. They have one daughter.

80. Mary R. Gorton was born in Rock Island, Illinois, in 1844, and entered the Normal School in December, 1862. Having had superior advantages, she at once took high rank in her classes. She remained in school until June, 1865, when she interrupted her studies and taught a year in Rock Island. Returning in the fall of 1866, she completed her course, graduating in the class of 1867. After graduation, she returned to Rock Island and taught one year in the high school. Her career as a student and teacher had been so eminently successful that in 1868 she was called to a position in the Cook County Normal School, where she remained until April, 1871. She then accepted a call to the Normal Department of the Arkansas State University. In June, 1876, she was appointed principal of this department. In June, 1877, she tendered her resignation, and accepted an assistant's place in the Peabody branch high school, St. Louis. Here she remained until her death, November 15, 1878. Her appearance was unusually prepossessing; richly endowed in person and intellect, with a rare dignity of manner, quick sympathies, thorough scholarship, a genius for governing, and a noble ambition to excel. She produced a profound impression upon all who came within the circle of her influence. Dr. Harris, in a recent letter, paid a glowing tribute to her rare qualities of mind and heart. In the full maturity of a noble womanhood, she went out of this life into the infinite possibilities of the unseen.

81. Mary (Pennell) Barber taught in the model school the spring term of 1868, and again from January, 1869 to June, 1870. She spent the year 1870–1 at Vassar College; 1871–2 she taught in the Peoria County Normal school; from January to June, 1874, in the Polo high school; in 1874–5 in the Normal public school, and the fall of 1875 in the Tuscola high school. In December, 1875, she was married to A. H. Barber. They reside at No. 9 Langley Avenue, Chicago.

82. Onias C. Barber taught one year in Illinois, and two years in Mississippi. He has been on a farm most of the time since graduation. His health, feeble from childhood, has prevented severe labor. Since 1876 he has been clerking in Tamaroa, selling books and stationery.

83. John R. Edwards was born in Ohio, in 1839, and became a student in the Normal School in September, 1865, taking an advanced standing. He completed the course in two years, graduating with the eighth class in June, 1867. He was at once appointed to the princi-

palship of the Hyde Park schools, and remained there one year.   In
the fall of 1868 he was called to the principalship of the Evanston
schools; but in the spring of 1869 his failing health obliged him to
resign.   In August he was married to Miss Annie E. Downs, of Hyde
Park, and was elected principal of the third ward school in Peoria.
An injury received during the war had seriously broken his health, and
again his failing strength obliged him to give up his position, which he
did in March, 1870.   He removed to Hyde Park, where, after a lin-
gering illness of more than a year, he died, in April, 1871.   He was
of the thousands who escaped death upon the field of battle to die a
victim of the great war in the early years that succeeded it.

84. George E. Hinman has taught five years since graduation.
He has spent three years in Colorado, and four in Ohio.   He was
married in 1871, but lost his wife in 1876.   He is now living on a
farm near Granville.

85. Cyrus W. Hodgin was married to Emily Chandler in 1867.
They have one child.   For two years he was principal of the Richmond,
Indiana, high school, and for three years was principal of the Henry
County independent high school.   From September, 1872, to June,
1881, he was a professor in the State Normal School in Terre Haute.
He then resigned this position, and is now resting and doing institute
work.

86. Fred J. Seybold has not taught since graduation.   He acted
as book agent for Sherwood & Co., for a time, and subsequently was
admitted to the bar.   His address is not known.

87. James S. Stevenson was married in 1861; 1867-9 he was
principal of the Sparta schools; 1869-70 he had charge of the fourth
academic department, Washington University; 1870-2 he was principal of the Collinsville schools, and since September, 1872, he has
been principal of the Bates school, St. Louis.   His address is 1115 N.
Park Place.

CLASS OF 1868.

88. Ruthie E. (Baker) Scarrat was principal of Normal public
high school three years, and assistant in Alton high school one and
one-half years.   In April, 1873, she was married to Isaac Scarrat,
who died not long after.   She subsequently married his brother.
She taught one year in the Chicago schools, after the death of her
husband, before her second marriage.   Her address is Mrs. Nathan
Scarrat, Kansas City, Missouri.

89. Ann Eliza Bullock taught, 1868-9, near Tonica.   Subsequently she taught four terms in Bloomington, and five in Tonica.
She is not teaching now.

90. Jemima S. Burson taught four years in Richmond, Indiana,

and one and one-fourth years in Spiceland, Indiana, but is not teaching now, on account of ill health. Her address is Richmond.

91. Lydia A. Burson taught four years in Richmond, one-third of a year at Carthage, and one year at Spiceland, Indiana. Her health will not permit her to teach. Her address is Richmond.

92. Etta L. Dunbar, 1868-70, was principal of the Blackburn schools; 1870-74, of DeKalb schools. She was then obliged to give up teaching on account of ill health. Three years were spent in taking care of an invalid mother. She is now painting. Her address is Longmont, Colorado.

93. Anna C. Gates taught one year at Tolono, and since September, 1869, has been principal of the Gravvis school, St. Louis.

94. S. Grace (Harwood) Whitney has taught one year at Council Hill, two years as first assistant of Alton high school, and three years and a half at Clear Creek, Illinois. In April she was married to Ezra Whitney, of Livingston County, New York. She then conducted an educational department in the *Henry Republican*, and afterward devoted her attention to primary work. In 1879-81 she taught in Magnolia, and is now teaching in the Soldiers' Orphans' Home.

95. Lucia (Kingsley) Manning was, for three years, principal of the primary department of model school, and for four years was assistant in the Peru, Indiana, high school. She was married August, 1870, to G. G. Manning, of Peru.

96. Eliza A. (Pratt) Kean for four years was a teacher in the Bloomington high school. Her address is 99 Washington Street, Chicago.

97. Emma T. (Robinson) Kleckner has taught two years and two months. She was married in July, 1870. Her address is Freeport, Illinois.

98. Mary J. (Smith) Bogardus taught one year at Marengo, and two terms in Springfield. Her address is Mrs. S. Bogardus, Springfield, Illinois.

99. Cornelia Valentine was born in Indiana, in 1846. She entered the Normal School in September, 1865, and remained until her graduation, June, 1868. The year of 1868-9 she taught in Earlham College, Richmond, Indiana. The succeeding year, and until April, 1871, she was assistant in the Rushville (Illinois) high school, leaving this position on account of the sickness and death of her sister. The succeeding year she was an assistant in the Rock Island high school, and the year following (1872-3) she held a similar position in Aurora. She remained in Aurora only five months, ill health compelling her to resign. After several weeks of rest, she accepted the chair of mathematics in the Methodist College in Jacksonville, Illinois. Here she remained until the summer of 1874. In September, 1874, she returned to Rock Island, first as assistant, but soon after as principal of the high school. She remained until April,

1877, when a sudden attack of typhoid malarial fever obliged her to resign. She returned to her home in Richmond, followed by the anxious solicitude of loving friends. She endured her terrible suffering without a murmur, and on the twentieth of June, 1877, "entered into rest."

100. Clara E. Watts was one year matron of temporary Soldiers' Orphans' Home, for two years was teacher in Soldiers' Orphans' Home at Normal, and one year was principal of the intermediate department of the Normal public schools. She is now residing in Normal.

101. Stephen Bogardus, in August, 1868, married Miss Mary J. Smith. For two years he was principal of the Marengo schools. Since September, 1870, he has been proprietor of the Springfield Business College.

102. William A. McBane taught two years at Cairo and Metropolis, published a weekly paper three years, purchased a ferry franchise at Metropolis, and ran a steam ferry three years. He then went into the real estate business, and has taught but one year (1880–1 in Metropolis) since. His address is Metropolis, Illinois.

103. Henry McCormick. See page 50.

104. Jacob Rightsell was one year principal of a ward school, and for three years superintendent of city schools, at Little Rock. He was married in August, 1871. For two years he had charge of the H. R. library, Washington, D. C. He then was county superintendent of Pulaski County, Arkansas, one year. He is now principal of the largest graded school in Arkansas,—Peabody school—in Little Rock.

105. William Russell was married in August, 1868. 1868–9 he taught in Newport, Indiana; 1869–73 at Marion, Indiana; one year in Normal School at Terre Haute, and 1874–7 at Salem, Indiana. Since 1877 he has been teaching in Marion. He has charge of a township school six to seven months a year, and is employed in a Normal School about twenty weeks a year.

106. Elma Valentine was born in Indiana in 1849. She entered school in 1865 and graduated in 1868. Immediately after graduation she became a teacher in the Friends' Academy in Richmond, Indiana. She remained there until the latter part of February, 1871, when failing health obliged her to resign. Her position was very agreeable, and was not the occasion of her illness. In spite of medical assistance and the tender care of loving friends, she gradually sank away, until the fourteenth of April, when she passed from earth.

107. Annie M. (Edwards) Dougherty (H. S.) was married in December, 1871, to N. C. Dougherty. She taught six months in a seminary in St. Louis, and one year in the Princeton high school. Her address is Peoria.

108. R. Arthur Edwards (H. S.) graduated from the Normal Department with class of 1870. 1870–1 he was principal of Paxton

schools; 1871-2 of Monticello schools; 1872-3 at Dartmouth College; 1873-4 teacher of Latin and Greek in Rock River Seminary, Mt. Morris; 1874-76 was junior and senior in Princeton College, New Jersey, graduating in 1876; 1878-80 was acting professor of English literature and rhetoric in Knox College. He was married in December, 1879, to Miss Alice M. Shirk, of Peru, Indiana. He is now in a bank in Peru.

CLASS OF 1869.

109. Lizzie L. Alden, 1869-70, was principal of schools in Caledonia, Illinois; 1870-1 was assistant in Lena high school; 1871-4 she taught a country school near Brimfield; 1874-5 traveled in the east; 1875-7 taught in the Burton, Kansas, schools. She is now teaching in Sedgwick.

110. Melissa (Benton) Overman taught in Geneseo from 1869 to 1871. In the spring term of 1872 she taught in the Dixon high school, and in 1872-3 in the Freeport high school. In 1873 she was married to A. H. Overman. Address Mrs. A. H. Overman, care of Jansen, McClurg & Co., Chicago.

111. Ella K. Briggs taught one year at her home in Logan County, two years at Lincoln, one year at Delavan, one year at Jerseyville, and was two years principal of Cream Ridge, Logan County, schools. After resting one year she taught at Freeport two years. Her health failed, and she went to Minnesota, where she suffered a long and painful illness. Since June, 1879, she has taught two years in Freeport, Illinois.

112. Lucretia C. (Davis) Ramsey, 1869-70, taught in the primary department of Quincy College; 1870-1 in Rushville schools. Her address is Rushville, Illinois.

113. Jane (Pennell) Carter taught one year in Normal public schools; seven months in country schools in McLean County; three months in Bloomington schools, and one year in primary department of model school. Her address is Peru, Illinois.

114. Maria (Sykes) Nichols taught two years in Geneseo, one year in Kewanee, and was for four years principal of the Wyoming, Iowa, schools. She was married in 1876. Address, care of Austin Sykes, Kewanee, Illinois.

115. Helen (Wadleigh) Willis taught three years, one near Rutland, and two in Missouri. Her address is Neosho Falls, Kansas.

116. Ben. Allensworth was principal of the Elmwood schools, 1869-72; editor in Pekin in 1873, and taught three years in Minier. He is county superintendent of Tazewell County. His address is Minier.

117. Hugh R. Edwards was married in 1869. He taught as principal of the third ward schools, Peoria, one year; of sixth ward,

one year; of third ward, Sterling, one year; and of Byron schools, one year. For three years he ran the Edwards' Seminary, Sterling. The last five years he has been in the second ward school, Peoria.

118. Alfred C. Cotton, 1869–70, was principal of the Richview schools; 1870–1 of Buckley schools; 1871–3 of Gilman schools; 1873–4 of Grand Tower schools; 1874–6 of Griggsville schools. He graduated at Rush Medical College in April, 1878, and is now practicing at Turner Junction, Illinois. He is also lecturing in spring course at Rush. He was married to Miss Olive Rider.

119. Charles H. Crandell was principal of Petersburg schools one year; of ninth ward, Troy, New York, schools, five years; of Atlanta schools, one year; of Lexington, Illinois, schools, one-half year; of Hilliard, Ohio, schools, one year; of Worthington, Ohio, three years, and of Flint schools, one year. He was married in 1876, and is now in Worthington.

120. William R. Edwards taught in McLean, Illinois, three years. In the summer of 1870 he moved to Charles City, Iowa, where he married Miss Josie Bigelow. He remained there two years in the mercantile business. In 1872 he became principal of the New Hampton, Iowa, schools, remaining one year. He was for five years principal of Osage, Iowa, schools. In 1878 he resigned and returned to New Hampton, where he is in the mercantile business, and also editor of the New Hampton *Courier*.

121. Charles Howard.

122. Isaac F. Kleckner was married in July, 1870. For four years he was superintendent of Stephenson County. In 1873 he was elected county clerk, which position he now holds. Address, Freeport, Illinois.

123. George G. Manning, 1869–70, taught at Fulton; 1870–1 at Jacksonville, Illinois. In the summer of 1871 he was made superintendent of Peru, Indiana, schools. He is still there. In August, 1870, he was married to Lucia Kingsley.

124. George W. Mason was married in August, 1875. He was principal of Paris high school three months; of Charleston high school six months; of Kramer schools, Little Rock, one year; of Pekin high school two years; of Hannibal high school three years, and taught at Lewisburg, Arkansas, one year. Since 1878 he has been engaged in the study and practice of medicine. For a time, he was house physician in Mercy Hospital, Chicago. He is now practicing in Bloomington.

125. Charles W. Moore, 1869–72, taught in Fremont; 1872–4 was principal of Ridott schools; 1874–5 of Cedarville schools; 1875–6 of Lena schools; 1876–7 in country schools in Stephenson County; 1880–1 was principal of Storm Lake, Iowa, schools. He is now employed in the postoffice at Storm Lake. He was married in 1871.

126. Christopher D. Mowry was principal of the Pecatonica

schools 1869–72, and of the Anamosa, Iowa, schools 1872–4. He then entered Rush Medical College, and graduated in 1876. To recover broken health, he spent the following year on the plains and in the mountains. For four years he practiced at Osage, Iowa. He is now in Aurora, Illinois. He was married in 1869 to Fannie E. Alderman.

127. James W. Hays in 1869–70 was principal of a grammar school in Paris, and the next year was principal of the high school in the same place. Since September, 1871, except one year when he did not teach, he has been principal of the Urbana schools.

128. Gratiot Washburn (H. S.) immediately after his graduation, he joined his father, Hon. E. B. Washburne, in Paris. He remained there most of the time until his father returned to America. He then entered the New York Custom House, and was there at last report.

CLASS OF 1870.

129. Louisa C. (Allen) Gregory was principal of the Alton high school one year, and for two years was assistant in the Peoria County Normal School. In June, 1874, she was elected professor of domestic economy in the Champaign Industrial University, which position she resigned in June, 1880, and is now in Washington, D. C. In 1879 she was married to Dr. John M. Gregory, Regent of the University.

130. Barbara Denning taught in Shawneetown in 1870–1, and in 1871–3 in Cedar Point, LaSalle County. In 1873 she went to Rosario, Argentine Confederation, as mission teacher. She will return to her home soon.

131. Alice Emmons was the daughter of Judge Sylvester Emmons and wife, and was born in Illinois in 1848. She entered school in September, 1865. Her course was interrupted by occasional terms of absence, so that she did not graduate until 1870. She began teaching in Cairo the following September, but after three weeks of school work her health failed, and, very much to the regret of the Board, she was obliged to resign. The year was spent at her home in Beardstown. The succeeding year she returned to Cairo, but after two weeks in the school room she was called to the death-bed of a dear friend. She returned to her home seriously ill, and in a few days she passed away, October 2, 1871. A brilliant scholar, thoroughly conscientious and faithful in the discharge of every duty, all had anticipated for her a future of rare usefulness. Though a decade has passed away since her death, the memory of this beautiful girl is as though but yesterday she had gone out from her schoolmates to her brief career.

132. Cara E. Higby taught 1870–1 in the Skinner school, Chicago; 1871–2 in the Blow school, St. Louis; 1872–7 in the Skinner school, again, and 1877–80 in the West Division high school, Chicago. She

is now employed in the West Side high school.   Her address is 374 West Jackson Street.

133. Emma A. (Howard) Gardner taught in Warrensburg, Missouri, 1870–1; in Carbondale, Illinois, 1871–2, and in Los Angeles, California, 1872–4.   In January, 1874, she was married to Henry I. Gardner.   Her address is Orange, California.

134. Margaret (Hunter) Regan from September, 1870, to June, 1874, taught in the Mississippi State Normal School; the last three years she was principal of the school.   In 1874 she was married to L. T. Regan, of the class of 1870.   Their home is Morris.

135. Maria L. (Kimberly) Perry taught two years in Warrensburg, Missouri, and one year in Fort Smith, Arkansas.   She was married in 1874.   Her address is 164 Canfield Street, Detroit.

136. Mary D. LeBaron, in 1870–1, taught in Oneida; 1871–2 in DeKalb County; 1872–9 in the Rolling Mills schools, Chicago, and for one year she conducted a private primary school in Chicago.   She has not taught since June, 1880.   Address 741 Dixon Street, Chicago.

137. Letitia (Mason) Quine, immediately after her graduation, commenced teaching in the Pontiac high school, where she remained one year.   The winters of 1871–2, 1872–3, 1873–4, were spent in the Woman's Medical College, Chicago, from which she graduated in the spring of 1874.   By request of the Woman's Foreign Missionary Society, in the fall of 1874, she went to Kin Kiang, China, to establish a medical dispensary.   She remained two years, when she was obliged, by ill health, to return.   She succeeded during her stay, however, in permanently establishing the dispensary.   In November, 1876, she was married to Wm. E. Quine, M. D., of Chicago.

138. Adella (Nance) Shilton taught three and a half years in the aggregate, in Wethersfield, Galva, and Moline.   In 1874 her eyes became so weak as to oblige her to leave the school room.   In 1879 she was married to Mr. C. A. Shilton.   They reside in Kewanee.

139. Adelaide V. Rutherford taught one year in Missouri, one in Texas, one in Plainview, and one in Chetopa, Kansas.   In the meantime, she spent one year in Michigan University.   After 1877 she was at her home in Girard, caring for her invalid mother.   She remained at home until August, 1880.   She then returned to Ann Arbor high school, where she expected to graduate in June, 1832, but was compelled to leave in April on account of sickness at home.

140. Fannie (Smith) Cole, in 1870–1, taught in Paxton, and in 1871–2 in the intermediate department of Woman's College, in Evanston.   For the next two years she taught "good manners and the etiquette of occasions" in various institutions.   In 1874 she became the "paying teller" in the office of the treasurer of Cook County.   She remained there until her marriage to Madison B. Cole, in July, 1875.   She has done some teaching since her marriage. Their present residence is Galveston, Texas.

141. Armada (Thomas) Bevan taught three years in Lincoln, one year in Jerseyville, and two years in Delavan. In 1877 she was married to John L. Bevan, of Atlanta. They have one daughter.

142. Marion (Weed) Martin taught one year in Loda, and one year in Lacon. She was married in 1872, to Irwin A. Martin, of New York. They have one daughter. Her address is 36 West Forty-Sixth Street, New York.

143. Ben. W. Baker was principal of the grammar department of the model school for four years. Since then he has been preaching. He is married, and has three children. In 1881 he went to Denver, Colorado.

144. Joseph Carter, while pursuing his studies, was for two years principal of the grammar department of the model school. After graduation, he spent two years in farming, and studied law and edited a paper for two years. He became principal of the Normal public schools in 1874, and remained in that position until June, 1878, when he resigned to accept the superintendency of the Peru schools, where he still remains. In 1870 he was married to Miss Jane E. Pennell, of the class of 1869. In addition to the above work, Mr. Carter has done a large amount of institute work in Woodford, McLean, and LaSalle Counties.

145. Robert A. Childs was principal of the Amboy schools for three years. He was admitted to the bar in 1873, and since then has been practicing in Chicago. In December, 1873, he was married to Miss Mary Coffeen. They have three children. · Their home is in Hinsdale.

146. James W. Dewell, 1870–2, taught near Carrollton; 1872–3 at Barry; 1873–4 at Elm Grove; 1874–6 in Kane. In 1876 he bought a farm near Franklin, in Morgan County, and resides there. He rents his farm and teaches, having taught three years in the same school. He was married in 1872.

147. Samuel W. Garman, 1870–1, was principal of the Mississippi State Normal School, at Holly Springs. 1871–2 he taught in Lake Forrest Seminary. 1872–3 was spent in the Rocky Mountains with Prof. Cope, of the United States geological survey. Since 1873 he has been connected with the Agassiz museum, in Cambridge. He has traveled quite extensively, having spent some time in South America, especially in the Titicaca Valley. At last accounts he was engaged in "deep sea," and similar work.

148. John W. Gibson, 1870–2, was principal of one of the schools in Belvidere. He was married several years ago. Since the summer of 1881 he has been in business.

149. Benjamin Hunter taught one year in Oneida. Subsequently he practiced law in St. Louis. Present address is unknown.

150. John W. Lummis, 1870–1, taught in Clayton; 1871–2 in Elm Grove. In the fall of 1872 he was married, and moved to a

farm near LaPrairie, where they still reside. With a single exception, he taught every winter until June, 1880, since which time he
has not taught. His teaching has all been done in Adams County,
except in the winter of 1879–80, when he taught in Hancock County.

151. John H. Parr taught in Cedarville four years, and in Mt.
Morris Seminary two years. He is now a student in the Chicago
Theological Seminary.

152. Levi T. Regan was superintendent of Logan County for four
years. 1874–5 he was principal of the Lincoln schools; 1875–8 of the
Amboy schools, and since September, 1878, he has had charge of the
Morris schools. Married Margaret Hunter, July, 1874, of same class.

153. Wade H. Richardson was married to Lydia Corbett in August
1870. He taught in Kankakee and Rantoul 1870–2. From October,
1872, to June, 1882, except one year which he spent in the south, he
was principal of a ward school in Milwaukee. In 1878 his wife and
one child died of diphtheria. Two daughters survive her. In the
summer of 1880 he was married to Mary A. Hawley, of the class of
1873. He is now a member of the firm of Fenn, Williams & Co.,
booksellers, stationers, etc.

154. John W. Smith was principal of the Pontiac schools four
years, and taught one year in California. For four years he was
engaged in business in Pontiac and McDowell. He was employed
during 1881–2 as teacher in the Illinois Reform School.

155. William Burry (H. S.) entered Harvard in 1870, and graduated in 1874. He then studied law, practiced in Chicago, and is now
a member of the law firm of Isham, Lincoln & Burry, of that city.

156. Wm. H. Smith (H. S.), 1870–1, taught at Granville; 1871–3
at Tonica; 1873–4 was in business; 1874–5 taught at Farmer City. . In
November, 1875, he was elected county superintendent of McLean
County, to fill unexpired term. He was re-elected in 1877. He was
married in 1870 to Miss Nellie Galusha. He resigned the superintendency in December, 1881, to become one of the proprietors of the
Saturday Evening Call, Peoria.

157. William Duff Haynie (H. S.) entered Harvard, and graduated in 1874. He studied law one year at Cairo, graduated from
Wesleyan law school in June, 1876, and has since been practicing
law in Bloomington.

158. Almira A. Bacon (H. S.)   No report.

159. Nellie H. Galusha (H. S.) was married to W. H. Smith,
and taught with him one year. Her address is Peoria.

CLASS OF 1871.

160. Charlotte (Blake) Myers, 1871–2, taught in the Carbondale
schools; 1872–4 in DeKalb; 1874–8 in the Normal public schools;

1878–9 in Metamora; 1879–81 in Streator; 1881–2 in Morris. In June, 1882, she was married to Edward Myers. They reside in Streator.

161. Isabella (Huston) Tabor taught one year in Atlanta, one in Lincoln, and one in Springfield. June, 1875, she was married to Rev. Manly Tabor. Her address is Middletown, Connecticut.

162. Julia E. Kennedy. See page 51.

163. Harriet (Kern) Walker taught five years in the Bloomington schools. In 1877 she was married to Mr. T. M. Walker, of Bloomington.

164. Celestia M. Mann. No report.

165. Frances I. Moroney taught in Minnesota in 1871–3. Since the spring of 1875 she has been teaching in the Bloomington, schools.

166. Frances (Rawlings) Cunningham taught in Centralia in 1871–2, and in Pekin in 1872–3, and in the Soldiers' Orphans' Home in 1873–4. In 1874 she was married to Dr. T. N. Cunningham. She taught one year after her marriage, in Topeka, Illinois. Her address is Sheffield, Illinois.

167. Isabel (Rugg) Reed taught one year in Odell, and two in Pontiac. In 1873 she married N. H. Reed. Their home is in Pontiac, Illinois.

168. Francis (Shaver) Thompson taught in Chicago until the great fire, and finished the year in Woodstock. In 1872–3 she taught in Pekin, and in 1873–4 in Chicago, until her marriage, which took place in December, 1873. Her address is Mrs. J. T. Thompson, 146 Twenty-Seventh Street, Chicago.

169. Emma G. Strain taught in the Bloomington schools for seven years, and finally resigned on account of ill health. Her address is Louisville, Kentucky.

170. Frances (Weyand) Latham taught three months in Somanauk, six months near Belleflower, and two in Bloomington. She was married in February, 1874, to W. A. Latham. They reside on a farm near Osman, in McLean County, Illinois.

171. W. C. Griffith, on leaving school, took charge of the Taylorville schools and retained the position for five years. In 1876 he resigned and accepted the general agency for Indiana of the Aetna Life Insurance Company. Mr. Griffith was married to Miss Elnora Libby, a high-school student, in 1871. He resides at Indianapolis.

172. Henry F. Holcomb entered the Normal School from Lake County, September, 1867, and graduated in 1871. Immediately after graduation, he commenced teaching, but after a few weeks was suddenly stricken down, and died in a few days. He was a man of unusually good health, and was full of life and physical vigor.

173. Andrew T. Lewis taught only two years. He was admitted to the bar, but has not practiced, having been engaged in publishing

a newspaper most of the time since graduation. In 1879 he went west and engaged in teaching in Central City, Nevada. In 1880–1 he was principal of the Deadwood schools, and since has been in Colorado, Utah, and Montana. He is now in Urbana. Mr. Lewis was married some years ago, but lost his wife a few months after leaving Illinois.

174. T. A. H. Norman taught four years, and then took the course of study in the American Medical College, St. Louis. He practiced for a time, and then returned to teaching, having been employed for three years near Martinsville, Illinois. He was married, shortly after leaving school, to Miss Pauline Bartholdt, a lady who will be well remembered by the students of 1870–1. He has retired to a farm near Martinsville.

175. Edgar D. Plummer has taught but one year, his health having failed during his school course. He is engaged in business in Heyworth, Illinois.

176. James O. Polhemus was a classmate of the two preceding, and entered school in September, 1868. After graduation he taught in Panolia; Chester, Ohio; near Paxton, Illinois; and in Ludlow, Secor, and Gridley. At the close of his work in the last-named place he was quite ill. He had a distressing cough which soon developed into hemorrhage of the lungs. He survived the attack about a month, dying August 15, 1877. His widowed mother resides in El Paso, Illinois.

177. James R. Richardson taught in Sparta, seven months, in 1871–2; six and one-half months in Arcadia, in 1872–3; nine months in district schools, in 1873–4; seven months in district schools, near Jacksonville, in 1874–5; at Mauvaisterre, in 1875–7; at Union Grove, in 1877–8; at Woodson, in 1877–9; five months near Jacksonville, in 1879–80; at Woodson, in 1880–1; at Franklin, in 1880–2. All the above work, except the first, was done in Morgan County. In 1877 he was married to Miss Sarah M. Williams, a former student of the Normal School. His address is Jacksonville, Illinois.

178. R. Morris Waterman entered school in September, 1867, and devoted four years to his work, taking the classical course in order to fit himself for teaching the ancient languages, and graduating with the class of 1871. He spent the summer with his parents on the farm near Barrington, Illinois, and in July was appointed to the principalship of the Blue Island schools. A few days before the schools were to open he was somewhat indisposed, and the beginning of the term was deferred. He gradually failed, and in three weeks died. Mr. Waterman was an especial favorite while at school. The students of ten years ago vividly recall the quiet, unassuming gentleman with a keen sense for humor, a kindly word and willing hand for any enterprise that promised good to the school or his society—the Wrightonian. Having fitted himself for any position in the schools of the State, much

was expected of him; but at the beginning of his career, standing on the verge of manhood, crowned with the love of friends and the sincere respect of all who knew him, he died.

179. John X. Wilson was principal of the sixth district in Peoria, 1871 to June, 1879. He has not taught since the latter date. Mr. Wilson was married in 1866.

180. John P. Yoder, 1871–2, was principal of the Blue Island schools; 1872–3 he was in business in Chicago; 1873–4 he taught a district school in McLean County; 1874–80 he was principal of the Danvers schools. In September, 1881, he became principal of the Bushnell schools. He is married, and has three children.

181. Alice C. Chase (II. S.) Chicago.

CLASS OF 1872.

182. Anna G. Bowen, her health not having been such as to permit her to teach continually, has taught thirteen terms, and expects to resume her work as soon as she is able. Her present address is 78 Aberdeen Street, Chicago.

183. Martha A. Fleming, from September, 1872, to June, 1876, was principal of a grammar department in the Hyde Park schools. She resigned to accept a position in the Peoria County Normal Schools, where she remained until 1878. Since that time she has been teaching in Chicago. For one year and a half, she was connected with one of the leading seminaries for young ladies—Park Institute. She resigned this position in September, 1880, and in the following month took a position in the primary department of the Oakland school, where she remains. Her address is 37 Oakwood Avenue.

184. Lenore Franklin taught in the Normal public schools for five years; in the Delevan schools for two years; in the Rockford schools part of 1876–80; in Pueblo, Colorado, schools, 1880–1, and in Princeton in 1881–82. She is now teaching in Belvidere.

185. Mary C. Furry, for three years succeeding her graduation, taught in the Normal public schools. She then taught one term in a family school; one year in the Sterling schools; two years in a country school near Sterling, and since September, 1880, she has been teaching in Sterling.

186. Clara (Gaston) Forbes taught one year in La Porte, Indiana. On Christmas day, 1873, she was married to Prof. S. A. Forbes, Director of the Laboratory of Natural History, at Normal. They have three children, two girls and one boy.

187. Anna M. Gladding entered the Normal School in September, 1868, from McLean County. She had been for some time a student in the model school, and by the singular sweetness of

her disposition, and by her patient fidelity, she had won the esteem of all who knew her. She finished the course in 1872, and at once began her work as teacher, spending the first year in Vienna, Illinois. The two succeeding years she taught in district schools; in 1875-6 she did not teach, but resumed her work the succeeding year, teaching at Galva. Never robust, her strength was insufficient for the wearing life of a teacher; she therefore relinquished her position and removed to Vineland, New Jersey. Nothing was known of her ill-health until the news was received in April that she had passed away.

188. Rachel Hickey taught in Ramsey in 1872-3; in DeKalb in 1873-4, and in Bloomington in 1874-5. Since September, 1875, she has been teaching in the grammar grades of the Indianapolis schools. Her address is 48 Cherry Street.

189. Sara C. Hunter has taught in the Lakeview schools constantly since her graduation. Her address is Englewood, Illinois.

190. Alza (Karr) Blount taught in Atlanta, Illinois, 1873-4, and in Forreston, 1874-6. In August, 1874, she was married to George Blount, of the same class. They reside in Macomb.

191. Martha G. Knight, from September, 1872, to June, 1879, taught constantly. The first four years she taught part of the time in country schools, and the remainder of the time in Henry, and in Bloomington. From September, 1876, to June, 1879, she taught in the Bloomington city schools. She did not teach in 1879-80, but is now principal of the Clear Creek school, in Putnam County.

192. Julia F. (Mason) Parkinson entered the model school when quite young, her parents having moved to Normal to educate their children. She entered the Normal Department in September, 1869, and graduated with the class of 1872. The year after her graduation she was principal of the Winchester high school. The succeeding year she was first assistant in the Lincoln high school. In September, 1874, she took charge of the model department of the Southern Illinois Normal School, where she remained until December 28, 1876, when she was married to Prof. D. B. Parkinson, of the same institution. For some years her health had not been very good, and in the summer of 1876 her husband took her to the mountains of the west, hoping, at least, to prolong her life. At first she seemed benefited by the change, but she soon began to fail, and died in August, 1878, at San Jose, California, leaving one son.

193. Emma A. Monroe, 1872-3, taught in Virgina, Illinois, and 1873-5 in Bloomington. From June, 1875, to September, 1878, she did not teach. In September of the last named year, she resumed her work, and has been employed constantly in the Bloomington city schools.

194. Julia (Moore) Byerly has not taught. At least, no report has been received.

195. Mary V. Osburn, 1872–3, taught in the Lebanon schools; 1873–4 was principal in the primary department of Elleardville school, St. Louis; 1874–5 first assistant in the same school; 1875–6 rested; 1877–82 in the same school. In March,, 1882, she was promoted to the Everett school.

196. Flora Pennell. See page 51.

197. Alice B. Phillips, 1872–5, taught in the Normal public schools. She has not taught since June, 1879. Her address is 88 Fort Greene Place, Brooklyn.

198. Louisa Ray taught in St. Soseph, Missouri, in 1872–4; in 1874–8 she was head assistant in the Peoria County Normal School. She was an invalid for two years. Since September, 1881, she has taught in Oakland high school.

199. Alpha Stewart taught in Stanford in 1872–3; in Oak Grove in 1873–5; in Mount Hope in 1875–6; in Oak Grove in 1876–7; in Mount Hope in 1877–9; in Normal in 1879–81. She is now teaching at Atlanta.

200. Gertrude (Town) Beggs was assistant in the Henry schools in 1872–3; she was employed in the Bloomington city schools in 1873–5; she was assistant in the Wilmington high school in 1875–6. In September, 1875, she was married to Robert H. Beggs of the same class. They reside in Denver, Colorado, where she is teaching.

201. Edith (Ward) Roache taught one year in Elgin, two in Hyde Park, and one in California. She was married in 1877. Her home is in Watson Valley, California.

202. Robert H. Beggs, 1872–5, was principal of the Virginia, Illinois, schools, and 1875–80 of the Wilmington schools. Since September, 1880, he has been principal of a ward school in Denver, Colorado.

203. George Blount, 1872–3, was principal of the Adeline schools; 1873–7 of the Forreston schools; 1877–8 of the Lexington schools; and since September, 1879, has had charge of the Macomb schools. August, 1874, he was married to Miss Alza Karr, of the same class.

204. James M. Greeley was principal of the Elmwood schools 1872–3. 1873–6 he taught winter schools aggregating fourteen months. His health failing, he went to Kansas, and in October, 1879, he was elected county treasurer of Saline County. His address is Salina.

205. Frank W. Hullinger taught two years in Bloom, Cook County, one year in Granville, and one year in Homewood. He studied in Oberlin College, and Chicago Theological Seminary, and in July, 1879, was ordained and began the work of the ministry. He was pastor of a church in Dundee, Michigan, for two years, and is now pastor of the Congregational church, in Milton, Rock County. He was married in December, 1873.

206. Elisha W. Livingston spent 1872–3 in Beloit College. He was principal of the schools in Caledonia station for four years. His failing health obliged him to resign. Since 1879 he has taught two terms, and is now farming.

207. Thomas L. McGrath taught one year in Litchfield, one in Equality, and one in Butler. He is now city attorney in Mattoon.

208. Samuel W. Paisley was born in Golconda, Illinois, in 1846. Orphaned at the early age of three years, he was reared by an uncle. His early life was devoted to manual labor, and his circumstances were such that he enjoyed few opportunities for educating himself. His ardent nature responded to the call for volunteers, and although very young, he entered the Union army. After the close of the war, he attended the academy at Friendsville, and for several years thereafter alternately taught and attended school, striving, with characteristic energy, to fit himself for his chosen profession. In September, 1868, he entered the Illinois Normal School, and graduated with his class in 1872. During his life as a student he won the high esteem and confidence of his instructors and fellow-students. He enthusiastically identified himself with every noble enterprise. No student ever responded to the roll call of his *alma mater* who lived upon a higher plane than he. Scrupulously faithful to every requirement, brilliantly successful in his studies, loving and tender in his nature, he was fitted as few men or women are, to perform the delicate and difficult task of teaching the young. Immediately after graduation, he was appointed principal of the Watseka schools, having been united in marriage in August, 1872, to Miss Helen Clute, of Normal. Into his work he threw all the devotion and enthusiasm of his loyal heart. His ambition was unsatisfied with the mere teaching of text-book facts, and he aimed to impress upon his pupils the lessons of gentleness, reverence for the true and beautiful, and obedience to the highest promptings of their natures. His success was abundant. Like every true teacher, he was an indefatigable student. Upon the foundation acquired at school, he was steadily building a broad and liberal education, thus fitting himself for whatever position might await him. After four years of intensely active work at Watseka, he took charge of the Lexington schools. With a kind of fierce energy he threw heart and soul into the duties of his new position. The sequel could have been forecast with almost unerring precision. After three or four months of labor, he was suddenly prostrated with hemorrhage of the lungs. He relinquished his position and returned to Normal, the home of his wife's mother. Here he slowly rallied, and regained so much of his original strength as to take charge of two of the classes in the Normal School. But he was unequal to the task, and the dreadful hemorrhage returned about the first of November. Hoping to stay the progress of the disease, he went to the mountain region about Chattanooga, Tennessee, and for a time seemed to gain strength in the bracing atmosphere. His last let-

ter, addressed to President Hewett, was full of hope and good cheer; but on the morning of February 4, all were shocked by the unexpected tidings of his sudden death. His funeral took place at Normal on February 7, and was attended by a large number of students and friends. His remains were gently laid-to rest under the trees of the sad city of the dead. Thus upon the threshold of a noble career, with a heart full of hope and love and good will to men, with his eager face aflame with high aspiration and courage, he halted, and laying aside the garb of the toiler, obeyed the summons of the Master, and "entered into rest."

209. Frank E. Ritchey taught two years in Milwaukee and one in Illinois. He commenced the practice of law in St. Louis, but received such flattering propositions to relinquish this business that he left St. Louis in 1879, and is now engaged in stock business in Ford County. His address is Campus, Illinois. He was married in 1879.

210. Espy L. Smith was principal of the Granville schools in 1872-3; of the Camp Point schools in 1873-4; of the Wenona schools in 1874-5; of the Minonk schools in 1875-9. He spent a year on a farm and is now studying medicine in a Homœopathic College in Chicago.

211. John H. Stickney was principal of the Altona schools from 1872 to 1877, five years, and of the West Side schools in St. Charles for three years. In September, 1880, he again took charge of the Altona schools, where he is at present.

212 William R. Wallace entered from McLean County in April, 1868, and graduated with the class of 1872. The succeeding year he was principal of the Piper City schools, and in 1872-3 he held a similar position in Pinkneyville. His health, never good, warned him to leave teaching, so he went into the drug business, first in Bloomington, and subsequently in Heyworth. His health grew gradually worse, however, and in December, 1876, he died. His parents reside near Hudson.

213. James M. Wilson was principal of the Bloomington, Indiana, schools, for three years. In September, 1875, he entered upon his duties as professor of mathematics in the Indiana State Normal School, at Terre Haute, which position he occupied until June, 1881. In August, 1873, he was married to Miss Sallie Tomlinson, an undergraduate of the Illinois Normal.

214. Edwin F. Bacon had nearly completed his studies in 1865, when he left school and went to New York City. He taught there in 1865-6.. For two years, 1866-8, he had charge of a large school in Norwalk, Connecticut. In the fall of 1868 he entered the scientific department of Yale College, and graduated in 1871. He taught Latin and German, in Wilmington, for one year. In 1872 he received his diploma from this Normal School, and shortly after he went to

Germany and studied and taught two years. In 1873 he returned to New York, and has since been engaged in teaching German, in which he has become very successful. His address is box 296, Jersey City.

215. Charles D. Mariner was principal of the Byron schools two years, of the Marengo schools one year, of the Duraud schools three years. He taught, also, a country school one year. Since June, 1880, he has taught twelve months in Winnebago Township. He was married in 1871. His address is Winnebago.

216. Chalmers Rayburn (H. S.) taught in Vienna, Illinois, two months, in Sperry, Iowa, four months, in McLean County one year, in Hudson two years, and at Money Creek two years. His address is Towanda.

217. Newton B. Reid (H. S.) taught two years at St. Paul and Albion, Illinois. He is now practicing law in Bloomington, Illinois.

CLASS OF 1873.

218. Lura (Bullock) Elliott, during the spring term of 1874, taught near Tonica; 1874–5 was principal of primary department, Tonica; 1875-6 was principal of Tonica schools; 1877–8 was assistant in Macomb high school. She was married in 1879, and is now living on a farm near Tonica.

219. Mary M. Cox taught one year at Belleville, one year at Greenville, California, and five years at Watsonville, twenty miles from Santa Cruz. In the summer of 1881 she went to Europe, where she is still studying. Her address is number 14 Wieser Strasse, Hanover, Germany.

220. Ellen S. Edwards taught one year at Lexington, five months in Rock River Seminary, and was for two years assistant in Normal School. In September, 1877, she entered the Boston School of Orators and completed the course in 1879. Her address is Princeton.

221 Ida. L. Foss taught six months at Homer, and for three years was assistant in Rossville high school. Since September, 1877, she has had charge of the high school at Rushville.

222. Mary (Hawley) Richardson taught six months in Naples, one year in Beardstown, and five years in Milwaukee. In August, 1880, she was married to W. H. Richardson, of Milwaukee.

223. H. Amelia Kellogg, after graduation, taught constantly in Chicago until November, 1881. Her health failed, and she went to Texas. She is at San Antonio. Her address was 29 Oak Avenue, Chicago.

224. L. Effie Peter, immediately after graduation, went to San Juan, California, and taught near that place one year. 1874–5 was teacher in the grammar school in Mason City; 1876-7 assistant in

the high school at same place; 1877-9 was first assistant in Lincoln high school; 1880-1 taught in Larned, Kansas; and since, has been teaching in Cimarron, Kansas.

225. Anna V. Sutherland taught the Mt. Prospect school two years, taught in Bloomington two terms, in Heyworth one year, and in LeRoy two years. Her address is LeRoy.

226. Mary I. Thomas, for three years taught at Atlanta. She has not taught since.

227. Emma (Warne) Hall, 1873-4, was assistant in DeKalb; 1874-5 was principal of Blackberry schools. Her health failing, she did not teach again until January, 1877, when she took charge of a grammar school at DeKalb. She was married in 1877 to E. Hall, superintendent of the S., C. & C. R. R. She resides at Sycamore.

228. L. P. Brigham was principal of the Tolono schools in 1873-4; of the Arcola schools 1875-7. He then studied one year at Indianapolis. In 1878-81 he was principal of Farmer City schools. He was married in 1878. In 1881-2 he attended Rush Medical College.

229. Charles DeGarmo. See page 50.

230. Jasper T. Hays was married in December, 1875. In 1873-4 he taught in Whiteside county; in 1874-6 in Lee county; in 1876-7 in Morrison and Delhi; 1877-8 taught four months in country school; 1879-81 taught in Kansas. He is now farming. His address is Elivan, Kansas.

231. E. R. E. Kimbrough taught at Golconda in 1873-4, and is now practicing law in Danville. In 1878 he wrote: "One boy eight months old, a few briefs, and a Democratic nomination for State Senate, Thirty-First district." He was defeated for Senator, although receiving a very complimentary vote, his district being strongly Republican.

232. George W. Lecrone taught three months at Moccasin and was principal of East Side schools at Effingham one year. He then served as deputy clerk of Effingham County. He is now publishing a paper at Effingham, Illinois.

233. Walter C. Lockwood married Elizabeth Peers in 1874. He was three years in the hardware business in Ottawa, two years on a farm near Rankin, taught one winter near Rankin, and went to Kansas in 1879, where he is engaged in the hardware business. His address is Marion Center. He paid his tuition in full, after graduation.

234. DeWitt C. Roberts married Miss Fannie Pace in July, 1875. He was principal of Beardstown schools 1873-6, professor of mathematics at Cape Girardeau Normal School 1876-80, and is now principal of Broadway school, Denver, Colorado.

235. Arthur Shores taught six months in Minnesota, three months in Glencoe, in that State, nine months in Taylor's Falls, and

six months in district school in Tazewell County. He is now practicing law in Minneapolis, Minnesota, 921 Eighth Avenue.

236. John B. Stoutemyer continued studies two years. He taught one month at Covel, and two months near Bloomington. He is now farming two miles west of Bloomington.

237. Felix B. Tait taught one year at Woodstock Seminary, and was admitted to the bar in June, 1876. He is practicing in Decatur, Illinois.

238. J. Lawson Wright, 1873-6, was principal of Adeline schools; 1876-80 of Forreston schools; 1880-1 of Savanna schools; 1881-2 of Cedarville schools.

239. M. Louise Abraham (H. S.) has taught constantly since graduation. 1873-5 in Spencer, Indiana; 1875-7 in Illinois, near Gilman; 1877-8 in Spencer; and since September, 1878, in Edinburg, Indiana.

240. Edmund J. James. See page 49.

241. J. Dickey Templeton (H. S.) worked in the State museum for a few months. Since 1875 he has been employed in a bank in Bloomington.

CLASS OF 1874.

242. Emily Alden taught in Loda in 1874-5. In 1875-6 she was principal of schools in Princeville. She did not teach in 1876-7. In 1877-8 she taught in Kent, Iowa, and since 1878 she has taught in Afton in the same State.

243. Lida (Brown) McMurry taught in Sublette in 1874-6; in Arcola in 1876-7; in Clear Creek in 1877-8; and two months in Decatur in 1878-9. In the summer of 1878 she was married to Wm. P. McMurry, of the same class. Their home is in Normal.

244. Eunice Corwine taught in the country near Lincoln in 1874-8. Since 1878 she has been teaching in the Lincoln schools.

245. S. Alice Judd has been employed constantly as assistant in the Decatur high school since her graduation.

246. Sarah M. Littlefield was principal of the Rushville high school in 1874-5; she taught in the Beardstown schools in 1875-6; she was again principal of the Rushville high school in 1876-7, and in 1877-8 she again taught in the Beardstown schools; she taught in the Galva schools in 1878-9, since which time she has not taught. Her address is Beardstown.

247. Mary (McWilliams) Burford taught in Logan County in 1874-5, and in Farmer City in 1875-6 and 1877-8. She did not teach in 1876-7 on account of poor health. In September, 1879, she was married to Will F. Burford, of Farmer City, where they now reside.

248. M. Ella Morgan has taught continuously since graduation, in Washington, D. C. Her address is 1114 Tenth Street.

249. Elizabeth (Peers) Lockwood has not taught. In September following her graduation she was married to Walter C. Lockwood, of the class of 1873. She discharged her obligation by paying her tuition in full. Her home is in Marion Centre, Kansas.

250. Emma V. (Stewart) Brown entered school in September, 1870. One year was spent in teaching during the course, so that she did not graduate until June, 1874. She taught in Rochelle in 1874–5; • in Peru, Indiana, 1875–6, and 1876–8 in Wichita, Kansas. August 9, 1868, she was married to I. Eddy Brown, of the same class, and removed to Decatur, where Mr. Brown was employed as principal of the high school. Her wedded life was brief. August 1, 1880, a little less than two years from the time of her marriage, she died of puerperal fever. She left a babe, but it survived her only a few weeks. The closing days of her life were singularly beautiful. Conscious of approaching death, she arranged all of her affairs with the serenity and fortitude 'of the hero of a hundred fields. Loving life as only the young blessed with all that is beautiful can love it, she submitted to the inevitable with calm composure, and even greeted it with a happy smile.

251. Maggie (Woodruff) Evans, 1874–6, taught in Savannah, Illinois. In 1876 she was married to William A. Evans, of the same class. Her address is Leavenworth, Kansas.

252. I. Eddy Brown immediately after graduation was elected principal of the Decatur high school. He retained this position until June, 1880, when he resigned to accept the State Secretaryship of the Y. M. C. A. In August, 1878, he was married to Emma V. Stewart, a sketch of whom is given above.

253. Francis W. Conrad, the first year after graduation taught in the Maine State Normal School. Warned by failing health, in the summer of 1875 he went to California, where he has been teaching constantly since. In September, 1877, he was elected principal of the Montecito schools, Santa Barbara, which position he still retains.

254. John N. Dewell, 1874–5, was principal of the Barry schools; 1875–8 of the Litchfield schools, and 1878–81 of the Hillsboro schools. His present address is Bloomington, where he is in the insurance and real estate business.

255. David S. Elliott, 1874–5, was principal of the Caseyville schools. In 1875 he joined the Methodist Conference and preached for a while, teaching, in the meantime, four months in Mackinaw, three months in Groveland, and two months in a private school. 1878–9 he was assistant in the Centralia schools. 1879–81 was principal of the same schools. He is now principal of the Bunsen school, Belleville, Illinois.

256. William A. Evans, since graduation, has taught two years in Illinois, and four in Kansas. At present he is teacher of history and natural science in the Leavenworth high school.

257. Thomas E. Jones, 1874–6, taught in Troy, Kansas; 1876–8 he was principal of the Mt. Pleasant, Missouri, schools; 1878–9 he had charge of the Hillsdale, Kansas, schools; 1879–80 he spent as a traveling salesman, 1880–1 he was again principal of the Hillsdale schools, where he is at present.

258. William P. McMurry has not taught. He studied law, was • admitted, spent a few months in Texas, and then returned to Normal. He is now employed in the office of the Phœnix nursery, Bloomington.

259. Elinzer H. Prindle, 1874–6, taught in Centreville. 1876–8 he was principal of the White Hall schools. In the summer of 1878 he removed to Kansas, and engaged in farming and stock-raising. In November, 1879, he was elected county clerk of Hodgeman County. He is now teaching in Larned, Kansas.

260. Carlton H. Rew, 1874–7, was principal of the Pontiac schools, and 1877–9 of the Fairbury schools. 1779–80 was spent in study. Since September, 1880, he has had charge of the Wilmington schools. In 1878 he was married to Miss Ada Casley, an undergraduate of the Normal School.

261. William J. Simpson has taught six years since graduation, most of the time in country schools. He is now farming near Sigel. Mr. Simpson has been married twice. His first wife, whom Normalites of 1873 will remember as Alice Buchanan, died in 1877. He was married again in 1880.

262. Harry A. Smith, 1874–5, was principal of the Lena schools, and 1875–8 of the Rock Falls schools. In 1878 he entered the ministry, and is now in charge of the Baptist Church, in Tampico.

263. Jasper N. Wilkinson, 1874–9, was principal of the Buda schools. 1879–80 he was principal of one of the ward schools in Peoria. Since September, 1880, he has been principal of the Decatur high school. He was married in Buda, in 1879.

264. Adele (Cook) Sample was married to A. Sample in September, 1875. Her address is Paxton, Illinois.

CLASS OF 1875.

265. Margarita McCullough, 1875–6 taught in Edinburg, Indiana. She has since taught at South Evanston, having lost but one day since graduation.

266. Josephine McHugh, 1875–7, except spring term, was assistant in the Galena high school. The spring term of 1877 she taught in Omaha; 1877–80 in Warren; 1880–1 in Shellsburg; 1881–2 in Dwight. She is now teaching in Bloomington.

267. Florence Ohr, with the exception of the spring term of 1881, when she attended the Normal, has taught constantly in the Soldiers' Orphans' Home since graduation.

268. Henrietta Watkins taught a short time—a few weeks—in Decatur. She is now at home in Normal.

269. Mary A. Watkins has not taught. Her address is Normal.

270. David Ayers, 1875-6, taught a district school near Sweetwater; 1876-7 taught near Elkhart; 1877-81 was in charge of the Sweetwater schools. He married Miss Anna Martin in November, 1881. He is now in business. His address is 734 Forty-Third Street, Chicago.

271. Robert L. Barton, 1875-7, was principal of Mound City schools; 1877-8 he taught four months at Farmer City; 1878-81 at Rossville. He has since been superintendent of the Galena schools.

272. Albert D. Beckhart, 1875-7, taught in Cerro Gordo; 1877-8 in Buffalo, Sangamon County. He was married in December, 1876, to Miss Jennie H. Baker. In 1877 he joined the Illinois Annual Conference, and is now preaching. He is located at Nilwood.

273. Lewis O. Bryan, 1875-6, taught in Salem; 1876-9 in Van Buren, Arkansas. He was admitted to the bar in February, 1880, and is now practicing at Van Buren, Arkansas.

274. W. T. Crow has not taught. He is postmaster at Cotton Hill, and proprietor of Sugar Creek mills.

275. James Ellis was principal of Winnebago schools, 1875-6; 1876-7 he taught four months in Boone County; 1877-80 was again principal of Winnebago schools. Since September, 1880, he has been principal of the high schools at Sharon, Wisconsin.

276. Judd M. Fiske taught one year, 1875-6, at Armington, Illinois, and two years at Naples. He married Miss Harriet A. Hunter. For two years he taught in district schools. 1880-1 he taught at Ridott, and is now teaching there.

277. Justin L. Hartwell was principal of the Dixon schools in 1875-7; 1877-8 ran a business college at Dixon; 1878-80 was principal of Odell school. He has since been principal of Barry, Illinois, schools. He was married in 1873.

278. Josiah P. Hodge taught six months. His business is law and real estate. Address, Golconda, Illinois.

279. U. Clay McHugh was born in Monroe County, Ohio, July 16, 1850. He entered school from McLean County, January, 1872, and graduated in June, 1875. In 1875-6 he taught in Pleasant Hill. During the summer of 1876 he entered Rush Medical College, Chicago, and remained there until March, 1877, when he returned to his home in Lexington, and taught a further term of three months, continuing his medical studies meanwhile. In the summer of 1877 he returned to Rush, and graduated in February, 1878. He returned to his home, but was stricken down by sudden illness, and died July 11, 1878.

280. W. S. Mills, 1875-6, was principal of the grammar department of the model school; 1876-80 of a ward school at Joliet. In

May, 1882, he graduated from the law department of Columbia College. His address is 73 Pine Apple Street, Brooklyn.

281. James N. Mosher, 1875–6, taught near Odell; 1876–7 he had charge of the Watson, Missouri, schools; 1877–8 of the Van Buren, Arkansas, schools; 1878–9 he did not teach; 1879–80 of the Watson schools. Since September, 1880, he has been principal of the Edwardsville schools, Kansas.

282. John L. Shearer taught at Rockport in 1875–6 ; taught a country school near St. Louis in 1876–7 ; a country school in Henry² County in 1877–8 ; was principal of the White Hall schools in 1878–9. He has since been principal of Napa City schools.

283. Benjamin F. Stocks was married in 1875.   In 1875–6 he was principal of Bethallo schools ; 1876–7 of Fairmount schools ; 1877–9 of Sullivan schools ; 1879–80 of La Moille schools ; 1880–2 of Cerro Gordo schools.

284. Ann S. Wheaton (H. S.), after graduating, went to Montreal to study French.   She returned to Normal in 1876 and continued her studies one year, when she went to Yreka, California.   After teaching a private school for a short time, she became a teacher in the public schools.   She purchased a home in 1880.

285. Nicholas T. Edwards (H. S.) graduated at Knox in 1879, and taught in Dover one year.   He studied Theology in the Chicago Theological Seminary and is now preaching.   He may be reached by addressing Princeton, Illinois.

286. Frank W. Gove (H. S.) graduated at Dartmouth in 1878. For six months he was professor of mathematics in Colorado State University.   He is now surveying in the mountains of Colorado.   He was married in July to Miss Ida Cook.   His address is Rico, Colorado.

287. Emrich B. Hewitt (H. S.) entered the high school in 1871, from Forreston, Illinois, and graduated with his class in 1875.   He entered Harvard University in September, 1875, and remained one year, when failing health obliged him to give up his college work and endeavor to regain his strength.   He remained at his home, in Freeport, for a few months, but failing to receive any benefits from medical attendance, he went to Colorado, hoping that a change of climate might prove beneficial.   He gradually declined, however, and finally died in March, 1879.   Universally esteemed, ambitious to excel as a scholar, and surrounded with all that tends to make life desirable, his early death was peculiarly sad.

CLASS OF 1876.

288. Mary L. Bass, since graduation, has been teaching in Oakland school.   Her address is 3655 Vincennes Avenue, Chicago.

289. Louisa C. Larrick, in the fall of 1876, taught at Gibson ;

1878-9 at Middletown, Virginia. She has since been teaching at Pontiac, Illinois.

290. Amanda M. Pusey, 1876-80, taught in Champaign; 1880-1 she taught in Ottawa, Kansas. She has since taught at Neosho, Missouri.

291. George II. Beatty taught six months near Clinton, six months in Midland City, six months near Clinton. 1879-81 he was principal of the Heyworth schools. He is now at Maroa.

292. Daniel S. Buterbaugh, 1876-7, taught at Money Creek; 1877-9 at Camargo and Pesotum; 1879-80 near Clinton. Since 1880 he has been principal of the Danvers schools.

293. William II. Chamberlain, 1876-9, taught at Ridge Farm, Illinois; 1879-80 he studied at Normal; 1880-1 at Ridge Farm. Since 1881 he has been principal of the Rossville schools.

294. Asbury M. Crawford, 1876-7, taught in Mechanicsville; in 1877-8 he studied law in Bloomington. He then went west, and is now in the nursery business at Helena, Montana.

295. George W. Dinsmore taught one year in Shelbyville, Tennessee, and one year in Illinois. His health would not permit of further teaching. He went west, settling at Lyons, Kansas, and engaging in the hardware business. He married Carrie Wallace, in Houston, Texas.

296. Lewis C. Dougherty, 1876-8, taught at Lacon; 1878-9 taught four months in Rising, Neb. Since September, 1879, he has been principal of the Minonk schools.

297. J. Calvin Hanna, taught one year in Toulon, three months near Monica, Peoria County, two months in Wooster, Ohio. He graduated from Wooster College in June, 1881, and has since been teaching in the Columbus, Ohio, high school.

298. Benjamin S. Hedges was born in Virginia, in 1852. He entered the Normal School in September, 1873, and graduated with the class of 1876. He secured a State certificate about the time of his graduation. Shortly after graduation, he was appointed principal of the Rochelle high school. A part of the summer of 1876 was spent at the Centennial Exposition. He returned to his home in the early fall, expecting to begin his work, but contracted typhoid fever in the home of a friend, who died of the same disease, and passed away October 1, 1876, at the age of twenty-four years, five months ar ud twenty-seven days. He was a young man of high character and g eat promise.

299. Charles L. Howard, 1876-7, was principal of the Farmington schools; 1877-8 was agent for Johnson's Cyclopedia; 1878-9 was principal of the Centralia schools; 1879-81 of the Shelbyville schools. He is now principal of the Madison school, St. Louis.

300. John T. Johnson, 1876-8, was principal of the Millersburg school; in 1879 he taught a few months near Bloomington. He then

7

went into the hedge business. In 1880-1 taught eight months in New Boston. Since September, 1881, he has been principal of the fifth ward school, Peoria.

301. Claudius B. Kinyon has not taught. Graduating from a medical college in 1878, he has since been practicing in Rock Island.

302. Joseph F. Lyon, 1876-7, taught in Kansas; 1877-8 in Cumberland County; 1878-9 traveled and studied; 1879-80 taught in Altamont. Since September, 1880, he has been principal of the Odell school.

303. Truman B. Mosher taught seven months in a country school in Livingston County; 1877-8 taught at Sullivan Center; 1878-9 at Grouse, Kane County; 1879-80 in Livingston County. Since September, 1880, he has been teaching in Cherryvale, Kansas.

304. DeWitt C. Tyler taught two years at New Boston, and one year at Millersburg. He now practices medicine in Clifton, Kansas.

305. Leroy B. Wood is secretary and treasurer of the Plano Manufacturing Company, Plano, Illinois.

306. Arabella D. Loer (H. S.) is in Mexico, Missouri.

307. Charles A. McMurry (H. S.), 1876-7, continued his studies at Ann Arbor; 1877-8 taught at Armington; 1878-9 at Clear Creek; 1879-80 at Clifton for five months, returning to Ann Arbor in the spring; 1880-81 taught at Littleton, California; 1881-2 in Denver, Colorado. He is now in the University of Halle, Germany, making a specialty of political economy.

CLASS OF 1877.

308. Mary A. Anderson has taught in the Bloomington high school since graduation. Her address is 605 West Front Street.

309. Agnes E. Ball, 1877-8, taught near Girard; 1878-80 in Girard; 1880-1 in Virden; 1881-2 in a district school near Girard, Montgomery County.

310. Emma E. Corbett has been teaching at Milwaukee constantly since graduation.

311. Nettie (Cox) Smith, 1878-9, taught in Hudson; 1879-81 in a district school near Hudson. She was married in 1881.

312. Adeline M. Goodrich, is traveling in the interest of the Woman's Christian Temperance Union. Her address is Freeport, Illinois.

313 Anna L. Martin, 1878-9, taught near Washburn; 1879-81 in the Normal public schools. She was married in the fall of 1881, to David Ayers. Her address is 734 Forty-Third Street, Chicago.

314. Selina M. Regan taught a district school three months; 1878-9 she taught the same school six and one-half months. Since January, 1880, she has taught in Morris, Illinois.

315. Laura A. Varner, 1877–9, taught in country schools near Freeburg. 1879–80 she taught in Marissa. She has since been principal of the Marissa schools.

316. Wilmas (Varner) Metzger, 1877–8, taught four months in Marion County. In April, 1878, she moved to California, and taught constantly until her marriage to J. E. Metzger, in November, 1880. Her address is Healdsburg, California.

317. Emily Wing spent two years at Wellesley College, taught one year in Collinsville, and one year in the Female Academy, at Jacksonville. Her address is Collinsville.

318. Levi D. Berkstresser is employed in banking and the clothing trade. His address is Buda, Illinois.

319. W. Irving Berkstresser, 1877–8, taught in Bryant's Commercial College, Chicago. He is now preaching in Decatur.

320. Richard G. Bevan taught, 1877–8, in a district school six months; 1878–9 in the same school six months, and 1881–2 he taught six months near Atlanta.

321. Edward R. Faulkner has been principal of the Frankfort, Kansas, schools, since graduation.

322. Hiram R. Fowler has taught in Cave-in-Rock constantly since graduation.

323. Frank B. Harcourt taught part of 1877–8 in Logan County. In 1878 he returned to Normal and finished the high school course. His address is Chestnut, Illinois.

324. George L. Hoffman was married in 1879 and is practicing law at Mt. Sterling, Illinois.

325. Albert Swan taught in Toulon in 1877–8 ; in N. Wyoming in 1878–80 ; in Castleton, Illinois, in 1880–2.

326. Levi Spencer taught during the summer term of 1878, and winter term of 1878–9, in Piatt County ; summer term of 1879 in Macon County ; then two terms Piatt County. He has since taught at Oronogo, Missouri.

327. Edward R. Levett is practicing law in Chicago. His address is 132 LaSalle Street.

328. Sarah (Coolidge) White (H. S.) was married in the fall of 1879. Her address is Springfield.

329. Jennette Kingsley's (H. S.) parents moved to Normal when she was a little child. She entered the lowest department, and completed the course, graduating from high school with the class of 1877. After a few months of rest, she became a teacher in the Normal public school, and remained there until June, 1879. Very soon after the close of school she went to Denver, in order to be present at the competitive examination of teachers in that city. Brilliantly successful, she received an appointment, and in September commenced her work She had been in the school room but a few weeks when she was stricken down with the dreadful typhus fever, and survived but a few

days. Her body was brought back to her old home, and laid to rest in the cemetery at Bloomington. Miss Kingsley was one of those to whom nature had been peculiarly generous. Possessing an unusually sunny disposition, superior intellectual attainments, rare personal beauty, and the rarer gift of a devout and loving heart, she won the respect and affectionate regard of all with whom she came in contact.

330. Sabina F. Mills (II. S.) taught nine months in Granville, and three months near Mt. Palatine. Since June, 1879, she has taught in El Dorado, Kansas.

331. Laura Sudduth (II. S.) is at Wellesley College, and will graduate in 1883. Her address is Normal.

332. Fremont C. Blandin (II. S.) was at Ann Arbor in 1877-9. He since graduated from the Wesleyan law school. His address is Rutland, Illinois.

333. George A. Franklin (II. S.) taught in Butler in 1877-9; was for some time foreman of a printing office in Rockford; is now running a cattle ranch at Forest City, Iowa.

334. Theodore T. Hewitt (II. S.) is in a bank at Freeport, Illinois.

CLASS OF 1878.

335. Mary M. Baird, 1878-9, taught at Naples. Ill health compelled her to rest until 1880, since which time she has taught at Mendota, Illinois.

336. Evangeline (Candy) Mitchell taught at Chestnut, Illinois, one year. Her present address is Arcola, Illinois.

337. Jessie (Dexter) Benton taught one year at Lexington. She was married in the summer of 1879.

338. Eugenia Faulkner taught in the Frankfort, Kansas, high school two years, and has since taught at Marysville, Kansas.

339. Flora M. Fuller, 1878-9, taught in the Carrollton high schools. She is now teaching in the Millersburg schools.

340. Sarah C. Martin, 1879-80, taught at Washburn, and in 1881-2 in the same place.

341. Ida (Philbrick) Gaston taught three months in Baileyville. She married Frank Gaston, of Normal, in December, 1879.

342. Frances Preston entered the Normal School from Lee County, in September, 1874, and graduated in 1878, taking the full Latin and Greek course. The year 1878-9 she taught in Centralia. In September, 1880, she commenced work in the Mendota schools, west side, and remained there until the following spring, when failing health compelled her to resign. She returned to her home in Amboy, but she rapidly declined, and died May 3. She had an intense desire to acquire knowledge, and doubtless hastened her death by over-study and severe exertion as a teacher. She possessed

an unusual amount of individuality and originality, and by her careful preparation was especially fitted to occupy a conspicuous position. Her ample success as a teacher indicated that if her life had been spared she would not have disappointed the high hopes of her many friends.

343. Florence Richardson entered school in September, 1875, and graduated with her class in 1878. Immediately after graduation she became an assistant in the schools of Millersburg, Mercer County, where she remained one year. In September, 1879, she entered the Bloomington corps, where she remained until her death. The following sketch is taken from the Bloomington *Pantagraph*, for which it was prepared by Rev. J. W. Dinsmore:

" A very great company attended the funeral of the above-named young lady, at the Second Presbyterian church, yesterday afternoon. It is creditable to human nature that so great public interest should be shown in a simple school teacher. Many a millionaire has been carried to his grave without a tithe of the respect and sympathy that were shown yesterday for the memory of this modest girl. * * * From our public schools she entered the Normal University, and having made a very successful course, she graduated in 1878. Having become a teacher in our city schools, she rapidly advanced until she became mistress of the highest room in No. 1. and some months ago was promoted to be principal of No. 3. To this creditable distinction she was borne, not by the strong hands of influential friends, but by the simple force of real merit and industry. She was thoroughly devoted to her calling; talented, diligent, painstaking, and full of a sustained enthusiasm. She gave much promise of a brilliant career in her chosen work. She was a faithful member of the Second Presbyterian church, being a pupil, and lately a teacher, in the Sunday school, much admired and respected by her pastor, and by all who have knowledge of her ways of life. Her loving and sacrificing devotion to her foster parents was beautiful and noble. No less was she devoted to the mother that bore her, although necessarily living mostly at a long distance from her. She was called away suddenly, just as promise was budding into fulfillment, as hope was waxing into realization. A highly intelligent, attractive, amiable, and whole-hearted young woman,—a sincere disciple of Jesus Christ,—well qualified to live, well qualified also to die. Peace to her ashes, while her memory will be long and lovingly cherished by many who knew her in life. This little tribute is gladly laid on her grave by one who knew her well, and valued her highly."

344. Helen L. Wyckoff, 1878–9, taught in Centralia; 1879–81 in Roberts, Illinois. Since February, 1882, she has been teaching in Bloomington.

345. Osci J. Bainum, 1878–80, taught at Parkersburg. Since September, 1880, he has been principal of the Olney high school.

346. John T. Bowles, 1878–80, was principal of the Naples schools. He was married in November, 1879, to Miss Clara Webster; in 1880–1 he taught at Gridley; in 1881–2 he was principal of the Metropolis high school. He is now superintendent of the Metropolis schools.

347. Oliver P. Burger, 1878–9, taught in country schools near El Paso; 1879–80 at Crittenden, New York; 1880–1 taught at Spring Bay; in 1881–2 he was principal of the Secor schools. He is now at Maroa, Illinois.

348. Gilbert A. Burgess, 1878–81, was principal of the schools at Monticello. He was then appointed county superintendent.

349. Arthur C. Butler, 1878-80, was principal of the Normal public schools. Since then he has been principal of the Virginia, Illinois, schools.

350. Andrew W. Elder, 1878-9, taught at New Boston; 1880-1 taught; 1881-2 was principal of the Centralia schools. He is now teaching in Denver, Colorado.

351. Willis C. Glidden taught from the time he entered until graduation. He graduated from the Homœopathic Medical College, Chicago, in June, 1879, and is practicing in Beloit, Kansas. He was married in June, 1881, to Miss Leager.

352. C. Guy Laybourn, 1878-80, was principal of the preparatory department of Markham's Academy, Milwaukee. In the summer of 1880 he visited Europe. On his return he entered the Ann Arbor law school, and remained there one year. He was admitted to practice in Iowa, and is now a member of the firm of Wilson & Laybourn, Creston, Iowa.

353. Edwin H. Rishel taught at Adeline in 1878-9. He is now teaching in a colored university at Selma, Alabama. He was married in the summer of 1880.

354. William N. Spencer taught three months in Piatt County; one year in Hardin County; one year in Blandville, Ky., and the last year at Carterville, Missouri.

355. George I. Talbot taught in Victor in 1878-9; in Shabbona in 1879-80. In December, 1881, he was elected county superintendent. His address is Shabbona.

356. Rachel M. Fell (H. S.) taught in Normal public schools two years. She is now working in labratory of natural history.

357. Annie Sudduth (H. S.) is at her home, Normal, Illinois.

358. Dorus R. Hatch (H. S.), 1878-9, was principal of the Barry schools. He held the same position until January, 1880, when his eyes became so weak that he resigned and commenced treatment. Since then he has been railroading. He is now in Chicago under a physician's care. His address is 13 Avon Place.

359. Theodore W. Peers (H. S.), 1878-9, taught in the "colored department" of the Collinsville schools. He is now at Ann Arbor, Michigan.

CLASS OF 1879.

360. Annette S. Bowman, since graduating, has taught as assistant in the Rock Island high school.

361. Amanda M. Crawford is continuing her studies at Normal.

362. Mary S. Cummings taught in district schools nine months. She is in the millinery business at Macon.

363. Daisy (Hubbard) Carlock, 1879-80, taught at Roodhouse;

1880–1 she taught in Morris. In the summer of 1881 she was married to Mr. Carlock. Her address is Hudson.

364. Harriet E. Morse, 1879–80, taught at Pekin, and has since taught at Oregon, Illinois.

365. Nettie (Porter) Powers, 1879–80, taught in Mendota; 1880–1 in Omaha. In the summer of 1881 she was married to Horace E. Powers, of Omaha.

366. Lizzie Ross, since graduation, has taught at Pekin.

367. Julia Scott, 1879–81, taught in Mendota. She was assistant in Normal University from January, 1882, to the end of the year. Her address is Pecatonica.

368. Emily (Sherman) Boyer, 1880–1, taught in Astoria; 1881–2 in Normal public schools. In July, 1882, she was married to E. R. Boyer. They live at Lewistown, Illinois.

369. Jennie A. Wood, 1879–80, taught in Minonk; in Perry, Ohio, ten months, and is now teaching near Perry.

370. Emanuel R. Boyer, 1879–81, was principal of the Astoria schools. He has since been principal of the Lewistown schools. In July, 1882, he married Emily A. Sherman.

371. C. R. Cross has been principal at Sparland, Illinois, since graduation.

372. Silas Y. Gillan was principal of the Galena schools in 1879–81, and has since been principal of the Danville high school. In the summer of 1880 he was married to Lizzie K. Harned.

373. Horace E. Powers graduated from Ann Arbor law school, and is now practicing in Omaha. In the summer of 1881 he married Nettie B. Porter.

374. William C. Ramsey, 1879–80, taught at Galt, California; 1880–2 at Stockton. He now has charge of the Normal Department of the Stockton Business College.

375. Fannie C. Fell (H. S.) is at her home, in Normal. She taught a few months at Streator, Illinois, but ill health compelled her to resign.

376. Hattie Follette (H. S.) is at her home, in Normal.

377. Mary Sudduth (H. S.) is continuing her studies at Vassar College.

378. Nelson K. McCormick (H. S) graduated from the Wesleyan University in 1881, and is now at work in the State laboratory of natural history, Normal.

379. Frank M. McMurry (H. S.) taught five months near Farmer City, and four months at Empire. He is continuing his studies at Ann Arbor. His address is Normal.

380. Oscar L. McMurry (H. S.) taught four months near Clifton, and then went to Ann Arbor. His address is Normal.

381. Thomas Williams (H. S.) is in the stock business in Kansas. Address Bloomington.

CLASS OF 1880.

382. Elizabeth Baumgardner, for two years, taught the primary department of the Gardner schools.   She is now principal of the same schools.

383. Helen Baxter, since graduation, has been teaching at Griggsville.

384. Lillie M. Brown, during part of the year 1881, taught in Mendota. She is now teaching in Berea, Kentucky.

385. May Hewett, since September, 1881, has been teaching in Oak Park.

386. Helen F. Moore taught in Decatur until December, 1881, when she resigned to go to Albuquerque, New Mexico.

387. Isabel Overman, 1880-1, taught in Gardner; 1881-2 she taught six months in Piatt County.   Her address is 2715 Wabash Avenue, Chicago.

388. Mary E. Parker, 1880-1, taught in Eskridge, Kansas; 1881-2 in McPherson, Kansas. She is now teaching in Gardner.

389. Grace W. Weeks, 1880-1, taught in Dwight. She spent the summer of 1881 in Normal. She is now in the south.

390. James W. Adams, 1880-2, taught in Forrest.

391. Andrew L. Anderson, 1881-2, taught near Chandlerville, Cass County.

392. Alpheus Dillon has taught a school near home five months.

393. James M. Harper, 1880-2, was principal of the Gardner schools. He is now teaching in Milford, Illinois.

394. Woodman R. Marriett, 1880-2, was principal of the Port Byron schools.

395. Carleton E. Webster taught two years in the Ottawa township high school.   He is now principal of the Dixon schools.

396. Edgar Wyatt, 1880-1, was principal of the Chapin schools.

397. Alice C. McCormick (H. S.) taught one year at Naples. She is now continuing her studies at Normal.

398. Frances Ohr (H. S.) taught one year in Gardner, one year in Centralia, and is now in the Normal public schools.

399. F. L. Lufkin (H. S.) is continuing his studies at Ann Arbor.

400. Herbert McNulta (H. S.) is in Annapolis Naval Academy.

401. George K. Smith (H. S.) taught in Maroa one year, and is now working in a railroad office in Denver. His address is 296 Lincoln Avenue.

CLASS OF 1881.

402. Sarah A. Anderson is teaching in the Delavan schools.

403. Clara A. W. Bowles, since graduation, has been teaching in Metropolis, Illinois.

404. Mary R. Gaston taught two months in Mendota, and since in Astoria, Illinois.

405. Addie Gillan taught in the Harvard schools, 1881-2.

406. Mary J. Gillan taught one year in Farmer City. She is now at Danville.

407. Belle Hobbs is teaching in the Metropolis schools.

408. Annie P. Knight; health does not permit her to teach.

409. Helen Middlekauf is continuing her studies at Wellesley, Massachusetts.

410. Celia S. Mills taught at Mendota in 1881-2. She is now in Normal.

411. Carrie Rich is in the Shawneetown schools.

412. Mary A. Springer is in the Elizabeth, Illinois, schools.

413. Lizzie P. Swan taught but five months at Metropolis, resigning on account of ill health.

414. William H. Bean taught one year in Blue Mound, and is now at Ann Arbor.

415. Isaac L. Betzer is principal of East Side schools, Champaign.

416. Elmer E. Brown is principal of the Belvidere schools.

417. James B. Estee taught one year at Woodstock, Illinois.

418. G. Frank Miner is principal of the Hennepin schools.

419. Wendall Puckett studied one year at Normal.

420. Edward Shannon is principal of the Payson schools.

421. Elmer E. Shinkle died of malarial fever in August, 1881.

422. John H. Tear is principal of the Astoria schools.

423. Nathan T. Veatch is principal of the Butler schools.

424. Charles Walter, Alton, Illinois.

CLASS OF 1882.

425. Mattie V. Bean.

426. Matilda Glanville teaches at DeKalb, Illinois.

427. Camilla Jenkins teaches at Butler.

428. Lida Kelly teaches in Normal public schools.

429. Cora A. Lurton teaches at Elgin.

430. Mattie B. Maxwell teaches at Plainfield, Illinois.

431. Lillian Pillsbury teaches in the Belvidere schools.

432. Mattie L. Powell teaches in Amboy.

433. Florence Hubbard Reid is at Normal.

434. Louisa M. Scott teaches at Magnolia, Illinois.

435. Lettie J. Smiley teaches at Gardner, Illinois.

436. B. Bayliss Beecher (H. S.) teaches in McLean County.

437. Charles Fordyce teaches in McLean, Illinois.

438. Jessie F. Hannah teaches in Peru, Illinois.

439. James V. McHugh is principal of the Normal public schools.

440. Murray M. Morrison teaches at Adeline.

441. George W. Reeder teaches at Mt. Pulaski.

442. Milton R. Regan teaches at Auburn, Illinois.

443. Edwin E. Rosenberry teaches at Franklin Grove, Illinois.

444. Charles N. Smith is studying medicine in Danville.

445. William J. Smith teaches at Oak Hill.

446. Evens W. Thomas teaches in the Normal Department of the University of Colorado, at Boulder.

447. Franklin L. Williams teaches in Loda, Illinois. .

PHILADELPHIAN SOCIETY.

The State Normal University was opened October 5, 1857, in Major Block, in Bloomington, with an attendance of nineteen, of whom six were males. Four days after the opening of the school, October 9, 1857, the male students (by this time their number had increased), "desirous," as the preamble to their constitution reads, "of forming a society for the purpose of extending their social relations, and for the elevation of their moral character and intellectual attainments," called a meeting in a small room on the second floor of the building. The room was lighted by one miserable old tallow candle, and, as Mr. Gastman says, "Harvey J. Dutton had a fearful time in trying to induce the old thing to burn." C. D. Irons, of Peoria, was chairman, and H. J. Dutton, of Metamora, secretary *pro tem*. After a lengthy discussion of the object of the meeting, Mr. Pope and Mr. Harper were appointed a committee to draft a constitution, which was presented and accepted on the following evening, fixing the name of the society as the "Normal Debating Society." The following names were immediately affixed to the instrument:

Henry H. Pope, Taylorville, Christian County; E. D. Harris, Monmouth, Warren County; J. G. Howell, Duncanton, White County; John Hull, Salem, Marion County; C. D. Irons, Peoria, Peoria County; J. L. Spaulding, Metamora, Woodford County; H. J. Dutton, Metamora, Woodford County; Peter Harper, Peoria, Peoria County; Edwin Philbrook, Vandalia, Fayette County; E. A. Gastman, Hudson, McLean County; B. F. Rawolt, Canton, Fulton County; Silas Hayes, Bloomington, McLean County; L. L. Lightner, Thebes, Alexander County; J. D. Kirkpatrick, Princeton, Bureau County.

The meeting then elected C. D. Irons, president, J. L. Spaulding, vice-president, H. J. Dutton, secretary, and John Hull, treasurer, and selected their first question for debate, which was as follows: "Is a lawyer justified in defending a bad cause?" supported by Messrs. Hull, Howell, Harper, Philbrook, and Kirkpatrick, on the affirmative, and by Messrs. Pope, Dutton, Hayes, Spaulding, and Webber, on the negative.

The peculiar and interesting parts of the first constitution read as follows:

Preamble.   Whereas, we, the undersigned students of the Normal University, of the State of Illinois, desirous of forming a society for the purpose of extending our social relations, and for the elevation of our moral character and intellectual attainments, pledge ourselves to be governed by the following constitution and by-laws:

ARTICLE I.   This Society shall be known as the Normal Debating Society.

ARTICLE II.   The officers of this Society shall consist of a president, vice-president, secretary, treasurer, librarian, critic, marshal, editress, and chorister.

ARTICLE III.   The exercises of this Society shall consist of debates, etc.

ARTICLE XII.   It shall be the duty of each member to attend all the regular meetings of the Society, and to perform such other duties as the Society may impose upon them.

ARTICLE XIII.   Four regular meetings shall constitute a term.

ARTICLE XX.   Should any member move the dissolution of this Society, he shall thereupon be expelled.

The name of the Society, especially after the ladies were admitted, was not perfectly satisfactory, and October 15, 1858, notice was given by Mr. Hull that two weeks from that time a proposition would be made to change the name. Accordingly, October 29, it was moved that Article I be so amended as to read: "This Society shall be known by the name of 'Social Friends.'" This change did not seem to meet the wants of the members, and it was tabled for one week, when it was taken from the table, voted on, and lost. At last, Miss Jennie G. Michie, now Mrs. Dr. Fox, of Lyons, Cook County, Illinois, proposed the name "Philadelphian," as expressing the idea that we are a band of brothers. This was finally adopted, after much discussion and filibustering.

The first few meetings are interesting, on account of the variety of exercises they present in contrast with our present meetings. The exercises consisted, as per Article I of the constitution, of debates, etc., and if the minutes are correct, the "etc." part of the programme must have been irregular business. The entire literary part of the programme, in those days, consisted of debates, and if one did not occupy the whole evening, the members often proposed another, and went to work on it, making it sometimes the best debate of the evening. The roll was often called, and members were expected to respond by speaking on the subject. What a sensation that would produce if practiced now!

Attendance on all regular meetings, and performance of duty, were compulsory then, and the Societies were always called to order on time, probably because of the fine attached to tardiness. At that time members of the Society acted as critics, which custom prevailed up to about 1865, when gradually the professors came to fill that position, and now a student as critic is seldom seen. It was formerly the custom to have special critics for papers and debates. At first the critic was one of the officers, chosen at the regular election. It was also customary, the evening of the installation of officers, for the out-going presidents to appoint one or two persons (ususally ladies, for at that time the presidents were always gentlemen, no lady being bold enough to aspire to the presidency) to conduct the president elect to the chair. At that time members were not afraid to do work, as is manifested by the fact that the same persons were on debate every evening for nearly a whole term. According to the constitution, the Society held its first meetings Wednesday evenings, but the first amendment to the constitution changed that to Friday evenings. This continued to be the time until after the formation of the Wrightonian Society, and after the bitter feeling that existed between the two Societies had subsided enough to permit them to act together, when the Philadelphians would meet Friday night, and the Wrightonians Saturday night, and *vice versa* the next week. After many changes in the time of meeting, the present plan was finally adopted.

The manner of conducting their exercises appear to us as rather peculiar. In those exciting times the Society was of the first importance; marks and graduation were secondary affairs. There were fewer members and as much work to be done as now, and each one had to do his part toward pushing forward the Society.

The solid debates, in which the members engaged with a great deal of zest, were lightened here and there by a humorous one, in which the professors were not loath to engage. This dignified subject was once discussed:

Resolved, That we most horribly protest against, vigorously condemn, obstreperously denounce, and aguishly shudder at the influence of such historical literature as,—

> "Jack and Gill went up the hill
> To get a pail of water.
> Jack fell down and cracked his crown,
> And Gill came tumbling after."

Supported on the affirmative by Professors Hewett and Sewall, and on the negative by Professors Stetson and Edwards.

And again, "*Resolved*, That the poem commencing, 'High Diddle Diddle, the Cat and the Fiddle,' etc., is utterly unworthy of belief," supported by gentlemen Sewall and Baldwin, and denied by gentlemen Hewett and Wright. The question was decided by a committee appointed by the chair to examine a copper tossed by the president. The committee consisted of gentlemen Hull, Liversay, and Gilwie.

Again, "Ought men to shave?"

The following preamble and resolution was presented by Mr. Hewett, in a joint meeting, March 1, 1862, and received with much applause:

"WHEREAS, We are credibly informed that the president of the

Wrightonian Society has this day become the possessor of a fine horse and buggy; therefore, be it

Resolved, That we are jointly and severally tickled."

During the war, and the exciting times before and after it, questions of more than usual interest were discusssed with more than the usual earnestness. Questions such as,

Resolved, That it is just and expedient at the present time for congress to declare the liberation of the slaves of those in rebellion against the government." September 28, 1861.

"*Resolved*, That the slaves emancipated by the United States government should be colonized on this continent." May, 1862.

"*Resolved*, That the appointment of General Halleck in place of Fremont was unjust and impolitic."

"Is it expedient to colonize the freedmen?"

"*Resolved*, That the States in rebellion should be reduced to the condition of Territories."

"*Resolved*, That Jeff. Davis should be hung." December 2, 1865.

"Has a State a right to secede?"

"*Resolved*, That congress should declare the slaves free."

"*Resolved*, That Lincoln's proclamation is unjust and impolitic."

Gradually, other exercises found their way into the Society. First, declamations, then orations, and when the ladies were full-fledged members they started a paper, called "The Literary Paper," which consisted of several departments,—under as many editresses,—as the "political," the "social," and the "religious departments," which continued to exist for some time.

Our "Ladies' Garland" was first known as "The Student's Manual," and was entirely in the hands of the gentlemen. In February, 1858, the name became just "The Garland," yet in the hands of the gentlemen, but in August of the same year it came into the hands of the ladies, and has since been known as "The Ladies' Garland."

Debates, considered the object of the Society at first, gradually lost ground, except during the war, until now our exercises consist of "etc.," and debates, in the face of the old constitution. The gradual growth of the present class of exercises is plainly seen in the minutes of the meetings, where the whole programme is usually recorded. Shakspearian readings were practiced considerably, which lightened the exercises very much. These the teachers conducted as they do now. The professors frequently lectured before the Societies. Often their lectures have been published at the expense of the Society, and copies distributed among the members. The usual lecturers were Professors Stetson, Sewall, and Cook, and Doctors Hewett and Edwards. During the war, tableaux illustrating scenes from military life were given.

During the early days of the Society, only Normal students were admitted, but on April 29, 1862, the Societies agreed to draw the students of the model school, who were of the age required for admission, into the Normal, but they could not hold office, nor vote, and were not subject to tax. Later, they were admitted on the same terms as the Normal students. At this time they were among the most active members of the Society. There were frequently contests between the two departments, and very exciting ones, too, for, on the whole, the Normal students did not win much glory. Although ladies were not admitted at first, despite the opposition of a few, led by Mr. Harper, on October 16, 1858, it was moved and carried to invite the professors and ladies to attend and take part in the exercises, and soon afterward the constitution was so changed as to admit them. The opposition were not conquered, however, and January 20, 1860, Mr. Harper, as Mr. Philbrook says, "a persistent Englishman, and a bachelor," introduced a motion excluding ladies from the Society, giving as the principal objections, that their presence would embarrass the beginners and leave all the talking to a favored few, and that many young men would attend the exercises simply to accompany the ladies, and disturb rather than assist the meeting. The motion, however, failed, and no more was heard of the opposition. The ladies quietly grew into power and began to hold office. As officers, they crept gradually up from chorister and editress to the position of secretary, which office was first filled by Miss Scott, in December, 1861; and to the position of president, in the winter term of 1870, which office was filled by Miss Alice Emmons, who had a hard fight for the position, having been defeated the term before. The election of a lady caused dissatisfaction, and a committee was appointed to test the election, and it was finally declared illegal. R. A. Edwards was chosen to fill the vacancy.

The following is a list of the presidents, and the order in which they served, from the organization up to the winter term of 1882:

1. C. D. Irons,	49. C. W. Hodgin,
2. Edwin Philbrook,	50. J. R. Edwards,
3. Peter Harper,	51. L. A. Chase,
4. Henry H. Pope,	52. Joseph Carter,
5. E. A. Gastman,	53. William M. Bane,
6. John Hull,	54. William Edwards,
7. J. G. Howell,	55. B. W. Baker,
8. E. D. Harris,	56. A. C. Cotton,
9. L. H. Hite,	57. Alice Emmons,
10. J. F. Ridlon,	58. Alice Emmons,
11. J. M. Burch,	59. James H. Hovey,
12. M. R. Kell,	60. William C. Griffith,
13. T. F. Willis,	61. George Blount,
14. E. A. Gastman,	62. Lottie C. Blake,
15. Edwin Philbrook	63. Frank Richey,
16. J. G. Howell,	64. N. B. Reed,

17. J. Little,
18. Mr. Waite,
19. John Hull,
20. M. I. Morgan,
21. J. G. Howell,
22. E. A. Gastman,
23. T. F. Willis,
24. Edwin Philbrook,
25. E. F. Bacon,
26. J. Little,
27. M. I. Morgan,
28. Ira Moore,
29. Ira Moore,
30. Mr. Waite,
31. J. Little,
32. M. I. Morgan, .
33. Mr. Waite,
34. I. D. Scholes,
35. John F. Gawdy,
36. J. H. Thompson,
37. C. F. Childs,
38. C. F. Childs,
39. D. Fulwider,
40. C. H. Crandall,
41. W. L. Pillsbury,
42. Mr. Robinson,
43. H. C. Karr,
44. Joseph Hunter,
45. E. C. Hewett,
46. A. T. Ewing,
47. F. J. Seybold,
48. W. L. Pillsbury,

65. Louise Ray,
66. J. D. Templeton,
67. I. E. Brown,
68. F. B. Tait,
69. J. N. Wilkinson,
70. S. L. Spear,
71. Ella Morgan,
72. Elma J. Webster,
73. Lewis Bryan,
74. C. O. Drayton,
75. Mary A. Anderson,
76. D. C. Tyler,
77. Charles McMurry,
78. W. C. Glidden,
79. Miss F. Preston,
80. Miss A. Stahl,
81. H. E. Powers,
82. Jessie Dexter,
83. G. A. Burgess,
84. C. E. Webster,
85. W. C. Ramsey,
86. John Humphrey,
87. Jesse F. Hannah,
88. W. H. Chamberlain,
89. Austin C. Rishel,
90. Frank Tyrrell,
91. E. W. Thomas,
92. May Parsons,
93. L. Messick,
94. M. R. Regan,
95. F. L. Williams,
96. J. L. Hall.

Of the faculty not before mentioned, Miss Flora Pennell was secretary in the spring of 1870, and vice-president in the winter of 1872; Mr. De Garmo was chorister in 1871; Mr. Hewett was treasurer in the summer of 1863; Miss Bandusia Wakefield was secretary during the winter of 1865.

The constitution has suffered many changes. During its history, there have been seventy changes or amendments, three of which have been complete revisions. The first change was proposed the same evening the constitution was adopted.

Members were formerly elected to the Society on their application. The first account of any "drawing" is recorded as happening during the winter term of 1859, when a committee was appointed to see to it. Even then they had to pass through the form of an election before becoming full members. This was abolished by a change in the constitution soon afterwards. Thus far no mention has been made of the organization of the Wrightonian Society.

On the evening of February 26th, 1858, during the presidency of E. A. Gastman, after a very exciting debate, and during a very stormy time among the members, which prolonged the exercises very much, as there was a rule which made it the duty of the president to fine any member who left the room without permission of the presiding officer, C. D. Irons, H. J. Dutton, and J. L. Spaulding requested permission to leave the room. As the session was nearly over, Mr. Gastman asked the gentlemen to remain until the adjournment. This request was answered by their promptly leaving the hall, and the president ordered a fine of twenty-five cents to be entered against each of the refractory gentleman. This action was the beginning of a trouble that led to the founding of the Wrightonian Society. The next step is best shown by the minutes of the meeting which are as follows:

BLOOMINGTON, February 27, 1858, 3:30 p. m.

Special meeting; roll called; society resolved itself into a committee of the whole; Mr. Gastman was chosen chairman of the meeting, Hite acting as secretary. Gentlemen Irons, Dutton and Spaulding appealed to the house from the decision of the chair, in the case of the fine imposed upon them. After considerable wrangling, the question, "Will the Society sustain the president?" was put, and decided in the affirmative. Motion was made by Mr. Pope to expunge the fine from the records. Carried. On motion, the society adjourned. March 5th, the resignations of the gentlemen were handed in and acted upon. Spalding's and Dutton's were accepted, but on motion of John Hull, C. D. Irons was expelled from the Society. On March 6th, however, Iron's resignation was accepted, and on March 7th, their request for an honorable discharge was granted.

At the beginning of the spring term, in 1858, an unusually large class entered the University. Among them were J. H. Burnham, P. R. Walker, Aaron Gove and H. B. Norton. "We noticed," says Mr. Gastman, "that these men came into our Society, but manifested no desire to join. In a short time it was whispered around that Dutton and Irons were going in with these men to form a new society. It was also hinted that this new society would receive the aid and sympathy of Simeon Wright, then an honored and respected member of the Board of Education. It seems quite ludicrous to me now, when I remember the tremendous excitement this announcement produced among us. The leaders of the opposition were quiet workers, and it was sometime before their real plans were disclosed. When it was generally known that a new society was formed, and recognized by the president of the University, we were somewhat disgusted with the uncertainty of human affairs. As I remember it, the new society came into existence with the name of 'Wrightonian,' and it was always understood that it was conferred on account of the gratitude that the members felt toward 'Uncle Sim' for his kindness at a time when they needed all the help they could get." We thus see that the real founders of the Wrightonian Society were our first president, vice-president and secretary.

Perhaps it is worth while to repeat an old joke that gave some of us considerable satisfaction at the time. Between Ira Moore and the members of the new Society, there was considerable gall and wormwood. They did not like him, and certainly no love was lost. Neither party took pains to hide the feelings that raged within. When the rooms were fitted up in the University, some of the boys were puzzling their brains over the motto on the door of the Wrightonian Society—*sapere aude* (dare to be wise). The discussion attracted quite a number, and just then it happened that Prof. Moore passed along, and some one called on him to translate the motto. Without a moment's hesitation he said, "Sap heads and adders," and passed on. For quite a time it was altogether sufficient to set a Wrightonian raving to ask about the meaning of the motto on the door.

The first meeting recorded as being held at Normal was that on September 22, 1860, and was in one of the lower rooms. The first meeting held in the Philadelphian Hall was on October 20, 1860. January 5, 1861, arrangements were begun for dedicating the hall, which were carried out July 2, 1861. The minutes of the meeting are as follows:

PHILADELPHIAN HALL, Friday Evening, July 2, 1861.

The Society assembled for the purpose of dedicating this hall. The Wrightonian Society attended in a body, and many other visitors were present, including members of the State Board of Education, filling the hall to its utmost capacity. The following programme was successfully carried out, viz.:

1. Prayer by the Rev. Mr. Ames, of Bloomington.
2. Music—"Washington's Birthday."
3. Dedication address by B. F. Taylor, of Chicago. Subject, "Going Away from Home."
4. Dedication Ode, written by Miss Sprague. (Tune, America.)

> Come, brothers, sisters, sing;
> Let all our voices ring
>   In concord sweet.
> To dedicate this room,
> Our Philadelphian home,
> We hither gladly come
>   With joyful feet.
>
> To progress, social joy,
> And truth without alloy,
>   This hall we give.
> The pleasures tasted here,
> With friends to us so dear,
> Shall yield us mem'ries dear
>   While each shall live.

8

Before we close our song
We'll greet the coming throng
  Who hither move.
As time new years shall tell,
Oh! may the members swell,
Our name still proving well,
  "Fraternal Love."

RECESS.

5. The unfortunate quarrel among Uncle Sam's girls: Prudence (away down east), Miss Sprague; Ruth (middle States), Miss Dunlap; Carolina (the sunny south), Miss Stevenson; Katrina (prairie land), Miss Puffer.

6. Music—"The Crystal Spring."

7. Oration—"Our Society," by John Little.

8. Music—"Over the Mountain Wave."

DISMISSION.

E. F. BACON, Secretary.   M. I. MORGAN, President.

The manner of gaining our room is worthy of mention. When this building was ready for occupancy, there was some dispute in regard to the choice of halls. So one day the boys lifted Prof. Moore to their shoulders, and let him through the transom of the south hall, which he preëmpted in the name of the Philadelphian Society.

On the eleventh of May, 1867, the Societies received their charters from the Legislature, of which they were justly very proud. Mr. Gastman says: "We felt that we were somebody; we could sue and be sued. We put on a good many airs in consequence of it, and attempted to intimidate the faculty when they threatened to close up the halls if the Societies did not keep better order."

For a number of years but little improvement was made on the halls. They were warmed by the pipes which are still here, but for years have not been used. The pipes had a habit of beginning suddenly, and without warning, a most disagreeable popping and cracking, more or less, throughout their entire length. This often occurred when some flowery orator was in the midst of his most effective burst of eloquence. There was no help for it. Business had to be suspended until the pipes stopped their noise, which they usually did in a short time, and about as suddenly as they began. An improvement was made in the pipes, which thenceforth prevented this noise, and soon afterward stoves were brought in. For two or three years the halls were not carpeted. Our first carpet was a red-and-white Brussels, selected and purchased with the greatest secrecy. It was presented to the Society by Professors Hewett, Moore, and Hovey, and a few others of the Society, and cost about two hundred and fifty dollars. It was desired to have it laid without the Wrightonians knowing anything about it until the following Saturday night, when we expected to dazzle their eyes with a beautiful new carpet, in striking contrast to their own bare floor. But we missed it. It was deemed that the only time to get the carpet into the hall unobserved was during devotional exercises. As the boys were taking it in at one of the windows, they were discovered by a tardy Wrightonian, and by Saturday evening the Wrightonians had a carpet laid ready for use. That red-and-white Brussels was sold when the old one sold this year was purchased.

The platform was formerly at the opposite end of the hall. The one now used by the critic was placed upon another, about two and one-half feet wider. On the upper and smaller one the president was perched, and the person addressing the Society stood on the narrow projection of the lower one, if he did not step off, which a high-flown orator would sometimes do, just as the eagle was soaring to its highest altitude. When the platform was first changed to its present position, the lower part extended entirely across the room, and the upper part not so far. The piano stood on the lower part, and made it necessary for the musicians to ascend two steps, and descend one, to get to the instrument. It was soon changed to its present form, thereby conforming to the plan of the Wrightonians, who had taken the start of us in at least one improvement. When the change in the platform was made, it became necessary to ornament the windows behind the president's chair. The expense of fixing it as it now is, was nearly one hundred dollars in those times of high prices. The walls have been twice frescoed, once in 1868, during the winter term, at a cost not less than one hundred two dollars, but how much more is a mystery. When the hall was frescoed the second time, is not definitely known. The first frescoing was badly damaged by the leaking of the roof, and by a careless carpenter, who pushed his foot through the ceiling.

Our rooms were first lighted by tallow candles, then by wall lamps, and lastly by chandeliers, two sets of which have been used. In the early days, the Normal University boasted of but one piano, the little, old one now used in the primary room. This the societies used alternately, carrying it up and back again each Saturday evening. The societies not having any instruments, oftentimes regaled themselves with comb music and the like. At last a bold strike was made, and in 1864 a new and expensive piano was purchased, and dedicated with appropriate ceremonies. On November 4, of the same year, the Wrightonians, hearing of our intention and being determined to keep even with us and have a piano of some sort, bought a second-hand one, which soon wore out, compelling the purchase of a new one. The music in the early days consisted most commonly of hymns, and to aid in the singing, hymn books were furnished the members. The chorister, or his assistant, usually led in this exercise, which quite often was somewhat of the character of congregational singing in churches,—either too fast or too slow, too high or too low, and always full of discords.

Many of our pictures were donated to us, but the larger number were purchased and hung between the years 1868 and 1873. Previous to 1867, the chairs used were carried up from the recitation rooms, not then being fastened together as now. When we had an influx of visitors, the president would ask some of the gentlemen to step down stairs and bring up some more chairs. They were not always promptly returned, and President Edwards often became quite indignant in consequence. In 1866 a union festival was held, at which all kinds of gambling known to the moral and religious world were resorted to, such as grab-bags, ring-cakes, fish-ponds, etc., as well as many other perfectly legitimate means, for the purpose of raising money. By this festival three hundred and ten dollars was cleared, and arm chairs were purchased February 23, 1867, at a cost of five hundred dollars. After furnishing and beautifying the rooms, a re-dedication took place. This was during the administration of Loring A. Chase.

Janitor's fees for the care of the hall have varied largely. About fifteen years ago the members took turns in caring for the hall, free of charge. The work has several times been let for eighteen cents per week; once for seventeen and three-fourth cents; then for twenty cents, thirty cents, and sixty cents. We pay now seventy-five cents. For a long time previous to the removal of the stove, one dollar and a quarter was paid.

It was formerly the custom to leave all wrappings in the dressing rooms, when coming up to the Society, as we now do when up coming to school. Society meetings were more like sociables.

Our library started with a few pamphlets belonging to members, or donated by them. Shortly after the organization of the Wrightonian Society, the Societies received from the Board of Education the books belonging to the district school libraries, Nos. 1 and 2. No. 1, consisting of sixty-three volumes, fell to the Philadelphian Society. Only a few of the sixty-three volumes are valuable. Among them were Macaulay's History of England, four volumes; Irving's Works, four volumes; Bayard Taylor's Travels, and Webster's Unabridged Dictionary. In every possible way the members sought donations. Members pledged themselves to give books. Committees were appointed to solicit books, and in May, 1863, an exhibition was given in Phœnix Hall, Bloomington, for the purpose of raising funds to purchase books. Among the many donors is the name of Senator Trumbull. A catalogue of books was printed, in connection with the Wrightonians, at a cost of $84. The catalogues were disposed of at the rate of twenty-five cents each, and as none are left to tell the story, they must have been in demand. The number of books reported in the library at that time was eight hundred and fifty-six. We now have about three hundred less than that number. Formerly the office of librarian was important, for he received a salary.

In the early times it was customary to elect honorary members. Every one who took an active interest in the University received an honorary membership, and for the honor conferred it was expected that in times of great need, from one dollar to ten dollars would be forthcoming. When necessary, taxes were imposed on the members, from five cents to a dollar. Sometimes only the gentlemen were taxed. The strength of the Societies has alternated. There was formerly great strife between them. The members of one Society were not found in the halls of the other for months at a time.

"At the contest, in 1868, the Wrightonians had a very strong quartette of male voices. We called them 'the four pirates.' The question of the hour was, What can we do to beat them? We finally hit upon the plan of choosing two young, sweet-looking girls to sing against them. The plan worked successfully, as the judges, in those days, were men. They could not decide against the girls, and we swept the board. The folks on the other side always claimed that we bought the judges."

The Societies used regularly to have a union exhibition at the end of the winter term, and a union lecture at the end of the spring term. They had a picnic each spring in the grove between here and the standpipe. They had an annual custom in connection with the school as a whole, of serenading the teachers. They would hire the Bloomington band at a large expense, and follow it around to each teacher's house. One summer, as usual, the faculty were requested to retire from the assembly-room, so that arrangements might be made for the serenade. The usual motion was carried, and the serenade committee appointed, when some one moved an amendment to the motion, supporting it by a vigorous speech. Times were hard; it would cost forty dollars to hire the band to come out, and it was a tiresome tramp to follow it all over town in the night. They could effect a great saving by hiring a big wagon and taking the faculty to the band's headquarters, where they could be serenaded at one-third the expense. He (supposed to be Joseph Carter) was followed by two or three vigorous speakers, cocked and primed for the occasion, and through their efforts the amendment prevailed. The committee on arrangements failed to do their duty, consequently the faculty received no serenade.

Without relating any more stories concerning the school at large, let us return to the subject of our sketch. In 1871 the Philadelphian Society stood on a good financial basis. Harmony prevailed among its members, and the barriers and obstructions that impeded its progress were rapidly disappearing. At this time we had cash on hand to the amount of $50.97, and a prospect for a large increase. Times were good, and everybody seemed willing to contribute freely toward any enterprise with a noble purpose. Dues were raised from fifty cents to one dollar per term, and tickets sold like government bonds at a premium.   By 1872 we had an abundance of wealth, and were enabled to purchase new curtains and a beautiful carpet.   With these new additions our hall began to assume the appearance of a royal manse, and we were very anxious to make it a model of perfection and beauty; but after due consideration, we banished our extravagant notions and applied ourselves to business.   During the year we handled no momentous questions, but we introduced a great many novelties. Burlesques, exciting tragedies, comic lectures, beautiful tableaux, etc., were the great attractions.   Strangers read our programmes with protruding eyes and gaping mouths, and when the time came we usually "took them in" for a dime.

In 1874 we experienced considerable difficulty in the management of uninterested parties, who were at times inclined to interrupt our exercises by loud talking and ill-mannered actions.   The propriety of adopting a ticket system, which would exclude disorderly persons, was discussed with much earnestness.   It was proposed to issue as many tickets as there were seats in the hall, and to give them only to respectable people.   This measure failed after a stubborn fight, but it was the means of securing our present ticket system (adopted in 1877).

Soon after settling the ticket question, we became involved in a spelling war, for which we made ample preparation.   We had great faith in our ability to conquer words and in consequence of this we were war-like, and ready at any moment to meet an enemy.   The anticipation of a battle and the glory that was to follow, fevered us with excitement, and when the mania had a firm hold, we received word from our neighbors, who by the way were affected likewise, that they could cure our disease on the homeopathic principle.   The result was a contest.   We met at the appointed place in due time, and tested our knowledge of words.   Fortunately for us, we gained a victory which secured for us an elegant picture and a good deal of confidence.

Having conquered the "Wrights," we pursued the even tenor of our way for a while, unmolested by outside factions.   But this calm, if such it may be called, was of short duration.   Many of our most active and energetic members belonged to the famous "Liberal Club," and they succeeded admirably in giving prominence to their thoughts. They exercised a powerful influence, and to a certain degree they controlled our finance and made our laws.   When it was time to nominate a candidate for the presidency in the spring of 1875, they had a man selected who was well qualified to fill the office.   He was not a liberal in his views, but owing to the friendly relationship that existed between him and different members of the club, he consented to be their candidate.   An exciting campaign followed, and party feeling ran high. Not unfrequently did the conciliatory members of the faculty recommend measures of peace, but all in vain.   Both parties were persistent, and a compromise was as unfavorable as a treaty.   Finally, after a long and careful canvass the votes were cast, and the decision announced. According to the official report, the liberals had a majority. The Christians, however, were dissatisfied with the result, and called for an investigation. The examining board failed to discover discrepancies of a serious nature, but so much dissatisfaction prevailed that it was deemed best to hold a new election. The second election again proved successful for the liberals. Their candidate received a handsome majority, but, unfortunately, he resigned just after his inauguration. The history of the "Liberal Club" receives more attention in our "chapter on reminiscences."

After the "Liberal Club excitement" had cooled down, the Society concluded that the hall was in a condition for repairs. It was never fully determined whether this was due to the faction battle or not; nevertheless, the hall was thoroughly repaired. The walls and ceiling were artistically frescoed in oil, and the wood work received a fresh coat of paint. The expense incurred was not less than $215, but what was that to a band of loyal "Phils," who had the confidence of the public. Our entertainments were giving universal satisfaction, and the payment of so small a debt was simply a question of time, not of resource.

In the fall of 1879, we purchased a new piano, costing $250 and the old one. One year from the above date the Society made an investment in furniture. We purchased three costly chairs for the convenience of the president, secretary, and critic. Our hall, at present, is equal in splendor to any of its kind in the State. The new carpet of 1881, costing over $300, the richly dyed curtains swinging from the arch, the beautiful scenes of life portrayed by master hands, and the costly chandeliers, cast in a model of rare design, command the admiration of our friends and the respect of our rivals.

Before closing this brief and imperfect history, let us notice an amendment to the constitution which has worked with good results. Until 1881, it was the duty of the president to arrange and publish a programme for each regular meeting. This necessitated much time and labor. It over-burdened the ambitious student who worked for "marks" and "society fame," consequently a change was necessary in order to secure good talent for the chair. It was our object to make the office one of honor. With this intention, we appointed a committee of three to revise the constitution. After long deliberation, they proposed the establishment of an executive board (consisting of the vice-president, acting as chairman, and two directors) whose duty it was to solicit exercises for the meetings, and to report to the president of the Society the exercises for each meeting previous to the Wednesday evening preceding said meeting. According to this amendment, we gained our object. Everybody seemed pleased with the change, so we incorporated the amendment as a part of our constitution.   At each regular election now we have several aspiring candidates for the office who (according to their campaign speeches) are willing to perform the *duties* of the office to the best of their ability.

This history must now end, incomplete as its records are.   We have done our best to gather the facts of interest.   We have searched the archives, and sought for treasures in the secret vaults, sometimes with success, sometimes with failure.   The records, though imperfectly kept, have aided us in our work, and old students have generously responded to our call.   In many instances, however, we have been disappointed.   Those who could have given us valuable information have failed to do so, but we have no word of fault.   We are content.   Old Philadelphia will live and hold her sovereign sway.   The historians of to-day have not done her justice, but we trust that future men, with ampler means, will pay her a more deserving tribute.   With bright hopes for the future, and kind wishes for her friends, we say adieu.

WRIGHTONIAN SOCIETY.

The following address was delivered in the Wrightonian Hall, December 18, 1880.   Through the courtesy of J. H. Burnham it is inserted here: It was my fortune to be one of the pioneers of the Normal, and you know pioneers are a privileged class.   Hence, while you allow me the pleasure of telling stories, please have the kindness to remember that in matter and manner the Normal pioneers are not to be criticised by the strict rules of modern scholarship. The Normal institution entered upon its career in October, 1857, at Major's Hall, in the city of Bloomington.   Some time in the course of the first few months, the students in attendance organized a literary society, the lineal ancestor of the present Philadelphian Society.   During the winter, this Society grew and prospered, being, perhaps, all that the size of the Normal would at first justify, the number of pupils amounting, perhaps, to seventy-five or eighty at the end of the first winter term.   I entered the Normal at the beginning of its first spring term, April, 1858, in company with about forty students, who were organized into classes "D" and "E."

At the close of school, on the second day of the term, the members of the entering classes were invited to one of the class rooms, where they were told that the time had come to organize a new literary society.   The principal speakers were old students, who were, or had been, members of the existing Society.   There were only four or five of them, and as the entering students were, as yet, strangers to each other and to the subject, the arguments used were mostly furnished by the older members, who displayed at the same time their want of appreciation, to say the very least, of the society privileges which they had been enjoying. Their remarks were so ill-natured that some of the entering class discovered they could not rely upon these representatives, and it was suggested that before organizing a new society it would be well for all to attend the existing Society at its next meeting, when we could judge whether it would be advisable to take steps to organize another, and a rival society. This idea at once became popular, and in spite of all that could be said by those who had organized the meeting, it adjourned.

Upon the following Saturday, some of the new students took a walk from Bloomington to the new Normal building, then in a state of practical suspension—its foundation walls only were erected, and the financial panic of the previous year had apparently given the enterprise its eternal quietus. The eye of faith told us that the great State of Illinois would, sooner or later, complete the building, and in imagination we could almost view the beautiful structure since erected upon that foundation. Some one in the company possessed a plan of the proposed building, upon which the two Society rooms were shown exactly as they are now finished. The fact that here would be good halls for two literary societies, prepared us for the part we subsequently took, and, no doubt, proved the turning point in the minds of some who were, perhaps, a little ambitious of organizing a society which might become one of the permanent institutions of one of the earliest Normal Schools in the great west.

It was the bad fortune of the organization, now called the Philadelphian Society, upon its first meeting in the spring term of 1858, to make a very poor exhibition of its literary ability, and the new students were so much disappointed that it required very little argument to convince the majority, that classes "D" and "E" had the ability to organize and carry on a society which would be, at least, on a par with the organization then in existence.

Tradition asserts that the members of these classes were, in their own estimation, a very superior class of beings. Posterity is unable to vindicate the great claims or these individuals, but it should be remembered that posterity had no vote at that particular crisis, and hence it was easy, at the adjourned meeting of the "D" and "E" classes, to pass a resolution to organize a new literary society. It was at first organized as the "D and E" Society, and it is unfortunate that your present records do not show this fact. History requires me to state that our by-laws provided for the admission of members who were not of our classes, and we actually required the four or five old students—the originators of our enterprise—to obtain honorable discharges from the old Society before admission to the new organization. This being the case, they were not eligible to office at the first election, and all positions were filled by members of the entering classes.

It is proper to state that the two Societies were at this time—and for a long time after—rivals, contesting for existence, and that the best of feeling did not always exist between their members. The new organization did not at first have the formal consent of the principal. He allowed it to organize as a temporary expedient, and often explained that the time might soon come when both Societies might be broken up, and when two new institutions might be organized upon an entirely different basis. The temper and spirit shown by each was not exactly such as he wished, and for the proper development of the Normal, he was of the opinion something different must be attempted. Thus matters stood during the spring term of 1858. The Philadelphians thoroughly believed their organization was altogether the most permanent, and that only the new Society was in any danger of disruption. They were allowed their choice of evenings, and our Society used the same hall on the night which they rejected. Instead of being depressed by this little circumstance, the elastic public spirit of the new Society declared it possessed the most desirable evening of the week. A very laudable degree of interest was shown by the members of the new Society. There was a zeal and ambition unknown in the other, and it was not long before we could discern symptoms that the ruling powers were disposed to treat the young fledgling as being almost a grown bird. For this change of treatment we were largely indebted to Simeon Wright, then a member of the State Board of Education, who took a deep interest in the welfare of the new Society. He boldly advocated our right to live, and took the ground that we were entitled to equal rights with the Philadelphians, and it was popularly believed that his whole influence was given in favor of the continuance of our organization.

At first our by-laws required an election of officers every four weeks. P. R. Walker was the first president, and your humble servant was the first secretary. There are those present who can appreciate my deep mortification at being compelled to take this position. No other person would accept; my excuse of poor penmanship being considered a mere pretext. Being determined to do my whole duty, I took up the pen, but have a distinct recollection of receiving no ballots for the office at the next election. When told that our first record-book is now lost, I confess to a secret satisfaction at the disappearance of such formidable evidence against my penmanship. Three years in Normal did little to improve my handwriting, even though I enjoyed the benefit of a course of lessons from Professor Washington Irving Vescellius, the great American card writer, who taught the whole school, in 1860, the full beauties of the "shyrographic curve." Thus you see one illustration of the peculiar advantages enjoyed by the pioneers of the Normal.

During the first term the *Oleastellus* was started and named. Miss Ross was the first editor, and was instrumental in selecting the name, which was suggested, I think, by Mr. E. P. Clark, then principal of the Bloomington high school. I think we devoted more time to debate than is given at present, and that we did not possess the talent to carry on such a variety of exercises as you are able to enjoy at present. The most of us were truly pioneers, having never seen a literary society before. At that time we obtained no benefit from the teachers of the institution, who did not join the literary societies until 1860, when, by agreement of the faculty, they were equally apportioned to the two organizations.

For fear of foundering upon the rock of parliamentary discord, and with a shrewd desire to acquire the confidence of the principal, we provided a by-law, under which, in case of disputes within our Society, we would agree that our "umpire" should be the principal of the Normal. I believe he was never appealed to, and eventually, becoming a little more confident of our internal harmony, we repealed this provision. Before reaching this stage, however, we had demonstrated our disposition to maintain good order at our meetings. The first election contest in our ranks grew out of the determination of a few resolute members to maintain good order. Our meetings being in the city, free to the general public, and not necessarily attended by our teachers, became the resort of triflers and idlers, and threatened to become unmanageable. The election of a strict disciplinarian for president came near being lost, and was only carried by very close campaigning, and the bringing out of every possible law-and-order voter. A certain energetic member, who now lives near the Rocky Mountains, saved the day by escorting to the meeting an extraordinary number of woman suffragists. As he brought them separately, the trouble did not begin till the meeting adjourned, when he suddenly found his contract rather unprofitable. I am inclined to think that the literary work of the Society was more easily performed during this first term than it was a year or two later. At that early day, no standard of excellence had been formed, and we were too easily contented, perhaps, and yet our simple performances were a severe strain upon a few of the most active members. These had enlisted for the contest, and preferred to succeed in the Society, even if they failed in the class room, and it was no uncommon event for these persons to deliberately accept low class-standing rather than see the new Society fail of surpassing the standard shown by its neighbor. The action and reaction being equal, it is probable these strenuous efforts exerted a most beneficial effect upon both of the literary Societies, and that the influence of those early times has not yet wholly disappeared. Among the most active and useful early members, I can give you the names of several now occurring to my mind. There was the conscientious and devoted P. R. Walker, who gave days and nights of unceasing labor, and whose interest in your Society is of an undying nature. W. H. Avery, a talented

young man, was the most fluent debater of our early times, and
contributed much towards our success. H. J. Dutton, H. C.
Prevost, L. D. Bovee, James R. Fyffe and James H. Bailey
were among our best members. Of the ladies, there were Misses
Town, Carter, Clark, Dennison, Ross, McKinstry, Collom, Ives,
Boughton, and many others who assisted, by their pens, their
voices, and their presence, and who are entitled to your remembrance. I have here a printed list of all who were members at the
close of the year 1858, including the large number who entered in
September, and have indicated the names of all who were charter

MEMBERS:

GENTLEMEN.

James H. Bailey,*	John P. Curtiss,	William H. Avery,*
L. D. Bovee,*	George B. Robinson,	Lewis P. Cleveland,*
J. H. Burnham,*	E. Aaron Gove,	W. Duncan,
J. R. Fyffe,*	C. J. Gill,	Harvey J. Dutton,*
William T. Law,*	N. M. Carter,*	Duncan G. Ingraham,*
John B. Miller,	Edwin B. Fiske,*	J. L. Spaulding,*
Hermes S. Payn,*	H. C. Prevost,*	L. L. Lightner,*
Byron Sheldon,*	Robert L. Duncan,	John Walton,
Rufus W. Angell,*	H. B. Norton,	N. D. Stevens,*
P. R. Walker,*		

LADIES.

P. R. Butler,	Phebe W. Jones,	Mattie Havens,*
Ann R. Collom,*	Kate Zorger,	S. Stewart,
Fannie S. Dennison,*	Sarah E. Fell,*	Jennie Bryant,
Julia A. Ives,*	Mary E. Moore,	Helen Ross,*
Sarah E. Town,*	Caroline Moore,	Martha L. Fay,*
Susan H. Wright,	Lydia M. Young,	J. McCoy,
Emily A. Carter,*	Mary Brigham,*	Ellen I. Boughton,*
Martha J. McKinstry,*	Lizzie Wakefield,*	Lizzie Clarkson,
Amanda O. Noyes,	Hattie E. Hoover,	Mary J. Scoggan.*
Anna B. Roberts,		

Our officers were at first chosen for one month, and could you
examine that lost record you would be surprised to see the care and
facility with which the honors were distributed. I was soon
promoted to the position of vice-president, and while filling that
office was called upon to preside at a very critical period. Our name,
that of the "D and E Society," was found inconvenient, and when
compared with the dignified title of our rival, suffered very materially.
Besides it was seen that the members of D and E classes would some
day pass to the upper grades. Brains were busy devising a name
which should out-shine or out-*sound* the Philadelphians; but for

weeks we wrestled with the problem in vain. Our knowledge of the dead languages was too limited to devise an original word, and we fell back to first principles, and declared that the genius of the Normal required an expressive name of English origin. Name after name was proposed and rejected in our secret conclaves, and we were fast approaching serious disagreement, and were fearing our best efforts might end in ridiculous failure. At this juncture some one of our number, E. Aaron Gove, if I remember rightly, who well knew of the great assistance rendered us by Simeon Wright, and who was well-informed as to that gentleman's interest in our welfare, suggested that we name our Society in his honor. Mr. Wright, as you all know, had been one of the earliest friends of the Normal. He had traveled all over Illinois as agent of the Illinois State Teachers' Association; had addressed public audiences; had exerted himself to the utmost to mould public sentiment in favor of a State Normal School, and when the institution was founded, was selected as a member of the State Board of Education. In our Society's early struggle for existence, he had spoken words of encouragement, and unless we were entirely misinformed, he had influenced the president of the Normal, Charles E. Hovey, to "let the boys go on with their experiment." Hence, in our perplexity, the proposition to call the "D and E Society" the "Wrightonian," found many warm supporters. In order to change our name, a by-law must be amended, and the proposition laid on the table one week. During this week the amendment was discussed and grew in favor. When the vote was taken, it was my fortune to be called to the chair in the sickness or absence of the president. There were eleven votes in favor of the proposed name, out of seventeen members who were present. Our constitution required a two-thirds vote to change a by-law, and in the excitement of the occasion I decided that eleven was two-thirds of seventeen, and that the amendment was adopted. Historical accuracy requires the statement that at the moment I reflected that even if mathematical accuracy required eleven and one-third votes, that third of a vote was an impossible quantity, and I was doing no violence to the rights of voters, even if I was making a bad ruling for one who was a little proud of his class-standing in mathematics. Inasmuch as the six members who had voted *no* were tolerably sure they were legally and mathematically entitled to the right of defeating the amendment, they promptly appealed from the decision of the chair. The whole matter was discussed, and I was given an opportunity to revoke my decision. By this time I had discovered that the question of a name was very difficult to manage, and that it should be settled in some manner as speedily as possible, and it occurred to me that if a majority sustained my decision, the Society would be permanently named, as I saw that even if we failed of possessing the fraction of a vote required, we at least had the matter where a majority held the power to settle the question by upholding my decision, and I insisted on allowing it to stand as given. As a majority voted to sustain me, there was no help for the minority, and they very soon accepted the situation, although they afterward, very properly, asked me very exasperating questions in mental arithmetic.

As the summer term drew near its end, and plans were being discussed for the entertainment of the public at the end of the first academic year, our principal proposed a joint contest meeting between the two Societies. The exercises consisted of music, and a paper from each Society, and a debate. The latter was decided by judges, while the other exercises were left to the decision of the general public. Not being considered a very ornamental debater, as I had already been found lacking as a secretary, I was not chosen as one of the disputants, and that labor was thrown upon W. H. Avery and P. R. Walker. Just twenty-four hours before the time appointed for the public meeting, Avery positively declined the position, although he had spent over a week in preparation. No one else would take the position, and, as in the case of the first of the organization, my assurance and audacity were equal to any emergency, and I accepted the place. My preliminary rehearsal before Mr. Walker, in the shades of Blooming Grove, was a dismal failure, and my colleague's heart failed him entirely. For once it was evident his high estimate of my versatility was entirely at fault, as he was in favor of abandoning the contest. I thought the audience was entitled to the privilege of seeing us defeated, and that the performance should proceed as per programme. In some unaccountable manner, it happened that my public rehearsal was rather better than my failure under the trees, and the Wrightonians were not specially disgraced, as they won the debate, and closed the term with flying colors.

The important question of the admission of new members at the beginning of the next year was uppermost in the minds of the leading members of the Wrightonian Society. Very quietly they formed their plans, and began to lay wires to secure, during vacation, the best of the new members who might attend in September. Our efforts during vacation, and at the beginning of the new year, were so successful that we were about to secure a very large majority of the new students, and were in a fair way to deal a terrible blow to our rivals, when a new rule was promulgated—that of alphabetically dividing the entering class, which ingenious device is, I believe, still in existence. Chagrined and disappointed, we were forced to acquiesce, though there would have been a tremendous satisfaction in showing our success in proselyting. Again your narrator will boldly introduce his own experience, and again will you perhaps draw the conclusion that he should be ashamed to expose his actions to the light of day, even if twenty years and more have elapsed. It was my fortune to fill the presidential office at the time of drawing these new members, in September, 1858, while Hon. Luke H. Hite, now of East St. Louis, was the Philadelphian president. There was one very talented student in the entering class,—Henry B. Norton, of Ogle County,—now, as you all know, one of the faculty of the State Normal in California. His early friend, P. R. Walker, one of our most valuable members, had filled his mind with a desire to join the Wrightonians, and those of us who knew his peculiar talents, were anxious to secure the new member. I procured a list of the names, of the entering class, and exercised my best ingenuity in arranging them in such alphabetical order that Mr. Norton would fall to our side, but my best efforts were unequal to the occasion. With a sad heart but deceitful countenance, I took the precaution to request Mr. Hite to meet me in private, where we could draw the members without interference from any of our associates. As I expected, we lost Norton, for whom I would have given two dozen ordinary members. Before separating, I tried one last expedient. Norton was my room-mate, and I told Hite he was very anxious to belong to our Society, and that a young man named Kester, whose sister was a Philadelphian, was, I thought, anxious to be exchanged from the Wrightonians. I proposed we make the trade. "What kind of a fellow is Norton?" queried Hite. I gave my room-mate a good recommendation, but did not see any call for telling the whole truth. Just at that moment I pointed him out, crossing the hall with his well-known "kangaroo" stride. "What! Is he that tall, gauky-looking fellow? You may have him." Thanking Mr. Hite very kindly, I soon proposed we report our list to the principal, and kept the secret for some months, but before the beginning of the next term it leaked out, and such exchanges were afterwards rare, or impossible.

Our Society made good use of all its new members, but it is hardly saying too much to assert that this one acquisition gave us the best society man that ever entered the Normal University. During the second term of our existence, we were officially recognized as the equal of the older Society. Both Societies were then obliged to use the same hall, which was the school room, but we were allowed our choice of Friday or Saturday night for one term, while at the next term the other Society took its choice, and so on, alternating, until the completion of the new building.

During the spring term of 1858, our library was founded by Simeon Wright, who secured for each Society the donation of one of Moore's district school libraries, of over one hundred volumes each, with five library cases. He also donated, personally, quite a number of valuable books, so that from the very first our library was considered the best of the two, although in this, as in my other statements, it may be proper to bear in mind that twenty-two years have not proved sufficient to dampen the ardor of an original Wrightonian, and I may occasionally exaggerate. During the whole of the second year both Societies made considerable progress. Both were fortunate in possessing a membership that took pride in striving after the highest possible excellence. The Philadelphians were the most quiet. They were less ambitious than their rivals. While the Wrightonians were less tractable, they were the most enthusiastic. They were the most thoroughly imbued with a love for their Society, and appeared to have the highest appreciation of the design and scope of the Normal institution. To us, it seemed as if the Philadelphians disliked change, even if in the direction of progress. To our rivals, we seemed too ready to try experiments, and too willing to trust our own untried judgment. I have no doubt that both were partly right, and partly wrong. In the progress of time it is natural that the two Societies should lose many of their distinctive traits, and they are now, perhaps, more nearly alike than at the time of which I am writing.

The Wrightonians never ceased plotting for the supremacy, and at the close of the summer term of 1859, found themselves once more ahead of their antagonists. They decided that the annual examination should be signalized by some event besides a Society contest, and fixed upon a lecture before their Society, and the whole institution, as one of the events of the last week of the year. They therefore very quietly secured Phœnix Hall, and engaged Benjamin F. Taylor, then editor of the Chicago *Evening Journal*, and a poet and lecturer of some considerable note, to give a public free lecture, to which should be invited the Board of Education, the Philadelphian Society, as well as the general public. When our plans were fully matured, we found, to our surprise, that the president, Mr. Hovey, refused his consent. He declared we had carried the spirit of rivalry too far; that were this lecture allowed, the Philadelphians would be made to appear before the public in a humiliating position, and that he was not sure whether the Wrightonians cared most for the merit of the lecture, or for the other feature of the event. It was in vain we urged that we had engaged the hall and the lecturer. The matter must stop. He, however, proposed that if we would join with the Philadelphians, he would engage that Society would unite, and that upon that basis the lecture might proceed. With some reluctance we consented, and when it was learned that our rival's treasury was unprepared for the sudden call, and that it would be in our debt for some months, this little circumstance, together with the satisfaction of having inaugurated an important custom, gave our society leaders all the credit they could reasonably desire. This lecture at the close of the summer term, was kept up for years, until other exercises more important occupied all the evenings at the disposal of the faculty.

In September, 1860, the new building was partially prepared for occupancy, and the Society's meetings were held in whatever room was most convenient, migrating from place to place until midwinter, when it took possession of its present quarters. During this first term at Normal, many of the students boarded in Bloomington, and the Society meetings were with great difficulty sustained, again throwing a severe strain upon the few energetic and ambitious leaders who had from the beginning known no such word as failure.

The present hall was dedicated January 24, 1861, at which time an original ode was one feature of the occasion, a copy of which I have furnished your president. The event was one of the proudest of our history, and our feelings on that occasion can be better imagined than described.

A band of workers, true and tried,
    In learning's toilsome way,
We've walked together, side by side
    Through many a changing day;
And hostile forces have essayed,
    With labor ever vain,
Our happy union to invade
    And break the clasping chain.

Chorus:

Then, comrades, linking hand in hand,
    A joyful chorus swell,
In honor of the gallant band
    That each has loved so well.

But now upon our waiting eyes
    A brighter star has shone,
Which points to where our pathway lies
    Through future years unknown;
And all that coming road seems bright
    With sunshine, song, and flowers,
As joyfully we come to-night
    To greet these festal hours.

Chorus:

So, brothers, sisters, gather all,
    A bright and smiling throng,
And dedicate our temple hall
    With joyful swelling song.

May mental treasures evermore
    Be poured upon its shrine;
May might and triumph, as of yore,
    Upon its banners shine.
And when this happy season 's fled,
    The parting hour draws near,—
When strangers in these halls must tread
    And fill our places here,

Chorus:

Again we'll gather, hand in hand,
    Our parting song to swell,
In memory of the gallant band
    That each has loved so well.

January 24, 1861.

9

At that time the library shelves which you now possess, though drawn upon the plan of the building, were still unfinished, and rumor declared that the want of funds would compel the building committee to leave these necessary adjuncts out of our new hall, and this rumor had an important bearing upon the circumstance which I now relate. Our library books, as well as the Philadelphians,' remained in the district school library case, in which they were presented two years before, and were situated in one of the lower halls of the building. Sometime in the month of January, 1861, the acting president of the institution, who, by the way, is not now a member of your faculty, gave an order to the presidents of the two Societies to transport the books, with their cases, to the new society rooms. Fearing that if this were done, the new library cases might never be finished, the two presidents counseled together and quietly resolved to ignore the authority of the acting president, and to take the position that they were not to be ordered, as presidents, to perform any labor which properly devolved upon the janitor of the building. This position was interpreted as being contemptuous insubordination, an interpretation which impartial history compels me to admit was one part correct. A peremptory order for the removal of the library cases was followed by silent inaction on the part of the presidents, and by a threat of throwing the books out of the window on the part of the acting president. At this juncture of affairs, several innocent members of each Society, ignorant of the motives of their presidents, performed the required duty, but too late to save the two officials from the wrath of offended majesty, as the next morning they were publicly suspended from the Normal University. The Wrightonians, with the impulsive promptness for which they were then famous, called a special meeting immediately and appointed a committee to report at the next meeting. This committee prepared a report, reciting the affront which had been put upon their Society, and the attempt to disgrace their president, by intimation, reflected upon the acting president of the Normal, and ended with a hearty endorsement of the Wrightonian Society's president, who could but feel that his position was fully sustained. No action was taken by the Philadelphians, and their president was left to guess at the estimation of his associates. In a few days both presidents were restored by C. E. Hovey, the president of the Normal, to their former standing in the school, but the trouble did not end here. The teachers of the Normal, now called professors, were equally divided between the two literary Societies, a proceeding which dates from the early part of 1860. The teacher who had suspended the presidents concluded that the vote of the Wrightonians, sustaining their presiding officer, was of such a rebellious nature that no member of the faculty could, consistently, retain his place in the Society, and he demanded that they withdraw from the Wrightonian Society, or compel it to expunge the proceedings from the records. By this time the excitement ran high, and a majority of this Society, acting upon their own impulses, would cheerfully have bid good-bye to the professors, and retained their resolutions and independence; but cooler heads and wiser counsels prevailed. Dr. J. Little, now of Bloomington, was the Philadelphian president at this crisis, and your humble servant was the other. I at once besought the Society to expunge the record, declaring that it had already done far more in my behalf than I deserved, and requested that action be taken which would leave the faculty at liberty to remain in our ranks. The matter was settled by cutting out the leaf containing the obnoxious resolutions, and presenting it to me with great formality, on the ground that in some future emergency I might need the document to establish my reputation if assailed by malice or ill-will. This record, perhaps the only official page of your early history now in existence, is still preserved by me with great care and affection. It is perhaps needless to add that twenty years of active life have as yet presented no crisis where the document has possessed any moral or financial value to its owner, or that the discussions or incidents of those exciting times compelled the finishing of these library shelves according to the original plan.

These excitements and diversions brought out the full zeal and energy of a body of active members. Pride and ambition conspired to build up a love for the Society that has never been excelled. Greater literary ability has, no doubt, since been witnessed here, but no greater devotion to the cause. I will give two more illustrations, which are in the nature of valuable history, going to show this devotion. In the spring of 1861, in order to add to the library, we formed a literary club, which met at private houses. The gentlemen were required to pay an admittance fee of five dollars, either in such books as the library needed, taken on a valuation fixed by a committee, or in cash, while the ladies gave three dollars, upon the same terms and conditions. This society, or club, had no written constitution or by-laws. Its principal officer was called the "tycoon," and possessed absolute power. He was the constitution, limited by one single condition, which was, that at any time the club might, by a majority vote, depose this official and order the election of his successor. Prof. L. H. Potter was the first tycoon, and so admirably did he manage the club that no notice was ever given of a new election. The meetings of this society, all held at private residences, were, to my mind, the most delightful and valuable gatherings I ever attended. In addition to the social and literary advantages gained, our library received an addition of over one hundred much-needed volumes of just the books we desired, and but for the outbreak of the civil war, and the diversions and dispersions of the times, it is probable that the impulse then given to the growth of your library would have continued until the present time, and resulted in State appropriations in aid of the Society libraries, or in their growth and upbuilding by other means. It must be admitted that the Society libraries have come nearer being failures than is pleasant to the contemplation of the pioneers of the Normal.

Near the close of the spring term of 1861, while all our efforts were being given to class study, Society work, and to the library effort before mentioned, a few of the most active members were startled to learn that the Philadelphians, whom we had apparently so far surpassed, who were unable to inaugurate any library, or other successful Society movement, were in reality carrying out a magnificent scheme which would, at commencement, enable them to throw open their hall to the public, and far outshine the Wrightonians, by the exhibition of a new Brussels carpet. Had the earth opened beneath us we should have been no less surprised, but we were compelled to keep our knowledge secret, and make no comment beyond a trusted, limited circle. History is silent upon the manner of acquiring this knowledge. Our information, which proved to be correct, told us that the Philadelphians were raising a fund of over two hundred dollars, and had ordered a carpet to be delivered at the end of the term. Possibly our information may have been derived from that sex which is said to be weak in the matter of keeping secrets, as there were then a few instances where Wrightonians and Philadelpians of opposite sexes so far forgot their prejudices as to be almost, if not quite, of one mind towards each other, and in some such a manner information crossed the lines and entered the Wrightonian camp. We at once determined to buy a carpet, and to buy it more secretly than our rivals. By superhuman efforts, as it then appeared, the two hundred and twenty-five dollars required was pledged, and the carpet ordered from New York by telegraph, to be sent to Bloomington by express. The Philadelphian carpet was shipped by a freight line, and ours arrived first. The secret was so well kept that the first knowledge of our movement gained by the Philadelphians was when the dray arrived at our door with the carpet, and it is safe to assert that Normal experienced a flutter of excitement to which the first gun at Fort Sumter, then one of the events of the times, was a tame and inconsiderable matter. When it is considered that a majority of the members of both Societies were in ignorance of what had been transpiring, you will readily see that the movement, in an institution which then counted but one-third of its present number, must have been a severe financial strain upon the two Societies, and will perceive that this incident is a good illustration of the intense rivalry existing at that early day—a rivalry which I now believe was rather too sharp to be healthy and profitable.

Looking back, as I can, to the day when this Society began its existence, and being identified closely with its history through a little over three years; having seen it emerge from infancy to a vigorous childhood, and living nearly twenty years in your immediate vicinity, where I often hear of your progress and success, it is with pride and respect that I now behold your polished and finished maturity.   ——————   J. H. B.

The following is a list of the presidents of the Wrightonian Society, in the order in which they served:

1. P. R. Walker,
2. W. H. Avery,
3. J. H. Burnham,
4. T. J. Curtis,
5. D. W. Beadle,
6. J. H. Burnham,
7. L. D. Boyce,
8. P. R. Walker,
9. E. A. Gove,
10. D. G. Ingraham,
11. William H. Fuller,
12. John X. Wilson,
13. H. B. Norton,
14. J. H. Burnham,
15. E. A. Gove,
16. P. R. Walker,
17. J. L. Spaulding,
18. H. B. Norton,
19. Dr. J. A. Sewall,
20. L. B. Kellogg,
21. Albert Stetson,
22. W. Dennis Hall,
23. Thomas Metcalf,
24. John W. Cook,
25. T. J. Burrill,
26. L. B. Kellogg,
27. O. F. McKim,
28. T. J. Burrill,
29. Aaron Karr,
30. John W. Cook,
31. Albert Stetson,
32. J. A. Sewall,
33. James Stevenson,
34. Edward Dunn,
35. L. T. Regan,
36. S. Bogardus,
37. B. C. Allensworth,
38. James Stevenson,
39. B. C. Allensworth,
40. G. H. Kurtz,
41. W. H. Smith,
42. G. G. Manning,
43. Hugh Edwards,
44. J. W. Hays,
45. Lewis Goodrich,
46. E. A. Doolittle,
47. Lou C. Allen,*
48. R. A. Childs,
49. Benjamin Hunter,
50. Marie Kimberly,
51. Owen Scott,
52. R. M. Waterman,
53. Henry Holcomb,
54. Alice A. Chase,
55. Belle S. Houston,
56. E. R. E. Kimbrough,
57. D. C. Roberts,
58. Emma Monroe,
59. T. T. Thompson,
60. James Carter,
61. Minnie Cox,
62. Nellie Edwards,
63. L. C. Dougherty,
64. Sarah Littlefield,
65. James Ellis,
66. R. S. Barton,
67. J. N. Cushman,
68. S. B. Wadsworth,
69. J. P. Hodge,
70. Adam Hoffman,

* First lady president.

71. Emily Wing,
72. Adeline Goodrich,
73. E. R. Faulkner,
74. Leroy B. Wood,
75. Flora Fuller,
76. Agnes E. Ball,
77. George Franklin,
78. Edward Swett,
79. Edgar Wyatt,
80. Ida L. Philbrick,
81. Andrew W. Elder,
82. Theodore W. Peers,
83. Silas Y. Gillan,

84. S. B. Hursh,
85. E. R. Boyer,
86. John H. Lear,
87. Beth L. Ford,
88. James W. Adams,
89. Elmer E. Brown,
90. W. H. Bean,
91. Nathan T. Veatch,
92. Edwin E. Rosenberry,
93. John N. Wayman,
94. Wendell F. Puckett,
95. William H. Heath.

When the Society was first organized, debating was considered its principal object, and debates continued to be a leading feature of the programme for many years. The records show that the debates were generally upon questions of the day. These debates, especially during war time, were often very spirited. It was voted at one time to make Abraham Lincoln an honorary member of the Society. Then followed a motion to add Jeff. Davis to the number. This served only to provoke a spirited discussion, and was voted down.

It was customary, in the early days, to have a standing committee on debate, whose duty it was to announce at each meeting the subject for debate at the next meeting. The monotony of the more serious debates was broken by the introduction of those whose whole aim was fun. The following are illustrations:

"The difference I ne'er could see
'Twixt Tweedle Dum and Tweedle Dee."

Question: "*Resolved*, That the sentiment of the foregoing lines is calculated seriously to impair the morals of the community." Messrs. Stetson and Metcalf supporting the affirmative, and Messrs. Edwards and Sewall the negative. And again:

"*Resolved*, That the proposed transit of Venus is inexpedient, and should be postponed till the times are easier," in which Mr. Burrington sustained his argument by copious extracts from Cæsar's Commentaries, and Dr. Sewall had a black-board brought in, and illustrated his remarks by appropriate sketches—with his own hand.

Again, "*Resolved*, That the progress of the nineteenth century is the greatest humbug afloat."

The programmes of the two Societies present, at present, a much greater variety of exercises than in former days. What is said in the Philadelphian history in regard to the gradual growth of these exercises is applicable to Wrightonia as well.

The lecture seems to have occupied great prominence. In the records of 1870, we find accounts of eight lectures. While some of these lectures were obtained from abroad, most of them were given by members of the faculty.

One of the most important events of 1867 was the refurnishing of the hall. It sadly needed renovation. Lou C. Allen, H. R. Edwards, and B. C. Allensworth were chosen as a committee to fix up things. The funds were largely raised by subscription, quite a number of the members subscribing ten dollars each. Something over three hundred dollars was raised. With this sum and the proceeds of an exhibition, the work began. Thomas Atkins was employed to fresco the ceiling and walls. This was done after a new style, as shown in the house then occupied by Mr. Hawley, and in which Mr. Pennell now lives. Tommy was quite an artist in his way, a great favorite with the committee, and warranted his work to stay on as long as the plastering stuck. The chairs and chandeliers now in use were purchased at this time. The piano (not the same one now in the hall) was selected by Prof. Metcalf while on a visit east. There was a special committee selected to buy the piano, at the head of which was that accomplished musician and royal gentleman, I. F. Kleckner. The only time Mr. Metcalf was ever known to reprove any one for being polite was when Kleckner, in ordering the piano, began a telegram with the word "please." The hall was finally ready for reopening. The committee was satisfied, and so was everybody else. Of course the Philadelphians had to follow suit in the way of fixing up. The project of framing the photographs of the presidents was at this time conceived and carried out. About this time the craze for dramas struck the two Societies, and the "curtain" was about the only thing that would draw the crowd. About the last night of the winter term of 1867 witnessed the culmination of the aforesaid craze. The presidents of both Societies had a special programme, each putting forth his best efforts to get the audience. The curtain was joint property, and mysteriously disappeared until recess, when it was spread to the breeze in Wrightonian Hall. The president of Wrightonia went home a happy boy that night.

The halls were first heated by means of steam pipes. These, however, proved insufficient, and a great nuisance, and Ruttan ventilating stoves were substituted. The stove was sometimes unable to warm the hall. Instances are found of adjournments on account of the cold. In 1878, a joint committee presented the matter of heating the hall to the Board of Education, and the hot air ducts on the west side of the building were continued to the society halls, and two registers put in each hall.

The constitution of the Society has undergone constant change. Even as early as the year 1869 the original framers of the instrument would not have known it. The present constitution was adopted in September, 1877, but has since been amended. Among these amendments are those providing for an assistant treasurer and a news gleaner.

Among many topics that deserve more extended notices, are the following: The presentation of the present secretary's desk by Aaron Gove, in behalf of Simeon Wright, in March, 1870; the "Sumner" meeting in 1874; the contests between the high school and the Normal Departments, in which the high school pupils compared favorably with their opponents; the gradual increase of contest expenses, and the spelling-match between the two Societies in March, 1875.

On November 20, 1876, occurred the death of Simeon Wright, at his home in Kinmundy, Illinois. His body was taken to Rock Falls, where it was buried with Masonic rites. The following resolutions were adopted by the Society:

WHEREAS, It has pleased Divine Providence to remove, by death, the founder and devoted friend of the Wrightonian Society, Simeon Wright; therefore be it

Resolved, That in his death we recognize the loss of the beneficent father of this Society, one of the most energetic workers in the earlier educational efforts of Illinois, and one of the warmest friends of the Normal University.

Resolved, That his generous character, manifested, as it was, by hearty sympathy and material aid in our behalf, shall ever be cherished by the members of the Wrightonian Society, and that we tender his relatives our deepest sympathy.

Resolved, That as a token of respect to his memory, the Wrightonian Hall shall be draped in mourning during the present school term.

Resolved, That our secretary be instructed to forward a copy of these resolutions to the bereaved relatives of the deceased, and also a copy of the same to the *Educational Weekly*, for publication.

The following is from the pen of a graduate of 1861:

It was shortly after the formation of the "D and E" Society that Simeon Wright appeared amongst us. Most of us had heard of him, many had seen him. He had been an ardent worker in the interests of common schools of the State, had traveled and lectured in nearly every county,—a task in those days of no small magnitude,—and as agent of the State Teachers' Association had contributed more than had any other man toward the upbuilding of that sentiment that has since helped to make Illinois one of the first common school States in the Union. I have been told that his career as State agent is the only instance, in our educational history, where a lecturer was employed at the voluntary expense of the teachers of the community to travel and lecture in the interests of popular education. Uncle Sim, as we soon learned to term him, called our attention to the need of libraries connected with the Normal School, and early espoused the championship of the "D and E" Society. Being as he was a welcome visitor, and intimate in the advices of the school management, I have ever thought that this espousal of the "D and E" was but a part of the plan whereby the principal of the school should be the patron of the elder, while Uncle Sim could foster the interests of the younger. Be this as it may, he urged us to proceed at once to the establishment of a library, and made what were at that time munificent offers towards its foundation. Two large library cases stood at that time in the school room. One of these was set apart for the library and was soon well filled with books. The other was offered to the other Society for a similar purpose. Thus it was that Uncle Sim was the real founder of the Society libraries. The increase in members of the school increased the roll of the Societies. The older Society found it necessary to amend their constitution, and admit ladies to membership. The re-christening followed close upon these movements, and the names Wrightonian and Philadelphian were assumed. The latter, in the light of subsequent events, should have been named for the first principal of the school. Uncle Sim now again stepped to the front and volunteered to procure a charter for the Society from the Legislature. He argued that as some considerable property was likely to come into posession of the Society, the title should be safely vested. At that time we fondly hoped to be able to erect a separate building for Society hall, and while that consummation is yet in the future, perhaps the next quarter century may find such an enterprise completed.

The rebellion opened in the summer of 1861. We had been in the new building one season, when principal, part of the faculty, and a majority of the Society enlisted for three years. Uncle Sim went with us as quartermaster of the regiment. It was during these years of camp and campaign life that we learned more than ever before to love the man. Now those warm, affectionate traits of his character had full play in caring for the interests and comfort of his boys. No position, save perhaps that of surgeon, and even that except in an engagement was second, offered such opportunities as did that of quartermaster for doing good to that youthful and immature regiment of soldiers. To him they looked for food and clothing, for protection from the inclemencies of the weather and from the dangers of disease. Uncle Sim was a true hero in camp and on the march. No man ever asked from him in vain. His labors were unceasing and unselfish. When others were sleeping, he was planning for their comfort. Did a man break down on the march, Uncle Sim had an extra horse for him to ride. Did one fall sick, Uncle Sim found transportation to some comfortable hospital.

As I look back at those days, I remember him with the utmost admiration and thankfulness. After the war I lost intimate knowledge of him, but managed to see him at least once a year, the last time a few months before he died, at his farm near Kinmundy. He was the same Uncle Sim Wright, fond of talking of his dear young friends, and ever putting above all other things the Wrightonian Society, which he seemed to regard with especial favor. I was ready to learn, at his decease, that he had remembered it substantially even to his end.

Few men have lived the peer of Simeon Wright in true friendship. His faults, like those of the rest of us, were apparent, but covered so deep by his graces that the former can barely be discerned at this writing, and in a few years more will be lost forever.

Whatever his private personal griefs may have been, I have never known. That he bore a burden of sorrow, I believe we always thought, but he bore them alone. No man ever heard him complain. He seemed to live for others, never for himself, and successfully prevented his intimate friends from sharing whatever of his pain, in his moments of solitude, saddened his heart. It is good for us who have left your halls forever, to know that kindly hearts still beat, and kindly remembrances still exist, for one who, despite his faults, had one of the largest and warmest hearts, and whose true friends are scattered far and wide over the earth. No poor student ever appealed to Uncle Sim in vain. No case of deserved charity ever passed his door unheeded; his hand, heart and purse were always open to the deserving. His memory will ever live in the hearts especially of the class of 1861.

Whatever may be the career of the Illinois Normal School, whether fortune or mishap be met, so long as memory can relate one item of its life, the relation of Simeon Wright to it and its interests will be a salient feature.

At the request of one of the young members of the Society, I am glad to write these few words in testimony of my affection for him, and my regard for his memory.   AARON GOVE.

In December, 1876, the Wrightonians were elated, and the whole school surprised, by the announcement that the Society had received a legacy of one thousand dollars, through the liberality of its founder. In due time the officers of the Society were notified of the fact that the last will and testament of Mr. Wright contained a bequest, as above stated. A committee was appointed to take the matter in charge, and act in the matter for the Society, and for nearly two years, from term to term, a "committee on the Simeon Wright legacy" was regularly appointed. But after a great amount of correspondence with Mr. Grove Wright, brother of the deceased, and other parties, the Society found it impossible to realize any part of the legacy, the estate of the grantor having been considerably encumbered, and the will having been changed in regard to one of the legatees, by interlining, after it had been attested.

The correspondence on this subject made the members better acquainted with the early history of their Society, and the interest which Mr. Wright took in its prosperity during the first years of its existence. By invitation of Mr. G. Wright, a committee of the

Society furnished an epitaph for Simeon Wright's tomb. He is buried in a picturesque spot in the cemetery at Rock Falls, which is situated on a high point of land, overlooking the valley of Rock River with its beautiful scenery, for miles. The deed of the burying lot in which his remains rest, is held by the Society; and the gavel now in use in Wrightonian Hall was made from a branch of Siberian arbor vitæ which stands at the head of his grave.

At the close of the fall term of 1877, Andrew W. Elder was elected Wrightonian president, and Miss Jessie Dexter Philadelphian president. It was decided that the regular union meeting of the term should be postponed till after the holidays, and both Societies assembled in the Normal Hall, on the first Saturday evening of the next term. The programme was a good one, and the feeling between the Societies was only such as to promise a healthful emulation. There were no indications of the storm that closed the term on the memorable ides of March, 1878.

At a joint meeting of the Societies it was decided to hold a union meeting, Saturday evening, March 16, 1878, and that no admission fee should be charged. This was unsatisfactory to many leading Philadelphians, and a meeting was called to reconsider the question of admission fee. It was argued by Messrs. Powers, Laybourn, Bowles, and other Philadelphians, that such a proceeding was in violation of their Society's constitution, under the provisions of which they could not hold a free meeting. The Wrightonian constitution was free from any such restraining clause, and it was thought, even if it were not, such clause would be null and void so far as the union meeting was concerned, for neither constitution ought to limit the action or fix the liability of the other Society. They met in the president's room after school, and a hot contest ensued. Miss Dexter occupied the chair. A vote was taken and the Wrightonians seemed to be in the majority. Motions were made to suspend, to amend, to lay on the table; points of order were raised, till the president, despairing of any peaceable settlement of the questions, called Mr. Elder to the chair and suddenly left the room. This was a signal for a "bolt," and the Philadelphians all followed. The opposition having left the room, of course it was soon decided to sustain the action of the previous meeting. The following announcement of programme appeared in the Bloomington *Leader*, Friday afternoon, March 15: "The union meeting of the two Societies, next Saturday, promises to be the great event of the season. The lovers of good music will surely be entertained; and every one will be delighted with the exhibition of chemical experiments by Prof. Seymour. The admission is *free*, and every one is cordially invited. The meeting will be held in the grand hall, and will be the last society exercise of the term. The following exercises will be presented:

Music, Misses Bradshaw and Manning and Messrs. Peers and
Ong; essay, Miss Knight; oration, "Echoes," P. R. Cross;
gallopade, violin and cornet, Messrs. Ong and Lufkin; declamation,
L. S. Judd; vocal solo, Miss Bradshaw; comic debate: *Resolved*,
That congress should take immediate action to prevent the present
threatened attack of spring weather.   Affirmative, Silas Gillan and
Dode Peers.   Negative, "Stephie" and Jim Byrnes; violin solo,
Charles Gaston; declamation, J. W. Adams; humorous reading,
Elmer Brown; oration, "The Devil's Yard-sticks," Silas Y. Gillan;
song, "Carve Dat 'Possum," Colored Glee Club.   The entertain-
ment will close with some brilliant experiments with the oxyhy-
drogen blow-pipe, by Prof. Seymour.
————— —————, Philadelphian President.
A. W. ELDER, Wrightonian President.

The above blank is explained by the fact that the Philadelphian
president is among the number of bolters who propose to have a
little meeting all to themselves."

The union meeting was all, and even more, than its friends
expected.   The great hall was crowded, there being hardly standing
room for the "bolting faction," some of whom responded to a special
invitation to come out of the adjoining room and witness "the
brilliant experiments with the oxyhydrogen blow-pipe," which, by
the way, amounted to nothing, for the blow-pipe was out of fix.
The following is taken from the autograph album of a loyal
Wrightonian of that day:

> Let " brotherly love " be thy motto,
>   Wrightonian decisions thy guide;
> And whether in mansion or grotto,
>   Refer to the " Union " with pride.
>
> In society rules so potential,
>   In joint rules, so easily spurned,
> Isn't there yet a "cream " (confidential)
>   That *bolters* will bring when well churned?
>
> Remember, in *flame* there's attraction,
>   In *gas* there's a wonderful "draw;"
> And, by these, one may wheedle a faction,
>   That openly sneers at a law.

March 20, 1878.   Yours in friendship,   JAMES BYRNES.

Among the traditions of the Society, is one to the effect that,
years ago, there was a regular publication conducted by "the boys,"
which was called *The Ventilator;* that it was vigorous and sprightly
and gradually grew so spicy that it burned itself out, and died for
want of editors brave enough to handle it.   However this may be,
certain it is that in 1877 some of the boys undertook to revive this
real or mythical publication; but the undertaking was not crowned
with perennial success.   Nothing of a startling character had occurred
in the field of journalism among the students since the phenomenal

event that marked the close of the centennial year, and the monotony began to be oppressive; besides, the boys concluded that there were a few things that needed regulating. Accordingly, a half-dozen of them set about the preparation of the "Great Illustrated Monthly, *The Ventilator*."

On the evening appointed for the reading of the "periodical," the Wrightonian Hall was crowded to its full seating capacity. A number of visitors from abroad, several members of the faculty, and many citizens of the town were in the audience. The editors were introduced after recess, and proceeded to unroll five or six yards of manuscript in one continuous scroll. As they read from one side of the paper, the crayon sketch illustrations were displayed on the other. Of the special points of excellence which characterized the paper, it is not necessary here to speak; suffice it to say that it contained some features of such unusual interest and merit that the boys received an invitation to read it entire the next Monday morning in the reception room to a select audience, consisting of the members of the faculty. After receiving this high and well-deserved attention, the editors were requested to file the original copies of the contributions and the names of the writers;* and, as a further token of the regard in which the faculty held them, the boys were granted a vacation for an indefinite time, which, however, was terminated at the end of one week, and Society matters once more flowed on in their accustomed channel. Yet, strange to relate, until this day no one has seen another copy of *The Ventilator*.

In the fall term of 1878, a certain lawyer of Normal, one Newton B. Reed, sent a bill of two dollars and twenty cents to E. R. Boyer, chairman of the finance committee, claiming that the amount was due from the Society to a certain grocer who had recently become insolvent and left the State. Mr. Boyer asked for an itemized statement, but this was peremptorily refused, immediate payment demanded, and a law suit threatened. After consultation with the other members of the finance committee and the officers of the Society, it was decided to "let him sue." Accordingly, Mr. Reed was duly informed that if he could show the bill to be a just debt, he could get his money by presenting the claim in a regular manner, otherwise not. A few days later, summonses were issued for E. R. Boyer, chairman of the finance committee, Silas Y. Gillan, president, and Miss Lizzie Ross, secretary, to appear in Bloomington. By unanimous vote of the Society, Mr. Gillan was appointed to take charge of the matter. A change of venue was taken to Judge Lawrence's court. The case was duly heard, and argued at some length by both sides, the Society's representatives claiming that the

*One of them, "Stevy's" article, remained among the archives of the University about two years.

bill could not be legally collected until regularly presented. Mr. Reed claimed to have an order on the society treasurer for the amount, signed by a former president, but up to the time of the trial he had failed to produce it. Mr. Gillan argued that if that were true, then the bill was already paid, the order having been accepted, and that as soon as such order should be presented to the treasurer it would be honored; but since Mr. Reed made no claim of ever having presented the order, it could not be held that the Society had refused payment, and that it must be presented before suit could be brought. Legal authority was quoted in favor of this opinion. Judge Lawrence postponed his decision for a few days to consult authorities. On the following Saturday he rendered a decision sustaining the points taken by the Society, and entering judgment for costs of trial against the party in whose name Mr. Reed had brought suit. There was, of course, universal rejoicing among the Wrightonians when the result was announced. They had undertaken the fight "for the principle involved," because they felt that Mr. Reed had been haughty and imperious, and that tamely to go to him to pay an order which had been accepted and never presented for payment, would be acceding to an unjust demand. This exultation was short-lived, however, for Mr. Reed appealed the case to the Circuit Court, and it came up during the winter term following. Mr. S. B. Hursh was then president, and Mr. Gillan was made chairman of the finance committee, with instructions from the other officers of the Society, sanctioned by a unanimous vote of the members, to take charge of the case, as before. On the day fixed for hearing the case, Messrs. Hursh, East, and Gillan, appeared for the Society, and owing to "the law's delay," had to wait three days before it was called. Mr. Reed, probably not caring to appear in so dignified a court with school boys for opponents, engaged another attorney to conduct his case. This time a jury trial was had. The jury did not agree on a verdict until near noon the next day, when they reported a decision adverse to the Society. The costs in the case amounted to about forty dollars.

Previous to May, 1877, the Society obtained funds by means of dues, which were one dollar per term. This fund they supplemented, when necessary, by a tax upon the members. No admission fee was charged at their meetings. By means of lectures and festivals, they raised money to make many great improvements. The amounts netted at these lectures and festivals show that they were well patronized. The committee on a union supper in 1875, reported the net proceeds to be one hundred and fifty-one dollars and ninety cents.

Wrightonia's enterprise in pushing forward such schemes was well illustrated in the management of an ice cream and strawberry festival in June, 1876. The evening proved stormy and cold, but nothing daunted by the weather, they secured a large attendance. Fires were put in all the stoves, and the temperature of the room was made such as to induce all to become patrons. The net proceeds were seventy dollars.

To prevent disorder, naturally resulting from free admission, as well as to provide an easy method of raising funds, the present ticket system was adopted. In the following resolution introduced by Silas Y. Gillan, and passed by the Wrightonian Society, in May, 1877, are embodied the principal features of the system:

WHEREAS, The current expenses of the Society are greater than can be met by the usual receipts; be it

Resolved, That the following measures be adopted:

1. The treasurer shall give to each Wrightonian who has signed the constitution and paid his dues for the current term, a ticket which shall entitle him to admission to all sessions of the Society during the present term.

2. Philadelphians who possess like credentials from that Society shall be admitted to any session of this Society, provided that the Philadelphian Society grants the same privileges to persons possessing tickets from this Society.

3. The president and chorister shall have power to give complimentary tickets, which shall admit the persons receiving them to one session of the Society.

4. Persons not possessing tickets of the above description shall be admitted on the payment of ten cents an evening.

5. It shall be the duty of the janitor to collect the admission fee from all persons who enter this hall, from whom said fee is due.

6. These measures shall be enforced after one week from adoption.

The term dues now are fifty cents, and these receipts of the Society are generally sufficient to meet all demands. During one term of the past year Wrightonia's membership was one hundred and forty, so that, notwithstanding the extensive improvements made during the past two years, the Society's finances are in good condition.

The society fight, of the fall of 1880, began with the discovery of some things that looked to Wrightonian eyes like irregularities in the selling of tickets by the Philadelphians. Season tickets admitted the holders to all regular meetings of both Societies during the term, and entitled them to a participation in society affairs. These tickets bore the following inscription:

1880.   I. S. N. U.   1880.
MEMBERSHIP TICKET
PHILADELPHIAN AND WRIGHTONIAN
SOCIETIES.
Fall Term.   Dues, 50c.

Persons not members of the school, and consequently not members of either Society, began to present these membership tickets for admission at the Wrightonian door. The doorkeeper reported to the Society officers, and a private investigation began. E. E. Brown was Society president. The pith of the whole affair was found in Article XIII, of the Philadelphian constitution, the first sentence of which read as follows: "All persons except members in full of either the Philadelphian or the Wrightonian Society, shall pay an admission fee of ten (10) cents to each regular meeting of the Society; except that upon payment of fifty (50) cents a ticket of admission shall be given, with the name of the person purchasing the same written thereon, and admitting said person to all meetings of either the Philadelphian or the Wrightonian Society (contest excepted), for the term during which the same may be purchased. In other words, the Philadelphian constitution provided that the "Wrights" should admit to all of their meetings, public and private, *any* person who should favor the "Phils" to the extent of fifty cents.

A joint meeting was held in room twenty-four, October 5. After the regular business of the meeting had been disposed of, a Wrightonian got the floor, spoke of the discovery, gave in a sentence or two a mild statement of his opinion about that Article XIII, and referred to the need of immediate action. A joint committee was appointed to examine and report on the subject. This committee, consisting of three from each Society, failed to agree. Another joint meeting was held, to which Wrightonian members went *en masse*. The committee gave two reports: the Wrightonian to the effect that the clause in the Philadelphian constitution must be repealed as a necessary condition of further joint action on the ticket question; the Philadelphian to the effect that the clause was justifiable. A certain Wrightonian moved the adoption of the Wrightonian report, which was followed by a spirited debate and a motion to adjourn. The Philadelphians found themselves in the minority on the vote to adjourn, and most of them left the room. They bolted. The Wrightonian report was shortly afterward adopted. Some of the Philadelphians complained that there had been trickery, in that they had not had due notice of the meeting. In reply they were told that their president had a hand in calling the meeting.

Many of the Philadelphians began to acknowledge the unreasonableness of Article XIII, but the majority seemed disposed to retain it, for fear its repeal would look like humiliating submission. The latter feeling lost influence, and near the close of the term, a committee from each Society framed a joint rule on the question, and Article XIII, of the Philadelphian constitution, was repealed.

The idea of uniting the two libraries was talked of in September, 1880. A Wrightonian urged the union of the two Society libraries with the University library, the setting apart of some convenient room, and the appointment, by the Board of Education, of a librarian. It was a part of the plan to make this librarian a salaried officer,—on duty one-half of each day,—and that the positions of librarian and university stationer be made *scholarships*, to be assigned to those of highest rank in certain work, and given to those only who intended finishing the course. This plan was presented to the Board, but at that time did not meet their approval.

In the spring term of 1880, the Society began a series of improvements which it has continued to the present time. During this time there have been purchased, curtains, at a cost of eighty-two dollars; a piano for two hundred and sixty dollars (the old piano, valued at one hundred and twenty-five dollars, being part payment); a new frame for Simeon Wright's picture, for thirteen dollars and fifty cents; a president's chair, for twenty-four dollars and fifty cents; a secretary's chair, for eighteen dollars and fifty cents; a president's table, for ten dollars; a critic's table, for eighteen dollars, and a chandelier, for twelve dollars. The hall has been repainted at a cost of seventy-five dollars, and the disabled chairs repaired for twenty-five dollars, making an aggregate outlay for the two years of five hundred and forty-two dollars. When it is remembered that this amount does not include the "running expenses" nor the cost of minor improvements, such as the covering of the books in the library, the rebinding of some of them, the hanging of curtains in the library windows, and others, it will be seen how ample are Wrightonia's resources. Composed of energetic and loyal members, she has but to see a want to have it supplied. For nearly a quarter of a century she has spread her banner to the breeze and a loyal band of heroes has ever been found gathered under it. Her triumphs have been many and well-earned. At times has come the chagrin of defeat, but the remembrance of the victories has kept away depression. Her growth has kept pace with favoring circumstances. Starting with but a score of workers, she has enrolled, through the years, three thousand, and boasts of a term-membership of nearly two hundred. Her library has been enlarged and her hall beautified. With new chandeliers and carpet, the probable improvements of the coming year, Wrightonian Hall will surpass in beauty any other in our State. This year, 1882-3, the quarter centennial of the Society's existence should be marked by such improvements.

INTER-SOCIETY CONTESTS.

1858. Debate: "*Resolved*, That compulsory attendance is beneficial." Affirmative, Peter Harper, J. T. Ridlon, Philadelphians; negative, P. R. Walker, J. H. Burnham, Wrightonians. In addition to the debate, there were on the programme, papers and music. The debate, however, was the only point contested and decided by judges. The debate was won by the Wrightonians. This contest was held in July. The time was changed the next year to December.

1859. Debate: "*Resolved*, That public opinion ought to restrict a teacher from expressing his political sentiments freely on public occasions." Affirmative, P. R. Walker and D. G. Ingraham, Wrightonians; negative, Howell and Little, Philadelphians. Misses Town and Clark read the *Oleastellus*, and Misses Washburn and Peterson, the *Ladies' Garland*. The judges awarded both debate and paper to the Wrightonians.

1860. Debate: "*Resolved*, That manual-labor schools are founded on correct principles, and are practicable." Affirmative, H. B. Norton and I. B. Kellogg, Wrightonians; negative, Edwin Waite and A. B. Keagle, Philadelphians. *The Ladies' Garland* was read by Misses Sprague and Whiteside; the *Oleastellus* by Misses Curtis and Baker. The judges awarded the debate to the Wrightonians, the paper to the Philadelphians. In this, as in previous contests, the literary exercises were interspersed with pieces of music, but the latter formed no part of the contest.

1861. No contest.

1862. Debate: "*Resolved*, That the labors of Pestalozzi in the educational field have been of more value to mankind than those of Horace Mann." Affirmative, L. Kellogg and A. McClure, Wrightonians; negative, E. F. Bacon and J. H. Thompson, Philadelphians. Wrightonian vocal music, a quartette by Misses McCambridge and Jones, and Messrs Hill and J. W. Cook. The Philadelphians presented a quartette. Sarah Stevenson and Mattie Burrill read the *Ladies' Garland*; Mary A. Fuller and L. A. Stevens, the *Oleastellus*. The judges awarded to the Wrightonians, the debate and vocal music; to the Philadelphians, the paper. Here we first notice music making a point in the contest. Owing to the absence of fixed rules, governing these contests, it was customary to agree to rules just before contest time. This often produced ill feelings. Here is a resolution adopted by the Wrightonians in November, 1860, which shows the lack of fixed rules: "The Wrightonian Society shall consider it their privilege to object to any judge appointed by the Philadelphians to serve at coming contest-meeting." It is worthy of note, too, that the above is the first "contest-meeting," the others being recorded as "joint" meetings.

1863. A disagreement and no contest.

1864. Debate: "*Resolved*, That Thomas Jefferson should be ranked higher as a statesman than William Pitt." Affirmative, F. J. Seybold and H. L. Karr, Philadelphians; negative, A. G. Karr and J. W. Cook, Wrightonians. Each Society furnished a quartette. The *Oleastellus* was read by Misses M. Little and M. R. Gorton; the *Ladies' Garland* by Misses B. Wakefield and E. A. Pratt. The Wrightonians won the debate; the Philadelphians, the paper and vocal music.

1865. No contest. A failure to agree upon a programme.

1866. Debate: "Ought the election franchise to be restricted to such persons as can read and write understandingly?" Affirmative, James S. Stevenson, Lewis Goodrich, Wrightonians; negative, Gifford S. Robinson, John R. Edwards, Philadelphians. Instrumental music, Lill Pearson, Philadelphian; Mary R. Gorton, Wrightonian. The *Ladies' Garland* was read by Mrs. Janette E. Gorham and Miss Annie M. Edwards; the *Oleastellus*, by Emma T. Robinson and Cora Valentine. Philadelphian trio, Myra G. Overman, Eurania Gorton, and Laura Fulwiler; Wrightonian quartette, Misses Moss and Howard, Messrs. Kleckner and Goodrich. The Wrightonians won the paper, vocal music, and instrumental music. The Philadelphians won the debate.

1867. Debate: "Should the congress of the United States regulate suffrage in the States?" Affirmative, Ben C. Allensworth and George G. Manning, Wrightonians. Negative, Loring A. Chase and Charles H. Fiske, Philadelpians. Instrumental music, Kate Anderson, Philadelphian; Fannie Smith, Wrightonian. Misses Barker and Nellie Galusha read the *Ladies' Garland;* Misses Benton and Lou C. Allen the *Oleastellus*. The Philadelphian vocal music, a duet, by Minnie Boyden and Julia M. Rider; the Wrightonian, a quartette, by Messrs. Kleckner, Waterman, Smith, and Manning. The judges awarded the paper to the Wrightonians, the debate and music to the Philadelphians.

1868. Debate: "*Resolved*, That Maximilian's career in connection with Mexican affairs shows that he possessed a noble character as a man and high abilities as a statesman." Affirmative, R. Arthur Edwards and W. C. Griffith, Philadelphians; negative, W. G. Myer and Ben. Hunter, Wrightonians. Instrumental duets, Jennie Roe and Marian New, Wrightonians; Fannie Smith and Onie Rawlings, Philadelphians. Mary C. Owen and Flora Pennell read the *Ladies' Garland;* Mary L. Kimbell and Clara D. Burns, the *Oleastellus*. Vocal music, quartettes. The paper and vocal music were awarded to the Philadelphians; debate and instrumental music to the Wrightonians.

1869. The debate was on the subject of "Free Trade."
Affirmative, H. F. Holcomb and John W. Gibson, Wrightonians;
negative, B. W. Baker and S. Kimlin, Philadelphians. The
instrumental music consisted of two duets: Wrightonians, Misses
E. Kingsley and Fannie Thomas, piano; Philidelphians, Messrs. J.
M. Trimble and T. A. H. Norman, violins. The *Oleastellus*, Alice
C. Chase and Isabel S. Houston. The *Ladies' Garland*, Alice
Emmons and Dell Cook. Vocal music: Wrightonian, a trio by
Misses G. Dietrich and F. Smith, and Mr. J. Miner; Philadelphian,
a solo by Mary Hawley. The oration for the Wrightonians was
omitted on account of the sickness of their orator, W. H. Smith.
The Philadelphian oration was delivered by R. A. Edwards.

The victory in the debate, vocal and instrumental music, was
awarded to the Wrightonians. The paper was awarded to the
Philadelphians. It is probably worthy of note, that the debaters
submitted the question for debate to the Society, instead of deciding
it themselves.

1870. Debate: "*Resolved*, That the United States should at
once pass a Free Banking Law; and that the banks established under
this law should be compelled to redeem their notes in specie."
Affirmative, Arthur C. Butler, Edmund J. James, Philadelphians;
negative, R. Morris Waterman, Samuel W. Paisley, Wrightonians.
Instrumental music, Philadelphian, Mrs. Lillie Moffatt; Wrightonian,
Josephine Mosley. The *Ladies' Garland* was read by Louise Ray
and Lottie C. Blake; the *Oleastellus* by Onie Rawlings and Lida T.
Howland. The vocal music consisted of two duets; Mrs. Lillie
Moffatt and Mary G. Eldridge for the Philadelphians, and Alice B.
Ford, and Flora D. Brown for the Wrightonians. W. C. Griffith
was the Philadelphian orator, and Henry F. Holcomb the
Wrightonian.

The Philadelphians gained the debate, instrumental music,
paper and oration; the Wrightonians, the vocal music. A day or
two before this contest, the Philadelphians told the judge appointed
by them that the other judges would make a great difference in their
marks, consequently that he should do the same. This judge marked
the Philadelphian debate 10, the Wrightonian 5; the Philadelphian
paper 10, the Wrightonian 5, and so on, thus making the general
average of the three judges, which up to this time decided the
contest in favor of the Philadelphians, who, otherwise, would have
been defeated. Before the next contest the rule was changed, so that
one judge could not out-mark the other two.

1871. Debate: "Is the policy of making land grants by general
government, in aid of railroads, a wise one?" Affirmative, James
Hovey and George Blount, Philadelphians; negative, J. M. Wilson
and J. E. Lamb, Wrightonians. The instrumental music was given
by Miss Roop, Wrightonian, and Miss Ware, Philadelphian. The

Oleastellus was read by Misses Franklin and Monroe; the *Ladies' Garland* by Misses Gaston and Karr. Miss Mary Stroud sang for the Wrightonians; Misses Compton and Town, and Mr. F. W. Conrad sang for the Philadelphians.

The Wrightonians won the debate and vocal music; the Philadelphians won the instrumental music and the paper. Shortly before the contest the Philadelphian orator was suspended, and the Wrightonian orator, through courtesy to the Philadelphians, refused to give his exercise.

1872. Debate: *"Resolved,* That it would not be wise for the State of Illinois to pass a law compelling all persons between the ages of seven and sixteen years, not otherwise well instructed, to attend school for at least four months each year, or for an equivalent amount of time.'' Affirmative, J. Dickey Templeton and Felix B. Tait, Philadelphians; negative, DeWitt C. Roberts and E. R. E. Kimbrough, Wrightonians. Libbie Peers, Philadelphian, and Anna Hughes, Wrightonian, were the contestants in instrumental music. The *Ladies' Garland* was read by Amelia H. Kellogg and Mary Hawley. The *Oleastellus* was read by Nellie S. Edwards and Emma V. Stewart. Each Society furnished a quartette for its number of vocal music. Walter C. Lockwood was the Philadelphian orator, and J. W. Smith, the Wrightonian.

The Philadelphian Society won the instrumental music, and the Wrightonians the debate, the paper, the vocal music, and the oration.

1873. The debate was on the question of the general government taking control of the telegraph lines. The Wrightonian disputants were R. S. Barton and E. R. Faulkner, affirmative; the Philadelphian, I. Eddy Brown and J. N. Wilkinson, negative. The contestants in instrumental music were Helen Stone, Wrightonian; Lula Brown Philadelphian. The *Oleastellus* was read by Misses Pace and Judd. Misses Morgan and Lillian DeGarmo read the *Ladies' Garland.* Julia Codding sang for the Wrightonians; Ida L. Aldridge for the Philadelphians. Mr. Cushman was the Wrightonian orator, and Mr. Conrad the orator of the Philadelphians.

The Wrightonians were successful in debate, paper and vocal music. The Philadelphians won the instrumental music and oration.

1874. Debate: *"Resolved,* That the bill known as the Civil Rights Bill, recently passed by the Senate of the United States, should become the law of the land.'' Affirmative, J. S. Shearer and S. B. Wadsworth; negative, A. D. Beckhart and C. O. Drayton. Miss M. M. Butterfield played for the Philadelphians, and Fanny Wright for the Wrightonians. Anna B. Simmes and Mary L. Bass edited the Philadelphian paper, and Hattie Smith and Agnes E. Ball, the Wrightonian paper. Lillian E. Hanford was the Philadelphian vocalist, and Lydia H. Clark, the Wrightonian vocalist. The orator of the Philadelphians was Charles McMurry; for the Wrightonians, R. L. Barton.

The Philadelphians were successful in debate, oration, and vocal music; the Wrightonians, in paper and instrumental music.

1875. Debate: "*Resolved*, That the law of Congress directing the resumption of Specie Payment in 1879, in that particular, is injurious to the best interests of the country." Affirmative, S. B. Wood and W. W. Brittain, Wrightonians; negative, Stephen L. Spear and DeWitt C. Tyler, Philadelphians. Instrumental music for the Wrightonians: a duet by Lilly Brown and Anna Pierce; for the Philadelphians: a solo by Amelia Stahl. The *Oleastellus* was read by Emma Corbett and Julia P. Codding; the *Ladies' Garland* by Mary C. Edwards and Jessie P. Codding. Adelaine Goodrich was the Wrightonian vocalist; Miss L. E. Sanders, Philadelphian vocalist. S. B. Hursh and C. Guy Laybourn were the orators of the Wrightonian and Philadelphian Societies respectively.

The Wrightonians won the instrumental and vocal music, and the oration. The Philadelphians won the debate and paper.

1876. Debate: "*Resolved*, That Chinese immigration to the United States should be prohibited by Congress." Affirmative, Silas Y. Gillan, C. W. Stevenson, Wrightonians; negative, George L. Hoffman, William C. Picking, Philadelphians. Edward R. Humphries was the Philadelphian instrumentalist; Clarence T. Hardin the Wrightonian. Mary Torrence and Mary A. Anderson edited the *Ladies' Garland*, Emily Wing and Frances M. Kosier the *Oleastellus*. Lillian S. Chapman sang for the Philadelphians; May Ross for the Wrightonians. Willis C. Glidden gave the Philadelphian, and Edward R. Swett, the Wrightonian oration.

The Philadelphians received the favorable decision of the judges on debate, and instrumental music; the Wrightonians on paper, vocal music and oration.

1877. Debate: "*Resolved*, That the United States Government should abolish all Protective Tariff." Affirmative, C. Guy Laybourn and John T. Bowles, Philadelphians; negative, Andrew W. Elder and William McCutcheon, Wrightonians. Instrumental music, Wrightonian, May Ross; Philadelphian, Lillian Peers. The *Oleastellus*, Flora Fuller and Mina C. Smith. The *Ladies' Garland* by Helen L. Wyckoff and Jessie Dexter. Vocal music, Alice C. Bradshaw, Wrightonian; Hattie J. Burgess, Philadelphian. Silas Y. Gillan was the Wrightonian orator, Horace E. Powers the Philadelphian orator.

The Wrightonians gained the debate, vocal music, and oration; the Philadelphians gained the paper and instrumental music.

1878. Debate: "*Resolved*, That the National Banking system should be abolished." Affirmative, Horace E. Powers and Carlton E. Webster, Philadelphians; negative, Samuel B. Hursh, John H.

Tear, Wrightonians. The contestants in instrumental music were Minnie G. Adams, Philadelphian; Hattie O. Hayward, Wrightonian. The *Ladies' Garland* was read by Lettie J. Smiley and Lou M. Allen; the *Oleastellus*, by Emily A. Sherman and Daisy A. Hubbard. Mary L. Criswell, Philadelphian, and Anna Lou Fisher, Wrightonian, were the vocalists. The Philadelphian orator was John Humphrey; the Wrightonian, Frank B. Harcourt.

The favorable decision of the judges was given to the Philadelphians on debate and instrumental music; to the Wrightonians, on paper, vocal music, and oration.

1879. Debate: "*Resolved,* That General Grant should not be elected president of the United States in 1880." Affirmative, Wm. II. Chamberlain and Austin C. Rishel, Philadelphians, and Rudolph Reeder and James. W. Adams, Wrightonians. The contestants in instrumental music were Charles D. Lufkin, Wrightonian, and David A. Hill, Philadelphian. The *Ladies' Garland* was read by Lida Kelly and Elizabeth Glanville; the *Oleastellus*, by Beth Ford and May Hewett. Emma Bookwalter was the Wrightonian vocalist, and Lizzie K. Harned, the Philadelphian. The orations were delivered by John H. Tear, Wrightonian, and Jesse F. Hannah, Philadelphian.

The favorable decision of the judges was given to the Philadelphians on debate, instrumental music, vocal music, and oration, and to the Wrightonians, on paper.

1880. Debate: "*Resolved,* That the United States should, in its tariff legislation, adopt the principle, 'A tariff for revenue only.'" Affirmative, David W. Reid, George Howell, Philadelphians; negative, Elmer E. Brown, James V. McHugh, Wrightonians. Instrumental solos, Minnie B. Potter, Philadelphian; Myrtie M. Freeman, Wrightonian. The *Oleastellus* was read by Jessie M. DeBerard and Addie Gillan; the *Ladies' Garland* by Lizzie P. Swan and Caroline A. Humphrey. Mattie L. Beatty, Philadelphian, and Margareth Dalrymple, Wrightonian, were the vocalists. James B. Estee was the Philadelphian orator, and William H. Bean, the Wrightonian.

The judges awarded to the Philadelphians the debate, instrumental music and oration; to the Wrightonians, the paper and vocal music.

1881. Debate: "*Resolved,* That the Irish people ought to accept the land bill as a solution of the Irish land question." Affirmative, Frank L. Williams and Murray M. Morrison, Philadelphians; negative, Walter J. Watts, and John H. Fleming, Wrightonians. Instrumental solos, Lida A. Kelly, Philadelphian, and Sadie A. Noleman, Wrightonian. The *Oleastellus*, Harriet Scott and Malvina V. Hodgman. The *Ladies' Garland*, May 'M. Parsons and Marie C. Anderson. Vocalists, Jessie A. Buckman, Wrightonian, and Lydia M. Reed, Philadelphian. Orations, Wm. D. Edmunds, Wrightonian, and George Howell, Philadelphian.

The judges awarded the Philadelphians the oration, paper, and instrumental music; the Wrightonians, the debate and vocal music.

INTER-NORMAL CONTESTS.

Some time in the latter part of the fall term of 1878, a certain student of the Illinois State Normal University suggested to a few of the leading society workers among his school-mates, the propriety of inaugurating annual contests between the students of the Illinois State Normal University and those of the Southern Illinois Normal University. The suggestion met with universal approbation, and when President Hewett was spoken to about the matter, he readily gave his consent, and approved the plan proposed.

Accordingly, on December 3, a meeting of all students interested in literary work was held in Normal Hall, to discuss the project. William C. Ramsey was made chairman, and Horace E. Powers stated the object of the meeting. On motion, a committee of five was appointed to send a challenge to the students of the Southern Normal. As such committee, the chairman named Silas Y. Gillan, Horace E. Powers, S. B. Hursh, Emily Sherman and Jennie L. Wood.

On December 4, the challenge was sent. The subsequent history of the contests may be gathered from the following:

NORMAL, ILLINOIS, December 4, 1878.
The students of the Illinois State Normal University, to those of the Southern Illinois Normal University, greeting:

Recognizing the importance of the culture to be derived from what is known as literary work, and wishing to add a stimulus to such work in the two Normal Schools of Illinois; believing that both of said schools will be benefited by a better acquaintance with each other; and on account of our relative stand as Normal Schools, being debarred from participation in the Inter-Collegiate contests, in a spirit of friendship, and not of rivalry, we hereby send you a challenge for a literary contest, to take place during the school week ending March 14, 1879, or as near that time as practicable; said contest to consist of a debate to be participated in by two representatives from each school, an oration, an essay, a piece of vocal music, and a piece of instrumental music from each school.

We further suggest the following conditions, subject to your ratification:

1. That the contestants shall be *bona fide* pupils of the schools they represent.

2. That the place of holding the contest be Normal or Carbondale (to be decided by mutual agreement hereafter).

3. That the time allowed for each exercise be as follows: Leaders on debate, fifteen minutes each for opening, and ten minutes each for closing; assistants on debate, twelve minutes each; orations and essays, twelve minutes each.

4. That to the contest meeting an admission fee be charged sufficient to defray expenses, including the traveling expenses of the contestants and judges.

5. That the decision as to the merits of the exercises be left to a board of three judges, one to be appointed by the State Superintendent, and one by each of the presidents of the two Normal Schools.

6. That the persons who participate in the first contest be a committee to draft a code of regulations for a similar contest annually.   COMMITTEE.

CARBONDALE, ILLINOIS, December 7, 1878.
The students represented by the two Societies of the Southern
Illinois Normal University, to those of the Illinois State
Normal University, greeting:

Realizing. equally with you the importance of literary contests, and recognizing the fact that such contests are never without beneficial results, we accept your challenge for a contest to take place during the school week ending March 14, 1879, or as near that time as may be practicable, with the following modifications:

That instead of four debaters, there be only two; and that the debate be limited to fifty minutes, the two opening speeches to be fifteen minutes each, and the two closing ten minutes each, and in place of the two other debaters, there be two declaimers, one from each school, each declamation not to exceed ten minutes; and that the programme consist of an oration, an essay, a declamation, a debate, one piece of instrumental music, and one piece of vocal music.

We propose this modification because it will afford a better representation of society work. Being the challenged party, we insist that the contest be held at Carbondale.

A. E. PARKINSON,
H. A. KIMMELL,
DORA A. LIPE,
A. C. BURNETT,
S. H. NORMAN,
W. E. MANN,
Committee.

NORMAL, ILLINOIS, December 10, 1878.
A. E. PARKINSON AND H. A. KIMMELL, Chairmen 'of Contest Committees, Carbondale, Illinois.

Gentlemen: Your communication is received. We accept the modification as to adding a declamation; but we think you will agree with us that it is better to have four speakers on debate; not only because such is the customary plan in society work, but also because such an arrangement making seven points, will obviate the possibility of a tie in the result. You will readily see that counting seventy-five minutes for debate, twenty-four for essays, twenty-four for orations, twenty for declamations, thirty for music, and ten for recess, the evening's entertainment will not exceed three hours in length.

We shall probably elect our contestants soon, and then they will take the place of our committee in making permanent arrangements for an annual contest between the two schools. In the meantime, however, we suggest the following: ·

That, of the proceeds of the contest each year, whatever remains over and above the expenses be divided equally between the literary societies of the school at which the contest is held; and in case the proceeds fail to pay the traveling expenses of the judges and contestants, the deficit be made up by the students of the school at which the contest is held. Such a plan will be an incentive to the students at which the contest is held to "work up" the matter by advertising, etc. Of course, this is on the presumption that when once inaugurated, the contests will be held alternately at Carbondale and Normal.

It will probably be necessary to have two boards of judges—one for music, and one for the literary work. Probably each year two of the judges can be selected from the residents at which the contest is held, thus necessitating the traveling expenses of but four judges and seven contestants, so that the necessary expenses each year, including advertising and the printing of programmes, will probably not exceed one hundred and twenty-five dollars. We feel confident that, with judicious management, an audience of five hundred, or more, can be secured for such an entertainment.

In respect to the question for debate, our rule here, in the annual contests between the two literary societies, is that the challenging party selects the question, and the other takes choice of sides, within a week after receiving the question. This rule has always been found satisfactory with us, and we suggest the propriety of adopting a similar plan.   Very respectfully,

SILAS Y. GILLAN,
Chairman of Contest Committee.

CARBONDALE, ILLINOIS, December 12, 1878.
MR. SILAS Y. GILLAN, Chairman of Contest Committee, Normal, Illinois.

Dear Sir: Your communication is at hand. Committee met and decided as follows:

1. That we insist upon only one debater from each school, for these reasons: (*a*) With four debaters, the exercises would be four hours long, exclusive of the time occupied in changing, which, at the

lowest estimate, would be thirty minutes. (*b*) In your first proposition, you implied six points, and in our reply, we implied the same number. We insist that the first proposition, as accepted, stand.

2. That we insist upon only *one* board of judges, for the reasons: (*a*) If the judges appointed are capable of judging the literary exercises, they will be capable of judging the music. (*b*) The probabilities are that the attendance will not be sufficient to defray so much expense.

The other propositions you make, in regard to expenses, choosing your question, etc., are agreed to. As soon as our contestants are elected, they will be the committee on further arrangements. Please let us know the question for debate as soon as decided upon.

Very respectfully,

ARTHUR E. PARKINSON,
Chairman of Contest Committee.

NORMAL, ILLINOIS, December 16, 1878.

MR. ARTHUR E. PARKINSON, Chairman Contest Committee, Carbondale, Illinois.

Dear Sir: Yours of December 12 is received. In reply, let me say: 1. The fact that our challenge included only six points, was an oversight. There ought to be an odd number of points, as you will no doubt admit. 2. It was with reluctance that we voted to include the declamation, as the aim of our Societies here is to give special prominence to *original work*. 3. We do not agree with you concerning the judges. On the contrary, we think the instances extremely rare in which one person is capable of judging intelligently of musical and also of literary performances. Yet we grant the possibility of finding judges who are thus capable.

There seems to be but three points on which we do not agree, and we propose the following compromise: Having already yielded to your wish in regard to introducing the declamation, we shall also yield the other point in regard to the judges, and agree to have but one board. We make these concessions, hoping that you will be so considerate as to yield in the remaining point, and agree to have two debaters on each side; for we deem it of importance that the contest be inaugurated, and we feel confident that when once the representatives of the two schools come together, they will be able to adopt permanent regulations that will be fully satisfactory to both parties.

In regard to the length of the programme, let me say, at our annual contests here, the exercises are not unfrequently three and a half to four hours long; yet our audiences are always large and never wearied. With a programme consisting of such a variety of exercises, an audience may easily be held for full four hours.

Very respectfully,

SILAS Y. GILLAN,
Chairman Contest Committee.

CARBONDALE, ILLINOIS, December 18, 1878.

MR. SILAS Y. GILLAN, Chairman of Contest Committee.

Dear Sir: Your letter is received. Committee met this p. m., and decided to yield in your favor in regard to the debate. In other words, we agree to the four debaters, but think the exercises will be entirely too long for a Carbondale audience. Please send question for debate as soon as possible. According to this programme there will be seven points. Reply at once.   Yours, etc.,

A. E. PARKINSON, Chairman.

NORMAL, ILLINOIS, January 13, 1879.

MR. A. E. PARKINSON, Chairman of Contest Committee.

Dear Sir: We submit the following subjects for debate, and ask your debaters to select one from them, and take their choice of sides:

Resolved, That the United States Government ought to take steps to secure such a modification of the treaties with China as would prevent further Chinese immigration.

Resolved, That our Government is a league of States, and not a Nation.

Resolved, That the present system of National Banks should be abolished.

Resolved, That the United States ought to adopt a system of Free Trade with all nations.

A word of explanation is perhaps due to you. We hope you will not think we have intentionally delayed the sending of this question for debate. We were not elected until Wednesday evening, and did not know the result until Thursday noon, on which day, and also on Friday, one of us was sick and out of school, so that we did not see each other until after mail time Saturday evening.

We expect that each of our pieces of music will be a solo. At present, we can not give you the full list of our representatives, as there is a probability that one of our musicians can not serve, and that we shall have to elect another. The election of essayist has been postponed until to-morrow. By next week we shall be able to give you the names of all.

Yours very truly,

SILAS Y. GILLAN, Leader on Debate.
HORACE E. POWERS, Assistant.

CARBONDALE, ILLINOIS, January 21, 1879.

MR. SILAS Y. GILLAN.

Dear Sir: Yours of the 13th instant is at hand. I should have answered sooner, but our debaters were slow in selecting the question. They decided to-day to accept the first question, and take the affirmative side, thus leaving you the negative.

Yours truly,   A. E. PARKINSON,

Chairman Contest Committee.

The Illinois State Normal *vs.* the Southern Illinois Normal, at Carbondale, Illinois, Thursday evening, March 13, 1879. Judges, Hon. J. H. Oberly, Hon. M. Weir, Hon. E. M. Prince. Dr. Robert Allyn, president of the evening. Programme: Music; prayer; music; debate: "*Resolved,* That the United States Government ought to take steps to secure such a modification of the treaties with China as would prevent further Chinese immigration." Affirmative, Wm. B. Train, Luther A. Johnson (*b*); negative, Silas Y. Gillan, Horace E. Powers (*a*); instrumental solo, "Rondeau Brilliante," Jeannie B. Morrison (*b*); instrumental solo, "Liszt's II Rhapsodie," Minnie G. Adams (*a*); oration, "Results of Doubt," Frank B. Harcourt (*a*); oration, "Republicanism in Europe," Arthur E. Parkinson (*b*); music; essay, "Let there be Light," Dora A. Lipe (*b*); essay, "Sermons in Stones," Daisy Hubbard (*a*); vocal duet, "O'er Hill, O'er Dale," Lizzie Sheppard, Lizzie Harned (*b*); vocal solo, "Going out with the Tide," E. Carl Webster (*a*); declamation, "The Maniac," Mary L. Beecher (*a*); declamation, "Lost and Found," Maggie Kennedy (*b*); music, Northern Normal (*a*), Southern Normal (*b*). Decision: On debate, instrumental music, essay, and declamation, the judges decided in favor of the State Normal; and on oration and vocal music, they decided in favor of the Southern Normal. Result: Five points to two points in favor of the State Normal.

CARBONDALE, January 14, 1880.

MR. J. HANNAH,

Dear Sir: We submit the following question for debate, viz: "*Resolved,* That the migration of the African race from the Southern States will promote harmony among their citizens and the prosperity of that section."
Truly yours,
E. L. SPRECHER,
Chairman of Committee.

NORMAL, ILLINOIS, January 17, 1880.

Dear Sir: The question proposed for debate does not seem clear to us in two points. There is doubt as to the meaning of the word *migration.* Do you mean the migration of the whole African race, or the present migration with all the uncertainties of the future? Second, we understand you to say this migration, whatever it may be, will promote harmony and prosperity in the States, from which the migration takes place. Is this your meaning? An answer in the form of a revised statement would be preferable.
Respectfully,
JESSE F. HANNAH,
Chairman Contest Committee.

CARBONDALE, January 20, 1880.

MR. J. F. HANNAH, Chairman Contest Committee: .

Dear Sir: Your letter concerning the question for debate came to hand to-day. We prefer to leave the question as it stands, and take the popular construction in regard to the meaning of *migration* of the African race from the Southern States. Putting this interpretation upon the question, it seems clear enough to us and seems to be in the proper form.   Respectfully,

CHARLES E. HULL, Secretary.

NORMAL, ILLINOIS, January 29, 1880.

MR. CHARLES E. HULL, Secretary Contest Committee.

Dear Sir: We have decided to support the affirmative of the question proposed for debate. Respectfully,   JESSE F. HANNAH,
Chairman Contest Committee.

Second Annual Inter-Normal Contest, Normal, Thursday evening, March 11, 1880. Judges, S. S. Lawrence, Esq., Pontiac, Illinois; William Hill, M. D., Bloomington, Illinois; T. T. Fountain, Esq., DuQuoin, Illinois. Programme: Quartette, "Carnovale" (*Rosini*), Normal Quartette Club; debate, "*Resolved*, That the migration of the African race from the Southern States will promote harmony among the citizens and the prosperity of that section." Affirmative, John H. Tear, Austin C. Rishel (*a*); negative, Charles E. Hull, Lauren L. Bruck; instrumental solos, "Last Rose of Summer," Miss Annie C. Wheeler (*b*), "Le Dernier Sourire," Miss Hattie Potter (*a*). Recess. Essays, "Want Stimulates to Action," Henry A. Kimmel (*b*); "Jean Ingelow," Miss Sarah Brooks (*a*); vocal solos, "In Quests Simplice," Miss Mary B. Walker (*b*); "Who's at my Window?" Miss Emma Bookwalter (*a*); orations, "The Desire of Eminence," Harold W. Lowrie (*b*); "Just Beyond," Jesse F. Hannah (*a*); declamations, "No Sects in Heaven," Miss Alice Krysher (*b*); "Rock me to Sleep," Miss Addie Gillan (*a*); quartette, "In this Hour of Softened Splendor," Normal Quartette Club. State Normal (*a*); Southern Normal (*b*). Decision: State Normal won the *whole seven points*.

The following persons had the honor of being elected for the third Inter-Normal contest: Debate, David W. Reid and James V. McHugh; essay, James B. Estee; declamation, Robert Elder; vocal music, Margareth Dalrymple; instrumental music, Minnie B. Potter; oration, George Howell.

NORMAL, January 12, 1881.

To DR. ALLYN, President of the Southern Normal University:

We send this question for contest debate: "*Resolved*, That the United States, in its tariff legislation, should adhere to the principle of a Protective Tariff." Respectfully,

(Telegram.)   NORMAL DEBATERS.

CARBONDALE, ILLINOIS, January 14, 1881.

E. C. HEWETT, LL. D., President Illinois State Normal University,
Normal, Illinois.

Dear Sir: I yesterday received a telegram, purporting to be
from the contest debaters of your University, stating a question for
debate and implying a desire for an answer.

I am at a loss about replying. But as our students have made no
movement in the matter of any future contests, and just now seem
wholly indifferent about doing so,—indeed, appear rather indisposed
to move,—I have deemed it best to say so much that you may communicate it to your contestants.

I may add that my opinion, personally, is decidedly averse to
more contests conducted as the two already had have been carried
on. I have scarcely named it to our faculty, but from casual words
dropped from time to time, I infer their opinions coincide with mine.
Our students, as yet, have made no arrangements for a contest, and
when I mentioned the fact of the telegram, seemed wholly apathetic.

I am, very respectfully and obediently,

ROBERT ALLYN.

ARMY LIST.

The following named persons, formerly teachers or students in
the Normal University, were in the Union army:

TEACHERS—NORMAL DEPARTMENT.

Charles E. Hovey,	Brevet Major-General, U. S. Vol.
(a)Dr. E. R. Roe,	Lieut. Col., 33d Ill. Inf.
Leander H. Potter,	Lieut. Col., 33d Ill. Inf.
Ira Moore,	Capt., Co. G, 33d Ill. Inf.
Julien E. Bryant,	Lieut. Col., 1st Miss., (C. V.)
*Dr. Saml. Willard,	Surgeon, 97th Ill. Inf.

STUDENTS—NORMAL DEPARTMENT.

Edward Allyn,	Private, Co. A, 33d Ill. Inf.
Jas. H. Beach,	Private, Co. H, 20th Ill. Inf.
*Wm. C. Baker,	Ord. Sergt., Co. A, 33d Ill. Inf.
Eugene F. Baldwin,	Ord. Sergt., Co. B, 12th Ind. Inf.
Wm. A. Black,	Private, Co. —, 87th Ill. Inf.
James H. Baily,	Gunboat Service.
(b)Charles Bovee,	Corp., Co. A, 33d Ill. Inf.
James M. Burch,	Capt., Co. —, 94th Ill. Inf.
Lorenzo D. Bovee,	Private, Co. E, 100th Ill. Inf.
George M. Berkley,	Corp., Co. C, 13th Ill. Inf.
Joseph M. Chase,	Corp., Co. —, 3d Ill. Cav.
Wilson M. Chalfant,	Private, Co. —, 104th Ill. Inf.
(c)Charles M. Clark,	Quarter-master, 2d La., (C. V.)

(d)Wm. P. Carter,   .   Corp., Co. C, 40th Ill. Inf.
*J. W. Cox,   .   .   Private, Co. C, 33d Ill. Inf.
Lewis P. Cleaveland,   .   Ord. Sergt., 1st Ala., (C. V.)
†Peter T. Crist,   .   Private, Co. F, 68th Ill. Inf.
Elmer F. Clapp,   Private, Co. C, 76th Ill. Inf.
Jesse Cunningham,   .   Private, Co. E, 78th Ill. Inf.
(e)Ephraim D. Carrothers,   Sergt., Co. —, 20th Ill. Inf.
John T. Curtis,   .   Hospital Steward, 97th Ill. Inf.
J. Harvey Dutton,   1st Lieut., Co. A, 33d Ill. Inf.
(f)Wm. H. H. DeBoice,   .   Private, Co. A, 33d Ill. Inf.
(g)Wm. Downer,   Sergt., Co. E, 70th Ill. Inf.
*Valentine Denning, .   Private, Co. G, 4th Ill. Cav.
James R. Fyffe,   2d Lieut., Co. A, 33d Ill. Inf.
Wm. M. Fyffe,   .   Private, Vaughn's Springfield Bat.
Wm. H. H. Fuller,   1st Lieut., Co. G, 84th Ill. Inf.
     Detailed as Signal Officer on
     Gen. McCook's Staff.

C. Judson Gill,   .   Capt., Co. B, 33d Ill. Inf.
James Gilbraeth,   .   Private, Co. —, 3d Ill. Cav.
E. Aaron Gove,   .   Adjutant, 33d Ill. Inf.
(h)Francis M. Gastman,   Corp., Co. A, 33d Ill. Inf.
Wm. A. Gunn,   .   Sergt., Co. K, 8th Ill. Inf.
†Charles Hayes,   Private, Co. K, 8th Ill. Inf.
Peter Harper,   .   Sergt., Co. G, 4th Wis. Inf.
John H. Hume,   .   Corp., Co. —, 11th Ill. Cav.
John M. House,   .   .   —— —— 110th Ill. Inf.
Otho H. Hibbs, .   Private, Co. E, 94th Ill. Inf.
*Ebenezer D. Harris,   .   Corp., Co. A, 33d Ill. Inf.
Charles E. Huston,   Private, Co. A., 33d Ill. Inf.
Wm. W. Hall,   .   Sergt., Co. —, 115th Ill. Inf.
Chas. D. Irons, .   Private, Co. —, 77th Ill. Inf.
Duncan G. Ingraham,   .   Corp., Co. B, 33d Ill. Inf.
Hiram W. Johnson,   Sergt., Co. E, 8th Ill. Inf.
(i)Fred B. Jones,   .   Private, Co. —, 77th Ill. Inf.
(j)Christopher Krebs,   Private, Co. B, 8th Ill. Inf.
John D. Kirkpatrick,   Private, Co. B, 93d Ill. Inf.
A. B. Keagle, .   .   1st Lieut., Co. D, 117th Ill. Inf.
Matthew R. Kell,   .   Private, Co. D, 49th Ill. Inf.
Wm. Law,   .   Com. Sergt., 47th Ill. Inf.
Dr. Jehu Little,   .   .   1st Asst. Surgeon, 24th Mo. Inf.
(k)Alvin T. Lewis, .   .   Corp., Co. A, 33d Ill. Inf.
Clark Leal,   .   .   Private, Co. A, 118th Ill. Inf.
*Moses I. Morgan,   .   Capt., Co. B, 33d Ill. Inf.
(l)Isaac N. McCuddy,   .   Corp., Co. A, 33d Ill. Inf.
Joseph R. McGregor,   .   ——, Irish Brigade.
†George Marsh,   .   .   Private, Co. K, 69th Ill. Inf.

Wm. W. Murphy,	Sergt., Co. —, 87th Ill. Inf.
G. Hyde Norton,	Capt., Co. A, 33d Ill. Inf.
*Marvin J. Nye,	Private, Co. A, 33d Ill. Inf.
Edwin Philbrook,	Quarter-master Sergt., 8th Ill. Inf.
Truman J. Pearce,	Private, Co. A, 33d Ill. Inf.
*James G. Pearce,	Private, Ottawa Battery.
Henry C. Prevost,	Sergt. Major, 94th Ill. Inf.
Edward M. Pike,	Ord. Sergt., Co. A, 33d Ill. Inf.
Henry II. Pope,	Capt., Co. D, 33d Ill. Inf.
George Peter,	Ord. Sergt., Co. A, 43d Ill. Inf.
Richard R. Puffer,	Private, Co. E, 8th Ill. Inf.
Orange Parret,	Private, Co. B, 77th Ill. Inf.
Logan H. Roots,	Quarter-master, 81st Ill. Inf.
Rasselas P. Reynolds,	Corp., Co. A, 33d Ill. Inf.
Geo. McClellan Rex,	Private, Co. I, 33d Ill. Inf.
Thomas M. Roberts, .	——, Co. B, 47th Ill. Inf.
*John H. Rhomack,	Private, Co. G., 68th Ohio Inf.
J. M. Stine,	Private, Co. M, 16th Ill. Cav.
†Justin S. Spaulding,	Private, Co. K, 8th Ill. Inf.
Gilbert L. Seybold, .	Private, Co. A, 33d Ill. Inf.
Byron Sheldon, .	——, ——, Ill. Inf.
Samuel Smith,	Private, Co. A, 33d Ill. Inf.
(m)Johnson W. Straight, .	Private, Co. A, 33d Ill. Inf.
Edwin Scranton,	Miss. Marine Brigade.
Frederick J. Seybold,	——, ——, Ill. Inf.
†Wm. A. H. Tilton, .	Ord. Sergt., 68th Ill. Inf.
John J. Taylor, .	——, Co. K, 20th Ill. Inf.
John H. Walker,	Private, Co. E, 58th Ill. Inf.
John X. Wilson,	1st Lieut., Co. F, 33d Ill. Inf.
Chas. E. Wilcox,	Sergt. Major, 33d Ill. Inf.
James E. Willis,	Private, Co. F, 87th Ill. Inf.
Peleg R. Walker,	2d Lieut., Co. K, 92d Ill. Inf.
Chas. W. Wills,	Capt., Co. —, 103d Ill. Inf.
Theophilus F. Willis,	Private, Co. C, 11th Ill. Inf.
Wm. Walton,	——, ——, Ill. Inf.
Cyrus I. Wilson,	——, ——, Ill. Inf.
J. R. Walker, .	Capt., Co. —, 28th Ill. Inf.

TEACHERS—MODEL SCHOOL.

(n)Joseph G. Howell,	1st Lieut., Co. K, 8th Ill. Inf.
*J. Howard Burnham,	Capt. Co. A, 33d Ill. Inf.

STUDENTS—MODEL SCHOOL.

Franklin B. Augustus,	Private, Co. A, 33d Ill. Inf.
Joshua Baily,	Ord. Sergt., Co. B, 73d Ill. Inf.
†John G. Dietrich,	Private, Co. —, 68th Ill. Inf.
†Joseph T. Davison, .	Sergt., Co. F, 68th Ill. Inf.

11

Arthur H. Dillon,	Private, Co. A, 33d Ill. Inf.
Ulysses D. Eddy,	1st Lieut., 4th N. Y. Art.
Richard Huxtable,	Private, Co. H, 77th Ill. Inf.
William Hogue,	Private, Co. G, 69th Ill. Inf.
Jas. F. Hough,	——, ——, 33d Ill. Inf.
†Robert McCart,	Sergt., Co. G, 68th Ill. Inf.
—— Mills,	——, ——, Ill. Inf.
(o)William A. Pearce,	Private, Co. A, 33d Ill Inf.
†Edward L. Price,	Corp., Co. F, 68th Ill. Inf.
Myron J. Peterson,	Private, Co. E, 75th Ill. Inf.
†Francis S. Rearden,	Corp., Co. G, 68th Ill. Inf.

REFERENCES.

*Resigned or honorably discharged, on account of continued ill health.
†Three months' service.
(a)Disabled by wounds at the siege of Vicksburg, and resigned.
(b)Disabled by five wounds, and honorably discharged.
(c)Mortally wounded at Milliken's Bend, Louisiana, June 7, 1863.
(d)Disabled by wounds at Shiloh, and honorably discharged.
(e)Killed at the siege of Fort Donelson.
(f)Died in hospital at Ironton, Missouri, February, 1862.
(g)Died July 23, 1862.
(h)Died in camp, on Black River, Missouri, March 23, 1862.
(i)Reported killed at the siege of Vicksburg, May, 23, 1863.
(j)Disabled by wounds at Donelson and Shiloh, and honorably discharged.
(k)Killed at Wilkinson's Landing, Mississippi, August 4, 1862.
(l)Died in hospital at Ironton, Missouri, October, 1861.
(m)Lost an arm in battle, and returned to Normal.
(n)Killed at the siege of Fort Donelson.
(o)Killed at the battle of Jackson, Mississippi, July 12, 1863.

RECAPITULATION.

Commissioned officers, 27; non-commissioned officers, 33; privates, 45; rank unknown, 12.

REMINISCENCES.

One of our early peculiarities was the possession of ninety acres of land for a model farm, and the existence of the idea that agricultural chemistry, if no more, was to be taught in the institution. With the laudable desire to spread a little agricultural knowledge over as large a surface as possible, the Board managed to secure a course of lectures on chemistry, with the intention of making, eventually, some kind of universal application of the principles to the agricultural improvement of the State, through the knowledge infused or injected into the Normal School. A lecturer was therefore employed, who gave us highly interesting discourses upon the principles of chemistry. He laid down the law at a galloping pace, took us below the crust of the earth and beyond the planetary bodies in a remarkably short time, pouring out knowledge at the rate of no one knows how many volumes per month.

Had we all been short-hand reporters, and had we been given time to write out and study his information, it is quite probable we might have acquired some knowledge of the great science of chemistry, and might at some future day, when teaching in the rural districts, have given the world some benefit from the lightning calculations. But as we knew nothing of the tricks of short-hand writing, and were not even allowed to take notes, and had no breathing spells allowed for that purpose, it naturally happened that the old adage pertaining to things that go in at one ear and out at another, had pertinent application. After a number of weeks of this treatment, some one, possibly one of our hard-working drill masters, with a weary experience of our general dullness, suggested that in all probability, the pupils were not fully appreciating the magnificent ideas cast before their feeble understandings. But our remarkable lecturer, who fully understood his own teachings, believed he had been so careful in his statements, and had made his way so remarkably straight and plain that the school had certainly mastered the subject as far as he had progressed, and refused to believe there was any doubt upon the subject.

It was then suggested that in order to test our knowledge, a written examination be sprung upon us without warning, and that the result would show our ignorance, though it might not prove his failure to give us an opportunity to learn. The lecturer at once fell into the trap, if trap there was. We were provided with blank paper in the ordinary way, and a list of questions was propounded in the ordinary way. In his anxiety to prove our thoroughness, he gave but a few simple questions. The latter were in many instances answered correctly, but as the pupils might have learned these points through general sources of information, the real test was considered to be the answers to questions of a technical nature. These were generally so far above the pupil's comprehension that very little stationery was spoiled by any attempt at answering, and the paper, like our minds, came out of the ordeal as blank as before. One question I shall never forget, though the proper answer has not been found in twenty years of extensive reading, "What is Allotropism?" Only three or four attempted to grapple with this terrible fiend. One believed it a system of medicine in opposition to homeopathy; one believed it a species of extinct mammalia; and one did actually show, by his answer, that the word had been railroaded into some previous lecture. I shall never forget the expression of our lecturer's face, as he read these answers which were to be taken as evidence of his admirable system, and which gave proof so conclusive that the lecturer's platform was after that generally vacant during the early days of the Normal.

Another theory was tested to the satisfaction of the school, but it never came to a full and final end in my time, and this was the idea that each and every person can be made a musician, or a teacher of music. Some of the members of the State Board went so far as to refuse to believe a pupil should be allowed to graduate unless he was able to teach music and lead in singing. Prof. C. M. Cady, of Chicago, was employed, with strict instructions to spare no pains to prove the correctness of the theory of the existence of universal musical ability. He divided the school into four sections. "A" was made up of good singers, those who had good voices, and also could read music readily by sight. "B" included moderately well-informed singers, and those who were capable of being rapidly advanced. "C" comprised all with a natural ear for music; those whose voices needed training to fit them for a place in the upper classes. According to popular report, section "D" was made up of "birds that couldn't sing, and that could never be made to sing." This class was small, but desperate. It labored zealously to grasp the rudiments of the grand art, but its best efforts were failures, and it became, in the course of a year or so, the laughing stock of the entire school. Being an early and constant member of this class, I have a right to mention its woes and tribulations, and to observe that it finally graduated from the pursuit of knowledge under these difficulties, by rising in a body and leaving the hall when the music hour arrived,—no permission being asked or given,—it being tacitly conceded that the pet theory of universal musical training had broken under the strain.

If any have never heard of the great and good Prof. Washington Irving Vescellius, or the great American card writer, they would thank me for the information that he was the first "professor" employed in the Normal University. Before his time, down to a somewhat later date, all our instructors were teachers, and they were unsparing in ridiculing the ordinary professors of the State. How the title ever took root here, after our experience with the great Vescellius, passes my humble comprehension. This remarkable professor gave general writing lessons to the whole school, much after the fashion of the agricultural chemistry class. Under his tuition, all the students were to be brought to the highest style of penmanship, and after graduation, were to be prepared to compete with other American card writers, and might be supposed capable of conducting an evening writing school. This accomplishment, when added like a mansard roof to the ability to teach music, would effectually dispense with the traveling professor, whose cards displaying impossible doves and eagles are hung up in the postoffices and other public resorts, and with the above-mentioned musical accomplishment, render writing and singing teachers extinct races, only to be met with in the lightest of light literature of the day. Professor Washington Irving Vescellius was considerably inflated by the promotion thus accorded to his merit, gave his whole soul to the work, and delighted himself and the school by the most brilliant blackboard exercises. Upon one unfortunate occasion he told the school the lesson of the day was to be the "shyrographic curve," and the general subject of "shyrography." I believe the gentleman wondered why this particular lesson proved so amusing to the school, and that he believed himself a much injured person, when the faculty soon after dispensed with his further services.

Music and penmanship were to be supplemented by the elegant accomplishment of drawing, and we were engaged three hours each week in this delightful pastime. Our instructor was a sedate Episcopal clergyman, whose home was at Springfield. He believed in training all the faculties, and was anxious we should acquire proper ideas of perspectives, and lines, and shades, and shadows, and become experts in some one branch of this delightful art. He conceived the idea of teaching the construction of capital letters on a large scale, giving blackboard exercises to the whole school by sections, in hopes, I suppose, that we might some day compete with sign painters. I remember that when his class was examined at the close of the winter term in 1860, our beloved professor requested section "C" to give an illustration of the method of constructing the letter "E." History compels me to remark that several of his pupils had attained such proficiency that they certainly were fully worthy of taking rank with second-class sign painters, and their capital letters were really almost capital specimens of art.

Our Mr. Hewett was perhaps as much given to bright sayings and happy retorts in those days as he is at present, and on this occasion he perpetrated one of his very best. Passing in review in front of the long blackboard in company with our professor, he quietly remarked: "Section C has performed to-day with great ease." (E's.) Our quiet teacher, not given to wit and humor, agreed with a gentle laugh, and through his mind there galloped no idea of the peculiar humor of the remark. During the evening of that day, at a social gathering of teachers and pupils, some one explained to our drawingmaster, with not a little difficulty, the real point of Mr. Hewett's little joke. When he thoroughly took in the situation, his joy and gratification knew no bounds. "Section 'C' performed with great E's," he repeated over and over again, and seemed at last to fully realize that something truly good had actually been said.

Scene: assembly room. McMackin standing at the dictionary-table looking up a word; no member of the faculty in the room, Dr. Edwards in charge, having stepped out; Frank Searles, going out to the reading-table, meets a greenhorn just in to enter school, who inquires, "Say, Mister, where can I find the president? I want to come to school." Searles directs him to "that man standing by the table," pointing out McMackin. He walks through the room and approaches Mc., with "Say, er you the president?" Mc. (very coolly and complacently), "Yes, sir; what can I do for you?" "I want to come to school." Mc. looks at him a moment in a dignified manner, "Oh,—ah,—yes; well, I never attend to matters of that kind myself; you'll have to see my private secretary."—[Enter Dr. Edwards.] "There he comes now; that bald-headed man. You just step to his desk; he will tell you what to do."

THE ECLIPSE OF THE MOON.

In the fall of 1874, on a certain Saturday evening, a total eclipse of the moon was advertised. The performance was to begin at one o'clock Sunday morning. After society meeting, those who were members of the "seventh hour class" strolled off in groups, two in a group, or whiled away the blissful moments discussing the critic's report, or the general topic of spelling; feeling all the while that eclipses were a grand, good blessing to those who found it difficult to frame excuses for occupying the parlor late at night and burning so much of the landlady's kerosene. The strictly steady ones went to bed; for, truth to tell, many of them had not heard that there was going to be an eclipse. A few boys, however, determined to "raise a racket" worthy of the occasion. Gathering about forty on the east side, they crossed the University campus to the west side, where were a large number of boys, "batching" and in clubs. Most of them were asleep. Collecting about the houses, the crowd would make night hideous until those within were prevailed upon to join the party. Re-crossing the ground, with numbers doubled, they reached the club house, popularly known as "Saint's Rest," next door to Dr. Hewett's residence, and quieter measures at first were resorted to in order to raise the boys, who were chiefly of the strictly circumspect sort. A committee of two or three went to each room, but some of those within, probably filled with visions of cruel hazing, resolutely refused to admit the callers. In vain the explanation was made that the intention was only to raise as large a crowd as possible, call out one of the professors and get him to "talk eclipse." One burly, broad-shouldered fellow displayed violent symptons of becoming unpleasantly pugilistic. All but two or three, however, yielded at last, and by this time the eclipse was coming on.

As to which one of the faculty should be called out, was the next question. Edwards wouldn't do. He would probably take it amiss. So thought several of the leaders of the party who did not happen to be on the most amicable terms with the president. "Doc." (Sewall) was just the man, but he was not at home. Professor Hewett was selected as the victim. The company of about one hundred ranged along the street in front of the professor's house. A committee of three "waited on him" by vigorously ringing the door-bell until he was wakened. It would seriously impair the writer's reputation as a truthful historian to say that Dr. Hewett was in full dress when he appeared at the door to inquire, "*What's the matter?*" With a word of explanation from the boys, he took in the situation in a moment. Said he had returned late in the evening from a trip by rail, and too weary and sleepy to sit up till the time of the eclipse, had gone to bed, but thanked the boys kindly for waking him. Then, putting on wraps, he came out, and for more than an hour entertained and instructed us with explanations and facts regarding the heavenly bodies. Altogether, it was probably the best remembered lecture on astronomy that any of those who heard it, listened to during their course in school.

THE LIBERAL FIGHT.

In the fall of 1874, the following young men, who were then students of the State Normal University, organized a society, termed the "Liberal Club," which originally consisted of John Shearer, Samuel Wadsworth, L. B. Wood, Stephen Spear, Charles Howard, Christopher Stephenson, George Snelling, Asbury Crawford, —— McPherson, —— Hume, Adam Hoffman, and Geo. L. Hoffman, which was subsequently joined by W. C. Gemmill, S. B. Hursh, J. N. Hursh, Cyrus W. Picking, George Beaty, Albert Snare, Dorus Hatch, —— Brown, a Hindoo, Charles Schwer, —— Merriett, —— Trenchard, and others. No one could become a member of this club unless he had met with the club for at least two evenings, and received the unanimous vote of all the members present at a regular meeting, nor unless the members were satisfied that the applicant for membership fully understood the nature and object of the club, which usually met in a small office on Main street, in Normal The object of the club being mutual improvement, and an impartial investigation, as near as might be, of such subjects as might be deemed beneficial and of common interest to the members of the club, and that free scope should be given to a proper discussion of any subject under consideration, each member feeling that his honest opinions could be frankly stated and his doubts expressed without restraint, and that no matter how diversified the opinions of the different members would be, each member and his opinions should be treated with respect, whether upon questions of education, politics, science, morals, or religion. Hence the name, "Liberal Club." To many, the name suggested that the club was antagonistic to orthodox religion, but this was primarily foreign to its object, although, incidentally, its members invaded the domain of orthodoxy, for opinions were freely expressed upon various phases of religion, its creeds, doctrines, and sects, as well as upon other topics of interest. The club work consisted in reading and commenting upon Tyndall's Belfast address, Draper's Intellectual Development of Europe, Huxley, Darwin, Winshel on Evolution, Herbert Spencer, Butler's Analogy, Theodore Parker's Discourse on Religion, and other books of like character. Besides, essays were written by the members, and read and criticised by the club. All the members were liberally inclined in their religious views, and frequently gave expression to their religious sentiments in the Wrightonian and Philadelphian Societies of the Normal University. Of this, the strict orthodox members of these Societies disapproved, and especially those belonging to the Young Men's Christian Association; consequently, they arrayed themselves against the Liberal Club, and recognized its members as antagonistic to religion and its institutions, and endeavored to tolerate no exercises in the Societies which tended to be at variance with orthodox doctrine. The Liberals, acting on the defensive, claimed that the Societies were secular institutions, and that there was no more impropriety in discussing theological subjects, in an honest and candid manner, than there was in treating other topics. This opposition to the Liberals brought about a zealous rivalry between the Liberals and their friends, and the Young Men's Christian Association and their sympathizers.

The strong opposition to the Liberals became clearly manifested in the Societies after the Liberals had arranged to prepare a programme for each Society, which was to consist of exercises given by members of the Liberal Club alone. The proposition had been accepted by Mr. Drayton, president of the Philadelphian Society, and Josiah Hodge, president of the Wrightonian Society. This was in the fall of 1874 or 1875. Adam Hoffman, who was a member of the Liberal Club, succeeded Mr. Hodge as president of the Wrightonian Society. It was during Hoffman's administration that the programme prepared by the Liberals for the Wrightonian Society was given. For admitting this programme, the president was censured by a majority vote of the Society. This motion was made and supported by members of the Young Men's Christian Association and others opposed to the Liberal Club. This motion called forth heated discussion for several evenings, and finally a motion to strike the vote of censure from the record prevailed, without a dissenting voice. Some of those who supported the motion of censure, after due deliberation, concluded that they were hasty. Thus, the trouble in the Wrightonian Society was ended, and harmony was restored. Soon after, the programme prepared by the Liberals for the Philadelphian Society, was given after some little opposition. No reasonable objection could be urged against the character of these programmes. They were in every respect commendable and worthy to be offered in the society halls. The opposition was to the privilege granted to the Liberals, rather than to the nature of their exercises. The leaders of the opposition to the Liberals were W. S. Mills, L. C. Dougherty, J. P. Hodge, James Ellis, B. F. Stocks, Kenyon and others.

The next contest took place in the Philadelphian Society at its spring election, when there were two candidates for president, viz.: Laybourn and Charles McMurry, the latter receiving the support of the Liberals, although he had no connection with them, and the former being the choice of the Young Men's Christian Association. There would have been no difficulty at this election had not Laybourn's supporters promulgated that the Liberal's were supporting McMurry, and that McMurry must be defeated. This caused an issue to be made between the Liberals and the Young Men's Christian Association, at this election. Both parties zealously engaged in securing voters and advocating their claims. On the day of election, when the result was announced, it was evident that Charles McMurry was elected, whereupon a few of Laybourn's ardent supporters charged fraud upon the judges, George Beaty, D. C. Tyler and Miss Mary Anderson, and, at the following meeting of the Society, succeeded in carrying a motion for another election, without first duly investigating the election. This arbitrary move was denounced as unjust and illegal by McMurry's friends. The excitement was intense for several days. Special meetings were called for the purpose of determining the proper mode of proceeding for an investigation of the election, but no terms could be reached other than that there should be another election without further ceremony. The McMurry constituents refused to yield their position, as well as their antagonists. The strife was growing fiercer, day by day, and no compromise could be effected, until finally some of the members of the faculty saw proper and necessary to advise. Upon their suggestion that it would be best to consent to another election without further difficulty, the Liberals and McMurry's friends generally, yielded, and another election was called. The excitement had risen to such a pitch that it interfered with the regular school work of those who were most interested. As soon as it was conceded that there would be another election, both factions at once proceeded to solicit members to pay their dues, so that they could vote. Before the close of the election, the number of voting members in the Philadelphian Society was more than doubled; and the election again resulted in favor of Charles McMurry. Both candidates were highly esteemed by the students, and either would have been satisfactory so far as they were individually concerned. But the fight was between the factions, rather than for their candidates. When McMurry's election was announced, a scene of wild excitement took place, after an interval, of stillness, during the counting of the votes. After this election, all differences were adjusted, and the waging factions ceased their hostilities toward each other, and it was generously conceded by the leaders in the fight that both parties were too rash, and acted imprudently. It is an event that will always be remembered by those who attended school during the period of the Liberal contest. After sallies of passion and burning remarks, came deliberation and candor. Whatever the Liberal or the orthodox may have said in the Societies which was of sufficient force to call forth comment must at last have been of mutual benefit, either in tempering or strengthening both in their respective convictions.

WORKING THE ROADS.

In the spring of 1877, about twenty-five of the boys were notified by the local authorities to work the usual two days on the roads. A meeting of the students interested in the matter was held in Dr. Sewall's room, and the subject was thoroughly discussed. It was decided that they should turn out in a body, each one taking three others to work on his time, thus putting in the required two days in half a day. A committee of five, consisting of Messrs. Gillan, Berkstresser, Faulkner, Boyer, and Bainum, was appointed to make necessary arrangements for the particulars of the plan. The committee drew up a code of regulations which all agreed to observe, to the effect that:

1. All were to come to school at the usual time the next morning, and remain until after devotional exercises and spelling, and when the classes passed out, file down stairs, form in line in front of the building, and march to the scene of the day's labor.

2. White shirts, collars, coats, and jewelry of any kind, were strictly forbidden to be worn.

3. As far as practicable, pantaloons must be worn inside of boots.

4. Each should be provided with whatever implement for digging he might be able to improvise.

The next morning a unique and motley crowd assembled, bearing a great variety of implements, from a grubbing hoe to a garden rake and a fire shovel. Edward Faulkner was chosen captain, and the company, consisting of eighty members, was divided into squads of eight, each commanded by a sub-boss. Forming in line, they marched to the place' designated by the roadmaster, just south of the iron bridge over Sugar Creek, on Main street. After working (?) about an hour, three of the "busy B's," Berkstresser, Bainum, and Burger, were sent to Bloomington to get a supply of liquid consolation, as the day was warm and the "work" thirst-provoking. Owing to the fact that the committee required so much time to "sample" the different varieties, it was near noon when they retured in company with a drayman and a barrel of cider. Sitting in the shade of the maples by the road side, the crowd by this time augmented to one hundred, or more, soon emptied the barrel. The remainder of the programme consisted in building a memorial mound of earth some six or eight feet high, in the middle of the road, making speeches, listening to vocal music by a colored man, who, passing by, was captured and urged to sing, although he protested that he had not time to wait, and the final homeward march. A large stone was selected from the creek near the Chicago and Alton railroad, and taken through the streets of Normal to the front of the city council's office, where it was planted by the sidewalk with appropriate ceremonies. In dedicating the stone as a memorial to the city council, Hoffman, Gillan, and Stephenson, were called on for speeches, and each one of the audience contributed a fitting sentiment as he put in his spadeful or hoeful of earth.

Two days later was commencement. By preconcerted arrangement, at the close of the exercises, the boys repaired to the west steps of the building, where, in a neat and appropriate speech, Mr. Edward Faulkner, in behalf of those who had worked on the road, presented the roadmaster with a hat, as a token of good feeling and respect, he having acted in the matter only in obedience to the legal direction of the city council, but having treated the boys in a most gentlemanly and generous manner.

DR. HEWETT'S BIRTHDAY.

A THREE-FOLD SURPRISE.

[From the Bloomington Pantagraph, November 2, 1878.]

Yesterday was President Hewett's birthday, the horologe of time having struck for him the half century. During the opening exercises, the members of the model department quietly gathered near the doors of the assembly room. The usual spelling exercise was begun, but after the president had pronounced three or four words, Silas Y. Gillan, of the senior class, arose and interrupted the exercise, saying: "I would like to put in a parenthesis right here in this exercise. For years and years this performance has been going on in just the same way; you have been drilling and drilling upon spelling, and yet, even here in McLean County, there are persons who cannot spell—a fact which conclusively proves the whole business of spelling to be a failure. [Applause.] Variety is the spice of life, and this morning we propose to have a little variety. Let it be recorded in the annals of the University, or at least become a part of the traditional history thereof, that on one morning, November 1, 1878, *the spelling exercise was omitted.*" Here the speaker drew from his desk an elegant gold-headed cane, and, continuing in a neat little speech, which was decidedly unique, abounding in humor and good feeling, presented the cane to Dr. Hewett, in behalf of the students of the school. It bore the inscription: "Pres. E. C. Hewett, LL. D. From the students of the I. S. N. U., Nov. 1, 1878."

Immediately on the first interruption, the doors on both sides were thrown open, and the pupils from the model school filed in. No sooner had the president begun to speak in response to Mr. Gillan, than little Jessie Davis came forward, carrying a beautiful bouquet, and said: "Mr. Hewett, please accept these flowers as a birthday present from the children of the primary department." Turning to make a double response, he was a third time interrupted by Mrs. Haynie, of the Normal Department, who, as representative of the faculty, held in her hand an elegant Bagster Bible. Mrs. Haynie's address was a model of delicacy and beauty, and was delivered with such evident feeling as to make it peculiarly impressive.

So successfully had the preparations been kept secret that the president had not the least suspicion of the affair, but was completely surprised. When at last he "got the floor," with voice tremulous with emotion, he thanked the good friends for their thoughtful kindness, on the day upon which he reached the "summit of life." In a short speech, which was full of good advice and good sense, he recalled the fact that just twenty-nine years before, he began his career as a teacher, and since that time, with the exception of a few months, he had been engaged in teaching, the last twenty years having been spent in this institution.

The members of the faculty were all called upon. Prof. Metcalf spoke at some length. Prof. Cook made a very witty little speech. When the president announced that the spelling exercise was over for the morning, the eyes of the students sparkled with delight, and they greeted the announcement with hearty applause.

THE SOCIABLE SQUABBLE.

The American of average pluck and combativeness has, among his most pleasant memories, the recollection of some parliamentary contest about society or class affairs. Wrightonians and Philadelphians of the spring of 1881, remember with special pleasure the sociable fight of the spring term. The opening of the spring term found both Societies in a healthy condition, with their ranks filled with earnest, plucky and able workers.

As usual, early in the term, arrangements were made for a union sociable. The night appointed was so stormy that few attended. Many now wished to hold the sociable the following (Saturday) evening. The older members objected to adjourning the regular literary exercises, and from this difference started one of the most hotly contested struggles of later years. As stated above, the contest was upon the propriety of adjourning the regular literary exercises for a joint sociable. The first joint meeting called to decide the matter was held March 22. In this meeting the sociable party carried their point, with but little opposition. It was now that the fight began.

At the close of the session on the twenty-third, the anti-sociable party called a meeting of the Wrightonian Society. Matters grew so interesting that about twenty members paid their dues before the meeting was called to order. Faces that had been long strange, and faces new in business sessions, now appeared. The anti-sociable party at this meeting were ably led by E. E. Brown, John Gray and others. The sociable side, by Walter Blake, and F. A. Houghton. The session was protracted and warm. The anti-sociable party argued that we could not afford to do away with the regular literary exercises for such a trifling thing as a sociable; that we get too little literary drill, even if every regular meeting is held. This was met by the new students retorting that there are more opportunities to do literary work than are taken advantage of; that drill in social courtesies is more needed by the majority of students than literary drill, and that the older students, having become acquainted, did not feel the need of a sociable, as did the newer students. At the final vote, by a majority of three, the anti-sociable party carried their motion to annul the action of the "joint meeting." Still the fight grew warmer.

The next meeting—a union meeting—met at 4 p. m., March 24, in Normal Hall. To those already spoken of as leaders of the sociable party in the Wrightonian session, we must now add the name of George Howell, a Philadelphian. At this meeting, David W. Reid was chosen by the two society presidents to preside. As the session was turbulent, it was found no easy matter to conduct the business expeditiously. The motion to reconsider previous action carried, and on reconsideration the joint meeting again declared in favor of the sociable by a vote of eighty-four to thirty-seven. This session lasted from 4 to 9:45 p. m.

At four p. m., March 25, another meeting of the Wrightonians was called in room twenty-three. At this meeting Mr. F. A. Houghton moved that we have a short programme, after which society adjourned for social exercises. This motion was seconded by E. E. Brown, and was unanimously carried. So ends the sociable fight, in which the "cream" and "scum" met in earnest but friendly conflict. Let us add that the sociable proved a grand success, and that one of the most pleasing incidents was the presentation of a beautiful bouquet by the ladies to George Howell, in token of their appreciation of his efforts in behalf of the sociable.

QUARTER CENTENNIAL.

NORTON'S LETTER.

DEAR OLD FRIENDS:

To my home on the summits of these Santa Cruz hills, by the Pacific, has come an invitation to write á few words upon the days when we dwelt and worked together. I was not exactly a beginner with the Normal University. I entered in the autumn of 1858, and found myself decidedly a junior, compared with a group, grave and reverend, of the real pioneers. John Hull, Joseph Howell, Enoch Gastman, Hayes, Ridlon, Augusta Peterson, Sally Dunn, Fannie Washburne, Edward Philbrook, whose hair parted in the middle, these were in the front rank of years and honors. We who entered in those September days of 1858, felt small and insignificant beside them. We were daily convened in the upper story of Major's Hall. I suppose that these younger generations of Normalites are not aware that such a building ever existed. The walls of the old house were rickety, and iron girders, with huge S's at the ends, held in place the brick masonry. Our assembling room was the third story. In the second story were recitation rooms, rather dark, and ill-adapted to our needs. Grocery and hardware stores occupied the first floor. The building was heated by a coal stove in each room, and as Illinois coal is gaseous and explosive, the stove doors were frequently blown open, with loud sounds and clouds of yellow smoke. C. E. Hovey was principal in those days, but Ira Moore was the one most directly in charge. Dr. Willard, looking very pale and frail, soon began to open his wonderful budget of philological knowledge. Hewett came within a month after my arrival, I think. He was a small man with a big head, in those days. He had very demonstrative boot heels, and especially hated cats, and went to sleep in Baptist meetings. He used to give us prodigious lessons in history and geography. He couldn't draw maps, but made us draw very nice ones. I remember his geography lessons, even unto this day. The names of the branches of the Amazon, the forms and heights of the Andean and Himalayan plateaus—these are mine yet, and will be to all eternity. My history work has not staid with me so well.

There was once a slight unpleasantness between my class and their teacher as to how General Greene got away from Cornwallis. It was quite a double-and-twisted business anyhow, and we inwardly vowed that we wouldn't learn it. The teacher gave us hard words and low marks, but our obstinate stupidity won the day. I am still densely ignorant as to whether it was the Chickahominy or the Nile that rose and fell in such a miraculous fashion, for the discomfiture of the British. Come to think of it, may be it wasn't Greene and Cornwallis, after all. It tires me to recall the matter. At any rate, somebody got away from some other fellow, and we wouldn't and didn't learn the particulars, and Professor Hewett considered us, very justly, a pack of ninnies.

We were called section "C" for awhile. There was a section B, including Burnham, Edward Waite, Fanny Grennel, Peleg R. Walker and others; a class which had entered some months before us, but they were soon incorporated with us. Gove, from Boston, John T. Curtis, Sophie Crist, C. J. Gill, Harvey Dutton, Moses Morgan— these stand out very conspicuously upon the tablet of memory as entering when I did. I had a peculiar psychological experience with Gove. It was a case of hate at first sight. He was very slim in those days, had a big nose, and used to laugh at people who made mistakes. I regarded him for some time with a silent, unspeakable hatred. Well, time mended all that. After these twenty-four years, I send love to Gove, whom I hated; to Dutton, whom I quarreled with; to Joseph Howell and Augusta Peterson, whom I respected and yet felt it my duty to regard with a certain dislike, because they were Philadelphians. From their heights of spirit-life may a benediction be wafted down, even to us, who struggled hard to make the name of Simeon Wright immortal!

There were two literary societies in those days. It is strange, but true, that the members used to quarrel. We had contest meetings, joint debates, and various occasions of conflict. After our removal into the "new building," we impoverished ourselves and incurred heavy debts, in order to buy better furniture and more books than the people of the other Society. On the door of the Wrightonian Hall was a motto, painted in blue and gold, "Sapere Aude." It was the occasion, to the Philadelphians, of many irreverent and disrespectful puns. As a loyal Wrightonian, I trust that this motto has disappeared, and that the Brussels carpet, gay with yellow roses, which reduced us all to bankruptcy who were concerned in purchasing it, has been replaced by the bounty of a younger and wealthier generation.

In 1858, Bloomington had a population of some 7,000 people. In winter, its streets were a sea of mud. "Come over here," once shouted Professor Wilbur, the geologist, to Uncle Sim Wright, across the street. "I can't," was the answer; between thee and me there is a great gulf fixed." Teams were daily mired down in the principal streets. There was a place called Pone Hollow, allusions to which were particularly in order, if any one would be called facetious. The crossings there were particularly dreadful when the long rains drenched the prairies.

"The gunpowder plot" was enacted in Major's Hall. Gove had organized a band of nocturnal serenaders, called the "Squallers." They used to go about with an awfully discordant orchestra of willow whistles. To blow these beneath the lattice of a slumbering maiden, was to induce in her spasms of palpitating fear and agony. The Squallers were wont to meet in Mr. Hovey's office, not to rehearse, but to form their plans. One of the boys had observed this, and longed to know what it all meant. He took into his confidence one Burnham, who wickedly betrayed him to the Squallers. Their plans were duly laid. Hidden in a box in the room, the inquiring youth heard the particulars of a plot which caused his "knotty and combined locks to part, and each particular hair to stand on end"—no less a scheme than the blowing up of the old building with gunpowder, in order to expedite the construction of the new one! The very box in which the spy was secreted was selected as the receptacle for this terrible explosive, and was turned over, rolling out upon the floor this inquiring youth. The tableau was unutterable; the muttered threats were dreadful. At last, after binding himself with more horrible oaths than Morgan, the anti-Mason, ever dreamed of, and making a liberal contribution for the purchase of gunpowder, he was allowed to go home, where he doubtless passed the night in dreadful expectancy, and came to school next morning, only to find an audible smile on every face. Well, he treated the crowd to apples, and we unanimously agreed not to tell his father of his misadventure; in pursuance of which pledge, his name appeareth not in these pages.

We were shabbily dressed in those days. I think my pantaloons were generally too short, and my coats seemed to have been made for some other person. We were very poor, but very plucky. We boarded ourselves, mainly on corn mush, washed the floors and built the fires at the Normal Hall, worked hard, lived hard, and were poorly provided with all things; our parents were sad-faced, struggling pioneers of the prairies; but we were cheery, resolute and happy in our life and our work. To the toiling youth of frontier homes, thirsting for knowledge, the Illinois Normal University opened the gateways of a new life. We loved it, rejoiced in it, and were thoroughly loyal to its name and fame.

The school saw but little of its principal in those years. Two miles to the northward, across the sodden prairies, in the rainy autumn of 1858, were clay pits, heaps of brickbats, half-complete foundations for a stately structure, yet in embryo. The construction fund was exhausted, the State heavily in debt, business everywhere

12

distressed and languishing; truly a somber prospect for the completion of a building, demanding, on the basis existing before the war, a hundred thousand dollars. It would be as easy to-day to raise a million. To secure these needed funds was the task which Charles E. Hovey set before himself. It was a labor for Hercules. His own fortune was pledged over and over. Had his plans failed, he would have been weighted for life with hopeless bankruptcy. This enormous task he undertook and carried through. He had a place on the programme of the school's daily work, but his classes generally wrought out their own salvation. But in the winter of 1860–1 the building was completed; the Legislature assembled; Governor Dick Yates delivered the dedicatory address; the State assumed the liabilities of the Board of Regents, and the enormous burden of debt rolled off the shoulders which had borne it so bravely. A new generation has arisen since those days, mainly ignorant of these events, and yet enjoying the fruits of those labors. It is for them that I make the record. We of the pioneering days, need no reminder of the grand work which could hardly have been performed by another than General Charles E. Hovey.

We were free in our conduct, to a singular extent. No school rules rested upon us. Our hours and methods were wholly our own. We lived as we pleased, formed our friendships and associations, made our calls, and managed our affairs, entirely at our own choice and pleasure. Very few schools were ever so slightly governed. I do not believe that our successors of to-day can be journeying under any similar slackness of rein. Nevertheless, the record of those years was a thoroughly Spartan one. We were from Puritan households, disciplined in self-restraint. Industry and poverty were our safeguards.

A magnificent park, stately buildings, a beautiful and prosperous city, methods well-ordered, and politics established, splendid museums and laboratories, a wealthier and more cultured generation of students —these are the pleasant things that greet the view as you gather to the silver wedding of our Alma Mater. It is not true that the former days were better than these, but we who saw the working out of the beginnings, had also our joys, struggles, and coronations; and we received a training which, if less orderly and exhaustive than that rendered now, nevertheless gave us some measure of fitness for our life-work.

From my home and class-room by the Pacific, I send hearty greeting to the teachers and pupils who worked in Major's Hall together. God bless and speed you all, dear old friends and comrades, and grant you such length of days that, in the seventh year of the twentieth Christian century, a few of us, if old, yet vigorous, if with snow on the head, yet with fire at the heart, may gather to our Alma Mater's golden wedding.   H. B. NORTON.

STATE NORMAL SCHOOL, San Jose, California, July 23, 1882.

ADDRESS BY GEN. C. E. HOVEY.

ALUMNI AND FRIENDS OF THE NORMAL UNIVERSITY:

We are here in obedience to a much honored custom, for the purpose of celebrating the completion of the first quarter-century of the Normal University; and I recognize the fact that I owe the honor of occupying the platform to-night to my early connection with the institution and a presumed acquaintance with the ideas on which it was founded.

It is no secret that this Normal School has achieved very considerable reputation in its department of labor. It is as well known in Washington as in Chicago. State lines have not walled in its fame, and I doubt whether Illinois can point to another institution which has done her more honor, except, always, her common schools. It, however, is one of these. The same men founded both, and maintained the right to support both at the public charge. They held that the Normal School was simply the head common school of the State.

I have thought I could not do better, on the present occasion, than to invite you to go back with me to the time when these measures, the establishment of free schools and a Normal School, were under consideration, and to introduce you to the men and ideas of that time. I admit the principle they contended about—the right to tax the whole property of the State in support of schools for the free education of every child in her borders—is no longer in issue. It has gone into your statutes and constitution, and gone there to stay. Indeed, he would be a brave man who should propose to take it out.

Similar laws, or laws for a similar purpose, more or less effective, are now on the statute books of every State and every territory of the United States of North America. By what right are they there? What right has government to take the property of one man to educate the children of another? Is not property an absolute natural right, as much as life, or liberty? When and how did government acquire the right to seize upon the property of the citizens for the support of schools—to take, by taxation, the earnings of the industrious and frugal to educate the children of the idle and thriftless?

At the time to which I invite your attention, a respectable body of the people of the State held that government had no such right, and they stoutly resisted, by words and votes, those who put forward the claim. They insisted that taxation for the support of common schools, if not tyranny, was at least an invasion of the rights of property, not warranted by anything in the social compact, and they challenged those who held the contrary opinion to an examination of fundamental principles of civil government. They pointed out the clause in the State constitution which declares "that a frequent recurrence to fundamental principles of civil government is absolutely necessary to preserve the blessings of liberty," and they invoked those principles in aid of their side of the question. Of course, the friends of free schools had no alternative but to accept the challenge, and for a quarter of a century the contest went on.

In 1825, the Legislature, under the lead of some far-seeing statesman, passed a school law, setting out with a preamble:

"To enjoy our rights and liberties, we must understand them; their security and protection ought to be the first object of a free people; and it is a well-established fact that no nation has ever continued long in the enjoyment of civil and political freedom which was not both virtuous and enlightened; and, believing that the advancement of literature always has been and ever will be the means of developing more fully the rights of man, that the mind of every citizen in a republic is the common property of society, and constitutes the basis of its strength and happiness; therefore, be it enacted, etc."

That is pretty good doctrine, even now. The law, that followed this preamble, established a system of common schools, and authorized a majority of the legal voters in any school district to levy a tax for the support of a school in that district. It was a local matter, and depended on the voluntary action of the voters. But it recognized a principle—the right of a people in neighborhoods to tax themselves for the support of free schools in such neighborhoods.

The next Legislature, 1827, amended this law, and provided that "No person shall hereafter be taxed for the support of any free school in this State, unless by his or her own free will and consent, first had and obtained, in writing." Here was a flat denial of the right of taxation for free schools. As amended, the tax section of the school law amounted to little more than a legislative permission "to pass around the hat." Of course, the legislation of 1827 was the death of taxation for school purposes, and it maintained a place on the statute book for many years. In process of time and changes it finally disappeared, but not until 1855 did the contrary principle take its place. Then was passed the first rough draft of the present free-school law. A two-mill tax was levied on "each dollar's valuation of all the taxable property in the State" for the use and support of common schools. In 1857, under leadership of a man who is no stranger to these halls, this law was revised and its provisions harmonized. I shall read from his speech, on reporting the bill to the House, before I get through.

From 1825 to 1855, or 1827 to 1857, if you prefer, the discussion among the people as to their right, in their collective capacity as a government, to impose a tax for the support of schools, went on. It was a memorable debate. I am sorry so little of it is now available. The most of it, so far as I know, and some of the best of it, was never in print. It was carried on in cabins, in shops, in town-halls, in churches, in school houses, on the stump and in the capitol. I remember its substance very well.

I should say in passing, that the plan of my address to-night excludes the idea of originality. I am inviting you to listen to the story as told by other men in other days, and in so far as I am compelled to vary from this rule, and to use my own words, it will be done sparingly and with a free knowledge that I am, to that extent, detracting from the historic value of the narrative. I am compelled, however, to begin the subject with some sketches in my own language. Here is one, wherein the right of taxation for education is deduced from the nature and objects of the social compact. I give it in outline only:

·The purpose of all human government is protection. Every man has an absolute natural right to life, and liberty, and such property as he has earned or otherwise honestly acquired; and he may properly defend these against all comers. If anybody attempts to murder him he may strike back, and if, in so doing, he kills his assailant, he is held blameless. In the absence of outside aid he must maintain his rights himself, or lose them. But he may combine with others for protection, thereby forming what is called the social compact; and this combination, or compact, or government, may undertake to protect each of its members from being murdered, or enslaved, or robbed; and it may do this by any appropriate means; for instance, it may establish courts, build jails, employ judges and sheriffs and policemen. These are held to be appropriate means the world over, but they cost money, and, as their purpose and effect is to protect all alike, all may properly be required to share in the expense of supporting them, each according to his ability. This is taxation. Nobody denies its propriety. It grows out of the necessities of the case. If men were angels the case would be different, and taxation might probably be less. But these repressive agencies are not believed to be the only means adapted to the protection of society. The inventive genius of mankind has been at work to discover others less repulsive. Of course, if other means or agencies or institutions can be found which tend to protect society, they will stand on the same ground as to their right to be supported by taxation that courts and jails do.

Assuming this theory to be correct, philanthropists have undertaken to find some such other means. Observation and experiment began a long time ago. It was discovered and recorded in a very old book that a child trained up in the way he should go, would go that way. It was ascertained that the patrons of jails and prisons were generally illiterate. Acting on these hints, wise men began to devise means for training children, and abolishing illiteracy. Colleges and universities were founded, and finally, after centuries of trial and experiment, the common schools. They are proposed as a substitute for the machinery of force, except as to the hopelessly incorrigible. Their effect is to do away with, or greatly abridge, the need of repressive agencies; and just so far as they do this, they protect society. The system is one of prevention. It undertakes to afford everybody's children an opportunity for elementary instruction and thereby help them to become good citizens, and to make free government possible. Such is an outline of the argument.

It assumed, of course, a variety of forms of statement. I remember one which struck me at the time as a little peculiar, but it was really grounded on the idea just stated. Perhaps I had better stop long enough to give this statement, as a further sample of the way the thinkers of the past generation reasoned about this matter of taxation for promoting the general welfare and the general safety. The statement to which I refer was about as follows:

The great Oxford professor, Dr. Blackstone, speaking of the absolute natural rights of man, groups them all together, under the general term, liberty. Now, liberty is the idol of mankind. Whoever can find out a means of promoting it is sure to be honored as a benefactor. For a thousand years the races to which we belong have been devising, and testing, and fighting for institutions which they believed would tend to secure for them and their posterity this supreme good. They began to formulate principles of government in the interest of liberty as far back as the middle of the eleventh century, when Henry II assembled a great council at Clarendon, and brought forward therein ordinances defining and limiting ecclesiastical authority. Half a century later, they made the plains of Running-mede forever famous as the place where the great charter of England was promulgated by King John, in the presence of the barons who had drawn it up, and a vast multitude of people.

This declaration was intended to define and protect the civil liberties of Englishmen. Its twenty-ninth chapter is regarded as the corner stone of the British constitution, and provides that no free man shall be taken, or imprisoned, or dispossessed of his property, or liberties, or outlawed, or punished in any other way, unless by the judgment of his equals or the law of the land.* Fitzwalter and the old barons did not declare for wild, unregulated liberty. They did not undertake to say that nobody should be imprisoned, or dispossessed of property or life. That was not their idea of liberty at Runningmede. But they did declare, and made their king agree, that none of these things should be done except in pursuance of law and the verdict of a jury. That was their idea of liberty six hundred years ago. It has not been much improved upon since.

Their great charter, amended and enlarged, was again promulgated in the reign of Charles I, and again on the accession of William

* "Nullus liber homo capiatur, vel imprisonetur, de libero tenemento suo, vel libertatibus vel liberis consuetudinibus suis, aut utlagetur aut exulitur, aut aliquo modo destruatur, nec super eum mittimus, nisi, per legali judicum parium suorum, vel per legem terrae."

and Mary, about 1688. In all these cases the people had been obliged to recover their liberties "by intrepid councils, or by force of arms," and they undertook, by formal declarations, to construct a barrier against future encroachments.

The institution they invented and chiefly relied upon for the protection of their civil liberties has come to be known as the common law; the old barons called it the law of the land. It made use of courts and all the officers and incidents necessary to ascertain and punish violence and fraud, and to settle disputes. They held it to be no invasion of the rights of property to compel every man, according to his means, to contribute to the support of these instrumentalities, and they were right. These agents were and are necessary for liberty and safety. But it can hardly be said that they are the only ones. There may be others. The test is protection to liberty. The machinery of the common law was devised to maintain liberty among men. The machinery of the common schools does the same thing. Both stand on the same ground. It will be seen that the soundness of this view hinges upon statistics. If it is a fact, and that must be shown by statistics, that the common schools do tend to decrease the enemies of social order, and to increase the number of good citizens, then the reasoning is sound.

I have before me a report of Hon. J. C. Dore, first superintendent of schools for Chicago, made about the time of the passage of the free school law, which furnishes some of these statistics. He says:

"The public has rights as well as individuals, and education is the surest protection to both. It is in a very great degree the prevention of crime.' Out of 28,000 convicts in the State of New York during the last ten years, previous to 1853, only one hundred and twenty-eight had received the advantages of a good common school education. More, than two hundred uneducated persons became convicts to every one who had received a common school education. In view of these facts, who will hesitate to acknowledge that our public school system is the security of the State, and that the public has a right to demand, and enforce, if need be, the attendance at school of every child of school-going age, until a common school education is insured? Suffering children to grow up in ignorance is doing violence to society. Who can tell how many thousands, pests to society, rendering necessary policemen by day, and sentinels by night, and courts of justice through the year for public protection, would have made inoffensive citizens had they possessed a good public school education? Who can number the murders perpetrated, thefts committed, crimes and misdemeanors of every name and nature, that never would have been, had the guilty availed themselves of the advantages of the public schools? * * * * * *

"In a country of free competition and equal rights, where 'every man is heir to the highest honors of the State,' a good education is indispensable to the full enjoyment of those rights. Places of honor, trust, and profit, can be filled only by persons qualified to perform the duties peculiar to such positions. It is in the public schools that the great majority of children and youth are to be educated, if at all. The question then comes home to every patriotic and philanthropic citizen, shall they be educated? * * * * * *

"The United States exhibit the relation of public education to free institutions. Their public school systems are the result of the grandest conception of modern times, and may yet make the tour of the world."

So said John C. Dore, nearly thirty years ago, and since that time the system has been spreading. And who shall say that it will not yet make the tour of the world? But I should mislead if I confined myself to a statement of fundamental principles and to the reports of school officers. There was an exceedingly practical side to the debate which cropped out, more particularly in State Legislatures. I am glad to be able to present this phase of the great common school contest in the words of one of its most celebrated combatants. (He did not reside in this State, and the speech from which I quote was a little earlier in date than the chief discussion here, but it covers the same ground. It was the same contest.)

Pennsylvania had passed a free school law, and the hosts of ignorance had rallied and demanded its repeal. In answer to that demand, Thaddeus Stevens said (I give only a part):

"Mr. Speaker: I will briefly give you the reasons why I shall oppose the repeal of the school law.

"It would seem to be humiliating to be under the necessity, in the nineteenth century, of entering into a formal argument to prove the utility, and, to free governments, the absolute necessity of education. More than two thousand years ago, the Deity who presided over intellectual endowments, ranked highest among the goddesses worshipped by cultivated Pagans. And I will not insult this House, or our constituents, by supposing any course of reasoning necessary to convince *them* of its high importance. If an elective republic is to endure for any great length of time, every elector must have sufficient information, not only to accumulate wealth and take care of his pecuniary concerns, but to direct wisely the Legislature, the ambassadors, and the executive of the nation, for some part of all these things, some agency, in approving or disapproving of them, falls to every freeman. If, then, the permanency of our government depends upon such knowledge, it is the duty of government to see that the means of information be diffused to every citizen. This is a sufficient answer to those who deem education a private and not a public duty —who argue that they are willing to educate their own children, but not their neighbors' children.

"The amendment which is now proposed as a substitute for the school law of last session is, in my opinion, of a most hateful and degrading character. It is a re-enactment of the pauper law of 1809. It proposes that the assessors shall take a census, and make a record of the poor. This shall be revised, and a new record made by the county commissioners, so that the names of those who have the misfortune to be poor men's children, shall be forever preserved, as a distinct class, in the archives of the country! Sir, hereditary distinctions of rank are sufficiently odious, but that which is founded on poverty is infinitely more so. Such a law should be entitled 'an act for branding and marking the poor, so that they may be known from the rich and proud.'

"Many complain of this tax, not so much on account of its amount, as because it is for the benefit of others, and not themselves. This is a mistake; it is for their own benefit, inasmuch as it perpetuates the government and ensures the due administration of the laws under which they live, and by which their lives and property are protected.

"This law is often objected to, because its benefits are shared by the children of the profligate spendthrift equally with those of the most industrious and economical habits. It ought to be remembered that the benefit is bestowed, not upon the erring parents, but the innocent children.

"It is said that its advantages will be unjustly and unequaly enjoyed, because the industrious, money-making man keeps his whole family constantly employed, and has but little time for them to spend at school, while the idle man has but little employment for his family and they will constantly attend school. I know, sir, that there are some men whose whole souls are completely absorbed in the accumulation of wealth, and whose avarice so increases with success that they look upon their children in no other light than as instruments of gain; that they, as well as the ox and the ass within their gates, are valuable only in proportion to their annual earnings. And, according to the present system, the children of such men are reduced almost to an intellectual level with their co-laborers of the brute creation. The law will be of vast advantage to the offspring of such misers. If they are compelled to pay their taxes to support schools, their very meanness will induce them to send their children to the schools to get the worth of their money.

"In New England, free schools plant the seeds and the desire of knowledge in every mind, without regard to the wealth of the parent or the texture of the pupil's garments. It is no uncommon occurrence to see the poor man's son, thus encouraged by wise legislation, far outstrip and bear off the laurels from the less industrious heirs of wealth. Some of the ablest men of the present and past days never could have been educated except for that benevolent system. Not to mention any of the living, it is well known that the architect of an immortal name, who 'plucked the lightnings from heaven, and the sceptre from tyrants,' was a child of free schools.

"But we are told that this law is unpopular; that the people desire its repeal. But, sir, much of its unpopularity is chargeable upon the vile arts of unprincipled demagogues. I do not charge this upon any particular party. Unfortunately, almost the only spot on which all parties meet in union is this ground of common infamy. I have seen the present chief magistrate of this commonwealth violently assailed as the projector and father of this law. I am not the eulogist of that gentleman; he has been guilty of many deep political sins; but he deserves the undying gratitude of the people for the steady, untiring zeal which he has manifested in favor of common schools. I trust that the people of this State will never be called on to choose between a supporter and an opposer of free schools. But if it should come to that; if that should be made the turning point on which we are to cast our suffrages; if the opponent of education were my most intimate personal and political friend, and the free school candidate my most obnoxious enemy, I should deem it my duty as a patriot, at this moment of our intellectual crisis, to forget all other considerations, and I should place myself unhesitatingly and cordially in the ranks of him whose banner streams in light.

"It is said that some gentlemen lost their election by being in favor of the school law. I believe that is true of the two highly respected members of the last Legislature from Union County. They were summoned before a county meeting and requested to pledge themselves to vote for its repeal as the price of their reëlection. But they were too high-minded and honorable to consent to such degradation. They fell, it is true, in this great struggle between the powers of light and darkness; but they fell, as every Roman mother wished her sons to fall, facing the enemy, with all their wounds in front.

"True it is, that two other gentlemen, and I believe two only, lost their election on account of their votes on that question. I refer to the late members from Berks, who were candidates for reëlection; and I regret that gentlemen whom I so highly respect, and whom I take pleasure in ranking among my personal friends, had not possessed a little more nerve to enable them to withstand the assaults which were made upon them; or, if they must be overpowered, to wrap their mantles gracefully around them and yield with dignity. But this, I am aware, requires a high degree of fortitude; and those respected gentlemen, distracted and faltering between the dictates of conscience and the clamor of the populace, at length turned and fled; but duty had detained them so long that they fled too late, and the shaft which had already been winged by ignorance, overtook and pierced them from behind.

"I am happy to say, sir, that a more fortunate fate awaited our friends from York. Possessing a keener insight into futurity, and a sharper instinct of danger, they saw the peril at a greater distance, and retreated in time to escape the fury of the storm, and can now safely boast that "discretion is the better part of valor," and that "they fought and ran away," "and lived to fight—on t' other side." Sir, it is to be regretted that any gentleman should have consented to place his election on hostility to general education. But will this Legislature, guardians of the dearest interests of a great commonwealth, consent to surrender the high advantages and brilliant prospects which this law promises because it is desired by worthy gentlemen who, in a moment of causeless panic and popular delusion, sailed into power on a Tartarean flood? A flood of ignorance, darker, and to the intelligent mind, more dreadful than that accursed pool at which mortals and immortals tremble! Sir, it seems to me that the liberal and enlightened proceedings of the last Legislature have aroused the demon of ignorance from his slumber; and, maddened at the threatened loss of his murky empire, his discordant howlings are heard in every part of our land.

"The barbarous and disgraceful cry 'that learning makes us worse; that education makes men rogues,' should find no echo within these walls. Those who hold such doctrines anywhere, would be the objects of bitter detestation, if they were not rather the pitiable objects of compassion, for even voluntary fools require our compassion, as well as natural idiots.

"In giving this law to posterity, you act the part of the philanthropist and philosopher. Those who would add thereto the glory of the hero, can acquire it here; for in the present state of feeling in Pennsylvania, I am willing to admit that but little less dangerous to the public man is the war-club and battle-axe of savage ignorance, than to the lion-hearted Richard was the keen scimetar of the Saracen. He who would oppose it, either through inability to comprehend the advantages of general education, or from unwillingness to bestow them on all his fellow-citizens, even to the lowest and the poorest, or from dread of popular vengeance, seems to me to want either the head of the philosopher, the heart of the philanthropist, or the nerve of the hero."

Such was the language of the men who fought the great battle of free schools. It was the same battle in Illinois as in Pennsylvania, and was won in the same way in both States.

Suppose you join me on a trip to Springfield, and having made yourselves comfortable in the gallery of the old capitol, as it was in February, 1857, turn your attention to the proceedings going on in the hall below. A man of medium size, wearing spectacles, rises to address the assembled legislators. It is evident that some measure of more than usual interest is about to be considered, or that some man of more than usual ability is about to speak; probably both.

The members have discontinued their letter-writing and are giving. attention:

"Mr. Speaker: As chairman of the House committee on education, it becomes my duty to explain the changes made in the present school law by the joint committee of both houses," began Hon. S. W. Moulton, of Shelby. "I believe I may say with truth that out of the one hundred members of this Legislature, there are none but are in favor of taxation for the support of common schools."

Recollect it is now in 1857. The great struggle of a quarter of a century culminated two years before when the two-mill tax was put upon the statute-book. The questions now at issue have reference to perfecting the law and distributing the fund. Mr. Moulton continues:

"The friends of this bill assume, as the true principles that should govern its distribution (the tax), that two-thirds be distributed upon population equally all over the State, and one third upon territory. Those who oppose this distribution adopt the amendment proposed by the late superintendent, viz.: That the amount of the two-mill tax collected in each county should be repaid to the several counties without regard to population, or other circumstances. This is the statement of the question.

"Mr. Speaker, I presume but little difference of opinion exists as to the true object of the two-mill tax—that of providing means for the education of all the children of the State, and that each child is of right entitled to an equal share of the tax, without regard to condition or locality, or from what particular part of the State it was collected. This principle has its foundation in the fact that every child has an absolute right to an education at the hands of somebody, to an extent that shall properly qualify him to discharge his duties as a citizen. Experience shows that when education is left to the voluntary actions of parents and others, it is greatly neglected, and amounts almost to a failure. Children come into the world in a helpless condition, and remain so for years. They cannot educate themselves any more than they can provide for themselves food and clothing. Hence, the duty and necessity of government, providing by general laws, ample means for their education. This can only be done by taxation; and I hold that, as this tax is collected by the same persons and in the same manner as all other State taxes are, it should be disbursed upon the same principle, without regard to where, from what person, or from what county or locality collected; and that any other principle of disbursement operates unequaly and unjustly.

"The tax being collected from all the property of the State, and the object being the education of all the children of the State, it seems to me that it follows as an irresistable conclusion, that each child is entitled to an equal *pro rata* share of all the money collected; that if the aggregate amount collected is equal to five dollars for each child, then that is the amount that each child is entitled to, without regard to any other circumstances, and especially whether one county pays more or less than another.

"If property is to educate the children of a State, then the rich counties ought to pay more than the poor counties, because they have more to pay with, just as the rich man pays more than the poor man. No county or individual has an absolute and unlimited control over property. It may be regarded as held in trust for certain purposes. The right of every child in the land to be educated is one of these, and of primary importance, upon which our government stands. This great principle, I trust, will never be subverted and lost sight of by the adoption of the principle that particular localities shall receive back just what they pay, which amounts to no taxation at all."

"Mr. Speaker, I desire only to say a word as to the result of the free school experiment in this State. Two years since the system was adopted, and it went into operation under not very favorable auspices. It was rather a novel thing to many of our citizens, some of them being greatly prejudiced against it; and besides, there were many defects and objectionable things in the old law. But, notwithstanding the many disadvantages of the old law, the expectation of its friends had been more than realized. The people have been aroused from the apathy that enthralled them; they have been brought into direct contact with the system, good or bad, for when a people are taxed for a thing, they become interested in it. The result seems to be that the great mass of the people everywhere are in favor of continuing the two-mill tax, and differ only about the details of the law. It is a remarkable fact, worthy of all remembrance, that no State or people who have once adopted a free school system ever abandoned it."

The chairman is supported by Dr. Gowdy and others, and opposed by Mr. Sparks and others, but his bill prevails and "is passed;" and from that event I date the real beginning of the grandest institution of the State, her free schools.

You will see that I have now called attention to early legislation in the State wherein taxation for the support of schools was directly drawn in issue; to the reasoning from fundamental principles of civil government by which the friends of free schools undertook to justify them; to a report of a school officer, Hon. J. C. Dore, twenty-seven years ago; to a speech on the merits of the free school system, by Hon. Thaddeus Stevens; and to a speech on perfecting and harmonizing our own system, by Hon. S. W. Moulton. This is as full and fair a presentation as I am able to make in the time allotted.

I now come to a separate consideration of the head school of the system, and I can not better introduce the subject than by stating the idea of a Normal School as understood at the time it was established.

Fortunately, I can do so in the words then used. I quote from the *Illinois Teacher:*

"The idea of Normal Schools is a very simple idea. It proceeds merely upon the ground that a man may profit by the experience of other men, as well as by his own; not by the experience of one predecessor alone, but of a whole lineage of them; not by the experience of one contemporary alone, but of any contemporaries who know more, on any common point between them, than he does. Now, the person who denies the utility of Normal Schools, undertakes to refute such a proposition. He affirms that one man cannot derive knowledge from the experience of others; that Tubal Cain made as good household or agricultural implements as can now be found in Chicago, reaping machines included. He undertakes to show that Fulton's first steamboat, which went from New York to Albany at the rate of four and a half miles an hour, was equal to those which now shoot, arrow-like, up and down the Mississippi. In a word, he denies that experience teaches, and that light enlightens. The object of Normal Schools is to teach teachers how to teach."

Such was a teachers' idea of Normal Schools as he wrote it twenty-five years ago. The Industrial League, an important organization, took a similar view of professional schools, as appears from its memorial to the Legislature in 1853. They say: "We, the members of the industrial classes are still compelled to work empirically and blindly, without needful books, schools or means, by the slow process of that individual experience that lives and dies with the man. Our professional brethren, through their universities, books and teachers, combine and concentrate the practical experience of ages in each man's life."

Such was their idea. These people seem to have thought that one man might learn something from the experience of another, and one generation from the experience of another generation; and that it was worth while to gather up these experiences and make them available. They thought they could do this, as the doctors and lawyers and ministers had done it; by establishing professional schools.

The great thinker and orator of that day, on these questions—the man who towered above his fellows like a Colossus—was Professor John B. Turner. His speech to the farmers and mechanics at Granville, in 1851, set in motion a movement which spread and strengthened until finally Congress responded by endowing professional schools for the industrial classes in all the States. From the first, Prof. Turner placed a Normal College at the head of the colleges or departments of his proposed university. The League was a unit on that question. Arny, Murray, Pennell, Kennicott, Rutherford, Minier—all agreed. A committee of the State Senate, to whom was referred their memorial, reported in 1854, I think, that

"In education, as in all other subjects, there are certain truths that are self-evident, or at least so nearly so, that they are admitted as axioms by all men acquainted with the subject. One of these self-evident propositions is, that the teacher must exist before the scholar can be taught. Whoever, therefore, would begin at the foundation of any system of public instruction must provide the means for furnishing a supply of competent teachers; and without these, it is equally self-evident that any system of common school instruction, however wise in its laws or ample in its expenditures, or free and accessible to rich and poor, will prove a useless tax on the one, and a waste of time, if not a nuisance, to the other."

How much have you improved on these "self-evident" propositions during the last quarter of a century? The statesmen who signed that report were George Gage, John D. Arnold and Joseph Morton.

I have drawn attention to the Industrial League because it had considerable influence in preparing the way for the Normal School. I must, also, refer to some facts about the State school funds. From time to time, as money accrued to these funds from the sale of lands, the Legislature appropriated it to the ordinary expenses of government; and directed the State Treasurer to enter on his books the amount, so appropriated, to the credit of the funds; and thereafter the State paid interest on the amount so taken and used, and applied it to the support of the common schools. There were three of these State school funds, but the interest on the college and on the seminary funds was consolidated with the interest on the common school fund, and disbursed for the support of the common schools.

Against this illegal diversion of the interest on the college and seminary funds, the League was the first to protest. In one of its memorials to the Legislature, it explains how the funds were being frittered away: "The annual interest on the university fund is about nine thousand dollars. If this should be divided between ten or fifteen colleges (as was proposed by some), it would give them only from six hundred to nine hundred dollars each per annum. Divided among one hundred counties (as was proposed by others), it would give them only ninety dollars each for a high school, or other purpose. Divided, as it now is, among the million of our people, it gives nine mills, or less than one cent, to each person."

Plainly the fund was not large enough to be of any great account to the common schools directly; and it was not intended by Congress to be so applied. In the special report to the State Senate, from which I have quoted, this matter was considered and the committee said:

"The universities and higher schools of Europe, and of the older States of this continent, were founded long before any attempt was made at a thorough system of common schools, and through them teachers were prepared to descend into, create, and instruct all departments below. If any State ever can secure a good system of common schools, for the people, by any other process, it is certain no one yet has done it, nor is it easy to see or imagine how it can be done.

"In accordance with this view, and in distinct recognition of this great fact, Congress granted to each new State of the west three separate funds,—university, seminary, and common school,—well knowing that the experience of the civilized world demonstrates the need of three departments in education as well as of three departments in the government of a free State.

"It is believed that no State but our own has ever attempted to reverse this decision of law, and our success so far in this enterprise is, to say the least, not very flattering."

So the report was adverse to the practice of applying the proceeds of the college and seminary funds to the support of the common schools, but it was made too late in the session for action, and the matter went over to the next Legislature.

Meanwhile, a new power had been growing up in the State. It found public expression through the State Teachers' Association. You know the men, Simeon Wright, Newton Bateman, S. M. Etter, D. S. Wentworth, William H. Wells, B. G. Roots, L. H. Potter, W. H. Haskell, J. Stone, Jr. I need not read the roll. It is a long one, and an honorable one. These men took counsel together at Chicago, in December, 1856, as to what had better be done or recommended. It was at a crisis in the intellectual history of the State. The free school law, then lately enacted, was on trial. It was crude in many provisions, and had some serious defects, chief of which was the total omission to provide any means for keeping up a supply of competent teachers, and the *esprit de corps* of the profession.

One result of that conference—that meeting of the Teachers' Association at Chicago, in 1856—became public a few weeks later, at Springfield, where the legislators had assembled. The bill, which disclosed the views and wishes of the Chicago conference of teachers, was entitled "An Act for the establishment and maintenance of a Normal University," and it called out a somewhat extended discussion of the nature and office of Normal Schools, and of their practicability and expediency. I have been unable to procure but one of the speeches delivered on that occasion, and from that must infer the tenor of the others—*ex uno disce omnes*. The speech which I have was made by Hon. C. B. Denio, of Jo Daviess:

"Mr. Speaker: "I had not intended to make any remarks on this bill, but since my name appears as one of the corporators, and after the unwarrantable insinuation of the gentleman from Union, that some gentlemen upon this floor are influenced in their support of this measure because their names are included among the corporators,

I deem it due to myself to state my position to this House, and give a few reasons for the hearty support I shall lend this measure. I happen, unlike the honorable gentleman from Union, to be numbered among those who, in early life, were deprived of the advantages of even a common school education. Had I enjoyed the advantages of that gentleman in my youth, and, sir, had I been favored with the long legislative experience of that gentleman, I might to-day realize less keenly than I do, my inexperience and want of these advantages; and, sir, I might be found battling on this floor, side by side with that gentleman, against extending to others those privileges which are the freeman's shield and the safeguard of the State. But, Mr. Speaker, in my time and in that part of the country where I was raised, one might travel a whole day and not find the sign of a school house; or, if he did, it would be only a little log hut, windowless and doorless. But, sir, a new era is dawning. Within two years, and since the passage of the law which the honorable gentleman only a few days ago voted against, school houses have sprung up in every part of the State, and by this time, perhaps, they have one even in Jonesboro.

"Now, sir, so far as the objection to this application of the interest of these 'sacred' funds is concerned, it seems to me that some gentlemen have all at once become wonderfully fearful that the 'sacred' fund (as they are pleased to call it) will be diverted from its legitimate channel. Why, sir, by reference to the journal of this Legislature some years since, I find that the gentleman from Union, and his political friends were feasting on oysters by appropriations from this same 'sacred' fund! And now, because it is proposed, after the lapse of nearly fifty years, to turn the interest of these funds to their legitimate course, the gentleman holds up his hands in holy horror.

"Mr. Dougherty: Can the gentleman from Jo Daviess state the amount belonging to these funds appropriated at any one time by the State?

"Mr. Denio: I will answer the gentleman by saying that, whether I can state the exact amount taken at any one time or not, does not matter, so far as the fact is concerned that the State has used up all these sacred funds, and grudgingly paid into the common school fund six per cent. only. And who are the gentlemen in this House mostly implicated in this matter? If you will go with me to the office below (the office of the Secretary of State was under the hall of the House) you will see by the names that the persons who are now so fearful that the school fund will be diverted from its legitimate direction, were in former years willing to pay themselves out of that fund; and chose to do so rather than take the responsibility of taxing the people. I suppose they acted in view of the fact that the little boys and girls could not vote, and their fathers could.

13

"What does this bill do? Sir, it proposes to educate teachers for the people's colleges. For these schools we must have teachers, and I think we should have western teachers, educated here at home. True, Governor Slade has done well in sending westward young women who not only make good teachers, but good wives. But I am not disposed to depend forever on such efforts. It is due to the State of Illinois that she take a nobler stand, and provide the means for educating her own young men and women to become teachers.

"The gentleman says we can not educate enough teachers to satisfy one-tenth of the wants of the State. I have not the slightest hope that this school can furnish a teacher for every school in the State; but it can and will, in a few years, furnish one, perhaps two, for every county. Their knowledge will become available to other teachers, and in this way the Normal School will multiply its usefulness.

"'But,' says my friend from Union, 'there is no guaranty that these men will continue to teach after they are prepared in this school.' In reply to this I have only to say that that will depend entirely on whether or not we are willing to pay them a reasonable compensation.

"Mr. Speaker, I am somewhat surprised that the speech just delivered by my friend from Coles should for a moment have disturbed or alarmed the friends of the bill before the House. It is true, he has made a speech against the bill; but this, to me, is a promise of a good time coming. I argue from the fact that he has spoken against the bill, that we may depend upon his vote with us for the bill. This has been the gentleman's way of doing business all winter. He has always convinced himself while speaking that he was wrong, and then voted against his own speech. I am not looking for a departure from his usual practice. I expect his vote for the measure."

I have a dim recollection that the gentleman from Jo Daviess once told me that the gentleman from Coles went back on him, and ruined his reputation as a prophet, by voting against the bill.

"There are certain reasons," continued Mr. Denio, "why I wish to see this bill become a law. It is not in all respects the thing I am in favor of, or have been in favor of. I have been, and am now, of the opinion that something like an Industrial University, on the plan of Prof. Turner, was demanded and should be adopted; and, acting on that opinion, I introduced the following resolution into the Legislature, in February, 1853, and it was adopted unanimously by that body:

"*Resolved*, by the House of Representatives, the Senate concurring therein, That our senators in Congress be instructed, and our representatives be requested, to use their best exertions to procure the passage of a law of Congress, donating to each State in the Union an amount of public lands not less in value than five hundred thousand dollars, for the endowment of a system of Industrial Universities, one in each State, for the more liberal and practical education of our industrial classes and their teachers.

"This resolution was presented to Congress by Hon. E. B. Washburn, of my district, and the lands were asked for, but nothing has yet been done."

I call attention to the dates. Prof. Turner outlined his plan for a University in 1851. In 1853, February 8, the State Legislature took action. These were the first steps taken anywhere, so far as I know, to procure an endowment by Congress for Industrial Universities in the several States.

"At that time, 1853, it was thought best to take a part of the University and Seminary funds to start such an institution. But there were too many 'old fogies' in the Legislature, and too many men in Congress who preferred to attend to the interests of railroad companies rather than the interests of the people and their education. So nothing was done. We now have a chance to do something to promote the welfare of the common schools, by furnishing them with competent teachers, educated at home. I shall give the measure my hearty support."

So spoke Denio. I have the speech of no other member, and did not, myself, hear the debate; but I understood, at the time, that it took a wide range, covering the theory of professional schools as well as the manner and means of their establishment and maintainance.

On the eighteenth day of February, 1857, this Normal University Act took its place upon the statute book "as an appendix to the school law; and on the fifth day of October following, its first class, or part of it, assembled for the first time. The meeting took place in the third story of a plain brick building, standing a little off from the principal street in Blooming ton, and known as Major's Hall. This hall had, theretofore, become historic as the birth place of a powerful political party in the State; and, more particulary, as the place where the grandest man of modern times had delivered an oration in behalf of liberty. It now became the scene of another event, quite unlike the former in outward demonstrations, but destined, I think, to be remembered as long.

Had you been there on that October morning, five and twenty years ago, you would have seen ten young men and seventeen young women grouped together on the benches, looking inquiringly towards Ira Moore and the principal sitting on the platform. That and there was the beginning. The names of those young people, or of some of them, head the column of your alumni. The two men on the platform saw, or thought they saw, in the faces before them a promise of coming honor to the institution. They believed in its growth, not as a sudden creation of a magic palace, but as the slow-coming result of hard work on a good plan. I think I may say, they, and their associates, were much in earnest. They had faith. Theirs was the glowing expectancy with which Romulus and Remus began to build, about the shepherds' huts upon the seven hills near the Tiber, the walls which afterwards sheltered imperial Rome.

In the quarter of a century of its existence, by the silent processes of a natural evolution, the Normal University has grown to be an important radiating centre of educational thought. Its graduates have gone abroad over the State, but loyally return from time to time to pay their tribute of affection and esteem. For them and for myself, I tender that tribute to-night.

ADDRESS OF RICHARD EDWARDS, LL. D.

When men are to be urged forward to the achievement of some high purpose, when the deeds under discussion are as yet unperformed, he who addresses a public assembly has need of skill in arranging his facts, and eloquence in uttering them. At such a time, the purpose of the speaker is to arouse his hearers into the right kind of activity, to awaken within them the required enthusiasm. But this is not our task to-day. Not of the future, but of the past, are we to speak on this anniversary. We need the spirit and bearing, not of the ecstatic seer, peering into the hidden depths of the time to come, but of the calm and truthful historian, reviewing the records of years gone by. And it is a positive luxury to feel that for once we are not to address ourselves to legislators, from whom an appropriation is expected, nor to a crowd of indifferent people whose torpid interest in education, or at least in the Normal University, it is necessary to kindle into life. Not that we have cause to complain of the way in which the appeals of the past have been met, either by citizens or law-makers. Both have dealt generously with this institution in the quarter century which ends to-day. Its friends have been grandly true to it, both in Springfield and throughout the State. But there is a refreshing sense of relief in the thought that we are discussing things accomplished, and not things hoped for. And the aim of this paper shall be to present as plain and impartial a statement as possible of the most significant facts in the history of the institution during the period—nearly fourteen years—of the writer's connection therewith.

That connection began on the seventeenth day of March, 1862, when I took the place on the faculty which had just been vacated by Mr. John Hull. My duty was to hear the classes in mathematics, and to give instruction in the Theory and Art of Teaching. At this time, Mr. Perkins Bass, a member of the Board of Education, was acting as temporary principal. On the twenty-fifth of June in that year, the Board, by a unanimous vote, elected me to the principalship of the institution, and my acceptance was sent in on the next day. The connection thus established was continued until January 1, 1876.

It is certainly no exaggeration to say that, in 1862, the prospects of the institution were gloomy. In the first place, it was a time of depression for all schools. The chief occupation of the people was war. Ambitious men and patriotic men—those who were seeking their own profit and glory, and those who were unselfishly seeking the good of the country, were for once engaged in the same outward pursuit. Home interests were for the time, in a state of suspended animation. Even business was neglected. The millions of the republic stood appalled in the presence of a terrible danger,—a danger the like of which had never before appeared. And the year just named will be remembered as the very gloomiest in all that perilous time. Military disasters had darkened the prospect. Bull Run had been the scene of two desperate defeats. Mr. Seward's ninety days had come and gone so many times, that the count of them began to be monotonous, and yet the rebellion was not crushed. Instead of that, it seemed mightier than at the beginning. Good reasons there seemed to be for expecting that several European governments would soon acknowledge the Confederacy as a nation. Under such a terrible pressure, men's minds dwelt almost entirely on one subject—the great question of preserving the nation's life. So that a discussion of educational topics—of schools and the means of sustaining them—seemed an impertinence.

And in regard to this institution, there were some special reasons for anxiety. Its faculty had been broken up by enlistments into the army. A large number of its students had also entered the service. In collecting the fragments that remained, and in organizing them into an effective school, the gentleman already named, Mr. Bass, had exhibited great energy, and no little skill; yet the minds of many continued to entertain grave and perplexing doubts. I remember that some of us talked very pluckily, but at the same time, felt a weakness in the knees that was not reassuring. And perhaps the principal cause of solicitude remains yet to be mentioned. It was the financial outlook. Great difficulties had been experienced in securing funds for the erection of the building. It is not strange that in the process debts should have been contracted. The Board, in their report dated December 20, 1860, state their liabilities at $65,000, and ask from the Legislature an appropriation of that amount, for the meeting of all obligations. The money was voted with the expectation that by the payment of that sum the institution would be left free of debt. But the result failed to justify this expectation. Claims to the amount of $42,000* or thereabout, were proved up against the University, after the last

* $10,000 of this was afterwards paid from the sale of swamp lands.

appropriation was entirely exhausted. Some of these claims were prosecuted in the courts, and judgments obtained. The defence had been offered that the building and fixtures were State property and therefore not liable to be taken on execution. But the courts decided otherwise, and a decree of mechanic's lien was issued in favor of one, at least, of the parties, empowering him to sell the building. Many incidents of that trying time recur to the mind. I remember attempting one day to bespeak the forbearance of the party holding the decree just mentioned. I strove to point out to him the great harm that would be likely to follow if the property should be sold, but the appeal made little impression upon him. He answered with much more of energy than of politeness or reverence of sacred things, and declared that he would sell the entire concern at any moment, whenever a purchaser could be found. His only difficulty arose from the fact that nobody wanted the elephant. Another, not financially interested, volunteered the cheerful remark that he hoped soon to buy the house for a corn crib. Another still, the principal of a private school in a county not far distant, foretold very confidently the approaching collapse of the Normal, and showed how his institution would come in for a share in the estate of the deceased. This kind of talk was very common all over the State. There seemed to be a confident expectation, very generally entertained, that the days of the Normal were numbered, and that soon the place that knew it should know it no more.

In view of all these discouragements, we took what still seems to me as the wisest course. It was resolved to ask for no more money at the beginning. For the time being, the current expenses, we knew, were provided for. The debt was therefore left untouched. It was resolved to concentrate every effort upon the work of instruction. The adverse gales were blowing, and the waves were dashing upon the good ship, and it was thought the best protection against the storm would be to make her thoroughly sea-worthy. I think we may say that no labor was spared. Every man, and every woman, cheerfully did what he could, and all he could. Nobody shirked a task; Nobody tried to escape hard work. Every one made the common cause his own. In the class rooms of the University, full hours were put in. But this was not all. Opportunities for outside work were utilized. Instruction was given at teachers' institutes. It was solemnly resolved that whatever could be done for the general advancement of education in Illinois, should not fail of being done, and that thus the school should vindicate its right to be. In all parts of the State, north, south, and middle, the members of the Normal faculty were to be found, cheerfully rendering such service to the teachers of the schools as they could. Nor should it be thought that this distant labor diminished the efficiency of the teaching at home. The work of classes was laid out with care for the time of the teacher's absence. And as the memory rises before me, I am strongly impressed with the belief that the hours of night were largely utilized for the purposes of travel. As far as possible, efforts were made to save the precious daylight for teaching.

Another instrumentality was used for extending the benefits of the institution to the teachers of the State. This was the State Teachers' Institute, whose sessions were held in the University building during the long summer vacation. The first session was held in September, 1863. It was attended by only fifteen teachers, and continued for four weeks. At the tenth annual meeting of the State Teachers' Association, held in December, 1863, this institute project at the Normal was commended to the notice of the teachers. Partly in consequence of this encouragement, another meeting was advertised for August, 1864. The number in attendance was 127. Prominent educationalists not connected with the Normal, were engaged as instructors, but most of the work was done by the regular faculty of the University. In 1867, another session was held, attended by 255 teachers; another in 1868, attended by 248; another in 1869, attended by 291. In 1870, 242 were present; in 1871, 215, and in 1872, 300. After that year, the meetings were devoted more exclusively to the study of science. In all these meetings, with perhaps but a single exception, the instructors labored voluntarily and without compensation. The time given to this work was the regular vacation allowed to members of the faculty after forty weeks of school work.

These labors were soon rewarded by very cheering indications of progress. The number of students at the University rapidly increased. The public sentiment throughout the commonwealth grew more and more favorable to us. The village of Normal began to be settled up with people who valued education enough to bring here their boys and girls, and to rent or purchase homes near the institution. In the principal's report of December 14, 1864, I find the following: "At present, we are suffering, for the moment, from a circumstance that seems to result from the high esteem in which the school is held by the community. So many persons have come into the neighborhood to reside in order to secure the benefits of the model school to their children, that real estate has about trebled in value during the last two years; and notwithstanding the unprecedented number of tenements recently erected, rooms for the use of students are as scarce as ever." I remember that one clear, moonlight night, about this time, a gentleman alighted from the train at what he had been told was Normal. No man was more familiar with the place as it had been two or three years before than he, but so great had been the changes, so numerous the added houses, that just as the train was moving out, he rushed wildly back upon the platform of the car, and consented to stop only upon the strongest assurance from the conductor that this was indeed his old home.* Of course, it ought not to be claimed that all the

---

*In June, 1862, the village contained about twelve houses, great and small.

financial prosperity that came to the village towards the close of the war, was due solely to the success of the school. Much of it no doubt arose from the general prosperity of the country. But the fact that so much of the general good luck came to this spot, was no doubt owing to the energetic life which had been developed within the school. One of the consequences of the returning prosperity was, that in February, 1865, the last dollar of our debt was canceled by an appropriation from the Legislature. From that day we breathed more freely. For the first time in its history, the institution owned itself, and had need to ask the people for nothing more than the means of paying its current expenses.

The progress of the institution during the period of which we are speaking may be indicated by the number of names on the catalogue for the successive years. These numbers in the Normal and model departments, respectively, were as follows:

For the year ending June, 1862, in the Normal, 152; in model, 133
For the year ending June, 1863, in the Normal, 205; in model, 226
For the year ending June, 1864, in the Normal, 304; in model, 279
For the year ending June, 1865, in the Normal, 282; in model, 411
For the year ending June, 1866, in the Normal, 270; in model, 502
For the year ending June, 1867, in the Normal, 327; in model, 580
For the year ending June, 1868, in the Normal, 413; in model, 630
For the year ending June, 1869, in the Normal, 462; in model, 318
For the year ending June, 1870, in the Normal, 429; in model, 328
For the year ending June, 1871, in the Normal, 464; in model, 255
For the year ending June, 1872, in the Normal, 460; in model, 317
For the year ending June, 1873, in the Normal, 437; in model, 293
For the year ending June, 1874, in the Normal, 450; in model, 316
For the year ending June, 1875, in the Normal, 467; in model, 312

From 1868 to 1869, the table shows a falling off in the model school from 630 to 318. This was due to a change in the status of that school. At first it was ungraded, having for its pupils the handful of children resident in the village, with a few others from other places. As the number of these residents increased, and as the school became better known, the attendance from both sources was greatly enlarged. The public moneys belonging to the local school district were paid over to the University authorities, and in return the children of the district were taught in the model school. But by the year 1867, there had been such an enormous increase in the population of the town, that it became impossible to continue the arrangement. On the seventeenth day of December, 1867, the board voted that at the end of the year, the connection with the school district should be terminated. By this action, the attendance upon the model school was diminished by something more than three hundred.

I pass on to note some of the most important results attained during the fourteen years of which we are treating; and I mention, first, the development of the model school. In 1862 it had been in part reorganized by my predecessor, Mr. Bass. Two grades had been established in it, the high school and the primary. At the head of the former was Mr. Charles F. Childs, who had been called to that position from St. Louis. The primary was under the care of Miss Livonia E. Ketcham. This arrangement continued until June, 1863, when both these teachers resigned their places. Mr. Childs' place was filled by the appointment of Mr. William L. Pillsbury, a then recent graduate of Harvard College. As principal of the primary school, Miss Marion Hammond, of St. Louis, was appointed about the same time. Soon after Mr. L. B. Kellogg was employed as an additional instructor. This last appointment was the germ from which sprung, in 1866, the grammar school grade. Until the autumn of this last-named year, the principal of the high school had general supervision of all the grades. After that time the grades were independent of each other.

The moving purpose in establishing the model school was to furnish to the Normal pupils an opportunity for practice in teaching. But, by the act incorporating the University, it is required that its maintenance shall not involve the Board in any expense; that is, the model school must pay for itself. The only way in which that result can be accomplished is by collecting tuition fees from its pupils. For some years it had been somewhat freely charged that the teaching imparted in it was of a poor quality. Mere pupil-teachers, so it was argued, could not, in reason, be expected to do as thorough work as well-qualified, regularly-employed, instructors. The natural effect of that objection would be to discourage parents from patronizing the school. As the readiest way of breaking its force, a number of gentlemen from Bloomington and elsewhere—persons well qualified for the work—were invited to give the school a thorough examination, and to report upon its condition and the character of its teaching. Two days were spent in the rooms, listening to the work, and a report was made, which effectually turned the edge of all that criticism.

One principal object aimed at in the management of the model school during these years, was the thorough fitting of boys for the best colleges of the country. This, it was thought, would help to give character to the institution in all its grades. A high reputation for sound scholarship, it was believed, would induce students to come, and would help to maintain good order among them after they were assembled. It was with this idea that the services of Mr. Pillsbury were secured. By some of the members of the Board it was thought that a man of stouter muscle than the pale student which he appeared to be, was required for the exigencies of the situation. They feared that the stalwart boys of rough exterior and boisterous ways would prove too much for him,—that his authority would be despised and his influence neutralized. But the result was quite the reverse of all this.

Closely connected with the model school is the training department. This has grown from very imperfect beginnings. Originally the pupil-teachers had very little supervision. The principal of the University was almost as much occupied in teaching as any of the other instructors. The principal of the high school had fully one man's work in the higher classes under his care. The regular instructors in the other grades were equally laden with duties. Systematic and efficient oversight of the fifty or sixty persons entrusted with classes in the three grades was a thing almost impossible to bring about. At first, the attempt was made by the principal of the University. Certain hours in the day were devoted to this work. As far as possible, the recitations were so arranged that his vacant hours came when the largest number of young people were engaged in teaching. Meetings of the pupil-teachers were appointed for the afternoon, after school hours. A record was kept of the classes and their work. Besides this record, each pupil-teacher was required to keep a diary, giving an account of every recitation, setting forth its subject-matter, the method employed in conducting it, the difficulties experienced, and the successes and failures encountered. In my report for December, 1873, I find a somewhat complete statement of the course pursued at that time and previously, in the matter of training the young teachers. But the great need of something better had been recognized. I had been all along convinced that this work required the full time and energy of one well qualified person. This idea had been repeatedly presented to the Board, but could not be carried out on account of the expense. At length, by the appropriation of 1874, the means seemed to be furnished. In June of that year, Prof. Thomas Metcalf was taken from the chair of mathematics, and installed in the newly-established department of practical didactics, or training. It was preëminently the right thing to do, both as to the proposed service, and the man to perform it.

The methods of professional instruction which prevailed during this period were introduced in the spring of 1862. The members of the class which had reached its third term in school, listened to a course of conversational lectures upon the Theory and Practice of Teaching, which they were required afterwards to reproduce, with such additions and variations as they wished to insert. These papers were examined by the instructor, corrected, and returned to the writers. At a later point in the course, several weeks were given to the history of education, and the biography of eminent educators. Besides this there were lectures upon the philosophy of education. About the year 1873, these lectures were discontinued, and in their place, that charming and lucid treatise, which has so won the hearts of the young people, Rosenkranz's Pedagogics, was substituted. This book, I understand, is still used, the authorities doubtless fearing that an attempt to put it out would provoke a rebellion.

In June, 1869, the Board adopted the plan of issuing certificates to such students as had completed the work of one or two years. This action was taken on account of the fact that a large number of the students were employed as teachers in the public schools before completing the entire course and securing diplomas. These teachers, claiming to represent the University, had nothing to show in confirmation of their claims. One consequence was that the community had no way of discriminating between the worthy and the unworthy, or between him who had mastered many studies and him who had mastered only a few. Each of the certificates contained an exact statement of the amount of work satisfactorily done by the holder.

Another department that has been developed and established upon a permanent basis during these years, is the museum, with its connected scientific work. In 1862, there was a very fine collection of specimens, considering the time it had taken, but it was owned by a private association—the Illinois Natural History Society. By their action as a corporation, all its work was done, and all its officers elected. At that time, the office of curator was filled by Prof. C. D. Wilber, who, we must not forget, had rendered very valuable service in making the collection. But it seemed desirable to unite this important interest under the same control as the school. In the year 1867, an appropriation of $1,500 a year was made by the Legislature for the salary of a curator, and $1,000 a year for additions to the museum. Prof. John W. Powell was elected by the Board of Education to the office of curator, and the election was ratified by the Natural History Society. This was the revival of an interest which had slept since the retirement of Prof. Wilber, in 1862, or thereabout. Prof. Powell shed luster upon the institution by his Rocky Mountain expeditions, and continued his connection with the museum until June, 1872, when the present faithful and efficient curator, Prof. S. A. Forbes, was elected. The divided jurisdiction which had hitherto obtained in this department, came to an end in June, 1871, when the Natural History Society made over its rights in the premises to the Board of Education. Thus all the interests within this building were placed under one management, and the purposes thereof were harmonized and unified. The development of this important department of the institution would of itself present an interesting history, and it is a history that ought to . be preserved as a part of the permanent records, but in this sketch it is not possible to present it in full. The proper person for that duty is the curator himself, who is familiar with all the steps, and able to set them forth in their true order.

Reference has already been made to the fact that the courts had decided that the Normal University was a private institution, belonging to the Board of Education as a corporation. The appropriations of money made to it seemed to be regarded merely as grants or gifts. The State was held not to be liable for the Board's debts. The property was not shielded from the demands of creditors by the sovereignty of the State. In some respects this was a disadvantage. Not, of course, in that it compelled the University to pay its debts. This, to an individual or a corporation, is not a drawback but a benefit. But it was an injury to the school to be thus shut out from the popular sympathy, to be severed from the great system of education for which the State feels a responsibility, and for whose wants, therefore, the Legislature is under some sort of obligation to provide. To remedy these evils, the first section of the act of February 28, 1867, ordains that "The State Normal University, established by an act approved February 18, 1857, is hereby declared a State institution, and the property, personal, real, and mixed, in the hands, and standing in the name of the Board of Education of the State of Illinois, is the property of the State of Illinois, and is by said Board held in trust for the State." Since the passage of that act, the Normal, with all its appurtenances, has been as much the property of the commonwealth as the State House or the great seal.

From the time of its establishment, the institution had received as an annual appropriation from the State, twenty-three twenty-fourths of the interest on a certain fund, called the college and seminary fund. The principal of that fund consisted of the proceeds, in part, of the sale of certain lands, given to the State by Congress, in the act admitting it into the Union. The revenue from this source amounts to $12,444.99 per annum. As our operations—the number of students and teachers—increased from year to year, it was reasonable that the expenses should also increase. This was, after some delay, recognized by the Legislature. In the appropriation bill, approved March 10, 1869, an addition of $9,000 per annum was made to our ordinary revenue for the next two years. Another appeal we were constrained to make to the Legislature, on account of the fact that in early years our appropriations had fallen behind in point of time, to the extent of some months. That is, every installment of money voted to us was used in part retrospectively. This irregularity was not corrected until 1873, when an appropriation of $6,915 was made to bring up the arrears.

It is said that when Dr. Johnson was reminded of the fact that the trees in Windsor Park were growing rapidly, he answered in his blunt way that they had nothing else to do, and therefore ought to grow. The same might be said of the beautiful grove now surrounding this building. But we can remember the time when there were no trees here, with the duty of growing incumbent upon them; and the converting of the bare prairie into such a noble forest as the eye rests upon here to-day was no slight undertaking. It involved a considerable expenditure of money. In 1867, $3,000 was appropriated to this purpose. Mr. Jesse W. Fell was appointed to superintend the work. It was done with his accustomed energy and skill. The winds were mighty and the situation was exposed. Many of the trees had to be reset; some of them more than once. I remember that this was true especially of the row of tulip-poplars just in front of the building. But Mr. Fell's intense love of trees carried him successfully through all the trials, and after a labor running through four years, he made his final report in 1871. It ought not, however, be thought that nothing had previously been done in the way of ornamenting the grounds. The line of trees along the margin of the enclosure were growing before my coming here. There was also a nursery of young evergreens which were utilized in the final planting.

The heating apparatus, as it was originally put in by Walworth, Hubbard & Company, was accepted by the Board in June, 1863, and was thought to be sufficient for the wants of the school. But as the number of students increased, and all parts of the building came to be continually used, two serious defects began to appear. First, the heating power of the apparatus was found to be insufficient, and secondly, the ventilation turned out to be worth very little. In the coldest weather it was found impossible to raise the temperature above fifty degrees Fahrenheit, and the condition of the air, when the windows could not be opened, became at last absolutely unendurable. Efforts were made to secure an appropriation for a new apparatus. It appears that in 1871, the sum of $4,000 was voted to us; but this was found utterly inadequate. This fact was made plain by a thorough canvassing of the whole subject. Another appeal was made to the Legislature of 1873, asking for an additional sum; but the request was not acceded to. In the emergency, the Board resolved to save the needed sum by curtailing other expenditures. This was done, and in the long vacation of that year a new boiler was put into the basement, and the present machinery for ventilation put up, at a cost of $8,500.

Among the lesser changes which took place may be mentioned this, that in June, 1866, it was ordered by the Board that the principal of the Normal University be hereafter officially known and called "president," and that the principal male teachers thereof be known as "professors." This was an accession of honor which had not been sought by the instructors, and I am not certain that they have all learned to appropriate it as yet. But the change was introduced into the catalogue from that time forth.

At all times since the school first went into operation, there has been criticism upon it and its work. It has often been charged that the graduates and pupils have done no appreciable amount of teaching, and that what they have done has been of an inferior quality. As early as 1866, statements to this effect had been somewhat industriously circulated in different parts of the State. In order to meet them, it was thought best to issue circulars of inquiry to the most prominent educators in Illinois, respectfully asking answers to the following four questions:

1. Have any of the graduates or pupils of this institution been employed as teachers in the schools of your vicinity?

2. What degree of success has attended their labors in teaching and governing?

3. In what repute is the University held by the people in your portion of the State?

4. According to your best judgment, is the University a benefit to the State, and is the outlay of money required to support it a judicious and profitable expenditure?

To this circular, thirty-eight answers were received, all of which, with the names of the writers, were published in full in the biennial report of the State Superintendent, and also in a separate pamphlet. Of these answers, Hon. Newton Bateman, in the report already referred to, says that they contain "a mass of testimony in relation to the standing and success of the graduates as teachers, which must be regarded as in the highest degree gratifying to the friends of the University, and a satisfactory proof that it is achieving the ends for which it was established. * * They (the letters) are from every portion of the State, and reflect the unbiased opinions of their various writers, founded upon personal knowledge and observation. With a unanimity and emphasis that is certainly remarkable, they affirm the superior ability, skill, enthusiasm, and success, of the graduates of the Normal University." These answers, thus warmly endorsed by the State Superintendent, were very helpful in maintaining and extending the reputation of the institution. Other inquiries of similar character have been since addressed to educational officials and others, with a view of exhibiting the amount of good which the school is doing. By a resolution passed by the House of Representatives, February 18, 1873, the State Superintendent was directed to obtain from the county superintendents the names of the graduates and pupils of the Normal University teaching in the different counties. By the returns made to this inquiry, it appeared that one hundred and twenty graduates, and three hundred and eighty-nine other pupils, were thus employed. They were teaching in eighty-six different counties. But it was easy to show that these numbers were far below the truth. This subject will be found discussed with some thoroughness in my reports to the Board of Education, presented in June and December, 1873.

The first specific appropriation for a reference library was made in December, 1862. The sum of $500 was voted at the beginning, and it was provided that $200 a year should be used in replenishing and enlarging it. Large purchases of books had been made before this, but they were chiefly of text-books for the use of individual students, to whom they were loaned. In this way, every student was furnished with every book that he needed to use in preparing his daily recitations. But this practice was found to be, in many respects, bad. In the early stages of the institution, when the attendance was small, this policy may have seemed wise; but when the numbers were greatly increased, the conditions were entirely changed, and the supplying of the students with all their books became an intolerable nuisance, entailing upon the institution an immense expense, and causing the teachers vast labor and trouble. But the abolition of the practice was gradual. As a general rule, books continued to be loaned until they were worn out.

In the war for the union of the States, the University bore an honorable part. The first principal became the colonel of the famous Thirty-third Regiment of Illinois Volunteers; and was promoted to the rank of brigadier-general. Many of the students had also entered the service. In all this there was a fitness. Institutions of learning are the natural homes of patriotism, as well as of other generous sentiments. Young men in pursuit of knowledge have always been distinguished by their sensitiveness to these higher appeals. In the report for December, 1866, I find the following statements:

Of the teachers and pupils of the University who entered the army, there were, as far as known, commissioned officers, thirty-four; non-commissioned officers, forty-two; privates, eighty-nine; rank unknown, ten; rank and regiment unknown, thirty-six; total, 211. The report closes with the hope that in the future a more complete list may be made out. Whether this has been done, I am not able to say. It must be remembered that the history of these enlistments belongs mostly, though not entirely, to the period preceding that of which we are now speaking. I remember that in the spring of 1862, the city of Springfield was thought to be in danger of an attack from the confederates. The rumor had been circulated in Bloomington and was quickly brought to Normal. The commotion was intense. A meeting was held in the northwest recitation room, and it was resolved to meet the foe in a manner worthy of American citizens. Farewells were impressively spoken, and I am sure that some tears were shed, but the whole turned out to be a false alarm, and the next day witnessed the return of the fiery youths to the dull routine of ordinary school duties. They had shown their willingness to serve their country, but their services were not then required. Many other events might be detailed, but it does not seem wise to take the time for them. A few may, perhaps, be simply mentioned without expansion or comment. For several years, the president of the University had no responsibility for the keeping of account books, or the disbursement of money, except a small amount known as the contingent fund. In 1869, a new set of books was opened, and in December of that year, the president was put in charge of them, and required to countersign all orders upon the treasurer. In June, 1873, the blanks, pay-rolls, and duplicates were adopted, which, I suppose, are still in use.

Several attempts were made to allow the Bloomington and

Normal horse railway to pass through the grounds, but the permission was not given until December 18, 1867. Even then, some of the members of the Board were doubtful of the wisdom of the measure.

Of the men and women who have been employed as teachers in the institution, I can give only a bare list of names. In the Normal Department, during my incumbency, there have been (naming them in the order of their appointment) Edwin C. Hewett, Joseph A. Sewall, Margaret E. Osband, Thomas Metcalf, Albert Stetson, Fannie L. D. Strong, Emmeline Dryer, Martha D. L. Haynie, John W. Powell, John W. Cook, Letitia Mason, Henry McCormick, Myra A. Osband, Rosalie Miller, Harriet M. Case, Stephen A. Forbes, Bandusia Wakefield.

As principals of the high school, there were Charles F. Childs, William L. Pillsbury, Mary E. Horton, Eliab W. Coy, Lester L. Burrington. Assistants in the high school, Lyman B. Kellogg, Oscar F. McKim, Melancthon Wakefield, Bandusia Wakefield, Thomas J. Burrill, John H. Thompson, Ruthie E. Barker, John R. Edwards, Martha D. L. Haynie.

Principals of the grammar school, E. P. Burlingham, John W. Cook, Joseph Carter, Benjamin W. Baker. Assistants in the grammar school, Mary Pennell, Lyman Hutchinson, W. S. Mills.

Principals of the intermediate school, Olive A. Rider, Martha Foster. Principals of the primary school, Livonia E. Ketcham, Marion Hammond, Edith T. Johnson, Lucia Kingsley, Martha E. Hughes, Gertrude K. Case, Jane P. Carter.

The members of the Board of Education during this period were Samuel W. Moulton, John P. Brooks, Perkins Bass, Newton Bateman, Walter M. Hatch, William H. Powell, George P. Rex, J. W. Schweppe, Henry Wing, William H. Wells, Simeon Wright, Thomas J. Pickett, J. W. Shehan, William H. Green, Calvin Goudy, Joseph Medill, John H. Foster, Walter L. Mayo, Charles P. Taggart, Benajah G. Roots, Thomas J. Turner, Kersey H. Fell, Thomas R. Leal, Jesse H. Moore, Elias C. Dupuy, Jesse W. Fell, Nicholas E. Worthington, Winfield S. Coy, George C. Clarke, Enoch A. Gastman, Charles F. Noetling, Edward L. Wells, Joseph Carter, Samuel M. Etter, J. C. Knickerbocker, H. Harrison Hill, Richard S. Canby. The treasurer was Charles W. Holder during all my connection with the institution. The janitors were Frank Nolle, and our good, honest, efficient friend, Peter Ketelson.

One of the most noticeable facts connected with the history of the Normal has been the permanency of its officers and teachers. While the controlling boards of other State institutions have been repeatedly legislated out of office, and other bodies created to succeed them, the Board governing this school has never been disturbed, but has gone on in the even tenor of its way. And in its very membership there has been unusual continuity. Hon. Samuel W. Moulton was president of the Board from July, 1859, to June, 1877, with a short interregnum. Hon. W. H. Green has been a member since about 1860. Dr. Calvin Gowdy was for many years a most faithful and efficient member, and the present president, Mr. Roots, has been for many years a most useful helper. Indeed, he was so before his appointment on the Board.

The transcribing of these lists, both of teachers and of members of the Board, has awakened a flood of precious memories. On the part of the instructors, I recall unflagging industry and faithfulness, and an ennobling faith in high ideals. Their work and their spirit have gone into the very bone and sinew of this great school, and have made it the grand thing it is to-day. All over this honored commonwealth, their influence is felt. They have been permitted to lay their hands, in a most effective way, upon the forces which affect its destiny. The Illinois of the future will be a different and a nobler entity, by reason of what these teachers have done for it.

And of the gentlemen, who, without fee or reward, have given of their time and their thought and influence, to build up here a power for the mental improvement of these mighty communities, to open here a fountain whose streams have helped to cover the land with the beauty and fruitfulness of culture, what shall be said? Nobly have they wrought. They have labored for permanent and not temporary ends. If this building should to-day be consumed in the flames, if the voice of instruction should be here forever hushed, their labor would not be in vain. Like good seed, the influence here planted would continue through the ages to reproduce itself, to the nourishing of mind and heart. And if this were a fit place for the expression of personal feelings, I might long engage you in listening to my grateful recital of the generous support and encouragement which I received from their hands.

Nor must I forget to say a word concerning the members of the Legislature, with whom I have had so much to do. I wish to say that my recollection of them is most pleasant. Many favors, many courtesies, have I received at their hands. On the whole, they gave us a liberal support, and I gladly express to them my thanks on this occasion, the last, perhaps, in which I shall ever publicly speak of the subject.

And the graduates and pupils of this school, how well they have carried out its spirit! How effectively have they recommended it to the good will of the citizens of Illinois! In a very important sense, they have made the Normal a success. Upon the flood of their successful teaching, the good ship has thus far floated, and weathered all the gales, and thus it must always be. The teachers may be faithful, the Board may be wise, and the Legislature may be generous, but all will go for nothing unless the out-going students are efficient in

14

meeting their responsibility. Every friend of the Normal ought to
be proud of the good service rendered by the boys and girls who
have migrated from its halls into the school houses of the land.

As a general indication of the progress made by the school
during the period which we have been considering, allow me to quote
a paragraph from the president's report of December 15, 1875: "The
progress of the institution for the last fourteen years may be shown
by several facts. For the school year 1861-2, the number of pupils
catalogued in the Normal School was 152. The number for 1874-5,
was 467; a gain of 207 per cent. The number catalogued in the
entire institution during the former year, was 285; during the latter
year it was 779; a gain of 171 per cent. The amount annually appropriated by the Legislature at that time was $12,445.99. For the
current period it is $27,200; a gain of more than 118 per cent. The
income from the model school at that time cannot be determined from
documents within my reach, but for the year 1862-3, it was $1,778.20.
Last year it was $4,488.04; a gain of 152 per cent. It will be seen
that the gain from appropriations, large as that is, falls far below the
gains in the number of pupils, or in the income from the model
school. There has also been vast progress in respect to the number
of our pupils found teaching and superintending, especially in positions of importance. The total number known to be teaching last
year (1875) was 777. Of those employed in Illinois, ten were
county superintendents, two were instructors in the Southern Normal University, two were professors in the Industrial University,
one was a teacher in the Peoria County Normal School, and two
were members of this Board (State Board of Education). Besides
these, there were many superintendents and principals of high
schools. Of those in other States, there were two county superintendents in Iowa, four principals of schools in St. Louis, one of them
a branch high school, and the others large grammar schools; one
principal of the city high school in Hannibal, Missouri; one teacher
in the State Normal School in Castine, Maine; one city superintendent in Denver, Colorado; one principal in Milwaukee, Wisconsin;
one high school principal in Warsaw, New York; two professors in
the State Normal School in Terre Haute, Indiana; one professor in
the State Normal School, San Jose, California; two professors in
the State University, in Fayetteville, Arkansas; one professor in
the State Normal School, in Cape Girardeau, Missouri; one city
superintendent in Little Rock, Arkansas."

The paper just read in your hearing refers exclusively to the
period of my own connection with the institution. It has been so
limited by the suggestion of the committee of arrangements for this
day. But I believe that on all proper occasions I have been prompt
to express my appreciation of the work done by my predecessors in
office, and I think I may claim to have missed no opportunity of

saying a good word for the school since leaving it. And perhaps I can not close this long paper in any better way than by a reiteration, in one word, of these sentiments, and by professing anew my personal loyalty to the Normal University, past, present, and future. May its power increase, and its friends be daily multiplied.

ADDRESS OF EDWIN C. HEWETT, LL. D.

Twenty-five years ago this summer, I made a journey to Illinois on a somewhat important errand. One year before I had made my first visit to this State; I came on what was not altogether a "voyage of discovery," but it was something like one. At any rate, my first visit gave occasion for the second, 1857, from which I returned to New England accompanied by a young woman. We had formed a kind of copartnership, which still continues. During this visit I heard considerable talk about the new, Normal School, which was about to go into operation. I had no suspicion, however, at that time, that the establishment of this State Normal School was a fact of any special significance to me, personally; my home was in New England; it had always been there, and I had no thought or expectation that it might not always remain there.

Another year passed away, and through the kind offices of friends, I had been spoken of to President Hovey, as a proper person to fill a place in the faculty of the new institution, then entering upon its second year. After some correspondence, extending over a period of a few weeks, I received a formal offer of the position. The salary, $1,200 per annum, did not promise an increase sufficient to tempt me much; but I had had some experience in the Normal School work, and decidedly preferred it to the work of a grammar school, in which I was then engaged. The result was that I closed with the offer, and the month of October found me a resident of Bloomington, and a teacher in the State Normal University. The connection thus formed has never been severed. I came here a young man, but I am reminded in many ways that I am a young man no longer. Whatever may be the ultimate period of my life, or whatever other work in the providence of a good God I may be called to undertake, it can hardly fail that, when my life work is finished, I shall find that the largest, the most important, and most characteristic part of it has been done here.

Nor does this probability, looked squarely in the face, cause me a single regret. I regret, indeed that I have not been able to do my work here better; but to have given my efforts, such as they were, to the shaping of this institution in its early days, its days of struggle and doubt; to have participated in its subsequent prosperity, and to have shared in the triumphs that have been set before you by a more eloquent tongue than mine; to have taught, for a longer or shorter period, every one who has gone as a graduate from its halls,—at least from the Normal Department,—leaves no room for regret that I have here spent some of the years of my youth and the best strength of my manhood.

I think there is little need that I should spend much time in relating facts of history concerning our institution. The story of its early days—its founding, the struggles through which it passed, the courageous self-sacrifice of its friends—has been given you better than I could give it; and it needs not to be repeated. My predecessor in the presidency has told you, with an eloquence that few can command, of its growth and prosperity in the years that followed its early struggles. The funny things connected with its history are to have a permanent place in the book now preparing, and you will all read them there.

When I came to the head of the institution, in January, 1876, it was firmly established; it had passed more than eighteen years of vigorous and successful life; its methods of work had crystallized, at least so far as such a thing is desirable; its character and aims had come to be well understood by a large part of the community; nor had it failed to have settled a large body of traditions such as grow up around every institution of learning. I had not to build the ship, nor to launch it, nor to mark out its voyage, nor to assign the duties of its officers and crew. It was already in full, successful and confident progress. Other men had labored, wisely and well, and nothing remained for me but to enter into their labors, and to carry them forward as best I might, on the lines of progress already clearly marked out.

It has been said that a time of peace and prosperity affords but a barren field for the work of the historian. Thus the historical part of this discourse may be soon dispatched. 1876 was about the middle point in the period of severe business depression through which our country has just passed. Our institution, in common with all others, had felt the effect of this depression. It was shown conspicuously in a considerable falling off in the number of its students. "Hard times," so-called, have a two-fold tendency to diminish the number of those who seek instruction in a Normal School. In addition to the difficulty of obtaining the money to pay current expenses at such an institution, a difficulty which it shares in common with all other schools, it has a peculiar influence to encounter from the following fact: When a diminution of revenues, and increased difficulty in collecting taxes, make it necessary that municipalities should diminish expenses, they are quite likely to be unwise in selecting the point of contraction. As the private individual is more likely to sacrifice his newspaper or magazine than his beer and tobacco, so our communities seem to be more ready to cripple their schools than to curtail expense for some other things that might be better spared. The heaviest item of expense for schools is the salaries of the teachers; moreover, this item of expense is one whose magnitude is fully known and appreciated by "Thomas, Richard, and Henry." Hence, the pruning knife of economy is likely to be felt here sooner than anywhere else. As a result, teaching becomes a very much less attractive field for prospective labor, and fewer will be found who are ready to incur expense in preparing themselves to enter this unpromising field. I think the reasons I have given fully account for the falling off in the number of students to which I have referred. For, with the return of better times, and a tendency toward a restoration of teachers' salaries, our numbers began to increase, and have continued to do so. Our enrollment in the Normal Department for the last winter term reached 369, an appreciably higher mark than had ever been reached before.

I am well aware that the excellence, efficiency or benefits to a community which belong to an institution of learning cannot be gauged by the the gross number of its students; but a large attendance is certainly presumptive evidence of efficiency and resulting benefit, and with many, perhaps most people, hardly any other test is applied.

Moreover, there are those in the Legislature and elsewhere, who are disposed to estimate the work of the school, simply by numbers, and at the same time to take into the account the number of graduates alone. Tried by this test, we suffer severely; for in fact, but about one-tenth of those who enter the Normal School take its diploma. Our course of study is more extended than that of most Normal Schools. We insist rigidly on our rule of requiring each one to reach a fixed standard of attainment in any study before he is allowed to pass that study. Many of our students, as some of you well know, are dependent upon their own exertions for means, and, before their course is complete, they are obliged to go out and teach. They may leave us with a full intention of returning to complete their course, but, if successful in their teaching, they are sorely tempted to remain in the school room instead of returning here to finish their work. Perhaps it may also be said that some do not appreciate sufficiently the advantages of a completed course and an enrollment among the alumni. From all these causes, it happens that the number of our graduates bears but a small ratio to the whole number of our students. I have hoped that, as the years go on, this state of things may change somewhat. I think it will; and still, much as I should rejoice to see a larger number of our students attain a place among the alumni, much as I regret to see that many do not seem to estimate the value of our diploma as highly as I think they should, I would not entertain for a moment the proposition to lower our demands in order to increase the number of our graduates. I do not want to see our diplomas any cheaper. Rather let the diploma mean as much as it does now, even if it must continue, as it has so long, that a large part—probably the largest part—of our influence on the schools of the State must continue to be exerted by our undergraduates.

The six and one-half years since January, 1876, have been years of harmony and prosperity. But very few changes have occurred in our faculty, nor have our relations to each other been marred by quarrels or bickerings such as afflict many faculties. Very few cases of severe discipline of students have arisen. I think they may all be counted on the fingers of one hand, and still have a finger or so to spare. Our interruptions by sickness of either teachers or students have not been very serious in any case, and but one out of the whole number of teachers and students in all departments, has died during that time. I commend this fact to the consideration of those timid people who fear that we are killing our people by hard work.

Our institution has never shown an undue haste in taking up new plans of educational work. We have never been over-anxious, I think, to forsake the old and well-tried for the new and experimental. I trust that we have not been unwilling to "prove all things," at least all things that were worth proving, but our strong tendency has been to "hold fast that which is good." Hence, there have been few radical changes in our plans and methods of work during the last six and one-half years. Three somewhat important changes are worthy of a passing notice. During President Edwards' administration, we had come to feel that our training work, the actual practice work of our students in the instruction of classes in the model school, was failing to do justice both to the pupil-teachers themselves and also to the young people who were placed under their care for instruction, and it was believed that this failure arose from the fact that their work was not always wisely planned nor properly supervised. The reason that this was so, was found in the fact that, with their multiplicity of other duties, no member of the faculty was able to give this work of planning and supervising the attention it required. Hence, in 1874, the office of training teacher was established, and our oldest professor was relieved from the duties of his chair and inducted into the new office. The wisdom of this step has been sufficiently demonstrated.

But another evil was found to exist, which a new device was necessary to remedy. Of course, we could not put classes into the hands of our pupils for actual instruction, until those pupils had had the benefit of our training for a few terms. But it was found that quite a large per cent. of our pupils remained with us but one or two terms, and left without ever having undertaken this practice-work. Nor had they received direct professional instruction or practice of any kind—nothing beyond what was incidental to the daily movements of the school and to their pursuit of the several branches of study in the class room. Hence, a lady competent to instruct young children philosophically, and also prepared, at the same time, to expound the philosophy of her work to others, was sought out and put in charge of the primary room, with the title of assistant training teacher. It was then ordained that all who entered the Normal School should spend one hour a day, during the first term, in observing her work with the children, or in listening to the exposition of her philosophy of the work that they had seen done. Moreover, they must keep a careful record of what they observed, and of what they were taught, and be examined in regard to the results. Thus arose the study called "Observation," among us, a study not popular with many at first, but against which I have heard no complaint now for a long time. Furthermore, many now ask to be allowed to pursue this work beyond the limits of our demands upon them; and generally such as prefer this request are among our brightest, best-prepared, and most promising pupils.

Secondly, our laboratories for the study of the natural sciences have been enlarged, improved, and much better supplied with apparatus than formerly. A quite important change has followed in our methods of teaching those sciences. In all of them, the work consists of experiments, to a much greater extent than formerly. Not simply nor chiefly seeing experiments performed by the professor, but the actual making of the experiments by the pupils themselves. In this way, we feel that we have come more into harmony with the theory and practice of the best modern teachers of science, and the results are correspondingly gratifying.

About three years ago, feeling that something might be done to bring more of the teachers of the State to share in the benefits of the Normal University, and at the same time to bring about a closer union between our institution and the body of actual teachers in the State who had never received instruction here, I proposed to our Board that we should cut down the regular work of our school year from thirty-nine weeks to thirty-six, and introduce a special term for actual teachers, four weeks in length, to be held in the month of August. My proposition met the approval of the Board, and the first such term was held in August, 1880. About two hundred teachers were present, a majority of whom had never been here as students before. These teachers, representing an immense aggregate of experience, took hold of the work with much enthusiasm, and expressed themselves highly pleased with what had been done for them. The next year, about thirty more came, and the term was equally successful. The third teachers' term is now in progress. The increase in attendance is a little greater this year than it was last, and the results promise to be quite as encouraging. I feel that the movement is fairly accomplishing the two-fold purpose I had in view when I proposed it to the Board.

The Illinois State Normal University has now completed a round twenty-five years of life and work. During the first four years, under the administration of President Hovey, aided by Moore, Potter, Sewall, and your speaker, together with others whose term of service was shorter, its foundations were firmly laid, the work received its impetus, and its scope and character were determined. After three years of hard nursing in old Major's Hall, in Bloomington, this spacious and commodious structure, erected in the face of difficulties that a man less full of pluck, persistency, and sublime audacity, than its first president, would not have overcome, was ready in the fall of 1860, to receive the school. Here, for one year, the work went on under the same managers, before the tempest-tones of war called the president, most of the teachers, and of the male students, to the field. Then followed a year of transition under the able management of Perkins Bass, aided by two of the helpers of his predecessor, together with some others. The times were troublous, the difficulties were great, but the work of the school was held firmly to the course already marked out, and in the model department, the high school work was well started under the guidance of the lamented Childs.

Before the year closed, a man came upon the stage here who was to play a conspicuous part at the head of affairs for the next thirteen years and a half. Early in President Edwards' administration, came Professors Metcalf and Stetson, and soon after, Mr. Pillsbury succeeded to the place of Mr. Childs, whom St. Louis had recalled. The story of President Edwards' administration, and of the succeeding one, I need not tell again.

During these twenty-five years, members of this faculty, men and women, have here invested the best of their powers, and of themselves, for periods of five, ten, fifteen, twenty years. No other Normal School on the continent has had, or has now, such an accumulation of teaching experience in its faculty. During this time, more than 5,000 young men and women have entered as students in the Normal Department, of whom 386 have received our diploma, and thousands of others have gone forth, bearing the training received here for longer or shorter periods, to take their places in the school rooms of the State.

What have been the results? I have no figures that will express them, nor can they be expressed in figures. But I am sure, after all allowances have been made, that a grand success has crowned our efforts—a success that has given the institution an enviable reputation, not only in our own State and in the neighboring States, but on the other side of the Atlantic, as well.

If I am asked to give the specific reasons for this success, I shall name the following as chief, in my opinion: First, the singleness of aim in all that has been done, viz., to fit young persons for the work of teachers in the school room. "This one thing" we started to do in 1857, and this one thing is the aim from which we have never swerved to the present day. Second, I would name the faithfulness, thoroughness, and singleness of purpose with which the men and women who have taught here have done their work. Third, I would include the fidelity with which such an overwhelming majority of our graduates and under-graduates have gone forth to redeem the pledges made to the State, by the devotion of their powers and their acquirements to the doing of the work for which they were trained here. Nor must I forget to mention, in this connection, the wisdom and faithfulness which have been shown by members of the Board of Management, some of whom have served in this capacity almost as long as the veterans among the members of the faculty.

If I were asked what peculiarities of the teaching here have done most to give our pupils the strength they have, and to crown our work with the success that has followed, I should not hesitate a moment to name two. First, the fact that our main strength has been given to the elementary studies. We believe in reading, arithmetic, and map-drawing, and we have some faith in spelling, as a worthy subject of school study, especially for teachers. It is at the foundation of the structure where the best work is needed, but where too often the poorest work is found. Second, I should name the intelligent thoroughness with which these foundation subjects have been preserved. We believe that work rightly done on the elementary studies can be made as efficient for training the mental powers, the essential part of an education, as any work in the whole field of scholastic pursuit. Our faith on these two points is no new thing, but a survey of the work done here for twenty-five years and the results of that work make that faith stronger to-day than ever before.

Yes, the Normal University has succeeded. The evidences of this fact are abundant and convincing. The past is secure. No mistakes of the future can obliterate it. Whatever of disaster may be in store for this grand enterprise, nothing can destroy what has already been done, nor annihilate the influences that have gone forth from this point as a center.

But our enemies are not all converted, nor are they all dead yet. From time to time, here and there,—often in the very places where we should least expect them,—are heard the same old questionings, assertions, and objections, and this being the case, perhaps I cannot better fill the remaining pages of this paper than with a brief presentation of the reasons why Normal Schools should exist, and should be supported at the public charge.

I shall assume that the necessity of free public schools for the education of the whole people is settled. I believe it is settled in the minds of the great American public in Illinois and elsewhere. Questions of detail may still·arise. Questions of the scope of the studies to be pursued, of the best methods of doing the work, etc., but I do not believe that our people will ever consent to discuss seriously the question of the utility and necessity of the free public school.

Now, it is clear that the value of a school depends upon the character of its teacher vastly more than upon anything else; yea, than all other things combined. If the teacher is good, the school will be good, whatever else may be lacking. If the teacher is worthless, the school is a total failure, although everything else may be of the best. Furthermore, it would seem to be clear that persons who are to do the best work as teachers must receive a special training for that work. As much as this is conceded for the proper doing of the commonest mechanical work. No man will send his old boot to be mended to any one who has not been trained to mend boots, although, perchance, the same man will put the training of his children into the hands of some green boy or girl who has never given one half-hour to learning how to do the work. Is the training of the future citizen, of the young immortal, at the critical, formative period of his life, so much simpler than the repairing of a broken boot? Experience in this country and in others, has fully shown that teachers trained in the philosophy and practice of their profession will not be forthcoming in sufficient numbers unless special schools are established on purpose to give that special training; hence, the necessity for Normal Schools. Normal Schools have been in existence in Europe almost one hundred and fifty years. They have existed in this country for about forty years. Now, the exact work and methods of a Normal School have never been settled, and perhaps they will not be settled for a long time to come, if ever; but the aim or purpose of a Normal School is simple and single, viz., to prepare prospective teachers for their work. Any school which has this for its sole aim, and does work which accomplishes this purpose to a reasonable degree, is a Normal School. Any school which aims at something more or less than this, or at something different from it, is not properly a Normal School, no matter how much incidental help for his future work the candidate for teaching may get there.

Recently, a whole brood of so-called Normal Schools has been spawned here in these western States, which have no right to the title, simply for the reason I have given. They do not make the preparation of teachers their special and single purpose. By their own published circulars, they are shown to be Normal Schools no more than they are "business colleges," or "schools of telegraphy," or "classical schools," or "music schools," or what not. They have chosen this word Normal rather than some other one out of half a dozen equally appropriate, to say the least, simply because those who have wrought in real Normal Schools have done such work as to give that word a greater cash value than any of the others, and so have made it worth "appropriating." Nor would it be an easy matter, if indeed it were possible, to keep a school dependent on popular patronage for its support, strictly and exclusively to the work of a Normal School; nor would it be easy to insist in such a school upon the work being done in such a way as best to accomplish that purpose; hence, a reason why Normal Schools should be established and supported and controlled by the State.

Prof. Payne, of Ann Arbor, in a recent article, urges the "enforced preparatory training of a prescribed kind for the few who propose to assume grave responsibilities, and to perform duties of extraordinary difficulty and importance." He says: "The only practicable safeguard against empiricism, against an ignorant and culpable trifling with the highest and dearest of human interests, is a training of a prescribed kind and degree for all who would assume such grave responsibilities and duties." Can such training as he here demands for teachers, be reasonably expected except in an institution established by government, under its control, and supported at its expense? Wise leaders of public thought have said "no," and hence they have advocated the establishment and support of State Normal Schools.

If, then, the value of our public schools depends upon their teachers, if these teachers require a special kind of training, if those having this required training are not forthcoming in sufficient numbers without government assists in their preparation, and if governmental authority and support are necessary in order that a school should give this training in the best way, it is clearly the duty of the State to establish and support such schools.

But, let it be clearly understood that government does this in order to further its own purposes, and for nothing else. Such schools may confer great benefits upon those who are instructed in them, but that is not the reason for their existence; they are in no sense to be regarded as charitable institutions. The money spent for such schools should be regarded as spent in the interest of public economy. Whatever is invested in our public schools is thrown away, if all the teachers are worthless. In whatever degree anything improves the efficiency of the teachers, just in that ratio it gives worth to the money expended for the schools taught by those teachers. Our State spends about $7,500,000 annually for its public schools; if, then, the work and influence of its two Normal Schools make the teaching in the State one per cent. better than it would be without them, then it follows that their cash value to the State is $75,000 per year. Whether their influence, direct or indirect, does make the teaching in Illinois one per cent. better or not, I will not assert; I merely say that, if it does so, they pay to the State an annual interest at the rate of more than fifty per cent. on the annual investment of less than $50,000 to support them.

And how much does this annual expenditure really burden the tax-payers? I made a careful calculation a few years ago, based on official data, and I found that a man that pays tax on $3,000,—and such a man, as we rate property for taxation, would be worth about $10,000,—this man pays less than twenty cents yearly towards the support of both these schools. This is a little less than the cost of two moderately good cigars! Can any one wonder that some of our economical politicians would be glad to blot us out, not, of course, because they love us less, but because they love the tax-payers more!

It is possible that some one might grant all that I have said, and yet ask: Why should not the State insist that the teacher should get his necessary preparation at his own expense? Why educate teachers at the public cost any more than lawyers, or physicians, or ministers? Are not the interests of the public health, the public morality and religion, and public justice, quite as important as the interests of public education? Without any attempt at discussing the last question, it is sufficient to say that the State puts itself into no such relations to these interests as it does to that of public education. It does not, by its constitution, appoint a State officer to have the oversight of these interests. It does not put its hand into the pockets of its citizens, willing and unwilling alike, and take out millions of money to promote these interests. Hence, it is not under the same obligations to do everything necessary in order that these interests may not suffer, and to provide whatever means may be requisite in order that the money it has taken from its people by force, and invested in its own way, be not squandered.

But we are still told sometimes that these young people will not teach, even after they have been prepared to do so at the public expense. However, recent careful statistics which so clearly prove the falsity of this charge in respect to all our students, save a very few, have caused this statement to become much less frequent.

One of the funniest points made by our opponents is, that whatever need there may once have been for State Normal Schools, they have now accomplished their work; they have outlived their usefulness. When it is remembered that about 20,000 teachers are needed for the schools of Illinois, and that the average period of their teaching is about three years, this statement appears very much like a huge joke. It would seem that the necessity for Normal Schools will cease at about the same time with the necessity for cradles and cribs, and not much sooner.

But we still hear it said occasionally, that our Normal School is a local institution, that McLean County derives most of the benefit from it. It is hard to understand how any one can talk thus, if he will take our catalogue, and observe how the residences of our students are scattered literally from Dunleith to Cairo, and from the Wabash to the Mississippi. I find by consulting the catalogues of the other Normal Schools of the country, that there is scarcely another one of which the charge could not be made with more force than of our own. If we are in good repute at home, that can hardly be set down against us; and it might be urged that the princely gift of McLean County to this institution entitles her to some favors. But it will be found that, under the rules of our Board, the only special privilege granted to candidates from McLean County is this: If they come to enter the Normal Department without appointment, they are required to show, on examination, that they are prepared more than forty per cent. better than candidates from other counties.

Friends, I have made no attempt to seize upon the poetry of this occasion, nor have the speakers who have preceded me. The temptation was strong to dwell upon the memories that this celebration is so well calculated to awaken, or to give free wing to fancy, and attempt to picture the glories that shall attend the completion of another quarter of a century, or to speak words of eulogy and of kind remembrance of those whose feet have grown weary by the way, and who have laid them down to their rest before reaching the meridian. We have attempted none of these things. We have given you the plain prose, but I close by expressing the hope that some of the poetry may be reached before the day is ended.

ADDRESS BY W. L. PILLSBURY, A. M.

The growth of·Illinois from 1850 to 1860, in population and in wealth, was immense. In the development of its material resources it made progress as great. Improvements in farm machinery, opening up coal mines and building great railroads, multiplied the number and enhanced the value of our farms, increased our farm products, and made markets for them accessible, and started us on the road to become what we now are, the greatest agricultural State in the Union, and what our friend, Mr. Jesse W. Fell, whose absence to-day we so much regret, says we shall be,—the seat of the greatest manufactories of the world. But the growth of that decade is not all recorded in the census reports and the transactions of the State Board of Agriculture. There was a growth of ideas as well. It is true that certain black laws, of which we hear much in every political campaign, were put upon the statute books of the State about that time; but it is also true that the same time gave birth to the movement and trained the man through whose agency all black laws have been swept from the statute books of this and all the other States.

We go, too, to 1855 for our first free school law, for the law that established common schools upon taxation of property, providing for the first time a State tax and a feasible and effective plan of local taxation in their behalf. And, following close upon this free school law of 1855, we find its corollary, the act of 1857, establishing the Illinois State Normal University to train teachers for the free schools. Hence, then, from this fruitful decade, this stately building on the prairie, this renowned school of teachers; hence these alumni, and this auspicious meeting.

But the whole of this subject, fortunately, does not belong to me. Gen. Hovey, last night, and Dr. Edwards, this morning, in eloquent words, have told you of the struggle for free schools and the Normal School, of the men and the arguments that prevailed, of the making the bricks in these walls,—not perhaps without straw but without what is more needful in these times,—money. They have told how the University grew and matured under their wise care, and Dr. Hewett has told you in fitting terms, of both its earlier and its later days, of which he has been so great a part. It is for me to speak more especially of the model school, that has grown up beside the Normal School from the beginning.

I have said that the law establishing the State Normal University was a corollary of the free school law of 1855. In like manner a training school, or a model school, is an essential part of a complete Normal School. I shall not elaborate this statement nor attempt to prove it before this audience, for I am sure that you all concede that it is true. There has been, and still is, a difference of opinion on the question whether this auxiliary of the Normal School should be a *model* school, or a *training* or *practice* school. It has been said on the one hand, that the purpose should be "to place before the pupil-teachers a correct model, a thing to be looked at, studied and imitated," and on the other hand, that the purpose should be "to send the pupil-teachers to the school to experiment and acquire practical skill in teaching." Doubtless much might be said on this question that would not be entirely out of place here, but I prefer to present the history, and to add only a few conclusions.

The purpose in the beginning here seems clearly to have been to establish a school to be observed and studied; and hence the name by which it has always been known—THE MODEL SCHOOL. The first allusion to the model school which I find in the proceedings of the State Board of Education, is in the report of a committee consisting of Messrs. Rex and Hovey, who had been appointed by the Board at its second meeting, "to visit the various Normal and high schools of the East, and report to the Board upon the subject of building, internal arrangements, etc." The Board adjourned from May 7 (this was in the year 1857) to June 23, and at the adjourned meeting of the Board, the committee, having meanwhile made the trip East, under the "etc." part of their instructions, I suppose, presented a careful outline of their "views upon the nature, object, organization, course of training, gradation and management of Normal Schools." In that report the committee say: "The third step is that indicated above; namely, to give practical skill by actual service under instruction in the school of practice, or model school. They should here be taught that there can be no real success in practice without a rational theory to which such practice can, at every step, be referred. They should be made to see and to feel that there must be a reason for every process in education, as well as in medicine, or engineering, or mechanics." [Proceedings State Board of Education, June 23, 1857, p. 10.]

At this same meeting of the Board, Mr. Hovey was elected principal of the Normal University, that was to be. At the next meeting of the Board, held August 18, it was resolved that the first session of the Normal University should begin on the first Monday in October; "also that the principal, should it be necessary, be authorized to employ a principal teacher in the model school." [Proceedings State Board of Education, August 18, 1857, p. 14.]

Pursuant to this resolution, Miss Mary M. Brooks,* who had been a primary school teacher in the Peoria schools, was appointed principal of the model school, the purpose being to begin with a class of primary pupils. In the report of the State Superintendent of Public Instruction, 1857–8, p. 392, I find the following, written by Gen. Hovey, in December, 1858, a little more than a year after the school opened:

"The model, or experimental school, is a necessary adjunct of a training school for teachers, and it was therefore determined to establish the primary grade at once. Miss Mary M. Brooks, a young lady of remarkable fitness for the place, was appointed principal.

"At first the success of the school was not very flattering, there being only seven pupils during an entire term, and one of these was received gratuitously. The second term opened with ten, and closed with fourteen pupils. But on the morning of the first day of the third term, every seat was filled, and over fifty applied who could not be received for want of room. So long as there was room in the Normal School for a class of twelve pupils of the intermediate grade, they were received and taught partly by the Normal students, and the proceeds of their tuition applied to the payment of the salary of the model school principal, and such assistants as it was found necessary to employ. This class, now grown into eighty pupils, has passed into the hands of Mr. G. Thayer. The receipts for tuition in the model school during the first year amounted to $439.50, and were wholly applied to the payment of teachers. The members of Section A have spent considerable time in this school as observers and teachers, and the members of the other sections or classes will, in turn, do the same."

It is, perhaps, fortunate, that the model, rather than the training school idea prevailed in the start, for had all the Normal School been permitted to assist in the nursing, I fear the infant might have perished in its cradle. Its trials would have been as terrible as those of that freshman class of one, to which Holmes says the sophomores

*See letter at close of this article.

and faculty of Harvard once devoted their attention for a year. But, happily, the child passed safely through the perils of infancy and has shown a lusty growth.

Perhaps I should say in passing, that Mr. Gilbert Thayer, who is mentioned by General Hovey in the extract above, was at that time keeping a private school in a building on the north side of the square in Bloomington, about where Fitzwilliam's store now stands, and that the connection between his school and the model school was never more than merely nominal. Mr. Thayer was never regarded as a teacher of the University. The model school continued on the same course for three years, until, with the Normal School, it removed to this building. It was mainly a school for observation, of the primary and intermediate grades, and the instruction was given by Miss Brooks, who received some help from two or three students who were called assistants. Miss Brooks left at the end of the third year, and the school began in this building with three new teachers, and some higher classes were started.

The year 1861-2 gave the model school for the first time a high school department. At the beginning of the second term, or about the first of January, 1862, Mr. Charles F. Childs, who came from the principalship of the Franklin school, in St. Louis, was made principal of the model school, and the high school was organized by him.

The school at this time grew rapidly, partly because of the increase in population of the school district in which the University is situated, the pupils of which attended the model school, and partly by an influx of pupils drawn by the reputation that the school already began to have. This growth in numbers, there being only two teachers in the school, changed very materially the relations between it and the Normal School. In the three lower grades it became more closely allied to a training school. How far this change had progressed, and the way in which the work of the pupil-teachers was done, and how it was made valuable to them by direction and criticism, is very clearly shown by the following, which I find from Dr. Edwards, in the State report of 1861–2, written December, 1862:

"One of the most prominent features of the Normal University is the model school. It is precisely what its name implies,—a model by which the students of the University may be guided in the teaching and discipline of their own schools. It is placed under the charge of instructors whose methods and skill in teaching and governing may be held before the uninitiated as the best known. The influence upon the minds of those about to go out as teachers, of having constantly before them a school of superior character, whose every movement they are required to inspect, and whose progress they may note, is certainly very great; but when in addition to this they are themselves required to conduct classes in such a school, and according to its high model, their work being carefully inspected and criticised by the regular teachers of both the Normal and model schools, we cannot fail to see that an opportunity for improvement in the art of teaching is offered by it such as is furnished by no other instrumentality. A plain statement of the method pursued in reference to the practice of the Normal students in the model school, will best illustrate the utility of this part of a teachers' seminary.

"At the beginning of each term, such members of the higher classes in the University as are designated by the principal for practice in the model school, have classes assigned to them for the term. Each student so designated has charge of one class in one study, and is therefore employed in teaching one hour in the day, the remaining time being appropriated to other work. For the progress of his class during the term, each pupil-teacher is held responsible, the principal and other teachers making from time to time such suggestions as the case seems to demand. As frequently as possible, however, the class, under its teacher, goes through an exercise before the faculty and the body of pupil teachers. This exercise is intended to be a fair sample of an ordinary recitation; or, if allowed to differ from that, it is in order to illustrate more fully some principle or method considered important. After a reasonable time employed in the exercise the class is dismissed, and the method and manner of the instructor are fully and freely discussed by all present,—their merits and demerits pointed out, and improvements suggested. In these discussions many principles are set forth and illustrated, and thus fixed in the minds of all present; practical suggestions are made just where they are most needed,—in connection with actual work; the objections that arise in any mind are presented, and, if unfounded, are answered; so that everything proposed is tried by the most natural and proper tests. It will be seen that in these exercises and discussions, the advantages of both theory and practice are combined in a very desirable and efficient manner. Without the practical illustration presented in the exercise, the general principles enunciated in the discussion would not be appreciated nor remembered; and without the discussion, the peculiarities of the exercise might be unobserved, or understood only as isolated facts, and their uses and relation to other facts remain unperceived.

"The model school, as here organized, is a very important auxiliary to the Normal University. But to make it efficient, it must be under the charge of skilful and earnest teachers. In this way there is presented to the Normal students a practical illustration of the teaching in any grade to which they may be called."

Many of you here present recognize the faithfulness of the picture. From the great increase in numbers, beginning in 1862, until 1874, there was no considerable change in the relations between the Normal and the model schools. For a part of the time the model school had been over-run with pupils, and four principals, one for each

15

department, and an assistant in the high school and the grammar school had been found necessary. But with the discontinuance of the connection with the district school there came relief; the grammar and intermediate departments were consolidated, and the school has continued thus organized up to this date. But these changes had brought no essential modification in the functions of the school as a model or training school. The instructors of the University, both in the Normal school and model school, had been more and more crowded with work. The duties of the president had multiplied. There was no one who could do more than snatch, from pressing duties, a little time to look after the work of the pupil-teachers, and they did not receive that careful and continuous supervision which is essential both for their profit and to the welfare of the pupils taught. The evil, which plainly existed, was met by the appointment of one of the teachers of the Normal school to the exclusive duties of a training teacher, and the principals of the primary and grammar school were styled, in addition to the title of principals, first and second assistant training teachers ; and the change in name indicated a corresponding change in a part of their duties,—a change which, it should be said, had to some extent already taken place.

Under the direction of Mr. Metcalf as training teacher, the work of the pupil-teachers has been most carefully systematized, and the training teacher or one of his assistants is constantly at hand to advise, to direct, and to note the faults and excellences. A further step has been made which carries us back to the idea of the model school. The pupils of the entering class each term visit, for observation, one hour a day, the class in charge of the principal of the primary department. The principal takes pains to explain her methods and the philosophy of them to her observers ; the whole is discussed, and subsequently the pupils preparing to teach are examined upon the work.

Viewing, then, the model school as an adjunct of the Normal school, we see it occupying these three positions: First, a model school for observation, with only a primary department ; next, the transformation having come about from an increase in the number of pupils, a school with a high school department, which was a model school, and lower departments, which were training schools; and, finally, the high school remaining a model school, the lower grades containing a training school for the pupil-teachers, so far as to have all the benefits that we may reasonably seek in a training school, unless we say that its pupils are mere subjects to be operated upon, and a school of observation for entering classes; while, at the same time, all is so carefully and so skilfully supervised that it is still a model school.

It appears to me that in this, as often in other matters, the truth has been found between the extremes, and I give it as my judgment that under the present regime, prevailing for the last eight years, the model school is more nearly, than ever before, accomplishing its part in furtherance of the legitimate purposes of the University. "But," some one will say, "this may be true enough so far as the grammar and primary grades go ; but why have a high school department?"

When I became principal of the model school in 1863, Dr. Edwards said to me that he wanted the high school developed upon a liberal plan and with a high standard to be attained. I believed he was right theoretically, then ; and as I read the results, there has been no conflict between them and the theory. Such an auxiliary school of a Normal school should be a model school. Would you have a headless model? Again show me a public school, I care not whether it be a city high school or a country district school, in which the teacher, or the school board, thinks that the teacher may be finished off and turned out with a diploma, and with about all the education they will ever need,—a public school that does not have constantly in view fitting boys and girls to acquire further education, either by their own unguided efforts, or in another school,—and I will show you a teacher and a school board that fail to comprehend what education means, and a school that fails to educate in the noblest sense of the word. And so I would have in our model school a high school in which fitting boys and girls for the college and the seminary and the scientific school shall be more prominent than preparing them to graduate. This I consider the main argument for our model high school. The idea of something beyond should be constantly presented by precept and example to those who are to become teachers of our youth. But I consider that there is, aside from this, abundant reason for its existence, inasmuch as it is unquestionably the high school in view that does much to fill up the grammar school; and because the principal of the high school has always been able to reciprocate, in a large measure, for the instruction of his pupils in Normal school classes, by receiving Normal pupils to his own classes.

So far I have spoken of the model school, and have given its history, viewing it as an adjunct of the Normal School. But it has had a history of its own,—a history that is apart from that which I have given. It has had a corps of teachers of whom, and of whose faithfulness and skill and ability and loyalty to the University, much might be said. But time forbids, and I can only ask you to pause a moment for a word of tribute in memory of some of those who have fallen.

Mary M. Brooks, the first principal of the model school, was a teacher of some experience, and of rare skill and power in teaching, winning and training children. She had a wonderful grasp of the principles of primary education; and it is the uniform testimony of those who were teachers or pupils in the Normal School during the three years of her principalship, that she filled her position most creditably, and that she made the school in her charge a model school in reality as well as name.

Among the six young men present that October morning twenty-five years ago, when the first session of the University began, was Joseph G. Howell, then about nineteen years old, the youngest of them all, I believe, who had come two hundred miles and more, from near Carmi, in White county, to prepare himself to be a teacher in the public schools. He continued a pupil for three years, graduating in the first class, and was immediately thereafter made a teacher in the model school, and at the beginning of the second term of the year, 1860–61, became principal. The catalogue for the year has this note: "From defects in the records, resulting from the hurried departure for the war of the principal of the model school, it is impossible to publish a correct list of the names in that department." And a later catalogue having a list of those who became soldiers says: "Joseph G. Howell, Company K, Eight Illinois Infantry; killed at the siege of Fort Donelson." These brief words tell of the quick response to the nation's call, and the swift-following death of as noble a youth as ever laid down his life for right and country. I have learned from his classmates that he was the son of a Presbyterian minister; that he was a young man of unusual mental power and promise; that he was by common consent the foremost man of his class. He was earnest and patient and ambitious; but he was always a genial companion, and his heart was filled with ready sympathy for every friend.

During his brief career as a teacher he won the hearts of all his pupils, as well as their respect, by his manliness and his ability. When the first call for ninety-day men came, he enlisted, the first from the University, a private under Captain Harvey at Bloomington, and was mustered in, April 25, 1861, at Springfield. His regiment, the Eighth, under Colonel Dick Oglesby, was the second in number of the War of the Rebellion (the first six were the numbers for the Mexican war); but it was organized the same day as the Seventh, which took the first in number, and Colonel Oglesby, of the Eighth, it was agreed should outrank Colonel Cook, of the Seventh. When the ninety days were up, Howell reenlisted at once, helped to reorganize company K, and was made first lieutenant. In the fight at Donelson, Colonel Oglesby was in command of a brigade, and Lieutenant Howell was detailed to act as a staff officer. While on duty he was shot in the eye and fell dead.*

---

*At this point, the speaker was interrupted by Dr. Hewett, who said he wanted to relate a little incident. Said he, "In the summer of 1861, Howell returned on a brief furlough, to visit Normal for the last time. One morning, as I was coming up the southeast walk towards the University, I met him returning from a farewell visit to his little friends in the model school. The sun was shining fiercely, but he was walking bare-headed, his soldier's cap in his hands filled with flowers that the little ones had given him. He paused and spoke a few words, then passed on, carrying tenderly the love-tributes of the children. It was the last time I ever saw him alive."

[It was an interesting fact that one of the little girls who contributed the flowers was present, in the person of Mrs. Flora M. Hunter, the dean of the Wesleyan College of Music.]

His memory belongs to the whole University, but a more fitting place for some memorial of him would be in No. 12, where he taught. I have in my hands five dollars that may be used for that purpose, and if there are those of his classmates or friends who will increase the amount, the recollections of his life may be preserved as a precious memory, to teach our youth a lesson of noble devotion and patriotism. The day after Mr. Howell's enlistment, he resigned his position as principal of the model school, and recommended, for his successor, Mr. J. H. Burnham, of the graduating class. His wishes were carried out. The summer session had been in operation about one week, and Mr. Burnham finished the term of twelve weeks, and graduated with his class by having his teaching in the model school counted as an equivalent for the studies of the last term.

As I have already said, about the first of January, 1862, Mr. Charles F. Childs came from the public schools of St. Louis to the principalship of the model school. A man about thirty-two years of age, a graduate of Antioch College while Horace Mann was its president, and a teacher of considerable experience, he had already a well-established name in the profession. Gen. Hovey had, in the outset, substantially outlined the plan of the model school, and Miss Brooks had most ably seconded him in developing that plan for the lower grade of the school. To Mr. Childs belongs the credit of the first organization of the high school. Under him the school rapidly won a reputation that has continued, and that has brought here the hundreds of pupils that have thronged the model school, coming from all parts of the State. Mr. Childs was an untiring student, and he made the model school a working school, for he had wonderful power in impressing himself upon all with whom he came in contact, and especially upon the young. He was a live man, abreast with the spirit of the times, and filled with a noble ambition to win a place and a name that should last. He left the model school at the close of the school year 1862–3, and became principal of the St. Louis high school. He staid there until his death, in February, 1866. I had hoped to make this meager sketch fuller, but have been unsuccessful in my search for material.

A little later, March 29, 1866, a memorial exercise in his honor was held in the hall above, and I am permitted by the author to read a few stanzas from a poem prepared for that occasion.

> While sluggards slept, he bravely sought to gain
>   The goal to noble workers ne'er denied,
> Who leave the noxious vapors of Life's plain
>   For Fame's far summit towering in its pride.
>
> The tireless Teacher! whose unbending will,
>   Forever active in the quest for truth,
> Played on his pupils' hearts with matchless skill,
>   And roused to worthy deeds the minds of youth.

Scorner of meanness, hater of pretense,
  Bold to avow convictions all his own,
He pierced deception's veil with keenest sense,
  And dared, when conscience bade, to stand alone.

Though sculptured pile, above his silent dust,
  With tongue of marble ne'er his fame should tell,
The souls he stirred and waked to manly trust
  Will keep the record of his labors well.

It is fitting, perhaps, that I should say a word of the high
school. The catalogue has shown usually but one teacher of the
school, or at most two. That has been to some extent misleading;
for, as you know, the pupils of the high school have been freely
admitted to all the classes of the Normal School; and thus, instead
of one or two teachers, the school has constantly had a full corps of
able instructors, having many special qualifications as teachers in
their particular departments. Taking this view of the case, I have
no hesitation in saying that it would be difficult to find in the country
a secondary school that has offered to its pupils a broader or a richer
course of study. I think the result of this has been apparent in the
pupils of the school.

I want here to note an error in the catalogue. It shows from
1862 to 1871, but a year's course in Greek. It should show a three
years' course. No pupil has ever graduated from the classical course
of study without doing three full years' work in Greek.

But what shall I say to-day for the nearly five thousand pupils
who have frequented the model-school rooms during the quarter of a
century whose limit we mark to-day? One thing should not be left
unsaid. No account of the teachers sent out from the University
would be complete that left them out. About half of the graduates
have taught, and have averaged about three years apiece, and the
under-graduates of the school who have taught have been numbered
by the hundreds.

The pupils of the model school, since it grew to respectable numbers, have always had a wonderful love for it, a great *esprit de corps.*
The school, though down stairs, and not the University nor the largest
interest in it, has always been jealous of its own good name and no
mean competitor of the Normal School for society and University
honors.

It is too soon to expect great things in the history of the world
of the pupils of a school begun but twenty-five years ago as an a b c
school, and whose first class was graduated since the close of the war.
But they are already to be found among the rising men of the
professions, among the merchants, the mechanics, and the farmers.
Many of the girls are worthy matrons now. If I mistake not there is
abundant promise for the future; and to that I think we may safely
leave the harvest.

In closing, I will only say that I am sure no school has ever had more loyal pupils than those of the model school, and that the Normal University has to-day no truer or stauncher friends than are to be found among those whose names have been enrolled upon the registers of the primary school, the grammar school and the high school below.

NORMAL, ILLINOIS, August 27, 1882.

MY DEAR SIR:

Soon after I came to the State in 1854, a young woman timidly introduced herself to me at my school room in Peoria, as Mary Brooks, from Brimfield. She was about the usual height, of rather large frame, a little gaunt, or poor in flesh, with a head to delight an artist, and a face so sincere and winning as to greatly impress, I will not say fascinate. the beholder. She was a Vermonter by birth, but her parents had settled in Illinois some years before. She said she wanted to engage in teaching and desired to pursue preparatory studies with me. She developed rapidly, serving as a pupil-teacher and as a full teacher in Peoria for about two years. Children loved her at sight. and the love was returned. It was genuine, and I think quite involuntary on both sides. Neither could help it. She had, or seemed to have, an intuitive knowledge of a child's mind at different stages of development, and a genius for inventing methods to aid its growth. I call this power intuition, genius, but I do not mean that it came to her without effort. She was a hard student of books and of nature. When a model school was determined upon as an incident and annex to the Normal University, the Board of Education, on the advice of the principal, invited Miss Brooks to take charge of it. Her class was composed of children. It was intended at that time chiefly as a model, and not as a school of practice for pupil-teachers. I shall not soon forget how Mary and her little friends got on together in their cramped and unsuitable room under a corner of Major's Hall, nor how the most learned man of the Board, Dr. Bunsen, used to sit for hours, sometimes whole days, watching Mary's work, as pleased as any of the children, and apparently unconscious of the lapse of time. The management and methods of the model school during this period, would repay study, if available. I do not know that they were ever described in print, and I cannot undertake to describe them now. After three years of successful labor, the first teacher in the model school resigned, to become Mrs. James M. Wiley, and died January 9, 1863, leaving two children, George and Katie.

Very truly,   CHARLES E. HOVEY.

To W. L. Pillsbury, Esq.

THE CELEBRATION.

As early as May, 1881, preparations were begun for a quarter-centennial celebration in 1882.

By correspondence, it was ascertained that a much larger number could attend in August than at the time of the annual commencement, in May. Arrangements having been perfected, the exercises began on the evening of August 24. After a cornet solo, by Charles Lufkin, General Hovey, now residing in Washington, D. C., delivered the address found in the preceding pages. The weather was very unfavorable, but the speaker was greeted by a large and enthusiastic audience, many of whom had been identified with the early history of the school.

On Friday morning the assembly room was crowded to its utmost capacity by a happy throng of old students, pioneer workers in educa-

tional enterprises in the State, and prominent citizens of Normal and
·Bloomington. Nearly an hour was spent in having a good, old-fash-
ioned sociable. The early classes were well represented. Harvey
Dutton and Lizzie ,Carleton had journeyed up from Missouri. Logan
Holt Roots had forgotten his banks and railroad schemes, and Mexican
telephones, and was there, the happiest of the happy. Anna Grennell
Hatfield paid the school her first visit since her graduation eighteen
years ago. These and scores of others had returned to the familiar
halls rendered sacred by hallowed associations, to greet old mates and
renew their allegiance to their "cherishing mother." Charles E.
Hovey was there, quiet and grave as of old, but with a twinkle of joy
in his eyes that spoke more than volumes. Richard Edwards was
the centre of a boisterous group of his boys and girls, and he the
youngest of them all, while E. C. Hewett, the shortest in stature but
the longest in service, put to shame all of his previous attempts at wit
and hilarity.

The early Thomas Metcalf broke his vacation off at the short end to be on
hand, and Albert Stetson, his co-worker for twenty years, was nowise
behindhand in promoting the general fun. Hon. Newton Bateman,
grown gray in the service, laid aside his cares for a day to greet old
friends and join in the general rejoicing. Father Roots, Hon. Charles
T. Strattan, Hon. Thomas F. Mitchell, Dr. E. R. Roe, Hon. Robert
Brand, and many others whose names are familiar to Normal students,
were in the audience. At ten o'clock, President Walker called the
assembly to order and announced the following order of exercises:

Piano solo, Mrs. Flora M. Hunter; address, Dr. Edwards;
reading of Henry Norton's paper, by John W. Cook; piano duet,
Mrs. Flora M. Hunter, Miss Minnie Potter; address, W. L. Pillsbury;
address, E. C. Hewett. These papers are found in the earlier part
of this volume. At three o'clock, the alumni business meeting was
held in the Philadelphian Hall. The chief item of interest was a subscription to provide a memorial for the lamented Howell, as suggested
by Mr. Pillsbury in his address. In a few minutes a sufficient sum was
collected to insure the success of the movement. A committee consisting of Silas Hays and Captain Burnham from the alumni, and Dr.
Hewett from the faculty, will have the whole matter in charge.

The event of events was, of course, the banquet. Miss Flora
Pennell, of the executive committee, had that part of the work under
her supervision. The executive committee asked Miss Carrie Pennell,
an under-graduate living in the village, to prepare the supper. She
undertook the task and the successful manner in which it was accomplished was a matter of universal comment. The large hall had been
elaborately decorated for the occasion. Festoons of evergreens connected the chandeliers; flowers were scattered about in profusion;
a shower from a fountain, in the center of the hall, fell upon a huge
circular basin filled with plants and blossoms; tablets on the walls bore

the names of, "our dead," and a fine large crayon portrait of Samuel W. Paisley occupied a place on the west side of the hall. Class pictures, crayon designs, and various other appliances completed the decorations. Humphrey's orchestra furnished delightful music for the occasion. At six o'clock the procession filed into the room, the alumni taking their places at the tables by classes. The guests were seated along the south side, facing north, and on the outside of the side tables. John W. Cook, of the class of 1865, acted as master of ceremonies. When all were seated, Dr. Edwards asked the blessing, and the assembled company, two hundred and twenty in number, entered upon the serious business of the evening—the discussion of the numerous delicacies spread before them. After this part of the business had been disposed of, the toasts were in order.

Gov. Cullom had indicated his intention to be present, but was taken sick in the train and was obliged to return to Springfield. Lieutenant-Governor Hamilton was on hand, however, and responded to the toast, "A true and tried friend of popular education." Dr. Bateman was "toasted" as "the man who first gave the schools of Illinois a national reputation," but the doctor had been obliged to return to Galesburg on the afternoon train. The sentiment, however, was greeted with loud cheers. "Our venerable friend, the president of the State Board of Education,—for a full half century the light of Egypt," brought Father Roots to his feet for a characteristic speech of ten minutes. Judge Reeves responded to the toast, "The Bar—the last resort of the school-master." The class toasts and speakers were as follows: "Our First Born—the Class of '60," E. A. Gastman; "The Class of '61," J. H. Burnham; "The Class of '62," Logan H. Roots; "The Class of 65," O. F. McKim; "The Class of '66," Sarah E. Raymond; "The Class of '68," Henry McCormick; "The Class of '70," Joseph Carter. Hon. Jesse W. Fell and Hon. A. J. Merriman were expected to tell "How McLean County got the Normal School.". Mr. Fell, however, was unexpectedly called to Iowa three days before the meeting. It was a serious disappointment to him and to the company, for his activity in securing the location is generally understood. Judge Merriman was a member of the Board of County Commissioners in 1857, and with his associates, Hiram Buck and Milton Smith, made the county appropriation of $70,000. The judge also had the distinguished honor of laying the corner stone of the building. Speech-making, however, is not in his line, and so Dr. E. R. Roe told the story in his stead, and, at its conclusion responded to the toast: "Our Early Teachers." General Hovey was called upon to let us know "how the building was erected," but instead, spoke as follows:

An intimation, more or less plainly stated, has several times been made, tending to show that the first presiding officer of this institution was substantially its founder, and that, at least, the building could not, or would not, have been built at the time it was without him.

I am glad of an opportunity to speak of these matters, and I may claim, I suppose, without challenge, that I was part of them. Right or wrong, the chief place in the beginning fell to me, and, with it, came an opportunity of influencing the trend of affairs in the institution, and, to some extent, out of it. I had done what I could to bring about the legislation which set the school in motion. Here, again, the accident of position* at the critical time enabled me to know and do what would otherwise have been impracticable. My advice as to plans for the proposed building was generally followed, and my services in and about its erection came to be in considerable demand before it was completed. But it would be a mistake to say that the Normal University owes its establishment, or conduct afterwards, to any one man or set of men. It was the outgrowth of the ideas and wishes of a majority of the people of Illinois, formulated and uttered by a large number of persons, and by at least two influential State associations. Prof. Turner and the Industrial League blazed the way, but they did not found the Normal University. The State Teachers' Association followed and secured for it a hearing, but the association did not found it. Father Roots tells you that Simeon Wright was the man who did the business, and I think myself his services were indispensable, but it would hardly be correct to say that he was the Atlas of the enterprise. The first superintendent of public instruction elected by the people, assisted in drafting the bill, but he did not enact it into law. His successor, the honored president of Knox College, stood guard over its interests at the gateway of danger for many years, and took care *ne quid detrimenti Normalis Universitas capiat*, but even he was not the sole Fidus Achates. Hon. S. W. Moulton, Hon. C. B. Denio, Dr. Calvin Goudy, and a majority of both Houses of the Legislature, voted for the Normal University Act, and Governor Bissell signed it, but they were not the founders of the institution; and yet, without each and all of these, I do not see how it could have been established at the time it was, and as it was. Each was a link in the golden chain, but only a link.

Nor do I see how it could have been located in McLean County without Jesse W. Fell; and yet Jesse Fell did not bring it here. A very modest and worthy citizen (Judge Merriman), who appears to be listening to me from a corner of the table to my right, and two other McLean County men (Messrs. Buck and Smith), were the heroes of that act. They took the responsibility and risk to themselves, politically, of involving the county in a debt of seventy thousand dollars to secure the location of the institution here. That act of

* Hovey was president of the State Teachers' Association, and editor of its "organ" at the time.

theirs required a high degree of moral courage, and entitles them to
a seat on the upper bench at the head of the table, along with Jesse
Fell.   But even these men must consent to a division of the honors.
Back of them stood the people of Bloomington with their subscription paper.   Without this paper, Jesse Fell and the County Court
would have had "to throw up the sponge" and yield gracefully, no
doubt, to Peoria.

Nor did Asahel Gridley risk any money in loans for erecting the
building, though my friend, Colonel Roe, gives him credit for making
advances.   True, Colonel Gridley furnished some money for that
purpose, but not a dollar came over the counter of his bank until he
had been amply secured by the promissory notes of citizens.   Such
men as S. W. Moulton, Jesse and Kersey Fell, Charles and Richard
Holder, Edwin C. Hewett, Joseph A. Sewall, Charles E. Hovey, and
others whom I do not at this moment recall, signed the notes.   The
banker risked nothing, and lost nothing, but gained interest.   The
men who signed the notes took the risk. ' But the merchants of
Bloomington stand on a different footing.   They did take risk.   They
gave the contractor for erecting the building, Mr. Soper, credit, to a
large amount in the aggregate, with no other security than my
promise to see them paid whenever there was anything to pay with.
They trusted the enterprise, and, to that extent, risked their
advances, and I take liberty to invite them to a seat on a bench a
little higher up than the banker's pew.

I must not leave this subject without naming the committee of
the Board under whose supervision this edifice was erected.   They
were Hon. S. W. Moulton, chairman; Hon. C. B. Denio, Dr. George
P. Rex, Hon. N. W. Edwards, Hon. William H. Powell, Prof.
Daniel Wilkins, and Charles E. Hovey.

Mr. Chairman, if you have been listening to me, I think you are
beginning to see that a goodly number of people have been engaged,
at one time or another, in one way or another, in founding this great
school, and in building its house.   Nor did one man make its course
of study, nor plan and limit its scope, nor give to the work so
mapped out that impulse which has thus far swept over, or brushed
aside, all adverse obstacles.   True, there was at first, as there has
been since and must continue to be, a head.   Somebody must decide
and direct, and the questions at the outset of any enterprise,
which clamor for settlement, are often numerous, and generally
important.   But the first principal was not left to solve these
problems unaided.   In addition to C. M. Cady, Dr. E. R. Roe, and
Rev. L. P. Clover, special instructors, and Charlton T. Lewis,
Samuel Willard, Chauncey Nye, and Miss B. M. Cowles, employed
from time to time, any or all of whom he could call upon for information and counsel,—I say, in addition to these, the first principal had
the good fortune to have associated with him, as co-laborers, Ira

Moore, Leander H. Potter, Edwin C. Hewett, and Joseph A. Sewall. A principal surrounded by such men need not set up for himself, or put on airs, or assume that he is the only considerable person on the premises. They were the peers of anybody in the profession. The principal had the benefit of their knowledge and experience, in determining the course to be pursued, and in formulating work to be done. These men made their mark on the school. I should not wonder if it could be pointed out even now. But they did not make the school what it is now. Presidents Bass and Edwards, and their associates, came later, it is true, but they served longer, and with no doubtful success. The proofs are all around me to-night. Their good deeds have been recorded, and were read to you this morning. I do not see how anybody can wipe out that record, and it is one on which they can afford to stand. But even these men and women must be content with having done a part. They did not do everything. After them came President Hewett and his associates, who are moving forward, bearing aloft the old banner, inscribed with mottoes indicating reliance upon plain, unpretentious, common-school work. I believe they are conducting this great school with judgment and efficiency. I know Edwin Hewett ranks high among the Normal-school teachers of America. But neither Hovey, nor Bass, nor Edwards, nor Hewett, nor all of them and their associates combined, have made this institution what it has grown to be. I will throw in the Board of Education, Father Roots, and all, and still I say there is an omission. The students must be added. They have carried the Normal University to a thousand school rooms all over the State, and have taught its classes there. I look upon them as non-resident professors. They have played no inconsiderable part in the work of the institution. I have not attempted to keep track of them, and what I happen to know has come to me incidentally. But right before mes its a well-known man who has been in charge of Decatur's public schools for twenty years; this morning a paper was read from a professor in California's Normal School; a moment ago a soldier, as well as teacher, addressed you; "shake," comes over the wires from the head school man in Denver; in front of me sits a citizen who, in addition to teaching, has twice represented his district in Congress; to my left sits a lady who for some years has been superintendent of public schools in Bloomington. A few years ago, at the reunion of the society of the Army of the Tennessee, in Chicago, a note was handed in to me, signed by a familiar name. I went out, and there met a remarkable woman in looks and attainments, a physician and professor of physiology in the Woman's College. I must not detain you by further recitals. All these, and a thousand more, are your boys and girls. They are the links in the silver chain that binds this school to the common schools of the State. But I must stop. I beg pardon for detaining you so long.

Dr. Edwards told "How the building was filled," and Dr. Hewett "How it is kept full." Hon. Thomas F. Mitchell, the staunch friend of the school in the Legislature, told "Where we get our munitions of war." He was followed by Hon. Charles T. Strattan, the member of the house from Mt. Vernon. "The Normal University abroad," was responded to by E. J. James, Ph. D. In the course of his remarks he read an extract from *Geschichte der Paedagogik, von Karl Schmidt*, which appears upon a later page of this volume.

Letters expressing regrets for unavoidable absence were read from Senator Logan, Senator Davis, Governor Cullom, Prof. E. W. Coy, Prof. Burrington, Miss Emaline Dryer, Dr. Sewall, Perkins Bass, Mrs. W. L. Pillsbury, George Howland, Superintendent Chicago Schools; S. H. Peabody, Regent Industrial University, and Hon. D. C. Smith, M. C. Thirteenth District. Aaron Gove, of 1861, telegraphed: "Classmates of '58, shake!" The following letters were also read:

SPRINGFIELD, August 25, 1882.

PROF. JOHN W. COOK, Normal.

Dear Sir: Your kind invitation reached me this morning. I am very sorry that I did not know of your meeting sooner; but it is impossible for me to go now. You will undoubtedly have a grand, good time, and my sincere desire is that the Normal school may prosper still more in the future than it has in the past. Its growth and success have been great so far, but it has its work still to do for the good of the schools of the State. There is no agency in existence that has done so much for the elevation of the schools as the Normal University, and my wish is that it may continue the good work for years to come. As you all know, I have been an advocate and friend from the start, and shall continue to do all I can in the future for the continuance of the school. There have been in the past many good, hard-working men and women connected with the school, as there are at present, who will never be forgotten by the people of this great State. The first president, General Hovey, deserves especial mention for the noble work he did in the start. Many of the students from the Normal have done good, noble work in various sections of our State, and we all hope to see this school not only continue, but to increase year after year. Remember me to General Hovey and others, and accept my best wishes. Yours Truly,

S. M. ETTER.

CHICAGO, ILLINOIS, August 23, 1882.

JOHN W. COOK, Corresponding Secretary.

Dear Sir: I am in receipt of your kind invitation to attend the quarter-centennial celebration of the alumni of the State Normal University. In reply would say that family sickness prevents my being present with you. Were it possible, nothing would afford me greater pleasure than to join in your festivities, and meet again some of the old friends and active workers who were the founders of that excellent institution,—the Illinois State Normal University. The old workers and the new workers all have my heart's good will. May God bless and prosper any agency that elevates and blesses humanity. With kind regards for yourself and all educators, I am,

Yours very sincerely,   JOHN F. EBERHART.

CARBONDALE, ILLINOIS, August 22, 1882.

PROF. JOHN W. COOK, State Normal University.

Sir: Your very kind and cordial invitation to me, asking me to be present and enjoy the twenty-fifth anniversary of the State Normal University, was received a few days ago. I should have replied at once, but for the fact that I was under a promise to do a little institute work in Pope county during this week, which I was then hoping to be permitted to turn over to another. That is found impossible, and I am therefore, at this late moment, obliged to send my regrets for an enforced absence, on account of a previously-made engagement. I am not able in words to convey my feelings of disappointment, for I know how much of interest centers around your noble pioneer Normal, and how large and enthusiastic a body of graduates, students and friends of education and virtue are rejoicing at your quarter of a century of success. It would have done me good, body, soul, mind and spirit, to have been with you, if only for an hour, to drink in new life and inspiration from the rehearsal of your noble history, and from the inspiring prospects before your grand University. But it may not be. I can only add, "May the first Normal University of Illinois continue first in war against ignorance, first in the peace which intelligence brings, and first in the memories of a grateful people." But let her remember that she must "run," if she shall "obtain" so great a boon, until her second quarter-centennial, for there is another child of the State, born and growing up, to do what she can.

I am very respectfully and obediently your servant,

ROBERT ALLYN.

SPRINGFIELD, ILLINOIS, August 25, 1882.

PROF. E. C. HEWETT, President State Normal University.

My Dear Sir: Deprived of the pleasure of attending your celebration to-day, I write this line to say that I am with you in spirit, and that I very much regret I cannot also be with you in person. I have watched with much interest the work of the State Normal University, from the time of its establishment twenty-five years ago until the present time. Early in its history I became satisfied that it did thoroughly and well what it attempted and professed to do; and I have long been of the opinion that the thoroughness with which work is done in the school has done much to improve the character of the instruction given in other schools; that the influence of the school, directly through its students and graduates, and indirectly by its example, is felt throughout the whole State in the improvement of the teaching done in its schools.

The friends of education in Illinois are to be congratulated upon having succeeded in securing the maintenance, for a quarter of a century, of so good a school for the training of teachers. May its influence for good to the schools of the State be augmented and long continued.   Hastily, but very truly yours,

JAMES P. SLADE.

CHICAGO, August 10, 1882.

JOHN W. COOK, Esq., Corresponding Secretary Alumni Association.

Dear Sir: Accept my thanks for your kind invitation to attend the quarter-centennial of your association. I regret to say that I find it impracticable to be present on that occasion. I should like to meet once more with those who stood "shoulder to shoulder" twenty-five years ago and struck out boldly for a higher plane of education in this State, and to enjoy with them in the retrospect what we then so much enjoyed in the prospect. Our anticipations have been fully realized; a glorious victory has been won, and Illinois to-day stands proudly among the foremost States of the Union in her system of popular education. And now, my young friends, men and women of a new generation, hold fast to the ground that has already been gained; strike out again; aim still higher; meet worthily the responsibilities that rest upon you; let the next twenty-five years witness still greater progress toward perfection, and you will have for your reward the consciousness that you are imitating the example of him who "went about doing good," and the thanks of the generations that are to follow.   Yours truly,   W. H. WELLS.

At the close of the exercises, General Hovey arose and stated that it had been his pleasure to attend a good many banquets at one time and another, but that he had never seen one in which the arrangements were more complete nor in better taste. This opinion was evidently the sentiment of all present, as it was received with loud applause. At eleven o'clock, after five hours of solid enjoyment, the formal part of the exercises closed, and the quarter-centennial celebration passed into history. Many lingered an hour longer saying good-byes.

All agreed that the celebration was an unqualified success. The early trains on Saturday bore away most of the visitors, and the institution settled down again to the routine duties that have made it what it is. There was a general desire expressed that a similar meeting should be held at least as often as once in three or four years, and there is no doubt that at least as early as the thirtieth anniversary there will be a gathering that will surpass the meeting of 1882.

THE STATE LABORATORY OF NATURAL HISTORY.

BY S. A. FORBES.

The long and close association of the establishment now known as the State Laboratory of Natural History with the Normal University, and the influence continuously exerted by it upon the pupils of the Normal School, and upon the teachers and pupils of the State at large, make it proper that a history of the Normal University should contain some account of the origin and development of the laboratory. The history of the latter institution has been one, not only of growth, but of metamorphosis, also. Commencing as the museum of a natural history society, it was afterwards transferred to the State, and served for a time the purpose of a state museum, but was finally converted into a natural history laboratory, made a center of operations and a source of supply for the State at large, but relieved from the necessity of maintaining a public display of specimens. While by far the most extended and useful part of its work has been done since its conversion into a laboratory, its actual beginning dates from the time of the formation of the old State Natural History Society of Illinois, an organization which had its origin in the same general progressive impulse which gave rise to the Normal University. The first public movement for the formation of this society resulted from a discussion of the subject had at a meeting of the State Teachers' Association, held at Decatur, in December, 1857. The society was actually organized at a convention held in Bloomington on the thirtieth of June, 1858. Prof. J. B. Turner, of Jacksonville, was chosen the first president; Dr. E. R. Roe, of Bloomington, treasurer; Gen. Charles E. Hovey, then principal of the State Normal University, secretary; and C. D. Wilbur, general agent. Letters of congratulation were read from most of the working naturalists of the State who were not present in person, and the new organization set out with every assurance of an active and useful life. This promise was abundantly fulfilled for several years. The annual meetings steadily increased in numbers and interest, and the work carried forward became of continually higher character, as shown by the papers contributed and by the large collection of specimens accumulated. These specimens were placed in rooms of the State Normal University, especially set aside for the use of the society by the Board of Education.

The scope and character of the scientific work fostered by the society may be inferred from the following partial list of the papers read at its various meetings:

By Prof. J. B. Turner, of Jacksonville, "On Microscopic Insects" and "The Great Avalanche of the Ocean;" by Dr. F. Brendel, of Peoria, "Forests and Forest Trees," "Meteorology in connection with Botanical Investigation," "On the Peculiar Growth of the Water Lily (Nelumbium Luteum, Willd.)," "Additions to Robert Kennicott's Catalogue of the Flora of Illinois," "Meteorological Table," and "Trees and Shrubs of Illinois;" by Dr. George Vasey (now botanist of the agricultural department at Washington), "The Mosses of Illinois," "Catalogue of Illinois Flora, with Three Hundred and Eleven Recent Additions," "Pernicious Weeds," "Range of Arborescent Vegetation," and "Additions to Illinois Flora;" by Prof. Cyrus Thomas, afterwards State Entomologist, "Orthoptera of Illinois," "Notes on Illinois Insects," "Catalogue of the Mammals of Illinois," and "Plan of a Natural History Survey;" by B. D. Walsh, the first State Entomologist, "Insect Life" and "Fire Blight;" by Dr. E. R. Roe, of Bloomington, "Some Features of the Drift Formation;" by Hon. James Shaw, of Mt. Carroll, "The Great Tornado of 1860;" by C. D. Wilbur, "Mastodon Giganteus" and "Fuel in Illinois;" by Richard H. Holder, of Bloomington (now of Freeport), "Directions for Collecting and Preserving Specimens in Ornithology," and "A Catalogue of the Birds of Illinois."

Most of these papers, with several others of similar character, were published in the State agricultural reports, notably in the third and fourth volumes, and many of them were reprinted in 1862 by the society in the form of a volume of transactions.

The principal donations of specimens made by members were those of Illinois birds, by R. H. Holder; of Illinois fossils, by C. D. Wilbur; of fresh-water shells and southern fossils, by J. W. Powell, and a fine series of Illinois plants, by Dr. George Vasey.

The society was formally chartered by the Legislature, February 22, 1862. The museum was at first supported by contributions of members and the regular income of the society, but as the collections increased in size and importance, the expense of caring for them became too onerous a burden for the small membership of the society, and the aid of the State was invoked. By section four of "An Act concerning the Board of Education and the Illinois Natural History Society," approved February 28, 1867, an annual appropriation of $2,500 was made for the salary of a curator and the improvement of the museum, and it was provided that this money should be expended under the direction of the Board of Education, by whom, with the advice and consent of the directors of the Natural History Society, said curator should be appointed. Under this act, Prof. John W. Powell, now in charge of the United States Government Surveys of the western territories, was appointed curator, March 30, 1867, and immediately prepared for an expedition to the valley of the Colorado River of the West. Appropriations were made for the expenses of his party by the State Board of Education, the State Industrial University, and the Chicago Academy of Sciences.

16

Collections of minerals, fossils, plants, insects, birds, and mammals, were made along his route from Council Bluffs to Denver, and thence to the canon of the South Platte, Pike's Peak, and the head waters of the Colorado, and this material was divided, at least in part, among the institutions sharing the principal expense of the trip. In the following year, Prof. Powell undertook a more elaborate exploration of the Colorado River, in behalf of which an appropriation had been made by Congress, and $1,000 had been voted by the Board from the income of the museum. Prof. Powell spent the next four years chiefly in the western territories in the further prosecution of his explorations, the principal expense of which is understood to have been borne by the general government. The affairs of the museum were in the meantime administered by acting curators in his pay. The appropriation of $2,500 per annum made by the Legislature in aid of the Natural History Society had been continued regularly up to this time, under the original conditions, but by an act approved April 14, 1871, this appropriation was made subject to the condition that the collections, cases, etc., of the State Natural History Society, then in the museum, should be made over to the State in such a way as should be satisfactory to the Governor. In accordance with this act, the transfer was authorized by the society, as is shown by the following transcript from its records:

"BLOOMINGTON, ILLINOIS, June 22, 1871.

"The Illinois State Natural History Society met, pursuant to adjournment, at the office of the city superintendent of schools, Vice-President Etter in the chair.

"On motion of R. H. Holder, J. A. Sewall was delegated as the agent of the society to transfer to the State Board of Education, for the use and benefit of the State, the collections in the museum, and other property belonging to the Illinois State Natural History Society, unconditionally."

The following is a copy of the instrument executed by J. A. Sewall, as agent of the society:

"WHEREAS, The State Natural History Society, at a meeting held in the city of Bloomington, and State of Illinois, on the twenty-second day of June, 1871, appointed the undersigned agent for said society, to assign and transfer all the property of said society to the Board of Education of the State of Illinois, in pursuance of the resolutions of said society; therefore, by virtue of said authority, said Natural History Society hereby assigns and transfers all its property of every kind, now in the Normal University building, to the said Board of Education forever.

This twenty-eighth day of June, 1871.

THE STATE NATURAL HISTORY SOCIETY.

[SIGNED.]   By JOSEPH A. SEWALL, Agent."

This conveyance was accepted by the following resolution of the Board of Education, extracted from the proceedings of their meeting held June 28 and 29, 1871:

"WHEREAS, The Illinois State Natural History Society did, on the twenty-second day of June, 1871, by formal resolution, determine and agree to transfer to the State of Illinois all the right and interest of said society in and to the property of the museum in the Normal University building, and did also then and there appoint and empower Joseph A. Sewall, as agent, to convey said resolution into effect; and,

WHEREAS, In pursuance of said resolution and authorization, the said Joseph A. Sewall did, on the twenty-eighth day of June, 1871, execute and deliver a conveyance of said property to the Board of Education in trust for the State of Illinois; now, therefore, be it

Resolved, That the Board of Education of the State of Illinois do hereby accept the said conveyance, and take possession of the property therein conveyed, for the use and benefit of the State of Illinois."

During the year following this transfer, Dr. George Vasey, then acting curator, made large botanical collections in various parts of the State, and added several hundred specimens to the museum herbarium from his large private collection. Specimens of fossils, minerals, woods, etc., were also obtained, and sets of minerals, geological specimens, woods, plants, and shells, were distributed to twelve of the principal public schools of the State.

On the twenty-eighth of June, 1872, the resignation of Prof. Powell was offered and accepted, and on the same day, Mr. S. A. Forbes was appointed to succeed him. A careful estimate of the contents of the museum was made at this time, with the following result:

Minerals, 1,500 specimens,		300 species
Plants, 9,000 specimens,		3,000 species
Shells, 5,000 specimens,		958 species
Fossils, 5,000 specimens,		1,200 species
Insects, 2,500 specimens,		1,500 species
Birds, 200 specimens,		191 species
Mammals, 30 specimens,		26 species

After the transfer of the museum to the State, no formal declaration of the views of the Board of Education concerning its relations and their intentions with respect to it was ever made, until the following resolutions were passed, December 15, 1875; but as these resolutions simply embodied the settled policy of the Board, in accordance with which the museum had been governed from the first, they may be properly introduced here:

"WHEREAS, Since the control of the museum of the Illinois State Natural History Society was transferred to the State Board of Education, no general declaration has ever been made by this Board of the relations and policy of the museum, or of the purposes of the Board concerning it; and,

"WHEREAS, It seems desirable that the students and friends of science should know definitely and authoritatively the nature, scope, and promise of the work of said museum, in order that they may intelligently coöperate with its officers for the promotion of the scientific interests of the State; therefore,

"*Resolved*, That we regard the museum as a State institution, devoted to the prosecution of a natural history survey of the State, to the encouragement and aid of original research, and to the diffusion of knowledge and habits of thought among the people.

"*Resolved*, That we consider it an important part of its work to supply collections of specimens to the public schools, as far as this can be done consistently with its own general interests, and especially to provide all needed facilities for the instruction of teachers in natural history, and in the most approved and successful methods of teaching the same; and,

"*Resolved*, That we cordially invite the coöperation of the scientists of Illinois, offering them the free use of its collections, library, and apparatus, and assuring them that whatever may be contributed to its cabinets or its funds, shall be used faithfully and impartially for the advancement of science throughout the State."

Until December, 1876, the establishment retained the obsolete title of "The Museum of the Illinois State Natural History Society;" but at that time the following resolution was adopted by the Board:

"*Resolved*, That the museum in the Normal University building, formerly the property of the Illinois State Natural History Society, but now under the control of this Board, be hereafter known by the name of "The Illinois Museum of Natural History."

The changed relations of the museum made it now proper that its operations should be confined chiefly within the limits of the State. It was therefore determined to put the large but disordered collection into condition for use as rapidly as possible, by classifying, arranging, cataloguing, and indexing the specimens and the library; to give immediate attention to filling up the most important lacunæ in both, with the view of ultimately accumulating sufficient material for a botanical and zoölogical survey of Illinois; to give much greater attention to the supply of cabinets of specimens to the public schools, and to encourage and aid, in every way that could be devised, the rational study of nature by the teachers and children of the State; to promote original scientific research, by bringing together the essential instrumentalities for its successful prosecution, and by providing for the publication of its results; and to assist in the solution of scientific problems bearing upon the industries of the people.

The sudden introduction, in 1872, of four new sciences into the common-school course, a knowledge of which was required of candidates for certificates, powerfully stimulated the study of natural history throughout the State, and made that part of the museum work relating to the public schools most pressing and important, especially as it soon became evident that the lack of preparation upon the part of teachers and school officers for the new duties which the law imposed upon them, threatened serious injury to educational interests, unless efficient help were given. Circulars were therefore issued from the museum, as soon as practicable, offering especial facilities free of charge to those who wished to fit themselves thoroughly for work in the new field, and proposing a series of mutual exchanges for the general benefit. While conducting these exchanges, all the available duplicates in the museum collections were issued to the schools which seemed most to need them. In continuation of this work it was determined, in the autumn of 1873, to attempt the organization of a new society of natural history, which should have for its leading purpose the supply of practical working collections to the schools, through the labor of the teachers and pupils of the schools themselves. With this view, after correspondence with several of the leading teachers of the State, the friends of the movement were invited to convene at Bloomington, Illinois, during the session, at that place, of the State Teachers' Association, in the Christmas holidays. The result was a large and earnest meeting of teachers, at which, after an animated discussion, a constitution was adopted, and the society formally organized by the election of Dr. Richard Edwards, as president, S. A. Forbes, curator, and Aaron Gove, secretary.

The purposes of this society were declared to be, to collect, study, and exchange specimens in natural history, to obtain for the schools with which its members were connected, suitable cabinets of specimens for study and reference, and to encourage and assist the rational study of nature by the pupils of our schools.

This society enlisted the teachers and pupils of more than forty of the colleges and public schools of the State, most of which did active work for the museum during the first two years. The duplicate specimens sent in, to the number of more than three thousand, were named and redistributed to these schools, and material to the amount of about four hundred and fifty dollars was added to the sets from the museum duplicates. This was largely alcoholic marine material, illustrating the sub-kingdoms, classes, and leading orders, representatives of which are otherwise beyond the reach of Illinois schools. A systematic check-list of these specimens, for use in making exchanges, was published during the winter.

Under the auspices of this association, a vacation school of natural history was held in the museum at Normal, in July and August, 1875. Instruction of a high grade, and good facilities for work and study, both elementary and advanced, were provided in the following branches: Systematic and structural botany of the flowering plants; cryptogamic botany, with especial reference to mosses and fungi; systematic and structural zoölogy, illustrated by mounted skeletons and other preparations, and by series of dissections made by the students under the eye of competent instructors.

A sufficient number of microscopes was provided for the use of students in the study of histology and the lower forms of life. Marine material was furnished fresh from the sea, and inland specimens of all varieties, in great abundance. Occasional excursions were made by the class to give opportunity for field-work.

The following gentlemen acted as instructors for the term: Prof. B. G. Wilder, of Cornell University, New York; Prof. W. S. Barnard, Ph. D.; Prof. T. J. Burrill, of the Illinois Industrial University; Prof. Cyrus Thomas, State Entomologist; Dr. J. A. Sewall, of the State Normal University; and S. A. Forbes.

It was found necessary to limit the attendance to fifty students, but within this limit the school was open to the teachers of the State. Over seventy applications were received, from forty-two different counties. The specimens selected for study were typical ones, and the dissections and examinations were so planned and conducted that the chief facts demonstrated were true, not of the species or genus only, but of the whole classes or sub-kingdoms, or else furnished notable exceptions to general statements about these larger groups.

The fresh water collections for study and dissection were obtained from Lake Michigan and the Illinois River, and the marine animals were collected, as needed, along the New England coast. The laboratory work was made, throughout, the basis of the course, and the lectures were designed chiefly to explain and complete the knowledge gained with the scalpel and the microscope. The study of the anatomy of vertebrates included careful dissections of Amphioxus, of the ganoid and common fishes, and the sharks, and skates; turtles, serpents, frogs, and salamanders; and birds, and mammals.

Invertebrate zoölogy was illustrated by dissections of star fishes, brittle stars, sea urchins, sand dollars, and sea cucumbers; earth worms, marine worms, brachiopods and ascidians; lobsters, crawfishes, crabs, beetles, and caterpillars; the common river mussel, several species of marine gasteropods, and the common squid. Besides these dissections of typical animals by the class, many alcoholic preparations and other specimens were presented for their examination.

The study of entomology was especially provided for. The students were taught the characters of the orders of insects, and afforded abundant practice in the determination of genera in the most prominent of these.

About seventy species of flowering plants were analyzed by the botany classes, representing some forty different orders. In structural and cryptogamic botany, the microscopes were in constant use. A key to the larger fungi was compiled by Prof. Burrill, and about half the session was given to these important but difficult and little known forms of vegetable life. The remainder was devoted to the ferns, mosses, algæ, etc., and to the study of the structure and development of plants. The students were incidentally taught to use the microscope, to mount objects, and to demonstrate important structures and processes. Considerable work was also done in ornithology, including the preparation of specimens. The lectures, thirty in number, were delivered one and two a day, and were brought into close relation to the laboratory work.

It will be seen that the amount of work done was tremendous; and yet it was so new, so varied, and intrinsically so interesting, that the students found themselves refreshed and rested rather than worn out, at the end of the term. The class separated delighted with the result of their studies, and expressing a lively desire to continue it in the future.

In accordance with a resolution of the Board of Education, adopted at their meeting in December, 1875, measures were taken to represent at the Centennial Exposition of the year following, the work done by the museum, for the benefit of the schools of the State. One set of specimens was prepared from those sent in by the schools connected with the School and College Association of Natural History, and another, intended to illustrate the character and condition of the material issued to these schools by way of distribution, and exchange, was made up from the museum duplicates then on hand for such use.

Concerning this exhibit, the State agent says in his report: "This case contained, so far as I know, the only exhibit of the kind in the whole exposition. The fact that it was thought worthy of a medal by the board of judges is an indication of its merits, and should afford strong encouragement to the Society of Natural History to persevere in its work."

During the year 1875, investigations were begun upon the food of the birds and fishes of the State, and a paper upon the former subject, giving the results of an examination of the contents of two hundred and twenty stomachs, was published in the Transactions of the Illinois State Horticultural Society for the year 1875. More elaborate preparations were made for the distribution to schools and state educational institutions of more or less complete sets of specimens of the zoölogy and botany of the State. With a view to the further development of work of this character, it was determined to abandon all attempts at a complete exhibition of specimens, to pack the material in the museum as closely as was consistent with its arrangement for convenient and ready reference, and to occupy the space thus vacated with tables for work and study; thus converting the establishment into a *biological laboratory* for the investigation of natural history subjects. It was further proposed, as a part of this plan, to establish in the new State house, at Springfield, a general exhibit of the natural history of the State, in connection with the collections of the State Geological Survey; and an act was passed by the general assembly, approved May 25, 1877, giving effect to this purpose.

By sections 8 and 9 of the act it was directed that the Illinois Museum of Natural History, at Normal, be converted into a State Laboratory of Natural History, at which, under the direction of the curator thereof the collection, preservation, and determination of all zoölogical and botanical material for said State Museum should be done. It was made a part of the duty of said curator to provide, as soon as possible, a series of specimens illustrating the zoölogy and botany of the State, to deposit them from time to time in the museum established by the act, and to furnish, as far as practicable, all zoölogical and botanical material needed by the State educational institutions for the proper performance of their work. It was also directed that one set of the duplicate zoölogical and botanical specimens then on hand in the Illinois Museum of Natural History, at Normal, which were not needed to illustrate the natural history work of the State Normal University, should be deposited, as soon as practicable, in the museum established by the act.

At the next meeting of the State Board of Education, directions were given for the necessary refurnishing and reorganization of the rooms and collection, the title of the Museum was changed to the "Illinois State Laboratory of Natural History," and sufficient appropriations were made to carry out the directions of the law in a liberal way. About two-thirds of the room was cleared of cases, those remaining were adapted to the systematic arrangement of specimens without reference to their display, and the space vacated was filled with the work tables and large cases of drawers.

This metamorphosis and reörganization of the establishment was the turning-point of its career, and amounted in fact to the founding of a new institution.

The following brief statement of its character and purposes, extracted from the report of its director for 1878, may therefore properly be introduced at this point.

"This is an institution whose chief objects are the prosecution and aid of original work on the natural history of the State (preference being given to subjects having special educational or economical value), the publication of the results of such work for the information of the people, the training and instruction of teachers of botany and zoölogy for the public schools, and the supply of the necessary scientific material to these schools, to the State Museum, and to the

State educational institutions. It affords a place to which any specialist or scientific student may come, with the assurance that he will find everything necessary for special study or original work on the natural history of Illinois, to which any teacher may come for preparation to teach these subjects intelligently, and upon which the officers of any school may draw for material to illustrate the scientific work of their school.

"Its operations are guided by the conviction that the spread of the knowledge and discipline of science among the people is essential to their highest prosperity; that this is a matter of public rather than of personal concern, and that it must be provided for by public rather than by private measures.

"To encourage the spontaneous and gratuitous labors of our scientific men, to assist them at least to the extent of supplying them with such facilities for work as are beyond the reach of individuals, and to furnish them a means of adding the results of their labors to the common stock of human knowledge, is obviously sound public policy. Without this class of workers, devoted to science for its own sake, no solid and valuable progress in science is possible. From them comes the initiative, the incitement. They are the root of the tree by which the raw elements of the natural world have been in all ages drawn together and made ready for the nourishment of the organism.

"As a means of putting the people in possession of scientific knowledge, museums and publications are necessary,—each serving similar ends in different ways,—the former instructing and arousing even the most ignorant as well as the most cultivated, but chiefly limited in its influence to those who visit it; the latter reaching a more widely diffused, but on the whole a better educated class. While the museum conveys instruction through the eye, and arouses, by a representative display of the natural history of the State, a popular interest in science which incites to study, and furnishes a basis of support for the higher scientific work, in the popular sympathy and intelligence, the laboratory is needed to provide ways and means by which this cultured interest may be converted into valuable knowledge and skill, and this, in turn, be bestowed upon the people through the press and the school.

"The functions of the museum and laboratory are too radically distinct to be successfully performed by one institution. The collections of the former are intended for display; of the latter, for study. The material, furniture, arrangement, and general equipment of the two must therefore be essentially different.

"It is also of great importance to the public welfare that the methods of work and habits of thought by which the achievements of modern science have been made, should be brought to bear as far as possible upon the daily life of all. For this, trained and intelli-

gent teachers of science are necessary, able to comprehend the work
of specialists, and to assimilate and adapt it to the needs of the community at large,—able also to translate the spirit and methods of
science into the work of the school, and through the school into the
pursuits of business and labor.

"But a practical knowledge of nature cannot be imparted by
books, or by word of mouth alone. The distinctive discipline of
science can only be got by the immediate exercise of the mind upon
objects and upon ideas directly derived from objects. Materials for
study, and named cabinets as the standards of reference, are the
sine qua non of work worth doing. To incite and reward natural
history work, nothing has been found more effective than skeleton
cabinets of representative species, which can afterwards be filled up
by the collections of teachers and pupils. The cost of these is
slight, the value very great. An easily accessible medium of mutual
exchanges, a center of authority to which difficult questions can be
referred for solution, are also indispensable to success.

"The pressing needs of these three classes, specialists in science,
the teachers and the pupils of the public schools, it is the principal
function of the state laboratory to supply.

"It is also evident that the large collections needed by the state
museum, and in the work of the great state educational institutions,
can be made more rapidly and much more economically by one
thoroughly equipped central laboratory than by the separate institutions themselves, since one set of apparatus, materials and men can
thus do the work which would otherwise require several. It is not
intended to take from those institutions any work of special educational value, but to do for them in the least expensive way what each
can not do separately without considerable special outlay."

To follow in detail the various operations of the laboratory since
its reörganization, would exceed the limit of this brief sketch, and a
general summary of the work accomplished must suffice. Zoölogical
and botanical collections have been steadily made in all parts of the
State, with a view primarily to accumulating material for a thorough
zoölogical and botanical survey of Illinois. In ornithology, a collection of two hundred and fifty species has been made, in northeastern
Illinois, near Waukegan and Chicago; in western Illinois, near Galesburg and Warsaw; in the central part of the State, at Normal; and
in Union, Jackson, and Alexander counties, in southern Illinois. A
good beginning has also been made in collecting a full series of the
nests and eggs of Illinois birds.

Insects of all orders have been regularly collected in northern
Illinois, from Galena to Chicago; in the central part of the State,
from Rock Island to Bloomington; and in southern Illinois
generally, except in the Wabash valley. The entomological cabinet
now contains about four thousand Illinois species, and twenty thou-

sand duplicates. With the appointment of the director of the laboratory as State Entomologist, in July, 1882, this department of the work assumed a new activity and importance.

The aquatic fauna of the State has been studied with especial care. The Illinois river and tributaries, from its headwaters to its mouth, have been thoroughly searched, as well as the lakes in the river bottoms. Rock river and its branches have been less carefully but sufficiently explored. The Mississippi and Ohio have been seined for weeks at Cairo, and numerous trips through southern Illinois have yielded an excellent collection from the lakes and smaller streams of that territory. Galena river, in northwestern Illinois, and the lakes in the northeast part of the State, have been exhaustively searched with seine, dredge, and towing net, and both the deep and shallow waters of Lake Michigan have been explored with dredge and trawl. These collections have included all orders of aquatic life, from fishes, amphibians, and reptiles, to the microscopic Entomostraca and Protozoa. Even the ponds and wayside pools have been searched everywhere for insects and minute Crustacea. Several large collections have also been made for the laboratory on the coast of New England, more especially for the supply of marine forms for use in our natural history schools, and for general distribution to the public high schools throughout the State.

The herbarium of flowering plants was already so large, that botanical field work has been confined chiefly to the cryptogams. An expert collector of fungi (Mr. A. B. Seymour) has been almost constantly in the field since July, 1881, and has sent to the laboratory about three thousand five hundred numbers, aggregating more than a hundred and fifty thousand specimens. About three thousand five hundred species of fungi have also been bought within this period, and eight hundred microscope slides of parasitic species have been mounted.

The laboratory has filled its function as a feeder to the State museum by supplying that institution with a series of three hundred and twenty species of mounted Illinois birds, each usually represented by male, female, and young, and a collection of sixty species of eggs; a good set of mounted mammals of species now occurring in the State, or known to have occurred here formerly; an extraordinary series of about fifty painted casts of Illinois fishes, together with about one hundred and fifty specimens in alcohol, and large cabinets of insects, mollusks, marine specimens, and plants, both flowering and cryptogamous. A series of mounted skeletons of mammals, birds, reptiles, amphibians and fishes, has also been sent down. To the Industrial University and the Southern Illinois Normal, good collections of fishes, insects, and plants have been given, with much miscellaneous material. Forty public high schools have been supplied with representative cabinets of fishes, insects, crustaceans, marine animals, and other objects, aggregating over ten thousand specimens, and the material is now on hand for the supply of about as many more. These cabinets are all issued under such conditions and with such precautions that it is known beforehand that they are needed, that they will be used, and that they will be properly cared for.

In the course of the investigation of the food of birds, over six thousand stomachs, representing two hundred and twenty-five species, have been obtained, and about seven hundred of these have been critically and exhaustively studied with the microscope. The food of fishes, both young and old, from all parts of the State, and during all seasons of the year, has been investigated on an equally elaborate scale. About two hundred and fifty insects have been dissected for a study of the food of certain difficult and important families, and the contents of their alimentary canals mounted as microscopic slides. The results of this work have been embodied in papers published in the bulletins of the laboratory, in the transactions of the State Horticultural Society, in the *American Naturalist*, and in various other reports and periodicals.

For the purpose of making the work of the laboratory available for the information of the general public, a series of bulletins has been published and gratuitously distributed. The fourth in number was issued in May, 1881, a fifth is now in press, and a sixth will be published during the coming winter. These bulletins contain only original contributions to a knowledge of the natural history of the State. Besides papers prepared at the laboratory, they include about one hundred and twenty pages of matter contributed by naturalists not connected with the institution. Three hundred and seventy-six pages have thus far been printed, and about two hundred more will be added this winter. Among the more important papers are an annotated catalogue of the birds of Illinois; elaborate reports on the food of the thrush family and the bluebird; complete catalogues of the fishes of the State, with studies of the food of old and young; a descriptive catalogue of the reptiles and amphibians of the United States east of the Rocky mountains, with a list of Illinois species; papers on the food of predaceous insects; a descriptive list of the Crustacea of Illinois; a list of our mosses, liverworts, and lichens, and various papers on Illinois fungi.

The library has grown in the meantime from a small and ill-assorted set of books, to a carefully selected collection of 1,200 volumes, and about 1,000 pamphlets on natural history. A card catalogue of authors is now complete, and a subject catalogue well under way.

Mention should also be made of a second natural history school, held in July, 1878, similar to that more fully described above, and equally successful in all respects.

From a movement initiated at this school, sprang a second State Natural History Society, organized in December, 1878, of which the director of the laboratory has been secretary from the first. This society holds semi-annual meetings,—one in June for field work, and one in February for the reading and discussion of papers. It is an active and flourishing organization, and gives every indication of a long and useful life. The educational value of the establishment is greatly enhanced by the fact that all its material and appliances are free for the use of such special students of science as wish to push their studies independently. Many capable teachers of science, and several promising young naturalists, have found here the means of entering upon their careers, or of adding largely to their resources.

And so the State Laboratory of Natural History, embodying the earnest and devoted labors of many whose names have found no place in this brief record, has grown and developed with the steadily increasing wealth and intelligence of this great State, by a slow and healthy enlargement of its field and building up of its power, until to-day it stands unique among all the state institutions of America. Its work will not be done until the life of the great and varied region which its operations cover, is known in all its forms and details, and understood as a whole,—until the general system of laws by which this complex aggregate of living things is unified and governed, has been mastered and made known. It is properly only at the real beginning of its career,—now first actually equipped for systematic and effective service. Its prime and essential function is not to do that which has been done before, nor even to teach that which is already known, but to push forward the bounds of human knowledge along certain special lines, and to apply the knowledge gained to the welfare of the people of the State. Its office is to enlarge that knowledge and mastery of nature which distinguishes the civilized man from the savage, and the support which it receives is to be regarded as a contribution to human progress.

FURTHER IMPROVEMENTS.

The foregoing article shows the development of the work in natural history during the last few years. But, in the mean time, other departments have been increasing their facilities and changing their methods of work.

When Dr. Sewall left the school to take charge of the Colorado State University, in 1877, he was succeeded by M. L. Seymour, of Blue Island. This gentleman had already won considerable reputation on account of his skill in devising simple apparatus to illustrate the work in the natural sciences. Under his management, a change has been effected in the appearance of the lecture room and chemical laboratory that would astonish the "old-timers." A steam pump that had outlived its usefulness, and had given way to one of more modern design, was transformed into an engine for working a pump to condense oxygen and hydrogen. It stands at the right of the door at the entrance to the lecture room. By its use, these gases are packed into cylinders and are always "on tap," to run the excellent lantern that has been added to this department of the school. The utility of this apparatus becomes apparent in many ways, especially in the study of anatomy and botany. Near the engine stands a three-story case, filled with beautiful and ingenious appliances for class use. At the back of the room is a commodious herbarium case, furnished with a large collection of plants for the botany classes. Large twenty-four-cell batteries illustrate the work in electricity, while the chemistry classes are assigned places at tables in the adjoining room, where the study is pursued by objective work on the part of the pupils themselves. A Bunsen filter pump adorns the south wall of the laboratory, and a lathe for wood and metal, a furnace, a bench and vise, numerous wash-bowls supplied with water from the cisterns in the roof, and many other conveniences are close at hand.

The work in physics has also changed its character to conform to modern ideas of teaching. A large case is filled with excellent apparatus from the establishment of James W. Queen and other manufacturers, and the pupils constantly use it in their work. This collection is increased from time to time by the liberality of the Board of Education. About a year ago, a four-inch glass was obtained from the celebrated house of Alvin Clark & Sons, and the astronomy classes are enabled to form a more intimate acquaintance with our celestial neighbors.

The room formerly used as the boys' play-room was remodeled about two years ago and is now used by Miss Rosalie Miller, the teacher of drawing. During the summer vacation of 1882, the dressing room in the southwest corner was converted into a class room for the observation classes, and the adjoining dressing room was furnished with cases and will henceforth be used as the library room. The part of the basement formerly occupied by the janitor was fitted up for the gentlemen's dressing rooms.

WORK OF THE UNDER-GRADUATES.

In Dr. Hewett's paper will be found certain statements respecting the attendance of pupils, and the reasons for the small percentage of graduates. The work of the under-graduates, however, is worthy of a large place in this volume. As has been stated, the reputation of the school must probably rest chiefly with them.

It was often charged by members of the Legislature, who were hostile to the institution, that students do not redeem their pledge to teach, but that, after receiving instruction at State expense, they enter other professions or other lines of business. The only way to reach just conclusions is to secure the facts in the case. To this end an attempt was made in 1878 to settle the question. Correspondence was opened with students, addresses were ascertained, and, by one device and another, reports were received from over nine hundred undergraduates who during the year 1878 were teaching.

It should be remembered that the canvass was necessarily imperfect, but it was demonstrated that more than one thousand of the pupils were actually teaching in the State at that time. This number is now undoubtedly increased very materially. When it is shown that one fifth of all the students that have attended the school are in the schools of the State twenty years after the establishment of the institution, it ought to settle the question forever as to whether or not the school is accomplishing its work. J. W. COOK.

[The following poem was written by H. B. Norton, and read by Lucy Curtis at the dedication of the Wrightonian Society Hall in 1861.]

ABSALOM'S PILLAR.

(2D SAM'L, XVIII:18.)

Young Absalom sat on the palace stairs,
  Sucking a julep through a straw,
And musing over his own affairs
  With a thoughtful visage as e'er you saw.
Absalom was a handsome fellow
  As human being could wish to view;
His hair was silken and long and yellow,
  Tied in a most miraculous cue.
    Let no mortal ever aspire
    In beauty to equal the dye of Tyre,
    Ophir gold, and Damascus blade,
    In which Prince Absalom sat arrayed.
    But the truth must be told at last—
    He was very decidedly fast.
    And yet, on account of his silken curls,
    His golden bracelets and glimmering pearls,
    His handsome face and his shining sword,
    By all young ladies was quite adored—
    Although Jerusalem's solid men
    Warned them against him with tongue and pen.

    But Absalom never yet had married;
    Year on year he had patiently tarried
    To step into the Governor's shoes
    As lawful monarch of all the Jews;
    Then some Princess as bride to win,
    Nobly endowed with the needful "tin."

And then, his wild oats being sown
Before he ascended the Hebrew throne,
He would establish a splendid reign,
And his memory last while the stars remain.

But David, without the slightest qualms,
Still kept singing those endless psalms,
And promised yet, in Absalom's fears,
To live to the age of a hundred years.
All things considered, his chance was fair
That yet he might bury his son and heir;
And the solid men of Jerusalem—
A joyful prospect was that to *them*.

So Absalom owned, with courage dim,
That his chance for the throne was decidedly slim;
And, in his desolate bachelor state,
Without a child or wife or mate,
He sighed that soon in the coming day
His very name should have died away.

But, struck by a happy thought at last,
He rose, and forth from the palace passed;
To an architect straight his course directed,
And showed the plan which he'd projected.
A mighty column he meant to raise,
Which should bear his name to the future days.
And so they reared it, stone on stone,
From the marble steeps of Lebanon;
Carved and fitted in every part
With the rarest power of the builder's art.
An obelisk was the column's form,
As suited best to outlast the storm,
Which, down the centuries yet to come,
Should bear the name of Absalom;
The name which its polished facets told
With inlaid letters of gleaming gold!
(He has been dead full many a year.)
He still kept on in his fast career.
Thus far had the work of the firm been done
Under the name of *David* and *Son*.
But our hero thought that he would rather
Change it to Absalom and Father.
But failing to make this grand progression,
At once decided upon secession;
And went to battle and perished there,
Because of the length of his darling hair.
But still, as my authorities say,
The Pillar standeth until this day.

A very decidedly similar plight
Was that of our much-loved Simeon Wright.
Years were creeping on apace,
Stamping their crow-tracks over his face.
Often the maxim at him was thrown,
That " no moss collects on a rolling stone."
But a better proverb had he than that:
"A setting hen is never fat."
And still he wandered o'er land and sea,
And never a chicken nor child had he.

Yet the children loved him—they loved to place,
Their rosy cheeks to his smiling face.
And countless friends o'er all the land
Rejoiced in the clasp of his genial hand.
Yet often—it cannot be denied—
Over his lonely lot he sighed;
And sang, in view of his situation,
Weeping Rachel's lamentation.
And so, as we've seen young Absalom do,
He upreared a pillar too.
Three long years has this column grown,
Stone upraised upon living stone,
Rising silently day by day.
We have heard our President say
Through what triumphs and toil and strife
This pillar has grown to its perfect life.
And now we have joyfully gathered here,
The topmost stone in its place to rear.

The years in their steady course will keep,
And he, our sire, with his sires shall sleep.
(But he will not perish, we surely know,
By allowing his hair too long to grow;
For the world beholds him every morn
Neatly shaven and trimly shorn.)
And if the moss, as the years speed on,
Should gather about the rolling stone,
We think he might with perfect propriety
Will it all to his pet society.

And the Pillar,—as ceaseless years roll by,
Still may it lift its head on high,
And bear to the centuries before,
The name that glitters on yonder door;
Standing ever, in strength sublime,
A signet ring on the hand of Time;
Stamping its likeness on hosts unborn,
Who its records may yet adorn.
Standing ever its founder's boast—
(We have offered this as a closing toast).

EXTRACT FROM THE FIRST PRINCIPAL'S FIRST REPORT.

"On the fifth day of October, 1857, the principal and Ira Moore opened the Normal University in presence of no spectators and the following students: Enoch A. Gastman, Jr., W. W. Higgins, Joseph G. Howell, John Hull, John D. Kirkpatrick, and Henry H. Pope—six; and Elizabeth K. Arnold, Hannah C. Bedell, Mary V. Davison, Sarah M. Dunn, Cornelia A. Gregory, Sarah J. Gregory, Helen F. M. Grinnell, Emily Junk, Elizabeth J. McMillan, Jane G. Michie, Jane F. Montgomery, Margaret C. Smith, and Kate I. Young—thirteen; in all, nineteen. Some others came in during the day, and on the ensuing morning the number had grown to twenty-nine. During the first eight days forty-three students (fourteen males,

17

twenty-nine females) were enrolled, our number for the first term."

Ira Moore, in *The Schoolmaster*, November, 1869, names James H. Dutton, Peter Harper, Silas Hayes, Charles D. Irons, Edwin Philbrook, Justin R. Spaulding, Fanny S. Denison, Annie M. English, Martha W. Fay, Martha A. Hawkins, Martha M. Marble, Frances A. Peterson, Matilda I. Reisings, and Bessie A. Strong, as also present in Major's Hall on the morning of the fifth day of October, 1857. It is probable these were the students who came in "during the day."

MRS. MARY FRANCES HULL.

Since the early pages of this volume have gone through the press, another member of the class of 1860 has passed away.

Mary Frances Hull was born in Bloomington, Illinois, June 3, 1841, and died in Carbondale, Illinois, August 19, 1882. She was the daughter of Amasa C. and Ann Washburn, both of whom survive her. She entered the Illinois State Normal School, January 4, 1858, at the beginning of the second term of the school, and graduated with the first class in 1860. Immediately after graduation, she was employed to take charge of the model school. She remained in this position about a year, when failing health compelled her to resign. Since that time she has been more or less an invalid. April 3, 1862, she was married to John Hull, a classmate, and now professor of mathematics in the Southern Illinois State Normal University. Two children survive her, a third having died some years since. Those who knew her will readily recognize the justness of the following extract from the remarks made by Dr. Allyn at her funeral:

"She had a rare degree of intelligence—a native genius, in fact, for acquiring knowledge and forming accurate judgments. Few have I found, in a very large circle of friends, who excelled her in ability and power to grasp facts and deduce principles; and in this estimate of her I was not alone. * * * * She had large ability to teach, and did succeed as few can. She had genius for thought which could readily have turned to authorship; but she chose the domestic circle, including wifehood and motherhood, the holiest and noblest of human relations—that higher plane which makes heaven possible for a human race, and which, as she presided in it, is the best type of a heaven of purity and improvement. And never should the hint that this was not her highest merit go without rebuke. Home was her kingdom, and she ruled it into peace and a school of virtue and power. Seldom have I known one so unselfish and considerate of others, so wise in words and especially in silence, so quick to form a judgment from obscure facts, and at the same time so accurate in conclusions, so charitable in judging of motives and actions, and so generous of quiet appreciative praise, or so sparing of censure."

WHAT AN EMINENT FOREIGNER THINKS OF THE NORMAL UNIVERSITY.

They (the Americans) are beginning to recognize the importance of the theoretical and practical training of teachers, and to establish Normal Schools to afford the opportunities for such training. At the head of such institutions stands the Normal University at Bloomington, Illinois: The large and very tasteful building was erected at a cost of $182,000. Two hundred ladies and one hundred gentlemen attended the school in 1864. The institution is intended to train teachers for the public schools by instructing its pupils in the art of teaching. * * * * In the third year of the course especial attention is devoted to methods of instruction and to practice in teaching. To afford opportunity for the latter a model school is connected with the institution. The present principal, Mr. Richard Edwards, is known far and wide as a prominent, able, and, in every respect, blessing-working man. He understands the dangers of slavish obedience to the text-book, and emphasizes properly the advantages of oral instruction."—*Translated from Dr. Karl Schmidt's Geschichte der Puedagogik, Volume IV, page 902.*

FINE

MERCHANT TAILORS.

A FULL AND COMPLETE STOCK OF

Foreign and Domestic Woolens

CONSTANTLY ON HAND.

All Work Made and Trimmed in the Best
Possible Manner. Perfect Fits
Guaranteed.

Prices as Low as Consistent with First-Class Workmanship.

DO NOT FORGET THE PLACE,

E C. Hyde & Son,

211 N. MAIN STREET, COR. WASHINGTON.

BLOOMINGTON, ILLINOIS.

WEDDING AND DRESS OUTFITS A SPECIALTY. SPECIAL
INDUCEMENTS OFFERED STUDENTS.

ILLINOIS
School Journal

NORMAL, ILLINOIS.

PRICE, $1.50 PER YEAR IN ADVANCE.

E. J. JAMES AND CHARLES DeGARMO,
EDITORS AND PROPRIETORS.

————THIS IS A————

32-page Monthly Magazine,

DEVOTED TO EDUCATION.

*It contains articles by the various members of the
faculty, besides communications from
prominent teachers of Illinois
and other States.*

——IT MAKES A——

SPECIALTY OF NORMAL AND STATE NEWS.

ROBERT A. SHAW,

Plain and Ornamental Plasterer.

KALSOMINING,

CISTERN BUILDING AND GENERAL REPAIRING OF PLASTERING

BOX 503, NORMAL, ILLINOIS.

RESIDENCE, CORNER CYPRESS AND ELM STREETS.

FOUR BLOCKS NORTH OF METHODIST CHURCH.

ILLINOIS

WESLEYAN UNIVERSITY

.

BLOOMINGTON, ILL.

NOTHING SUCCEEDS LIKE SUCCESS.

Twice in two years we have outgrown our college rooms.

On June 13, we graduated the largest class ever graduated in this section of the country, and gave four beautiful gold medals for merit.

Though only two years in existence, our graduates are already found in banks and other counting rooms, in business houses of all kinds throughout the country. Several members of our last class are engaged to teach in business colleges in different parts of the country.

During the last year a number of our students executed specimens of Pen Art that cannot be excelled in the west. A single drawing by one student was valued at $500.

IN SHORT-HAND,

We had, in 1881, more students than any other business college in the United States had in the last year reported by the Commissioner of Education.

IT MUST NOT BE DENIED that we can fit students for short-hand amanuensis work in from one to three months, and for general reporting in from three to six months, for we have repeatedly done it. Schools all over the country are taking up our system—Eclectic Short-Hand.

The Reporters' Bureau, of Chicago, wrote us:
"We have found positions for several of your students, as amanuenses, and every one of them has been a success."

Young Man, Young Woman!

If you want the fullest course of study and practice in Accounts, Penmanship, and Stenography, with a certainty of success, send for our College Annual, and prepare to enter at the opening of our fall term, September 12.

H. AUGUSTINE.   W. H. SCHUREMAN.

HOME NURSERY,

NORMAL, ILLINOIS.

AUGUSTINE & CO., Proprs.

WHOLESALE AND RETAIL DEALERS IN

*Fruit, Ornamental, and Forest Trees, Small
Fruit Plants, Grape Vines, Ornamental Shrubbery, Hedge Plants.*

SNYDER BLACKBERRY A SPECIALTY.

CORRESPONDENCE SOLICITED.

CATALOGUES FURNISHED ON APPLICATION.

OFFICE:

On Street Railway, near Railroad Crossing.

TELEPHONE NO. 198 WITH BLOOMINGTON EXCHANGE.

Take Street Car from L. E. & W. and I. B. & W. Depots, Bloomington, to reach Normal, at
the Junction of the C. & A. and I. C. Railroads.

PACKING GROUNDS TWENTY RODS WEST OF NORMAL UNIVERSITY.

———

POWELL'S LANGUAGE SERIES.

———

HOW TO TALK,

Introduction Price, 42c.
Exchange Price, 25c.

Introduction Price, 72c.
Exchange Price, 50c.

HOW TO WRITE.

———

These two books, prepared by W. B. Powell, A. M., Superintendent of Schools, Aurora, Illinois, are the result of many years of successful effort in training children to talk and write correctly.

Their purpose is to guide the young learner in the correct use of language at the time when he is *acquiring a vocabulary* and *forming habits of speech.*

The ordinary school grammars and alleged language text-books fail because they are only suitable for comparatively advanced pupils, who commence their study too late, after bad habits of speech, which books are powerless to correct, have been formed.

Pupils reading in a Second or Third Reader, can readily understand everything in the first book.

Specimen copies for examination, with reference to adoption, sent prepaid on receipt of the introduction prices, which will be refunded if either the books are adopted or returned.

Liberal terms for first introduction in schools. Send for descriptive catalogue.

Address,

COWPERTHWAIT & CO., PUBLISHERS.

F. S. BELDEN,
153 WABASH AVENUE, CHICAGO.

STATE NORMAL UNIVERSITY

NORMAL, McLEAN COUNTY, ILLINOIS.

This institution was established, by the General Assembly of the State, in 1857. Its sole purpose is to prepare teachers for the schools of the State. The several grades of the Model Department are established to aid in this work.

All students in the Normal Department are required to declare that their purpose in attending is to fit themselves for teaching, and all the work of the school is shaped to this single purpose. Probably no other Normal School Faculty in the country embodies so much of successful experience in Normal School work as ours.

Tuition is FREE to those who take a pledge to teach in the schools of Illinois; others pay tuition at the same rate as in the high school.

Our facilities for the study of Botany, Zoology, Geology, Chemistry, and Mineralogy, are excellent; and we now offer them to such as desire to make those studies a specialty at a very small cost.

THE HIGH-SCHOOL

grade of the Model Department offers the advantages of a first-class academy, and preparatory school. There are two courses of study,—the General and the Classical. Those who satisfactorily complete either course receive the Diploma of the University. The Classical course gives a thorough preparation for our best colleges; our graduates enter Harvard and Yale without difficulty. The General course offers excellent opportunities to those who do not have the time or inclination for an extended college course. Tuition in this grade, $30 a year,—or $10 a term. For particulars concerning the High School, address the principal, Edmund J. James, Ph. D.

THE GRAMMAR-SCHOOL

grade is under the charge of the Assistant Training Teacher; he does much of the teaching, sees that healthy discipline is maintained, and takes care that no improper or vicious pupils are admitted to the school. This school prepares pupils for the Normal Department, for the High School, or for general business. The instruction is given by teachers who are trained in the best modern methods, and who are under constant and efficient supervision. Pupils who complete the Preparatory Course are promoted to the High or Normal School without further examination. Tuition in Grammar Grade, $25 a year, or $8.33 a term.

For Catalogues and particulars, address

EDWIN C. HEWETT, PRESIDENT.

THE ☙ PANTAGRAPH ❧

ESTABLISHMENT

W. O. DAVIS, PROPRIETOR.

BLOOMINGTON, ILLINOIS.

ESTABLISHED 1846.

THE DAILY PANTAGRAPH.

The Daily edition is a neat 8-column folio, issued every morning (except Sunday); contains very full telegraphic dispatches of the Western Associated Press, reliable telegraphic market reports, and special telegrams and correspondence from all points in Central Illinois, covering the news field completely. It is received by Pantagraph agents in every town in this part of the State, on early morning trains, and furnished to its readers at 15 cents per week. Sent by mail anywhere for the same price. It is the best daily published for Central Illinois people.

THE WEEKLY PANTAGRAPH.

Its excellence is attested by the fact that its circulation is greater than any weekly published in a provincial city in Illinois. It contains a thorough condensation of all the news, foreign, general, state, and local, and correspondence from all parts of McLean and surrounding counties; accurate market reports, local and telegraph; choice stories and miscellany for home reading. Price, $1.50 per year in advance. All postmasters are agents to take subscriptions.

JOB DEPARTMENT.

This department of the Pantagraph Establishment has gained a reputation second to none in the west, for the execution of commercial, legal, school, and general printing. A specialty of stock work; no establishment in the world being better equipped for this class of work. Book and pamphlet printing in all the styles known to the "Art Preservative of all Arts." The following extract from a history of McLean County will bear republishing:

"In 1858, specimens of the Pantagraph job printing took the first premium at the great St. Louis Fair, at the National Fair in Chicago, the same year, and at the Illinois State Fair." "The job office of the Pantagraph is one of the best in Illinois, and the job printing is remarkable for its good taste."

Buying stock from the manufacturers direct, and having all modern machinery, enables us to compete with the world.

SCHOOL SPECIALTIES.

Under this head comes the Pantagraph Pen and Pencil Books, an article which has become as staple in the school room as the text-book. Wherever these goods are introduced, the noisy, screeching slate has been abandoned. A descriptive list sent on application. Special introduction discounts to schools. In addition to above, we publish Schureman's Township Treasurer's Books; Edwards' School Blanks, and many other like specialties.

BOOK BINDING.

It is not generally known that in Bloomington the metropolitan cities have a rival in this class of work. Bindings in all the various styles are here done at prices which defy competition. We submit the following testimonials in proof of these assertions:

NORMAL, ILLINOIS, September 23, 1882.
Having had a number of volumes bound at your establishment, I am happy to say that I am pleased with the whole job. The price was satisfactory, and the style and quality of the work metropolitan. Bloomington ought to be proud of your bindery. Yours respectfully, REV. H. R. PEAIRS.

BLOOMINGTON LIBRARY ASSOCIATION, September 25, 1882.
Having had considerable binding done at your establishment during the past two years, I take pleasure in recommending the style, durability, prices, etc. One of the best places to test the strength of the binder's work is in a public library. Respectfully, H. K. GALLINER, Librarian.

ILLINOIS STATE NORMAL UNIVERSITY, September 26, 1882.
I am pleased with the work you have done, in binding books belonging to our University Library, together with the few you have bound for my private library. Of course, the kind of binding was not such as to call for fine work so much as for plain, strong work. Your work seems to be strong and substantial, and I regard your prices as very reasonable. Yours truly, E. C. HEWETT.

ILLINOIS STATE LABORATORY OF NATURAL HISTORY, September 25, 1882.
The Bloomington Pantagraph Bindery has bound about 250 volumes for the library of this institution during the last two years. The work has been thoroughly well done, in every particular, and at prices as low as we could get anywhere. S. A. FORBES, Director.

ILLINOIS SCHOOL JOURNAL, NORMAL, ILL. September 23, 1882.
Having had many books bound at your establishment, it gives me pleasure to say that I have found the work uniformly handsome and substantial. It is also reasonable in price. So better or more elegant work need be desired than is done at your establishment. Yours truly, CHARLES DeGARMO, Assistant Training Teacher, Illinois S. N. U.

www.ingramcontent.com/pod-product-compliance
Lightning Source LLC
Chambersburg PA
CBHW021056030726
47496CB00006B/1873